The Cornelians

Also by Gillian Bligh

THE STICK MAN

The Cornelians

Gillian Bligh

Copperstone Books

Gillian Bligh
The Cornelians

This edition published 2003

ISBN 0-9544628-0-7

Published by
Copperstone Books

First published 2001 by Planetree

© 2001 Gillian Bligh

Author contact e-mail: gib@copperstone7.fsnet.co.uk

This novel is a work of fiction.
Characters and names are the product of the author's imagination. Any resemblance to anybody, living or dead, is entirely coincidental.

All rights reserved. No part of this publication may be reproduced, stored in a retrieval system, or transmitted in any form or by any means, electronic, mechanical, recording or otherwise, without the prior written permission of the author.

Cover design: Kaarin Wall

Printed in Great Britain
by
The Galliard Press
Great Yarmouth

Gillian Bligh was born and educated in Norfolk. She now lives with her husband on the Suffolk coast. She has two daughters and two grandchildren. When not writing she enjoys painting and researching her family tree and her links with William Bligh, Admiral of the Blue, probably better known for being involved in the famous Mutiny on the Bounty.

Author's Note

The Suffolk dialect is not easily read or understood by the uninitiated. For this reason I have used a diluted version – to retain a flavour of Suffolk without causing hardship to the reader.

Acknowledgements:

Very special thanks to:

My husband Michael

My sister Maureen

And last, but certainly not least, my daughter Suzanne, who asked me to write the book, deciphered my scribble, typed my manuscript and kept me inspired throughout.

For My Daughter

Suzanne

And

To The Memory of My Parents

Mildred and Frederick Bligh

Part One

The Foundling

Chapter One

Suffolk, England, 1846

The young girl sank back onto her pillows after the most exhausting three hours of her life.

Her skin was awash with perspiration, causing her long, dark hair to clump together, coil and cling, like glossy, black snakes.

She watched as the old woman cut the umbilical cord and, washed and bound the child with the quick efficiency that comes from a lifetime of experience. Fortunately, for the girl, the baby had been impatient to be born, so had made her ordeal shorter and easier by kicking his way into the world with an energy and exuberance that would have put a new born foal to shame.

Few words had passed between the old woman and the girl during the whole procedure. An onlooker would have deduced that the pair enjoyed such an intimacy that communication was almost telepathic.

Chapter Two

Twenty-two hours later in the village of Flinton, slightly west of the coastal town of Winford, the Reverend Richard Johnson and his wife Elizabeth, had just enjoyed a hearty breakfast, as was the custom at the Vicarage on Sunday mornings. The Reverend liked to breakfast early so that he could cast his eye over his morning sermon and make any last minute adjustments he deemed necessary. He had resided in the Parish of Flinton for the past twenty years, ever since he had brought Elizabeth to the village as a young bride. Now, as they sat at opposite ends of the table – which stood in the bay of a window overlooking the Vicarage garden – they were both lost in their own thoughts. The Vicar was wondering who to employ to repair the ancient pews that occupied the South side of the church. It was always a problem not appearing to favour one tradesman over another, especially in a small village like Flinton, which boasted two master craftsmen in carpentry. A fellow could land himself in a mire of trouble and discord if he did not apportion an equal amount of work to each man. Yes, he had better look over the parish accounts for last year before he summoned one or the other.

Elizabeth, a delicately boned woman in her mid forties, who could probably have done better in the marriage stakes than marry a young curate – as Richard had been – was toying with her teacup the contents of which now going cold. Although she was staring at the delicate artistry on the bone china, she was not really seeing it, she was reflecting on how quiet the house was now that she and Richard were its sole occupants. Their son, also named Richard, had recently taken a curacy at Illingham after a stay of six months at home. Illingham was not more than twelve miles away but she missed him terribly, looking forward to his weekly visits with almost a hunger. She now put her head on one side, as one does when trying to hear more acutely.

"Did you hear that, Richard?"

The Reverend dragged his mind back from parish business to look at Elizabeth's alert face. "Hear what, my dear?"

"A whimpering, I am sure I heard something whimpering. It sounded quite close by, under the window perhaps."

As she spoke they both rose from their seats to walk the short distance from the dining room to the kitchen, and so to the back door, which the Vicar opened with trepidation, expecting a wild animal or some such to scuttle into their home. As the distance between the door and the architrave widened, admitting nothing save a few petals from the early flowering cherries, that floated on a spring breeze onto the flagstone floor, they felt their senses relax sufficiently to allow a slightly wider opening of the door.

The Vicar, being at the front, was the first to espy the basket, which was resting undercover of their back porch. He immediately opened the door wide, allowing his wife to survey the unexpected scene. This time they both heard the sounds being emitted from within the basket – snuffling and whimpering that were unmistakably those of a human child. "It is a baby," said Elizabeth. "Why is it here, I wonder?" Both these utterances were made simultaneously with her reaching down, to uncover and reveal the face of a tiny a baby. The child had a shock of black hair and sparkling, blue eyes in a longish, honey coloured, plump face. It was a beautiful infant who, apart from the intermittent protestations, did not appear to mind that it had been abandoned under a strange porch on a Sunday morning, fortunately a very warm, sunny, Sunday morning.

A few of last year's dead leaves, together with the aforementioned cherry blossom petals had blown around and settled at the basket's base, making it quite a fetching scene. "Take it in Elizabeth, take it in," said the Vicar, "I will go out to the road to see if anybody is about, they would surely want to stay around to make sure we found it." And off the Vicar raced to search the road.

Mrs Johnson carried the basket and its contents carefully into her kitchen. She placed their extraordinary find on the large wooden table and proceeded to make a more thorough examination of the basket and infant.

The baby was indeed exceptionally endearing, looking up at its rescuer with an innocent, inquiring expression. Elizabeth unwrapped the child from its blanket and discovered that it was a boy. She had instinctively known the baby to be male, it had *looked* male, strong boned and strapping with a solid feel to him when lifted from his bed. Some babies tended to be loose-limbed and floppy when taken up. As she sat at the kitchen table, holding the infant in her arms, her husband re-entered the house in a bustle of consternation. "Nobody out there," he said, "save Old Shuffley and he has not seen anything suspicious, nothing much escapes Old Shuffley so we can assume the basket has not been left recently."

Old Shuffley had acquired his unusual name because of the short stepped way he walked, often not letting his feet lose contact with the road, but he seemed to cover an inordinate amount of ground considering his strange gait. Few folk could actually remember Shuffley being anything other than *old* , he had appeared to enter the world at around sixty years old and had remained unchanged ever since, save acquiring a few grey whiskers and a change of overcoat! What is more, he had no objection to his nickname.

"Well, they call tall folk 'lanky' don't they?" would be his only rejoinder on the subject so, 'Old Shuffley' he remained, liked and respected by all who knew him.

"I have prayed for another baby ever since our Richard was two years old," said the Vicar's wife with a dreamy, fulfilled countenance.

"The baby does not belong to us, we must find its mother, you must not assume that because it has been left on our doorstep we have any right to keep it. Face facts, woman, if God had wanted us to have more children he himself would have arranged it, not some desperate village girl who has got herself into straits she cannot cope with and who is probably weeping and wailing at this very minute about what she has done."

The Vicar had never before referred to his wife as 'woman', and the mere fact that he had used such a term revealed to his wife that he was unusually agitated. His face had taken on a purple hue and he had paced the same ten flagstones, back and forth, at least twenty times.

"I am sorry, I am sorry," he added almost at once. "I did not mean to lose my temper with you, my dear, it is just that this has all come about at a most inconvenient time. Here am I with a church service to conduct in two hours time but the child's presence cannot be ignored, we must do all we can to reunite the unfortunate little mite with its mother." As if at the mention of his mother, the little boy began to exercise his lungs a little more robustly until his wailing was at such a pitch that Mrs Johnson felt the need to place her finger firmly in his mouth.

"He is hungry," said the vicar's wife. "Why, he must be ravenous, we do not know when last he fed." She held her hand to her head, realizing that no suitable sustenance was at hand in their household.

"You must go for the mid-wife, Richard, at once, she will, no doubt, know of an available wet-nurse." She almost pushed her husband out of the kitchen door with her free hand, adding as she did so. "Collect the Doctor as well on your travels we should surely be able to sort the matter out between the four of us."

The Vicar made his way around the house, down the front path and so through the wicket, thinking as he did so that this must be the most hectic and problematic Sunday morning that he had ever encountered.

Dr. Miles lived just across the road from the Vicarage; in fact his house was a replica of the Vicar's own, having been built at the same time from the same plans. Even the Rhododendrons marking the front boundaries had been planted together and were a vision of splendour in early June when the milder weather exploded the buds. Today, though, Reverend Johnson had no thoughts of flowers or seasons as he made his way to the front door of his old friend and knocked loudly. It seemed an age before the Doctor finally opened the door wide and allowed the Vicar to pass through to the hall, where he recounted the morning's happenings.

Together they made their way back, across the road, where the Doctor saw for himself the abandoned child – still being soothed by Elizabeth's finger, but not now quite so content with it. After a thorough examination the Doctor proclaimed the child fit and healthy, he also informed the pair that the infant was no more than twenty-four hours old. The two men then left Mrs Johnson with her charge and proceeded to Mother Cooper's; who had brought more babies into the world than most folk had had hot dinners.

Mother Cooper lived about a quarter of a mile away but to the Vicar and the Doctor, who were both in their late forties, it seemed more like ten miles, such was the degree of urgency.

On reaching their destination a door was again banged on, bringing Mother Cooper to her front step in a fluster, wondering who could be trying to gain entrance with such forcefulness. After again relating the goings on of the previous hour, the Vicar looked to Mother Cooper for inspiration and direction. The plump woman was looking skywards, obviously making a mental search of her list of nursing mothers.

"Maggie Osbourne" she suddenly cried, "Maggie's the one to fetch, delivered a month ago she was and allust make enough to keep a young heifer happy. If she wont help you'd better ask young Sally Smith at Wood Farm, but Maggie's a good sight nearer to keep a commin' in."

Armed with this welcome information the two men set forth to find Maggie, whom they both knew well.

No.5 Fisher's Row was well within their sights as they turned away from the midwife but back in the direction of home. Two of Maggie's children were playing by her front gate, and they now ran ahead though the open front door to announce the morning visitors – who waited politely on the front step.

Maggie felt so honoured to have the Vicar *and* the Doctor

call on her, uninvited, on a Sunday morning, that she found herself unexpectedly tongue-tied as she ushered them into her tiny front room. Her husband Jack, a large, weather-beaten man with a leathery face, who laboured on Smith's Farm, came through from the kitchen where he had been blacking his Sunday boots, dipping his head as he did so, him being a tall man.

"We have come to ask for your assistance, Maggie," began the Doctor, "A baby has been left on the Vicarage doorstep for whom a wet nurse is needed urgently. Mother Cooper suggested we ask you as you – er – hem – well – we understand you have an abundant supply of milk, much in excess of your own baby's needs."

"Well," began Maggie, feeling extremely important all of a sudden. "Tis true I can feed another littlun, no trouble, shall I come now?"

"Now, now just you wait a minute," Jack Osbourne expostulated in the vernacular. "How do you know this littlun hasn't got somethin' that he'll pass on to our baby, you don't know who he belong to, he could have anythin' – what about if he's a carryin' the cholera?"

"No, no," came the Doctor "there has not been a case of cholera in these parts in years, you have no worries there Jack."

"Ah," said Jack, "but you don't know if he come from these parts. You don't know where he come from, a body can get a fair old distance in twenty four hours 'specially with the help of an 'orse 'n' cart," and he nodded his head knowingly as his neck shrank back into its collar from where it had been stretched. He felt pleased with himself for stating his piece, regardless of their exalted visitors.

"I have just examined the baby, Jack, he is perfectly healthy, there is no need to worry on that score, however, if you are that concerned we will ask somebody else if they would like to supplement their income in such an easy fashion."

At the mention of 'income' Jack's fears appeared to subside considerably. "Well if you know he isn't carryin' nothin' I s'pose it wont hurt none if Maggie help you out."

"Good," said the Vicar, "that is settled then, perhaps you will come along with us now, Maggie, you can bring your baby with you. I will see the rest of you in church in about half an hour, Jack, you can thank the Lord personally for your unexpected good fortune." With that the Vicar and Doctor exited the cottage with Maggie following not far behind.

What a morning, thought the Vicar, as he took his hunter from his waistcoat pocket for the umpteenth time that day, thirty minutes to go and he had not given his sermon even a cursory glance. Ah, well, he thought there would be plenty to announce from the pulpit this morning, he would ask everybody to search their minds for any information, however trivial, that might lead to the baby's mother.

The pair strolled back to the Vicarage in a slightly more leisurely fashion than they had departed, feeling pleased with themselves for having sorted out a problem of such magnitude.

The two men were easy in each other's company. The majority of village folk did not feel wholly at ease in the company of either a vicar or a doctor, so tended to treat them with a healthy respect. They only called on them if their professional services were required or exchanging niceties if, and when, their paths crossed in the village. Their respective children had grown up together, attended the schoolhouse together and freely entered the others' abodes enjoying all the social occasions together as a large family normally would, altogether it was a nice, comfortable interaction of convivial, like-minded people with only the width of the road between them. Their respective private lives rolled gently on, with not too many personal problems. They certainly had no anxieties regarding poverty or overcrowding, the like of which beset the majority of village dwellers, putting a strain on marriages and personal relationships, within the four walls of their – mostly tiny – cottages.

Mrs Johnson had reached a high state of tension and agitation by the time help arrived in the form of Maggie. Never had she been so relieved to see someone. Ushering her to an easy chair amid promises of a nice hot cup of tea and confections she herself had baked but yesterday, she relieved Maggie of her own child to replace him with the abandoned infant who now made up for lost time with a vengeance.

A timetable was sorted out that was convenient to both the wet-nurse and the vicar's wife. Then, and only then, did the Vicar go to his study to collect his sermon and left, with the Doctor, for church. This was the first time in twenty-four years that he had been late for his Sunday morning church service.

Chapter Three

Reverend Johnson and Doctor Miles walked hurriedly up the path between the tombstones, acutely aware that no other living person was occupying the churchyard. On entering the building the two men were astounded at the number of parishioners seated within; the place was full to capacity. The Vicar made a quick mental calculation of what the collection box might hold at twelve o'clock, and he was filled with a warm glow.

After the customary number of hymns and prayers, the hitherto neglected sermon was delivered, but foreshortened, to allow sufficient time for the Vicar to engage his congregation in assisting with the enormous task of discovering the whereabouts, and indeed the identity, of the child's mother. "I see the news of our morning discovery has spread like wildfire, but whatever the reason for our bursting seams this morning, it does me a power of good to see you all gathered here today and I thank you for coming for I can talk to you all at once. Indeed, yes, we found an abandoned infant on our back step at around eight-thirty this morning and we are at a loss to know of the circumstances surrounding his birth."

"Search your minds," he bellowed from the pulpit, "for any scrap of information that might help. Any of you may call on me, at the Vicarage, at any time. Do not be afraid to come forward, everything will be heard in the strictest confidence, I assure you. If any of you know something that could be important you will be doing the child a great service if you come to see me. The woman concerned could well be very distressed, not knowing which way to turn, fearing herself to be in dire trouble. Please help us to solve this mystery, it will be a good day's work done. God bless you all and I hope I will see as many of you again next Sunday. Now we will share a closing prayer."

During all the hymn singing and preaching that morning, one man in the congregation was feeling decidedly hot and uncomfortable under the collar. In fact his heart was thudding so loudly that he was sure his young wife could easily hear it, as she stood dutifully by his side. Every now and again he would look sideways to his right, but she would just smile up at him in a loving, possessive way which assured him, amazingly, that she was oblivious to his plight.

Daniel George Canham had married Louisa just nine months previously and they were blissfully happy, but he could see that their idyllic state would be short lived if she discovered the nature of his present thoughts.

Through the entire service Daniel had been painfully aware that the whole village was abuzz with gossip. The route to church had been littered with small groups of parishioners gossiping about the morning's happenings. It was inconceivable to think that there was a solitary soul in Flinton who had not heard about the baby, and not one over eight years old who would not give their eye teeth to learn the identity of the parents. The person who supplied *that* information would be as good as a national hero and remembered long after he or she had been laid to rest in the local churchyard.

For the past hour Daniel had been seeing disturbing flashes in his mind's eye; of laughing dark eyes, long black hair, a soft honey skin, warm inviting lips – a beguiling young lady, displaying such coquetishness that he once again found himself making excuses for not resisting her charms. He tried to convince himself that no man would have been stronger, but, even so, guilt overwhelmed him to such an extent that his legs went weak, his mouth dry, and his eyes darted about in his head as he struggled to stop himself running from the church, to take in vast amounts of clean fresh air to clear his head. And all the while the singers sang, the prayers prayed, the Vicar preached, and his wife smiled...

DANIEL GEORGE CANHAM, a voice was bellowing in

his head. YOU ARE GUILTY, YOU ARE GUILTY. OWN UP, OWN UP.

But Daniel knew that he would not be making the journey to the Vicarage, he was not brave enough, he liked his life the way it was. He would one day take over the farm from his father and, with Louisa at his side, they would have a good life together, a family and all the happiness that state brings. No, he could not go to the Vicarage but he would make amends to all he had sinned against, for he knew in his heart that the infant was the product of his youthful, fiery loins.

And so, as the congregation said their closing prayer, Daniel was saying one of his own.

He would attend church regularly. He would give generously to the collection box. Where the farmers usually donated five shillings annually to the local musicians, he would donate ten shillings. He would tend the farm, and keep the best set of accounts in the district, his father would be proud of him. He would take good care of Louisa and would be an excellent father to his children. He would curb his temper and be good to his workers. From here on in he would lead an exemplary life – but, he could not go to the Vicarage.

Chapter Four

Bright and early on Monday morning Thomas Foley, landlord of the Village Maid, made ready his horse and cart to visit the brewery. The dray cart was not due to deliver until Wednesday morning but Thomas had the feeling that the villagers were going to develop a great thirst in the meantime. Whenever there was a juicy bit of village gossip doing the rounds, Thomas found his takings increased accordingly and *this* bit of gossip, he judged, would take a mighty long time in dying down.

Thomas Foley, with his wife Sadie, had kept the Village Maid for the past thirty years. He prided himself on running a strict establishment. He did not allow over indulgence; anybody so doing would be shown the door of his alehouse. He was of the opinion that folks liked to congregate in his inn to have a gentle mardle and warm their insides, as well as slake their thirsts. He judged that what he lost on those he turned out, he would make ten fold on those remaining; they would be that indebted to him. So far this philosophy had served him well; he saw no reason to change it.

Thomas was a large, ruddy-faced man, be-whiskered, with a rotund figure, probably attributable to the enormous amount of ale he had consumed over the past thirty years. His wife was similarly built and had contributed to keeping the midwife in work by producing seven offspring, most of whom were dotted around the surrounding villages with families of their own.

Now, as Thomas led the horse, through the covered archway, out of the yard and onto Flinton High Street – a grand name for such a narrow thoroughfare, he thought – he espied a horse and trap approaching from the left, which he saw carried the Vicar, now slowing on approach.

"Mornin', Vicar," said Thomas cheerfully. "Another lovely

mornin' to be sure."

"Good morning, Tom, I do not suppose you have heard anything new to help solve our little mystery?"

"Sorry, Vicar, not a thing. I'm just off to the brewery to stock up on supplies which I feel I'll need tonight, you know how folks like to congregate and swap a piece of gossip, 'specially when there's a bit like this circlin'."

"Well, as you know, I bear you no ill, Tom, but I do wish they would do a bit more congregating in my church on a Sunday morning. It was a treat to see the place packed to such an extent yesterday, maybe they will all manage to drag themselves out of bed next Sunday. On second thoughts, it might be in our joint interests to keep quiet if we *do* discover anything." Both men laughed heartily at the thought of the potential advantage of milking the situation.

"Shame on you, Vicar, I would've thought it was just us mortal sinners that had ideas like that in our heads." They both laughed again.

"Well, I must press on Tom. I am off to Winford to ascertain the legal position of all this. Elizabeth is in her element at having a baby to fuss over again, as you can imagine, and she is enjoying all the interest. We have had at least half a dozen visitors already this morning calling on one pretext or another. There was obviously a lot of activity last night, of people clearing out their cupboards to see what could be given to the poor and needy. Next week they will have the excuse to call again when they realize that they need that old jacket, or whatever, more than they thought. Three young men have suddenly found the need to get married, I hope they have had the good manners to inform their sweethearts." They both laughed again at the hive of activity that was being generated by the poor little mite who was not even aware of it.

"Good day to you, Tom."

"G'day, Vicar."

Both men drove off in the direction of the coast road where they would then set off in completely opposite directions, for the brewery was in Denham, which was seven miles down the coast, whereby Winford was to the north, about four miles.

Reverend Johnson also intended to call at the registrars. It had been a lawful requirement for the last nine years that every birth, death and marriage in the land must be registered. These details were also recorded in London where a General Register had been set up for the whole of England. Of course the churches would still keep their parish records, but these new laws would prevent anybody from slipping through the net. All babies for instance did not make it to the church to be christened for one reason or another, but they now all had to be registered, even if stillborn. A long overdue piece of legislation, thought Richard.

Being only two days old, it was highly unlikely that the baby *had* been registered and the Vicar was acutely aware that it need not have been born locally anyway, but Elizabeth was fretting that they should give the child a name and he agreed it was necessary. Registration had to be carried out within three months of birth. The mother could well have come forward by then.

All these thoughts were going through the Vicar's head as he travelled to Winford on this lovely spring morning. Usually he would have been noticing how the hedgerows had sprung into life lately; the bare branches of Winter now covered with the lush green of Spring. Birds were calling to their mates with a new urgency and vigour, pheasants and partridges – alerted to approaching danger – scuttled back through the hedgerows from where they had been pecking in the verges. New shoots were visible, in what had been bare brown earth just a few weeks earlier, and white with snow just six weeks before that. But now the May blossom dominated the hedgerows, as the baby dominated the Vicar's thoughts.

It was amazing the effect that a child had on a woman, thought Richard, Elizabeth had completely metamorphosed during the last twenty-four hours. She was now vibrant, alert, bright eyed, and had a rosy glow to her cheeks as she bustled about doting on the infant. There was a new spring to her step. Altogether she was much more like the girl he had married, funny that, he had not noticed her skin becoming more pallid or her step slowing, or her eyes dulling. He wondered if he himself had changed much over the years and whether Elizabeth likewise had not noticed. Those notions saddened him somewhat as he journeyed on his mission so he did not notice that, as he had fallen into a reverie, the pony had slowed her pace.

His reflective mood remained until he reached Winford, where he looked around bemused, as one does, having made a journey one cannot recollect having made.

Collecting his thoughts he set forth to attend to his business, now being later than he had intended. He would first have a chat with old Mr Wilkinson-Kibble his solicitor…

Chapter Five

Elizabeth had indeed been given a new lease of life. She had not felt this good in years, or felt so needed. As a Vicar's wife, of course, she was kept very busy helping her husband. It was not unusual for her to visit the sick and needy herself, taking them flowers from her garden or homemade jam etc. She enjoyed her Christian duties very much but she had so longed for another child. She had felt cheated that they had not been blessed with one. So many cottages in the village were overcrowded, some seeming to have a new addition every eighteen months or so, she or Richard visited on every occasion, successfully hiding their own personal pain. Up until Sunday morning she had managed to count her blessings and accept life the way it was, but the baby had changed all that and she would use every feminine wile in her power to convince her husband they should keep him. She pushed to the back of her mind the fact that the child did not belong to them. Of all the doorsteps in Flinton he had been left on *theirs*. She felt her prayers had been answered at last, she had even chosen a name, of which she was sure Richard would approve...

Mr and Mrs Johnson employed only two people. Daisy Drew, a young girl from the village, came in on a daily basis as housemaid, and young Sidney Cartwright looked after everything outside. On this particular morning, Elizabeth, Daisy and Sidney had been exceptionally busy. Mrs Johnson had an inordinate amount of energy all of a sudden, wanting everything spick and span, inside and out. There was an air of expectant excitement pervading the house but no one knew quite what they were expecting, or who, or when, or if indeed anything at all! Daisy had never seen Mrs Johnson so happy and lively.

Sidney was used to his routine and usually attended to his

duties unsupervised, so he was surprised to find himself being asked to gather spring flowers by the basketful – augmenting them with blossom from trees – instead of blacking boots and mucking out horses. If this air of blissful existence continued he might just muster the courage to ask Daisy to walk out with him, a question he had been going to ask every day for the past six months but always heard himself floundering – his tongue refusing to obey his brain.

Sidney heard footsteps approaching from the house and looked up from his squatting position, beside the basket of daffodils and blossom. He felt the heat spread from his neck to his face and up to the very roots of his hair as Daisy came closer. As usual he became completely tongue-tied. Daisy stopped in front of him, putting all her weight on to one leg, causing one slender hip to gently protrude under her white apron. For some unknown reason to Sidney, this innocent posturing, together with the slight tilt of her head, sent his senses reeling again.

"Missus says, if you've filled the baskets you can come into the kitchen for some refreshment, we're all havin' a pot of tea, the baby's ever so nice and it doesn't cry at all. Missus is so happy it's a treat to be here. We're waitin' for Mr Johnson to come home, he's gone to Winford." She paused, "Will you come into the kitchen?"

Sidney nodded his now scarlet head. If she had led him to the slaughterhouse he would have followed. He picked up the basket and followed Daisy back to the house, another opportunity lost, he thought, staring at the nape of her neck where her damp curls clung.

Oh to be a damp curl, that close to Daisy's neck…

The house was indeed a treat to behold, having been brushed and polished from top to bottom. Windows had been thrown open to admit fresh, scent laden, spring air; vases and bowls had been filled with tulips, daffodils, forsythia, primroses and twigs of blossom. The baby slept contentedly in his basket while the happiest woman in Flinton sipped her tea and surveyed her domestic surroundings as she waited for her husband's return from Winford.

That evening, when the Vicar and his wife had the house to themselves at last, Richard related the details of his Winford visit. "Apparently, my dear, there is no reason why we cannot care for the baby for the time being, in fact, it would be desirous, because the mother knows where she has left it, therefore she is at liberty to come back and collect him if she so wishes. It is also obvious that you are enjoying the situation and it gives me great pleasure to see you so happy again. As for myself, I have no objection to giving the infant a temporary home, on the contrary, I would have been most offended if the desperate girl had *not* considered me to be the most appropriate person in the village to provide refuge to her son. The most important factor in all this is the child, and what is best for him. But, my dear, you must not allow yourself to grow so fond of him that you cannot part with him when the time comes to do so.

"I have familiarised the registrar with the facts, he will let us know if anyone in these parts during the next three months registers a male child born April the twentieth. In the meantime I suggest we give the child a temporary name and make the best of things."

"Thank you, Richard, I knew you would not make me part with him for no good reason. While you were about your business today I have been thinking of suitable names and, I would like to suggest that we call the child Matthew Luke Johnson, after the New Testament apostles, for I am of the firm belief that my prayers have been answered at last."

"That is an excellent idea, my dear, I whole-heartedly agree, the day has turned out well. I think we can be pleased with ourselves. The house looks beautiful, my wife looks beautiful, the infant is of a contented nature, what more could a man want? I think this calls for a glass of your best Elderberry, doesn't it?"

A quarter of a mile or so, along Flinton High Street, Tom and Sadie Foley were enjoying a brisk trade. Half the male population of Flinton had seen fit to grace their establishment that particular night. So full was their inn that Tom had placed benches out at the front, as he was wont to do on summer evenings. "Summer's come early this year," he remarked to his regulars, as he carried yet another bench outside. "At this rate we'll have the Village Green covered in no time an' I'll have to ask you all to slow down your mug-emptyin' while I traipse back to the brewery!" But Thomas was in good humour as his money drawer filled ever closer to the top.

Certain members of the community had their regular seats at the Village Maid. Old Shuffley, for instance, always sat in his high-backed chair in the chimney corner by the inglenook. He found the benches uncomfortable, probably on account of his spinal condition, which caused him to walk so queerly.

In the opposite corner was a settle, occupied now, as usual, by Amos Farthing – farmer of the parish – and his eldest son, Diggory. Diggory was thirty-five years old and still had not found himself a suitable wife, a fact of much consternation to old Amos and his wife Rosa. He was the last of their brood still at home, the other five all being settled and parents themselves.

At the small tables clustered around the chimney area, and on the seats under the windows – which looked out on the Village Green – were some other stalwart members of the community. Fingal Pardoe, stone mason, with sons Barnabas and Gabriel; Reuben Healey, the shoemaker; Silas Twybar, owner of Wood Farm; Zackery Renawden, blacksmith; Walter Fennell, builder and undertaker; Fergus Tooley, carpenter; Eli Penny, baker; Martin Partridge, butcher; Darcy Worthdale, carpenter; and Randolph Clarke who kept the general store, to name but a few. Others were seated elsewhere in the alehouse, and not privy to this particular conversation.

"Well, here we are again," said old Amos. "Settin' the world to rights as usual. I reckon we do more good and sort out more problems around this chimney corner than all those highfalutin members of parliament in London."

"I'll second that," agreed Walter. "All you need is a mug of good ale, a comfortable chair and some easy company and it's surprisin' what mysteries can be solved."

"I think we'll be a long time solvin' this one," said old Amos. "There's never bin a conundrum quite like this afore, not where none of us have an inklin' about it."

"That's a big word for you, Amos, so late in the day, conundrum, why, you go on like this you'll be in Westminster yourself," piped Darcy Worthdale, one of the younger members of the group, being only thirty-two years old.

"Thass the trouble with youngsters today," rejoined old Walter, "no respect for their elders, have they, Amos?"

"No respect for anyone, some of 'em," said Amos. "We never heard about littluns bein' left on doorsteps when we were young did we, Walter, we had to face up to our responsibilities, not hand them over to the Vicar."

"Why do you think the Vicar's door was chosen, thass what I can't fathom," said Martin.

"Thass not difficult to work out, I reckon thass about the best place to leave a baby – with a Christian man and his good lady," said old Walter.

"If you think thass a good place, Walter, maybe you know more about it than the rest of us," smiled young Martin.

"I shouldn't think it's anything to do with Walter," chuckled Darcy, "folks say he's a *handsome* little chap!"

"Cheeky little scoundrel, I'll give my business to Fergus the next time I need a job doin'," scowled Walter, pretending to be vexed. But everybody in the group knew Walter never employed a carpenter anyway. If you can make a coffin, he would say, you can make any piece of furniture – and so he did.

And so the conversation and banter went on, sometimes serious, sometimes light-hearted, everybody having their say, with plenty of nodding and shaking of heads.

"Are we goin' to have some lamps lit in 'ere tonight, Tom?" shouted Zackery, across the room. "I do declare Tom's takin' advantage of our good humour tonight and saving his wicks. I've missed me mouth three times already, it's gittin' s' dark."

As the night wore on the dialect grew broader. Most of the assemblage worked for themselves and their ladyfolk reminded them they should speak accordingly.

"Don't you go and show me up in that ale-house tonight," was a common instruction as they left their homes. "Just you remember you're a respected member of the community. Try to talk nice like." And try to talk 'nice like' they did, to keep their women happy.

" 'Pon my soul is that the time?" said young Diggory, looking up at the longcase, illuminated by one of Tom's recently lighted lamps. "I think I'll go and stretch me legs before turnin' in."

"And we know what direction you'll be takin' to do that don't we?" said Darcy. "Pound to a penny he'll be taking the route past Lydia Flowerdew's house."

Lydia was the Seamstress who kept a very neat cottage in Holly Lane, where she lived with her husband Nicholas – a junior solicitor with old Wilkinson-Kibble in Winford – and her three children, Suzanne, Megan and Leo, aged ten, eight and six respectively, very good looking youngsters, who were always immaculately turned out, as would be expected of a seamstress's children.

Lydia Flowerdew was thirty years old and had struck up a very close friendship with Miss Penelope Wyn-Jones, who had taken the post of Schoolmistress about twelve months earlier.

Most evenings Penelope would take in the evening air by going for a stroll around the village. She usually rounded off her walk by calling on Lydia, when the two young women would spend an enjoyable hour talking about those mysterious matters that interest young ladies. At around half past nine she would leave Lydia to walk back to the schoolhouse, which was situated in the High Street, about half way between the Inn and the Vicarage.

On his way home from the Village Maid, Diggory had to walk past Lydia's cottage. He liked to time it so that he was passing at around half past nine. This gave him the opportunity of offering to walk Penelope safely back home. An offer mostly accepted on dark nights, because she would need to pass the local inn, a task she did not relish. The fact that Diggory had to double back on his journey mattered not a jot to him, such was his infatuation with the Schoolmistress.

So now, as usual, Diggory rose from his chimney settle, trying, as he did so, to conceal his eagerness to leave.

"I don't know why you bother," said Zackery. "The Schoolmistress would never consent to marry you in a month of Sundays, Diggory, you're a nice enough chap and all that, but, would a young lady like that want to be known as Penny Farthing?" They all roared with laughter at the thought, totally ignoring the pain and embarrassment being suffered by young Diggory, who had spent hours and hours agonizing over that self-same problem.

So Diggory took his leave and the conversation drifted back to the case in hand.

"If you ask me," said old Shuffley, though no one had, "we should be concentratin' on the *look* of the bairn. I understand he's a bit foreign lookin' and the only foreigner about these parts that I know of is Mrs Haylett the merchant's wife, who used to live at High Point House. They all moved to Illingham last October. There were two lasses and a lad up there and they used to have an old lady stay with them at times. I think she was Mrs Haylett's mother from Spain. I heard tell that she liked to visit her daughter but got homesick after about a month, so kept goin' back home. Well, those are my thoughts on the subject anyhow."

As usual, Old Shuffley had said nothing at all for hours, then made a statement that made more sense than all the previous ones put together.

All eyes had now turned to Shuffley, eager to hear any other great revelations he might make.

"You make a lot of sense there, Shuffley," said Silas. "Maybe we should be lookin' in that direction. Do you know why they moved off so sudden like?"

"Well I heard tell it was more convenient for Mr Haylett's business, he had some ships you know, used to sail out of Illingham, but he wasn't short of a penny or two, he could well afford to keep another bairn."

"Thass a point, maybe we're on the wrong track after all," said Reuben disappointedly.

"I don't know," said Fingal, "some of us around here are a bit dark lookin'."

"Thass on account of us bein' out of doors in all weathers," rejoined Silas, "I don't think we were *born* that way!" More laughter followed this comment.

"Well the little mite isn't dark skinned but he has got very black hair," offered Reuben.

By now the conversation had become a bit fuddled.

"Well, the Spanish lady wasn't particularly dark skinned either although she did go darker in the Summer," said Old Shuffley. "I've done many an odd job up at High Point."

"My father built that house in 1806, I had a hand in it too," said Walter. "I was only twenty then, my, thass a fine house that is. We built several of them big houses, up on Winford Road, around that time. Then about ten years later we built the Doctor's house and the Vicarage, yes they must be thirty years old now. How time fly, I'll be pushin' up daisies meself before I know it, then it will be up to young Jarvis and Ambrose to keep the family name goin'."

Round and round went the little stories and reminiscences until it was time to go home and find their beds, which they would have to do ever so quietly, or they might get the wrong side of their good ladies' tongues, on account of the lateness of the hour.

"G'night, Tom, G'night, all," they called, as one by one they left the Village Maid.

It had been a good night and they had had a mighty fine time finding out nothing at all, but that fact probably would not dawn on them until they awoke the next morning – many of them with a very sore head!

Tom and Sadie waited until the last of them had departed then proceeded to bring in the benches and tally up their night's inflated takings.

A bit of gossip works wonders for trade, thought Tom.

Chapter Six

Four years later...

It was the twenty third of June and the inhabitants of Flinton were looking forward to the following evening – Midsummer's Night. The festivities traditionally began at around six o'clock on the Village Green – in the school house if the weather was bad – where there would be fun, games and music for the children of the village. At eight o'clock the Grand Midsummer Ball at the Manor would begin when Robert Kempton-Jones would throw open his grounds and house for the annual event. It was customary for him to send out one hundred and fifty 'inside' invitations for those of his guests who would be inside the house. These usually consisted of his friends, business acquaintances and prominent people from the village and surrounding areas. In addition to this he opened his grounds to admit any of the villagers who cared to attend. In fine weather the locals and fiddlers would congregate and dance on the huge lawns, but the large barns would be made ready, in case of inclement conditions.

Although a certain amount of food and drink was provided by Mr Kempton-Jones, each family was in the habit of taking extra provisions to ensure supplies did not run out. This year would be no exception; therefore most of the women of Flinton were busy in their kitchens.

The village boasted a merry little band of fiddlers, who supplied the music at all the festivities and gatherings, from weddings, to accompanying the carollers on Christmas Eve. They would make their way round, spreading a bit of Christmas spirit and hoping for a mug of warm cider to keep out the cold, and assist the dexterity of the fingers.

There were five main musicians, Amos Farthing, Eli Penny,

Walter Fennell, Reuben Healey and Fergus Tooley. Most of them had already trained up a young man to ensure continuity of the band, while one or two more were having lessons. An ability to play the violin ensured a welcome anywhere, and was an enjoyable way of earning a few coppers into the bargain. There was, therefore, a steady stream of young hopefuls always asking to be taught.

One such person was Matthew Johnson, who was just over four years old, but he had showed such an interest in the fiddle when he visited Old Walter Fennell with his father, that the old man had agreed to teach him. According to Walter the boy was showing great promise for one so young.

Naturally no one, to date, had told the little boy the unusual circumstances of his birth. He therefore believed Richard, junior, to be his older brother. Nobody had ever claimed him or even purported to be his mother, for which Elizabeth was immensely grateful. The Vicar himself had also grown to regard the boy as his son so, although he often wondered about Matthew's origins, it was no longer a burning issue to actively seek his parents. On the contrary, they both hoped the boy would remain with them.

By half past seven on Midsummer's Night, most of the younger, village children had been put to bed, after one and a half hour's of jollity on the Village Green. Their eyes were not long open after their heads found their pillows, a charming facet of childhood that, given the opportunity, many would choose to carry into adulthood. They were then left with their minders – often grandparents – while their parents made their way to the Manor House for a rare night out.

On this particular evening the road to the Manor was strewn with would be revellers, carrying provisions and – yet to be lit – lanterns. Every now and again they would cease their chattering and cluster toward the roadside to allow a carriage to pass on its way to the Ball. Everyone was in high spirits, anticipating a night to remember.

Daniel and Louisa Canham travelled to the ball in their

horse and trap, it was a fine breezy night. Louisa was wearing a new, blue frock, with a fetching scooped neckline that Lydia Flowerdew had made for her. Her pale gold hair was piled high on her head setting off her pretty, slender neck. Daniel was very proud to have her by his side, he intended to make the most of this lovely summer evening by dancing as much as possible with his beautiful wife. Being landowners, albeit in a small way, they had received an 'inside' invitation.

Daniel and Louisa had been married for five years. They had one child, Matilda Rose, who was three years old.

The little girl resembled her mother, being of a slender build with pale gold hair. Matilda was the apple of her parents' eyes. They hoped she was the first of several children. Tonight her grandparents, who also lived at the farmhouse, were caring for her. Dan Canham had not yet handed over the reins of the farm to his son, but he would have no hesitation in doing so when the time came, for his son had settled well into marriage and fatherhood. He had surprised his parents by his hard work and commitment to the farm and his family. Yes, Dan and Rose were very proud of their son.

As the hour approached eight the fiddlers were tuning their instruments at one end of the huge rectangular lawn where they had set their stools.

There was a good deal of bustle and noise as everyone found places in which to settle. Benches had been brought from the barns, but some had chosen to bring their own stools to ensure not having to sit on the grass, which might be damp of an evening, anyway they did not want to dirty their finery – they did not often have the opportunity to wear it.

As the church clock struck the hour of eight, the fiddlers outside, and the band inside, began their playing.

As Daniel whirled his wife around the dance floor he could not have been happier and for once his guilty conscience did not mar his enjoyment. Their own little group consisted of themselves with Richard Johnson, and Penelope and Diggory. Diggory still had his heart set on the Schoolmistress, but their relationship had never crossed the threshold from friendship to romance. It probably would have done, had his name not been Farthing. Diggory was considered quite a catch by the village maidens, which was just as well as he now had a rival for the affections of Penelope in the shape of Henry Miles, who had just returned home from his medical studies.

Flinton did not need three doctors, so Diggory was sure that Henry would be moving on fairly shortly, he could but hope. So Diggory was another who intended to make the most of the evening.

Daniel and Louisa returned from the dance floor as Penelope and Diggory got up to join the dancers.

"There are some pretty ladies here tonight Richard," said Daniel, getting back his breath, "I wonder if we can find you a wife amongst them."

"Everybody seems intent on finding me a wife, I wonder if you secretly envy my bachelor status." The young curate raised one eyebrow inquiringly at his friend.

"Good heavens no, I would not dare say so even if it were the case," Daniel cast a twinkling glance in the direction of Louisa. "It is just that I would not have to share my dancing partner quite so much if you had one of your own."

"I am sure Penelope will dance with me once or twice," said Richard, although he knew his friend was joking.

"Do not count on it, Richard, Diggory is quite possessive of her, it is such a shame they will not marry, after all, nobody calls Penelope, Penny, she will not allow it."

"I think perhaps there is a deeper reason for her spinsterhood," said Louisa as she watched her friend being danced around the floor by Diggory. "I think she intends to remain single by choice, after all, she has the village children all day, she probably would not miss having none of her own."

"It is funny," said Daniel, "I always thought you would marry Penelope one day, you are the best of friends."

Richard laughed, imagining the situation. "Why, if I were late home for dinner she would have me sitting in the corner for half an hour as punishment. No I love her dearly, but I could never be 'in love' with her. No doubt we are both destined to remain single."

"Well," said Daniel, "I am getting rather hot in here, we farmers are more used to being out of doors you know, so I will leave you to look after my lovely wife, while I go out for some fresh air. I will bring you back a report of how the outside festivities are progressing." With that he rose and left the table to cross the room in the direction of the French doors, which led onto the terrace.

As he watched the merrymaking Daniel smiled. Somehow, he thought, they always have a jollier time than we do indoors, they are less inhibited.

Amos and Walter were enjoying themselves immensely as they led their little band of musicians.

The dancers were in two long lines down each side of the lawn, clapping in time to the music while a couple holding hands were coming up the centre. When they reached the top they separated to each lead a line of dancers down the outside edge, they then formed an arch with their arms for everyone to pass through, so that a new pair found themselves at the top to dance down and up the centre. So the process went on, until everyone had had a turn…

From the terrace, steps led down to the lawn, flanked on either side by two huge statues. Daniel walked down, drawn towards the music and the dancing. He strolled to one side of the lawn where a gravel path and flower border led to another classical statue. From this vantage-point he had a clear view of both the outside dancers and the inside ones – visible through the French doors – he relaxed, his head falling gently back onto the cool stone. He vaguely noticed that the French doors were being opened again and a lady was passing through, fanning her face as she did so. At first he thought it was Louisa come to look for him. He followed her with his eyes as she lifted her skirts to descend the steps, for a closer look at the revellers on the lawn. As she walked towards him Daniel thought there was something familiar about her and then he caught his breath – it was Juanita, he was sure of it. He had not set eyes on her for about five years.

"Juanita," he called softly. The lady took her eyes from the dancers to focus on the young man, who appeared to have made her acquaintance. "Juanita, it is me, Daniel – Daniel Canham."

"Why, Daniel, how lovely to see you, I trust you are well?"

"Yes, very well thank you, but why have I not seen you for so long, ever since in fact…"

The lady cut him short, "My father moved us all to Illingham about five years ago," she explained. "He found it far more convenient for his business. He is a merchant, you may recall. Also, he wanted me to make a good marriage and thought there would be better opportunity in a large seaport. I am married now, you may have heard, to Alexander Fellstock. He is a barrister. We live in London. I met him while staying with my aunt – my father's sister – in Chelsea. I trust your own wedding went without mishap?"

"Yes, yes," blustered Daniel, surprised at the acquired poise and demeanour of Juanita, whom he remembered as fiery and flirtatious, with an infectious sense of fun. "I have not been able to forget you these last five years. I have hoped to meet you again."

"Well, now you have and we have found each other well," she said coolly. "You must not let me occupy your thoughts quite so much, your wife might object." She flashed her dark eyes at him and he realized she had not changed as much as he had at first thought. "I trust the nature of our friendship has not been bandied around the village?" She raised an inquiring eyebrow.

"Good heavens no, what do you take me for, but…"

Again she cut him off. "We are friends, Daniel, and if you would like us to remain so, you must not divulge the nature of our friendship to anyone. I would not like to have to defend my good name in the law courts of London. Good evening to you, perhaps our paths will cross again before I return home."

"Do not go, Juanita, please. I need to talk to you, what about your son, why did you leave him…?"

"Our son is in good hands, Daniel," she answered a little

sharply. "You really should not fret so, now I must return to Alexander, he will be wondering about my absence," she relaxed a little, then, she dipped her lovely head slightly and flashed him one of her sultry smiles. "You must call on us if you ever find yourself in London."

With that, she put her hand into her blue satin evening bag and handed him a small, embossed card bearing her name and address. She then lifted her skirts, walked up the gravel path, ascended the steps and disappeared back through the French doors of the ballroom.

Daniel's mood plummeted. On the surface, Juanita's warning had been gently chiding, but he sensed a more threatening undercurrent to her words especially as she had mentioned, in passing, that her husband was a barrister! He shuddered unexpectedly in the warm evening air. Now, he supposed, he would never be able to acknowledge his son, even if he wanted to…

Chapter Seven

"You have been outside a long time," said Louisa, on Daniel's return to the ballroom. "Are they having more fun out there than we are in here?"

"I rather think they might be, would you like to go out and take a turn at the dancing?" Daniel forced a smile, he did not fancy running into Juanita again in the ballroom.

"I think it will be a bit too energetic for me at the moment. Richard has been whirling me around the dance floor for the last half hour, I am feeling quite dizzy."

"Would you like to find a quiet area of the garden in which to sit?"

"No, no I am fine really, we are all going to take refreshments shortly while the band has a rest. Did you meet anybody interesting out there?"

"Oh, you know how it is in a village this size, one is familiar with just about everyone, but it is always nice to have a chat, it is a lovely evening. Are you sure you do not want to take a walk?"

"Really, I am."

"Where are the others?"

"Penelope and Diggory went outside about twenty minutes ago, and Richard is dancing with a young lady he met when she lived at Illingham, there, look, over by the window, they will be passing the band any minute, do you see them?"

Daniel's heart somersaulted, for Richard was dancing with Juanita. What should he do? Would Juanita publicly acknowledge him? He could feel himself becoming very hot but the palms of his hands were cold and clammy. He felt as he had done in Flinton church the morning the baby had been found. He silently prayed to God to get him out of this dreadful mess without arousing Louisa's suspicions. He willed the band to carry on playing, for, when it stopped, Richard would surely bring Juanita over to introduce her. He had looked forward to this evening so much, bringing Louisa to such a lavish occasion, being so proud of her, but it had turned into a living nightmare, from which he wanted instant escapement.

"Are you feeling alright, Daniel?"

"Yes, yes of course. It is a little hot in here do you not think?"

"You look quite pale, did you see them?"

"Yes, yes they make a handsome pair."

"She is very beautiful, I wonder if she is married."

"Will you excuse me, I need some cool air?"

"You cannot leave again, Daniel, you have only just come in, Richard will get the impression you are avoiding him, anyway they are coming over."

They were indeed heading straight for their table.

"Louisa and Daniel, I would like you to meet Juanita, a friend of mine, unfortunately I only have her on loan, from her successful barrister husband."

Hands were shaken or kissed and pleasantries and smiles exchanged. Juanita gave no indication of knowing Daniel, and so the nightmare passed, leaving Daniel feeling a bigger fraud than ever.

For those who did not have a guilty conscience, or a heavy heart, the journey home was magical. Hundreds of folk, who had just enjoyed one of the highlights of the year, tired but happy, wandering home, carrying their seats, empty bags and instruments, along the lane that led them from the Manor. The lanterns were now lit and held aloft, swaying gently from the movement of walking. The whole ensemble resembled a scene from fairyland. The horses and carriages, also with lighted lanterns, clip-clopped home quite tunefully. Cheery 'goodnights' were called out as, one by one, the villagers found their cottages while the remainder strolled merrily along, often breaking out into song. What a night it had been. The Midsummer Night's Ball would be a talking point for months to come. It would be the last chance to dance for most people 'til Christmas.

When Daniel arrived home that night he wondered what to do with the visiting card. He doubted he would ever call on Juanita but, perhaps he should keep it in case of emergency, Matthew could fall seriously ill, for instance, and no one else knew the identity of his mother. He took the small, embossed card out of his inside pocket and studied it carefully, then put it safely in a box with some other personal possessions.

Chapter Eight

"I am going up to Meadow Farm, shall I take Matilda with me to see the new piglets?" Daniel shouted to Louisa as he entered the kitchen door.

Matilda, like most three-year-olds, loved animals. They had no pigs on their own farm so she was always happy to go and see Mr Taylor's.

Daniel put Matilda on his shoulders and walked the short distance to the neighbouring farm.

Old Mr Taylor – he was not really old, but due to the fact that most fathers named their sons after themselves, one had to differentiate between them somehow – suffered with his feet. He now left the physical running of the farm to young Robert, while he himself concentrated on the bookwork.

It was 'young' Robert who greeted them today. "Hello, how is little Miss today then?"

"Little Miss has lost her tongue," said Daniel, tickling Matilda in the ribs to make her lose her shyness. "Perhaps the piglets have got it. What do you think, Robert?"

"I think we should go and have a look," he said, smiling at Matilda, as he took her by the hand to visit the new arrivals.

"Now, little Miss, which piglet do you think has got your tongue?"

"None of them."

"Oh, you have got it back then, now you can say 'hello' to me."

The little girl smiled shyly and hid behind her father, but she liked Robert Taylor all the same.

"No patter of little feet in your household yet, my friend?"

"Unfortunately not, I have asked Sally to stop making baby clothes, we have got drawers full, enough for three at least."

"It will happen, we waited two years for this little one and I can assure you she was well worth it." Daniel ruffled his daughter's hair.

"Well, I came to tell you that some of your fences went down in the gale last night. I have been up the top fields repairing mine today, oh, and to collect a ham for Louisa."

"Thank you, Daniel, I will go up there shortly to assess the damage – I will get your ham for you."

As Daniel carried Matilda home she was full of questions.

"Why do pigs have curly tails?"

"Because they eat a lot."

"Cows eat a lot too."

"Well, we will have to watch to see if their tails grow curly."

The little girl laughed at the thought of cows with curly tails.

Daniel held his daughter tightly. He was so lucky to have her and Louisa – luckier than he deserved. He took the child back indoors then went back to work. It was four months since he had seen Juanita and he could not get her lightly veiled threat out of his head. His thoughts flitted, he had better make sure everything was secure tonight before he went indoors; it promised to be another wild and windy night.

Later as Louisa lay sleeping beside him, Daniel was again being troubled by his conscience. He wondered why he could go weeks without thinking about little Matthew Johnson much at all, but then sometimes could not get him out of his head – tonight was one of those times. Did something jolt his subconscious occasionally? What triggered the old memories to come to the forefront of his mind? Daniel tried to think what might have triggered his thoughts today, if he could do that, perhaps he could avoid it happening in the future. Round and round went his musings. He *had* spoken to Robert Taylor about having a first child, maybe that was it.

How did he feel about little Matthew? He asked himself. He was a handsome little chap, very bright and alert, well-behaved, a credit to his adoptive parents. He saw him in church on Sunday mornings, he also saw him if he had reason to call on the Vicar and, although he tried not to stare at him, he knew he always did. It was as if the very fact that he should not be overly interested made him even more so.

Daniel's thoughts then drifted to his recent meeting with Juanita. Why had she seemed happy to talk to him outside, then treat him as a stranger when introduced to him inside?

He went over and over their conversation in the garden. She had appeared friendly, pleased even, to see him again, even so she *had* found it necessary to warn him. He mentally recounted their exchange of words until he thought it must be imprinted on his memory forever. Why did he torture himself like this, he wondered. Why not forget the whole business. But no matter how many times he told himself to forget the past and concentrate on the future, he persistently experienced days when his guilty secret haunted him to distraction, and of course the more he thought about it, the more indelibly it was printed on his mind.

Daniel looked sideways at Louisa as she lay in blissful ignorance. How he wished he could erase the past and feel worthy of the great love she had for him. He had made her happy, he consoled himself, they had one lovely child and would have others. He intended to never hurt her again as long as he lived. But was he not hurting her now? Her unawareness did not justify his deception. He could keep this secret until the day he died only to be exposed as a fraud after his death. He would then be in no position to defend himself, to tell her how sorry he was. She might grow to hate him. Round and round in his head went the hypothetical questions and answers until he felt he would go mad. Then he went over it all again from the beginning...

The evening before his marriage to Louisa, he had walked down to the Vicarage to see his best friend, Richard, who was to be his Best Man. After the usual pre-wedding teasing about losing his freedom, they had walked across the road to see their other good friends, Ben and Henry Miles, the Doctor's sons. All four had then wandered down to the Village Maid for a drink and a mardle. They had sat outside and reminisced about their school days and lives in general.

After an hour or so, Richard had said his goodbyes and taken his leave, with the excuse that it did not bode well for a curate to be seen over indulging in ale-houses. He was staying as a guest at his parents' house tonight and it would be rude to return at too late an hour.

The remaining three friends drank more than they should have, and occasionally cast an admiring glance or two at some female admirers, who were sitting opposite on the Green. The usual good-natured pre-wedding banter and teasing took place, which gradually, somehow, extended to the girls.

When the evening drew to a close, the young men gallantly offered to walk them to their doors. Unfortunately, one of the young ladies – dark, pretty and very flirtatious – said she lived quite a way up the Winford Road, so she would not trouble the young men. Daniel, feeling on top of the world – partly due to his forthcoming marriage and partly due to the quantity of intoxicating beverage he had consumed – said he could walk the young lady to her door then take an alternative route home which skirted the common. No trouble at all, he had said happily.

Amid a great deal of teasing – and an instruction to make sure he remembered he was virtually a married man – the friends had parted company.

Daniel had turned toward Winford Road but the girl had grabbed his arm, saying. "As I am lucky enough to have an escort tonight, would you mind if we went home by way of Common Lane it is such a lovely moonlit evening?"

"No, of course not, it will probably help clear my head if I have a longer walk."

"I heard your friends call you Daniel, do you not want to know my name?"

"Yes, I am sorry, I am forgetting my manners you must put it down to the fact I am getting married tomorrow." *He spread his arms wide as if encompassing the world.*

"It is Juanita."

"That is a very unusual name."

"It is Spanish, my mother is Spanish."

"I do not think I have seen you around the village before."

40

"I am not officially allowed to wander the locality, my father is very strict, he wants me to marry well. He does not want me to have the opportunity of falling in love with a farm labourer. But he may not object to a farmer's son," she added playfully, again holding his arm as she smiled seductively.

Daniel laughed. *"I am spoken for, but I know one or two others."*

They walked on in silence, still arm in arm, though Daniel was not really aware of it. His thoughts were with Louisa and how he felt with the world. After a while he noticed that Juanita had been quiet for some considerable time. Remembering his manners he inquired, "Are you alright?"

"Yes."

"If you are not allowed in the village why were you there tonight?"

"I go to the village whenever I can. The girls there have much more fun than I do. I like to go and talk to them, or even just watch them, but I have to wait until my parents are away from home, then I sneak out of my bedroom to go for a walk."

"Are you an only child?"

"No, I have a sister and a brother, both younger than me."

"Are you supposed to be looking after them in your parents' absence?"

"No, we have a housekeeper and a nanny."

The two had now reached the top of Common Lane. Ahead of them was the Common itself, where, in the distance, glowing red embers of abandoned fires could be seen. They drew to a halt, gazing ahead of them.

"We must be quiet," *said Daniel, putting his finger to his lips.* "The gypsies are here again, we do not want to set all the dogs barking."

"I envy the gypsies," *whispered Juanita,* "they are so free, I hate being so restricted, I am sure I shall run away one day if my father does not give me more freedom," *then,* "shall we run away now, Daniel?" *She flashed her dark eyes at him. Daniel chuckled quietly, it all seemed so unreal. Here he was in the moonlight, with a relative stranger, in the dark of night with the stars twinkling overhead and the fires glowing in the distance – the gypsy caravans looking romantic in silhouette against the night sky. He felt as if he were dreaming. He was quite enjoying the company, and the flirting, of the half-Spanish girl.*

"I must get home, Juanita," he said, turning to the right.

"No, please Daniel, let me stay with you a little longer, I do not want to go home yet."

"But I must go home, I am getting married tomorrow."

"Let me walk home with you then."

"No you cannot, you will then have to walk home alone."

"I will sleep in one of your barns and wait until it is light."

"You are mad." But he did not really mean it and he did not really care, he was happy tonight.

"I am not mad, I am lonely."

"I cannot let you do this," he said trying to sound authoritative.

"If you do not let me I will scream and wake the dogs, or I will run away now and you will have questions to answer as the last person to have seen me." Daniel gave in, after all, he reasoned, she would have walked home alone if he had not offered to escort her. He was not responsible for her in any way. He fancied she was a bit wild and did not want to spoil his good mood. He allowed her to accompany him as he wended his way home.

When they reached the farmyard he took her to the barn where the straw was stored. He was feeling very drowsy and muddle headed.

"Stay and talk to me for a while," the temptress pleaded.

"I cannot, it is getting late."

"Please," she gave him an injured look.

He allowed himself to be pulled down onto the straw, where, Juanita cuddled up to him temptingly and began to kiss him. He pushed at her several times in a playful fashion but he did not resist as much as he could have...he was drowsy and warm...Juanita was warm and inviting...the air was sweet...Juanita was sweet...she smelled so nice...he was getting married tomorrow...he was sleepy...he was happy...

When Daniel awoke the sun was shining through the cracks in the barn, he sat up and looked round, he was alone, had it all been a dream?

He was getting married tomorrow...

...no, he was getting married today!

He awoke with a jolt; he had dozed off after all and was now disturbing Louisa.

Chapter Nine

Penelope Wyn-Jones surveyed her class of children, acknowledging the privilege of being instrumental in their early education. She took her vocation very seriously. It was her intention that all her charges work to the best of their ability. She therefore kept a very strict schoolroom. She was particularly interested in the education of her girls. Girls, she felt, grew up to lead very disillusioned lives, watching their dreams and aspirations slowly evaporate as they took husbands, bore children and gradually lost their identity to the realms of domesticity, a fact which saddened her considerably.

The Schoolmistress had now lived in Flinton for twelve years. Most of the girls she had taught on her arrival were married, with two or three babies. She had watched as these girls had changed from happy, carefree youngsters, to work-worn young women with dull eyes and stooping shoulders, struggling to feed and clothe their families on the meagre earnings of their labouring husbands. Whilst she was aware that the young men of the area also led very hard, deprived existences, her compassion was, even so, mostly directed toward the girls. Penelope had had several proposals of marriage and had once or twice been tempted to follow her heart but, at those times, she would think of dull eyes and lost dreams. She would then straighten her back and strengthen her resolve to never succumb to the temptations of marriage. So far she had succeeded.

Some children were a pleasure to teach, being very eager to learn, into this category she put both Matthew and Matilda.

Matilda Rose Canham was an exceptionally beautiful child of ten years old. She had inherited the delicate bone structure and pale gold hair of her mother. She was beautiful but, as Penelope had found out, very strong minded for one so young.

The Reverend and his wife had raised Matthew Luke Johnson; he was now eleven years old. He was strong and sturdy. Dark as Matilda was fair.

The two children had never failed to intrigue their schoolmistress, for, ever since their inception at her school, they had been inseparable. They insisted on sitting next to each other in class and could not concentrate on their work if separated. When together they appeared to communicate as much with their eyes and expressions as with their voices. They were certainly no trouble to teach, both being exceptionally bright. If they associated with any of the other pupils at all, it was with John and Verity Miles, the children of young Doctor Miles. The four children were good friends but Matthew and Matilda were more like soul mates.

Matilda was showing great potential at the piano, while Matthew had, for some years, been having violin lessons from Old Walter Fennell, the undertaker. Matthew had frequently accompanied his father – he called the Vicar, 'Father' – when he visited old Walter on parish business. The two men met often, due to their respective professions, especially on the matter of funerals. Matthew had found an affinity with Walter, and chose to spend a considerable amount of his spare time with the old man, who taught him carpentry as well.

The Schoolmistress was overjoyed at having two such young, accomplished musicians in her charge. She gave them all the encouragement she could and enjoyed listening to the two of them performing together. Now, as she watched their heads bobbing over their work, she felt a great satisfaction at her contribution to their education. She hoped these two, at least, would make the most of their abilities.

Chapter Ten

The young Reverend Richard Johnson had, that evening, informed his parents of his intended marriage to Miss Jane Farley of Illingham. They had been delighted.

Richard was now thirty-three years old and was the Vicar of Winford but often preached at Flinton, his father having reduced his workload due to his age.

Richard was now on his way to tell his good news to his best friend, Daniel Canham. When Matthew heard that Richard was going to the farm, he had pleaded with him to take him along, he rarely saw Matilda – or Tilly as he called her – outside school or church and he had a present for her. It was a beautiful evening in May. The walkers reached the top of the hill, entered the farmyard on their left and knocked at the kitchen door.

The farmhouse was occupied by three generations. Old Dan Canham was now in his sixties but was still in charge of the farm. Dan and Rose, his wife, had given over most of their large house to young Daniel and his growing family. The arrangement worked well for all of them.

"Why, Richard, how splendid to see you," cried Daniel on seeing his friend. "What brings you up here tonight?"

"I have come to inform you of my intended marriage, Daniel. I am taking the plunge at last and I have brought my young brother with me, he wants to see Matilda."

Matthew now stepped into view from where he had been standing to one side of the door. "Hello, Sir," he said, politely.

"H-Hello, Matthew," said Daniel, looking at the boy intently. "Yes, yes, come in, we will find Matilda for you," he finished, regaining his composure. "Getting married, I never thought I would see the day," he blustered. "A confirmed bachelor, that is what I took you for."

"It has taken me longer to find the right person, that is all.

You were lucky, we all knew you would marry Louisa one day."

"Come on through, come on though," said Daniel, ushering his guests through the hall into the sitting room where they found Louisa, reading to the younger children.

"This is a surprise," she said smiling.

Richard quickly crossed the room to give Louisa a kiss on the cheek, while Matthew hung back shyly by the hall door, not knowing whether or not to enter.

Daniel informed his wife of the nature of the visit adding, " I think this calls for a celebratory glass of wine. Where is Matilda, she has a visitor?"

"What marvellous news, Richard," said Louisa, "I am so happy for you, will you excuse me for a moment?"

She crossed the room to greet Matthew. "Hello, it is lovely to see you, Matilda is in the garden sketching as usual. I know she will be delighted to see you, she talks of you all the time, Matthew, you must call on us again, anytime. Matilda finds you such good company." She opened up the back door to reveal Matilda sitting on a low garden wall, sketchbook in hand.

Matilda turned her head, then literally leapt onto her feet excitedly and ran toward Matthew, grabbing him by the arm and dragging him back to where she was sitting.

Louisa returned to the sitting room to collect the younger children for bed. She found them shyly enjoying all the attention of their Uncle Richard, as they called him. Uncle Richard was a favourite of them all.

On her return downstairs Louisa found the two men in very good spirits. "You are very honoured, Richard," she said now, "Daniel rarely touches alcohol, I think I must have had a good effect on him. I did not think he would settle quite so well into marriage and fatherhood." As she spoke she looked warmly across at Daniel; the two were obviously still very much in love with one another.

"When are you going to bring Jane to meet us? It is not fair of you to keep her all to yourself. It is so tantalising to hear so much of a person but never to meet them. Do please put us out of our misery, bring her over next time you visit – or perhaps you are concerned that our lively young family will dissuade her from motherhood?"

"Your family is delightful, Louisa, as well you know. You are to be envied and I am sure Jane will agree. Talking of children, I understand Matilda and Matthew are great friends. Penelope refers to them as soul mates. I hear they are two of her most promising pupils. She is particularly pleased that they have an interest in music, did you know that Matthew is quite an accomplished violinist?"

"Yes, we have heard," replied Louisa, "Matilda talks of little else but Matthew's virtues when she returns from school, they are certainly very close."

Daniel sat quietly, listening to the conversation between his wife and his friend, feeling a mixture of pride and consternation. There was nothing odd to *him* about the children's affinity with one another, it was no more than he would have expected between brother and sister, but he felt a tremendous sense of guilt that he had never been able to confide in Louisa about Matthew's background. He found the present situation terribly uncomfortable. Here he was, with two of his closest confidants – one his wife – talking about the unusually close friendship of two children who were bound to be close, given the circumstances. How would Louisa react if he told her that the young boy outside was his own? It was too late, he thought, he should have confessed to her before he married her. But then she may have called off the wedding and that would have devastated him, he loved her so much. But was it fair on her, he ruminated, he should have given her a choice. He had lived with this terrible burden for eleven years and it did not get any easier. He had sedulously endeavoured to push his secret to the back of his mind, but Matthew was becoming more and more a part of his life.

Due to his churchwarden duties, Daniel often called upon the Vicar, where he would come across Matthew. He also saw the child at church and often at old Walter Fennel's house if he had need to call. The boy was of such a nature that one could not dislike him. He had been well brought up, was always courteous. He was a handsome young lad, the sort you found yourself warming to after just a short time in his company.

There was no good reason why Daniel should discourage the children's friendship, but he had an uneasy feeling about it just the same and wished he could keep Matthew a bit more at a distance.

"You are extremely quiet, Daniel, have you nothing to contribute to the conversation this evening?" inquired Louisa. "Are you not also intrigued by your daughter's remarkable friendship with young Matthew?"

"I was thinking of the forthcoming marriage," lied Daniel. "And of how happy I am that Richard has found a wife. I wish you both every happiness. If you are only half as happy as Louisa and myself you will do extremely well for yourselves, so I propose a toast."

They both raised their glasses to their friend. "To Richard and Jane, may God bless their union."

Matilda was overjoyed at seeing Matthew.

"I cannot believe you are here," she said leading him towards the low wall. "I have so many things to show you on the farm and I want to take you to all my favourite places hereabouts."

"I do not think you will have time to do all that this evening," he laughed, "but I have good news. Your mother has just invited me to come here whenever I wish. We will have great fun, Tilly. Just think of all the time we can spend together."

They both fell quiet thinking of just that.

It was then that Matthew remembered the present he had for Tilly. He put his hand into the green baize bag he had brought with him and took out two little wooden boxes. They were each about two inches square and two inches high. They were made of oak. "I made these at Walter Fennell's," he said now, "I made one for me and one for you. I thought it would be nice for each of us to have an identical box."

"They are beautiful, how clever you are, you are kind to think of me so often, I will treasure this forever."

"You are not going to get away so lightly, I would like you to do something special for us too."

"Anything, what is it that you want?"

"I would like you to paint one of your oil pictures on the lid of each box. I thought that perhaps you could put flowers on yours and, maybe, a ship on mine. When you have done that I will take them back to Walter's workshop and varnish them."

Tilly was ecstatic. "I will ask Mother if I can borrow her oils, she usually lets me. I will do them as soon as possible. You are so thoughtful, Matthew, I love you so," she then put both arms around his neck and hugged him tightly.

He did not seem to mind.

Matthew put both boxes into the green baize bag and gave them to Tilly, who ran indoors to deposit them in the kitchen then she took her guest on a guided tour of the farm.

All too soon the friends heard their names being called from the back door. It was time for Matthew to return home.

Having waved goodbye, Matilda collected the bag containing the boxes from the kitchen. She showed her parents what Matthew had made and explained what they planned to do.

"That is a lovely idea," said Louisa, "of course you can borrow my paints, does Matthew have a special interest in ships?"

"He wants to travel, Mother, he wants to see the world for himself. He reads Reverend Johnson's books but that is not enough, he says he must go and see everything for himself. If he does not he will regret it for the rest of his life. I know how important it is to him because he tells me, but, it is difficult for me to explain it to you."

"I think I am beginning to understand," laughed Louisa, seeing the intense, serious expression on her daughter's face. "And I am sure he will achieve his ambition one day, now off to bed with you, it is getting very late."

That evening had set a pattern for the Summer. Matthew had so enjoyed himself that he often visited the farm, sometimes staying all day. The two friends explored the countryside together, shared their hopes, their dreams and if the weather was inclement they would either be in one of the barns or in the house, playing their respective musical instruments together – Matthew always brought his violin with him. Occasionally he would watch Tilly paint, mostly in water colour – the oils belonged to her mother – fascinated by the way she could bring a sketch to life. She was not yet accomplished, but she showed great potential, rather like Matthew with his carpentry. That was the most extraordinary element of their relationship, they complemented each other so perfectly. One could not say that either was handicapped without the other, on the contrary, they both had a lively, inquiring mind and special absorbing interests – he with his violin, carpentry and reading, she with her sketching, painting and piano playing. They both liked to go exploring and had a genuine love for the natural world.

One evening, shortly after Matthew's first visit to the farm, Matilda suggested that they go to Clancy's Wood – one of her favourite places.

The wood was on their land about half a mile across the fields. No one knew exactly why it was called Clancy's Wood, but old Shuffley had always claimed it was because a man called Clancy used to live rough in there many years ago. According to folklore he was so strange that the villagers used to avoid the place, preferring to lengthen their journeys by going round the edge, skirting the Common.

The last anybody had seen of Clancy was when he had left the village with a handcart piled high with his possessions saying he was 'gittin too old for the wood in Winter but would be back in the Spring, so no-one's to touch my house'.

Decades of avoiding Clancy's had resulted in a well-worn path along the side of the Common. By going cross-country it was possible for a walker to take a mile and a half off the journey to Winford. Anyway, not many people liked to go through the wood on their own, especially after dark.

To get to Clancy's Wood, one could either go along Poachers Way or cross the meadow and the poppy field, which were visible from the front windows of Uphall Farm.

The children had naturally elected to go across the fields.

As they crossed the meadow Matilda was enthusing to Matthew the beauty of the countryside, especially at this time of year. Ahead of them the poppy field was obscured from view by a high hedge which gave way to a stile on the right hand side of the field.

The children reached the stile and then stopped in wonderment, the view before them was breathtaking. The field of poppies was ablaze with colour, which varied in depth as the wind rushed across the top causing waves of vermilion to intermingle with a deep salmon. The flowers with their black centres, were ducking, diving and dancing. The field was a vibrant living mass of colour.

"Can we walk through them?" asked Matthew, "Every time I have seen them from Poachers Way I have wanted to walk through them."

"Of course we can, it is my usual route, but, do they give you a headache?"

"No, should they?"

"The scent gives some people a headache, I am glad it does not effect me, I love to walk through them." So they proceeded across the field with Matilda's hair also blowing wildly in the wind.

"You have lovely hair, Tilly, it is really beautiful. I will have to be careful when you are older that somebody does not snatch you from me and marry you. I would love a picture of you walking through the poppies."

The two friends had the habit of talking as though they would always be together. Each of their future plans always included the other; there was no question about it.

"I would never marry anyone but you, Matthew, nobody could know me as well as you do."

Arriving at the other side of the field they turned to look again at the fascinating, colourful scene, then turned, to enter the wood.

"Could we get lost in here?"

"Of course not."

"But it looks so big and all the paths look the same."

"It is quite large but I know it well, there is no need to worry. I have been playing in here for years; the trees are my friends. Listen, they talk to you."

The children stopped and listened. The trees did indeed appear to communicate as they swayed their huge branches in the wind, the leaves rustling and whistling, sometimes bending so low that the lower twigs caught at their bodies, as if to say. "Come on, talk to us, play with us, we love you." But it was impossible to stop for long when the trees in front were also calling and beckoning, tugging at their clothing, begging for company and ushering them along, and so the two walked on.

"The paths may look the same to you, but when you know them as well as I do, you will find they are all quite different. There are so many different types of trees in here, oaks, elms, beeches, sycamores oh, so many others too, but one is very special to me for it is just a sapling and the only one of its kind in the wood. It is in my very special place where I have taken no one before." As she spoke, the girl turned to the left down an almost obscured path. In many places it was nearly blocked by huge fronds of dense bracken but she parted them gently as she led the way, ever deeper into the wood. Another turn, this time to the right where there was no perceivable path, then, suddenly, they were faced by a huge oak tree with massive roots which laid along the ground, all twisted and intermingled, that had to be climbed over.

A little further, some more, dense bracken, then Tilly revealed her 'special place' and Matthew could see at once why she loved it so.

It was a clearing about twenty feet across, the ground was covered by long, lush, thick grass. Around the edges were intermingling bushes of blackberry and hawthorn with a large tree here and there, but toward one side, growing in the lushness, was a sturdy little sapling. The branches of the huge oak tree were swaying overhead merging with the branches of the other trees, giving a dappled sunshine effect to the whole area.

"It is beautiful, Tilly, no wonder you love it, I could live here forever."

"No doubt that is what old Clancy said, and why he did not leave the woods for years."

"What is the little tree?"

"It is a walnut, the only one I have found here, and now, Matthew, it is *our* special place."

It was a Thursday evening in August, during a period of particularly settled, fine weather that the children voiced the idea of a trip to Winford beach, for just the two of them.

Surprisingly their respective parents agreed to the outing with one or two provisos. Louisa agreed to pack a basket with a picnic and the Reverend Johnson offered to provide a lift with his horse and trap for the outward journey, if they would walk the two and a half miles cross country home. The arrangements were eagerly agreed.

At ten o'clock on the Saturday, Matilda presented herself at the Vicarage – picnic in hand. She had on a pretty, green frock and a straw hat that fastened under her chin with a ribbon, a necessity today for there was a fresh breeze blowing. Her long golden tresses were tied back neatly from her face.

Elizabeth Johnson greeted her, thinking what a lovely girl she was.

The children enjoyed a mug of milk and a home-made scone in the Vicarage kitchen, while Richard made ready the horse and trap. Elizabeth was quite taken with the young girl.

"Matthew has showed me the ship you painted for him on his box Matilda, you show great promise, I hear your mother is quite talented."

"Everybody says that Mother's paintings are beautiful. She is very good at flowers, we have lots of her pictures hanging on our farmhouse walls."

"And do you also paint flowers, Matilda?"

"Sometimes yes, but I like to draw and paint anything, the animals are the most difficult, they never stand still." She smiled under her hat while Elizabeth chuckled at the picture she had conjured up in her mind of a small child trying to coax an animal into a suitable pose, instructing it to stand perfectly still for half an hour.

"You must bring some of your pictures for me to see, dear, call any time. Your mother is most welcome too, I would be very happy to see you both, perhaps one afternoon next week?"

"Thank you, Mrs Johnson."

"Now I believe my husband is ready for you. Have a lovely time in Winford and remember, make sure you do not wander too far or get stranded by the tides."

"We will be careful, goodbye."

" Do not worry we will stay close to where there are plenty of people."

The children were eagerly anticipating their day at the seaside.

Chapter Eleven

The children made their way along the promenade admiring the huge houses that lined the way and wondering who lived in them. Every now and again a smart liveried footman would leap from a carriage and mount the steps to one of the impressive front doors, where he would knock and wait.

"They must be very important people," whispered Matilda, "we do not see half so many grand carriages in Flinton do we?"

"No, but there are even more in Illingworth," said Matthew. "When I have travelled the world and made my fortune I will buy you as many grand carriages as you want, I will buy you beautiful gowns and hats and ribbons for your hair. We will live in a large house and be very kind to our servants. On winter evenings we will build huge log fires and I will gather you and our children around me and tell you fascinating stories of all the places I have seen, and all the people I have met. You will play the piano and sing, I will play the violin and we will have lots of happy children. What do you think of that, Tilly?"

"I cannot wait, but I will miss you very much while you are gone."

"I will miss you too, but I will write, I promise, and we can think of each other whenever we wish, and every now and again I will come home to visit you."

And so the childish conversation and the making of plans went on as the children made their way along the seafront.

"I thought your father wanted you to train for the Church," Tilly said thoughtfully, as they settled themselves on the sands.

"Yes, he does, but I would rather not, I must travel. I will try to convince him that the Church is not for me. Richard is a vicar so he has one son that has followed in his footsteps. I do not want to argue with him, Tilly, he is such a good man, I do not want to upset him."

"But you will upset him if you go to sea, what does your mother say about it?"

"Mother tries to keep the peace, she says I will probably change my mind when I am older anyway, so it is not worth arguing with Father now, about something that may never happen. But I will not change my mind, Tilly, of that I am certain."

"But will you really want to leave your mother and father for months and months, maybe even years, and what about me. I do not think I could bear not seeing you and not knowing where you are or even if you are safe."

"It is not that I *want* to leave any of you, it is just a need to see the world, there are so many wonderful places to visit."

"I will try to understand, I *do* understand really. I am just being selfish because I like your company so much."

"Try not to worry, Tilly."

The children played and ran on the sands, they paddled in the sea with bare feet, laughing and shouting as the huge rollers chased them up the beach only to recede back again. It was as if the sea were playing a game with them, enticing them down to the water and then pursuing them back, trying to catch at their heels as it did so.

The picnic was eaten as their toes dried in the sunshine, and then they drew pictures with their fingers in the wet sand. Matthew's pictures left a lot to be desired.

All of a sudden he jumped up. "Let us go in search of stones. Old Walter showed me some stones he said he collected from Winford beach, they were a beautiful colour, much like your hair. If you wet them and hold them up, they are almost transparent, they are called Cornelians, come, I will show you."

Matthew picked up the basket, now empty save for the covering cloth and led the way down to the beach, negotiating the ropes of the bathing machines along the way. The further they walked, the stonier the shoreline became and they began to hunt for the stones in the shingle near the sea. When Matthew found one he held it up so that Tilly could see how translucent it was.

The afternoon flew by as the pair searched for the Cornelians. There were many amber coloured stones on the beach but only a few were the ones that they wanted.

The crashing rollers kept chasing them away from the shoreline making them laugh as they ran, time and again, up the beach, then followed the foam back to snatch another handful of stones to be sorted through. Sometimes they were not quite quick enough and the waves would break around their ankles, throwing the sparkling sea-spray over their hands and up into their faces, soaking their clothes as they screamed and caught their breath.

Never had the pair had such fun and many a lady and gentleman walking along the promenade stopped to watch, envious of their childish lack of inhibitions. The bathing machines were all on the sandy stretch of beach nearer to the town, so there were few restrictive objects to negotiate as they played.

Being August there were many well-to-do holiday makers about which added a leisurely atmosphere to the day. Eventually the children called a halt to the searching and sat down to count the Cornelians they had collected in the basket. There was a grand total of forty.

"I will keep them forever to remind me of our picnic," said Tilly.

The two fell into a companionable silence, as they played with the stones until Tilly grabbed Matthew by the arm. "I have an idea," she said excitedly. "Let us share out the stones between us and put them into our boxes, every time something happy happens in our life we will put a stone into the box and when something sad happens we will take out a stone."

Matthew laughed, "How can we put the first 'happy' stone in, if they are all in the box to start with?"

"I had not thought of that, well, we must take some out first and keep nearby. In a handkerchief perhaps."

"Yes, we will do it. How about taking out half. We will each put ten in the box and keep ten out."

It was a childish notion but one which fired their

imaginations.

"Just think, Matthew, even when we are apart we will be sharing all our happiest and saddest moments, just like we do now."

"And, Tilly, we can open the boxes and look at the stones each night to remind us of each other."

They began walking back along the shoreline, happy with their plan. Presently Matthew said, "Your hair looks like gold, the sun is making it sparkle, and look at the sea-spray, that is sparkling too."

As they left the town to begin walking in open countryside their conversation turned to family matters.

"Did you know that Richard and Jane are going to have a baby?"

"Yes, Mother told me. That means you will become an uncle. You are very young to be an uncle. Do you think the child will call you 'Uncle'?"

"I suppose so, I had not really thought, I will ask Mother. What else would one call their uncle?"

"Why do you think Richard is so much older than you, I am only four years older than Loveday and six years older than Edward."

"Perhaps that is something else I should ask Mother about," he laughed. "She will not let me come to the beach with you anymore if I ask so many questions on my return." And then he surprised her by asking, "Does your father like me?"

"I should think so, he lets you visit often."

"I find him looking at me strangely sometimes, as if he cannot see me properly, or is looking for something and is trying to find it in my face. Why do you think he does that?"

"Father is a very kind man, I think he is very fond of you. I know he admires your violin playing, he has said as much. Maybe it is when it is growing dark just before we light the lamps. Perhaps he cannot see you clearly."

"You are probably right," then changing the subject he said, "I have enjoyed today, it is one of the best days I have ever had and we have the Cornelians to remind us of it."

"Yes, I agree. When I look at the stones every night we are apart, I will close my eyes and see you on the beach, and I shall be able to hear the sea crashing onto the shore."

Chapter Twelve

As soon as Matilda arrived home from school with Loveday she knew that something was wrong. A horse, which she recognized as Reverend Johnson's, was tethered in the yard and her father's boots were outside the kitchen door. The Vicar, she knew, always tried to be at home when Matthew got home from school. It was their time together as a family. Matthew explained it was because Reverend Johnson was always so busy on Saturdays and Sundays.

Louisa met them in the kitchen. "Loveday, would you go into the garden for a little while and play with Edward, we have a visitor and I need to talk to Matilda."

Loveday did as she had been asked as Matilda turned to her mother. "Is anything wrong?"

"Yes, dear, I have some bad news to tell you."

Louisa put her arm around Matilda, guiding her to a chair, then gently told her that Jane had died in childbirth early that morning. The baby had not survived either.

Matilda started to cry. "I did not know this could happen, Mother."

"It does not usually."

"What will Richard do now, he must be terribly unhappy."

"He is devastated, dear, we must do all we can to help him through this."

"But they were so happy."

"I know. It seems very unfair."

"What will happen now?"

"Well, Richard will arrange the funeral. It will be at Winford."

"Will I go?"

"We thought we would leave it up to you. Matthew will go. Perhaps you would like to think about it."

"Yes, thank you. I think I will go to my room now."

Matilda went up to her bedroom and sat on her bed. She had not known Jane very well having only met her a few times, but she still felt very sad. Sad for them both and sad for Richard and Matthew. She knew she would not be seeing Matthew tonight as she usually did. He would be expected to stay at home.

She got up slowly and walked toward her dressing table, she opened the small drawer on the right hand side and took out her little painted box, she then removed her first Cornelian, she knew that Matthew would be doing the same.

The two families journeyed to Winford in their respective carriages.

When they arrived at their destination the children found the house filled with strangers, all wearing black. The window blinds had been pulled down, shutting out most of the natural light, making the whole affair seem even sadder. The children were relieved when it was time to go to the church. Again they did not go together. Matthew travelled with his brother and his parents while Matilda was in a carriage with her own parents, several coaches back. Louisa explained to her that close family always went first. The coaches and horses were adorned with black ribbons.

During the service Matilda noticed several people dabbing at their eyes so did not feel so ashamed of her own crying. Every now and again she would look at Matthew's back, where he sat a few rows in front of her, but he did not turn round.

At one point, the Vicar taking the service – it was not Reverend Johnson – paid tribute to Jane, to her lovely nature and to her unstinting support of her husband during her brief time as a vicar's wife. He went on to talk about her baby son who had lived such a short time.

It was at this time that Matilda noticed that Richard's shoulders were shaking as he sat in the front pew, with his head in his hands and she realized that he too, was crying and this knowledge made her cry all the more. She felt Louisa's hand on her shoulder, comforting her. She had never seen a grown man cry before. She had never been surrounded by so much sadness before; she longed to be in Clancy's Wood in the little clearing listening to the birds singing.

Later as she watched the coffin being lowered into the ground she looked around at all the other gravestones and realised that all these people buried here had been loved by someone at some time. They had all had a funeral service like the one she had just attended. She resolved to always be as happy as she could be and try to make other people happy.

She did not like all this sadness.

Chapter Thirteen

Three years later...

One morning, in late July, Richard Johnson asked to see Matthew in his study. Matthew knocked at the door and entered. He was now fourteen years old, tall and handsome. He was in fact as big as his father, but he was feeling nervous. Being summoned to his father's study usually meant that something serious was to be discussed.

Having opened the door wide he was surprised to see, not only his father but his mother too. Instead of sitting at his desk, the Vicar was standing close to where his mother was seated in an easy chair. Two more similar chairs had been put into the study from elsewhere in the house. His mother looked distressed as she sat, with bowed head, twisting a handkerchief she held in her hands. She now lifted her head to look at Matthew; there was a troubled expression on her face.

"Come and sit down, Matthew," said his father gesturing toward one of the chairs, "we want to talk to you."

"Am I in trouble?" Matthew sat tentatively on the edge of the seat.

"No, no of course not, it is nothing like that."

"Mother looks troubled."

"Your mother is a bit upset, yes, but we have some good news for you. I have managed to secure a place for you at a good school. It is in Kent. You will go at the beginning of September. It will be good grounding for the Church."

"But I do not want to go into the Church, you know I want to go to sea and travel the world." Matthew was distraught, "Mother, please help me, I do not want to go, please do not make me."

Elizabeth looked at her son with a helpless expression. "I do not want you to go either, Matthew but your father is adamant."

"But Richard has gone into the Church, surely we do not both have to. I will be so unhappy."

"You are not a baby," said the Vicar sternly. "It is time to prepare for your future. What sort of life do you think you would have at sea? Your mother would not have a minute's peace; she would worry about you day and night. Would you really want that?"

"I do not want to worry Mother but neither do I want to train for the Church. Please do not make me."

"You have already been accepted for the school, you are very fortunate, places there are limited."

"Then why not allow somebody to have my place who really wants it?"

"You are being silly, Matthew. You will attend the school and that is the end of the matter."

Matthew could feel his eyes smarting as he fought to hold back the tears that were threatening to turn him into a blubbering mess. His mother was sitting, crumpled, in the chair looking old and worried, she was now fifty-nine. She did not want her two loved ones to be at loggerheads but she did not want Matthew to go either. He had enriched her life for the past fourteen years; she could not bear to lose him. But she also knew that it was her duty to support her husband. She was in an impossible position. She now looked at her husband and said imploringly, "Could I be excused now, Richard?"

"I think you should stay."

"But you have called an end to the matter." She now began to cry openly.

"Elizabeth, how can I bring this matter to a satisfactory conclusion if you break down in tears?"

"But you know my feelings about this, surely you do not want me to lie?"

"Of course not but you must agree that the boy owes me this much after all I have done for him."

Elizabeth now looked desperate. "All parents do all they can for their children, surely we should not expect payment. We have Matthew's love and respect."

"We hardly have his respect if he is refusing to obey my wishes."

As Matthew stood and listened to his parents, he got the distinct feeling they had talked of, and disagreed on, this issue many times in the recent past. Why had he not noticed that something was afoot? Probably because he had pushed his father's wishes to the back of his mind and hoped they would be forgotten.

"You *do* have my respect and my love I assure you, but I need to travel while I am young," and then he got bolder. "If you insist on sending me to this school I will run away."

"You will do no such thing," his father bellowed. "I have never heard of such ungratefulness. We could have put you in the poorhouse, instead of that we raised you as our own son and look how you repay us."

"*Richard,*" Elizabeth was aghast. They had always intended to tell Matthew about the unusual way that they had become his parents, but not in this manner, not in the middle of an argument. "How could you?" she continued. "You are a man of God, how could you hurt Matthew in this way?"

Matthew stood bemused, he had totally lost track of the conversation, what were his parents talking of?

"I do not understand," he said quietly. "Why should you have wanted to put me in a poorhouse? What do you mean 'as your own son'?"

Elizabeth and Richard now looked at one another, each hoping the other would know what to say. As the silence hung heavy on the air Matthew said. "Please explain what you mean."

"Let us all sit down." Richard was trying to recover his composure. Elizabeth was crying again, dabbing at her eyes with the twisted handkerchief. "Let us all try to remain calm. I am sorry for what I said, I lost my temper and I am very sorry." He now moved toward Matthew, who was standing in front of his chair and experiencing an awful feeling of dread in the pit of his stomach. "Sit down, son. There is something else we must tell you before you hear it from someone else."

Matthew sat down as if in a dream.

Elizabeth and Richard then proceeded to tell him how he had been left on their doorstep as a baby. They told him very gently. Very gently indeed considering how high emotions had been running a short time ago. They told him how they had wanted to look after him and how, as time went on they grew to regard him as their own son, hoping against hope that nobody would claim him. Their prayers had been answered and they had been allowed to keep him.

Matthew sat in stunned silence, finding it difficult to take in. His smarting eyes had given way to a thudding heart and constricted throat. He felt weak and lost. His world, which had been perfect, this morning, was falling apart.

"We love you very much, Matthew," Elizabeth's voice was small as she peered at Matthew, trying to judge what his reaction would be. "You have given us as much as we have given you – please speak to me, Matthew."

"Do you have any idea who my parents are?"

"No, dear, I am sorry," said Elizabeth. "We thought if we kept you here and your mother changed her mind – well she would know where you were."

"So I was not wanted."

"You were very wanted by us."

"I could belong to anyone in the village."

"That is unlikely, someone would surely have known."

"Would you excuse me please, so that I can go for a walk?"

"Shall we have some lunch first?"

"I am sorry, Mother, I am not hungry. I could not eat. I would like to find Tilly."

"Yes, dear, talk to Tilly, you will feel better then, but please remember we love you very much."

"Thank you," Matthew's voice was very flat. He turned and left the room to go and look for Matilda.

Matthew went through the kitchen and out of the back door, then he stopped and turned around to stare at the porch, trying to imagine the scene that his parents had just described to him. He would never walk through this porch again without remembering. He turned again and walked around the house, down the front path and through the wicket. He then turned left into Flinton High Street. He looked at all the cottages as he passed, wondering if his mother was inside one of them. Slowly he made his way to the crossroads, then turned right into Hill Road. It was a good mile to Matilda's house but he was in no hurry, for he had a lot to think about, and it would give Tilly time to have her lunch.

When the farmhouse door was opened, in response to Matthew's knock, Louisa knew at once that something was wrong. Matthew was usually so bright but today he was deflated. "Would you ask Tilly to meet me as soon as possible in Clancy's, please, Mrs Canham?"

"Yes, Matthew, are you alright?"

"I am a bit upset, no doubt Tilly will explain later," and then he added. "Thank you, good bye."

Matthew turned out of the farm gates, he walked slowly across the road and up the path that ran along the side of the meadow. Ahead of him he could see the stile that led into the poppy field and beyond that, Clancy's Wood – his and Tilly's private haven. She would know where to find him; they always met in the clearing, by the walnut tree.

Matthew had just finished telling Matilda the awful news. They were sitting against a tree trunk at the edge of the clearing. All of a sudden they did not feel like children anymore. "Did you know, Tilly?" he asked needlessly.

"No, no I would have told you."

"Do you think your parents still remember?"

"Well, I suppose they must."

"That is the awful part. Everybody knows but me."

"It was a long time ago, it is probably not uppermost on peoples' minds."

"The villagers probably look on me with pity."

"I am sure that is not true, you have lovely parents who wanted to keep you. You are to be envied not pitied."

"I feel very humble. I argued with Father this morning and I should not have done. It is true what he says. I should repay him by training for the Church. I feel lost, Tilly, I do not know who I am."

She reached for Matthew's hand and held it tight, she then lifted it to her face and kissed it, then used it to wipe away the tears that were falling down her cheeks.

"Do not cry, Tilly. Do not cry because of me."

"You have always been my very best friend. I am *allowed* to cry for you. Your pain is my pain."

Matthew moved closer and put his arm around Tilly's shoulders. "I will have to do it, won't I? That is the least I can do for him when he has brought me up."

"You must do what you want to do."

"No, I must do what I *should* do."

"Your mother will be very unhappy if you go away. She brought you up too, and I shall be unhappy. How will I bear it?"

"My conscience tells me I must go. Then I will have repaid Father. Only then will I feel I can follow my own dreams. Please help me, Tilly. Write to me, it is so far away."

"I hear it does not take too long on the railway."

"Dear Tilly, what would I do without you?" He then got up and pulled Matilda to her feet. He put his arms around her and gave her, her first proper kiss, on her lips. They held each other tightly; both crying softly, their tears mingling, then they turned to leave the clearing.

Their idyllic childhood was behind them.

That night they each removed a Cornelian from their little painted boxes...

Chapter Fourteen

"You did not tell me that Matthew was adopted." Matilda did not direct her remark to either parent specifically but her father looked up sharply from his book.

"Did Matthew tell you he was adopted?"

"Yes, yesterday afternoon."

"How long has he known this?"

"His parents told him yesterday morning, he said that everyone in the village knows."

"How does he feel about it?"

"He is very unhappy. He does not know who his real parents are and, as if that is not enough, he is now to be sent off to school and he does not want to go, and *I* do not want him to go. Oh, Mother what am I to do without him?" Matilda flung herself onto her mother.

"Maybe it is for the best," said Daniel. "You are both growing up, you cannot go roaming around the countryside and the woods unchaperoned for ever you know, it had to come to an end one day. Matthew has got to prepare for his future and you must start acting like a young lady, you are thirteen now."

"But I can act like a young lady and still be friends with him."

"When does he go?" her father asked.

"At the beginning of September. We have only a month left. I cannot bear it. He is going to Kent."

"But you always knew Matthew wanted to travel, you knew you would be parted one day," said Louisa gently.

"I thought I would be older, I did not think it would be this soon, I tried not to think about it. Anyway this is not the same. If Matthew was going away to travel he would be happy and I would try to be happy for him, but he is not happy, so neither am I."

"Why did you not tell us all this yesterday?" asked Louisa.

"Because I was too upset. Who do you think his parents are, Mother?"

"I have no idea, nobody knows."

"I think it is very sad. Matthew says he must do as his father wishes to repay him for all he has done for him."

"Yes, it is very sad," said Louisa. "I cannot understand how anyone can abandon their own child. You must try to be brave about all this. You can write to Matthew while he is away and see him during the holidays. Now I think it is time for bed, dear." Louisa put her arms around her daughter and kissed her warmly.

"Well, I suppose he was bound to be told one day," said Louisa when Matilda had left the room.

"I am surprised he has not heard it from someone before now."

"I think our daughter is growing up, Daniel. I am sure I detect the symptoms of first love."

"But she is only thirteen."

"Thirteen and a half actually. That is not too young to fall in love, and it is so painful at that age."

"You are imagining it, they are just friends."

"You are like all men, you cannot bear your little girl to grow up and fall in love with another man." There was a gentle teasing in her voice, which Daniel ignored.

"What makes you think all this anyway?"

"They were holding hands as they walked back across the meadow last night, I saw them from the front window. It was so sweet, they are so young."

"Exactly, they are *too* young, it must be stopped at once." Daniel's voice had now risen and contained a slight panic.

"You cannot stop them seeing each other, especially now, Matilda is upset enough as it is. It would destroy her if they could not spend the next month together, they have been friends since they first started school."

"Friends yes, I have no objection about them being friends, but if they are holding hands in public and disappearing into the woods, then I think it must be stopped. It is unseemly now that they are older."

"I do not agree, I am her mother and I think we should leave things as they are for the next four weeks, holding hands can do no harm. The boy needs comfort and understanding, his world has just fallen apart, we cannot add to his unhappiness."

"On this particular matter I cannot agree with you, if she has silly notions in her head about marrying Matthew, we must discourage them at all costs."

Louisa was now becoming as angry as Daniel was. "I would have thought you would be happy if they married one day, they are perfect for one another. He is a vicar's son, he has been well brought up, I thought you were very fond of him."

"He has been well brought up I agree, but he is *not* a vicar's son, you do not know who's son he is."

"It does not matter, I am not going to forbid them seeing each other."

"Well I *do* forbid it. You must tell her tomorrow."

Louisa put her head in her hands and wept. She could not understand why Daniel was behaving in such a way. It was not like him, he was usually so amiable with his family.

"Please do not cry, Louisa."

"Then please do not make me. You know you are being unreasonable. You will alienate our daughter."

Daniel did not like to see his wife distressed and if he were not careful he would arouse her suspicions, ordinarily he would be happy that Matthew and Matilda were young sweethearts but this was no ordinary situation, he must diffuse the argument.

"Alright, if you insist I will allow them to meet until Matthew goes to school and we will not mention the matter to Matilda, but you must understand that I am not happy with the situation."

Louisa was pacified, superficially at least. She was, however, perturbed by her husband's outburst. It was not like him at all. Their household usually ran smoothly with Daniel at the helm on the farm, and she, mistress of the house. For the first time in their marriage there were signs of discord and she did not like it. She did not like it at all.

The children usually met in the evenings. School, music lessons and helping in their homes occupied their days but their evenings belonged to themselves and were something to look forward to throughout the day. Since the revelation of Matthew's adoption, their conversation consisted of little else other than their impending parting and the subject of Matthew's parents. Whilst they would both have liked to forget both matters to enjoy their last month together, it was not to be. Both issues were too big and too important for them to ignore.

Matthew became determined to discover his parentage and Matilda was so sympathetic to his dilemma that she vowed to help him in any way she could.

She tried to imagine how she would feel in the same situation but found it difficult, she was so lucky to belong to a happy family.

They sadly made their plans for writing to each other and vowed that nothing would ever part them. They had taken to holding hands as they walked in the countryside. Matthew would put his arm around Tilly when they were in the clearing. The clearing was still the place they went to most – where they shared their secrets and made their plans. They had grown up a little since the Vicar's revelation and their relationship had inexplicably moved on accordingly.

"Is that a bird?" Matthew asked one day as they sat in their favourite place, talking and listening to the sounds of the forest.

"Where?"

"Sshh, over there in the long grass."

They crept closer to the spot where he had indicated to find a jackdaw struggling to take flight.

"Its wing looks broken, we must take it home and care for it or it will not survive."

As they moved forward to pick up the bird it jumped through the hedge at the side of the clearing, flapping its wings awkwardly.

"We must find it," said Matthew, trying to part the tangled branches, while Matilda looked round for a branch or something to help them. After much struggling and scratching of their hands they managed to squeeze through after the bird by crawling low in the undergrowth, but what they found took them completely by surprise.

It was a little wooden house, a large shed really, overgrown with greenery but quite solidly built from logs. "It must be Clancy's house," said Matilda excitedly, fancy me coming here all these years and not knowing it existed. They then saw the bird fluttering against the bottom of the house. Matthew made a grab for it, and tried to calm it, as it struggled in his hands. Eventually he succeeded.

"Oh, Matthew, I am so glad we found this house before you went away. Let us bring a brush and some tools to clear it a little then we can meet here, even in bad weather. We could bring some old chairs too, there are several in the barns."

The two of them were happier than they had been for days.

They both agreed that the event warranted putting a Cornelian into their 'happy' boxes.

The next few weeks were taken up with caring for the jackdaw and, clearing and cleaning around, and inside, the little house. It was empty inside and Matilda knew she would be spending quite a lot of time there by herself when Matthew left. It was as if they were preparing their first home together.

"I will imagine you here when I am away, and I will envy you."

The time for parting was drawing nearer, until the time came for their last meeting at the clearing, which now incorporated a path through to the house.

"I have a present for you," said Matthew on their last evening together.

"And I have one for you, let's open them together."

They began unwrapping their presents, looking unusually shyly at each other as they did so.

Matthew unwrapped a small picture that Tilly had painted; of herself in the poppy field. He clutched her to him and held her tightly, tears streaming unashamedly down his face. "It is lovely, Tilly," he choked, "I will treasure it always. I will always have it with me on my travels."

Tilly's unwrapping had been interrupted; she now also uncovered a frame, which held a poem.

"I am not too good at poetry but I did my best," Matthew said modestly.

She now read:

Dancing on the Air
A poem for my sweetheart

The sun on her face
And the wind in her hair,
Golden as it dances
Dances on the air.

Strolling through the poppy field
With neither haste nor care,
Watching brilliance dancing
Dancing on the air.

Walking by the sea shore
Sun is glinting there,
Glinting on the sea spray
That's dancing on the air.

All at one with nature
'Neath her golden hair,
That's dancing in the sunshine
Dancing on the air.

Matilda was now crying as well. They held each other tightly.

"I too will treasure this, Matthew, I will put it with my Cornelians, for I feel it is too private to hang on the wall, is that alright?"

"Perfect, Tilly, I love you so much, I will always love you."
"And I'll always love you, Matthew."
She laid her head on his shoulder.
They then walked sadly from the clearing to make their way back home together for the last time until Christmas.

Chapter Fifteen

"Come into my study, Daniel, it is good to see you again." Reverend Johnson extended his arm to shake Daniel by the hand as he ushered him toward the door to the right of the hall. "How can I help you?"

"I am not here on Church business, Richard, it would be easier if I were, I trust you got Matthew settled at his new school?"

"Yes, although I am a bit worried about him, he was very quiet when we left him. However I expect he will soon settle down into his new routine. We arrived back home yesterday, how did we manage before the railway?"

"Matthew is the reason I am here."

"Matthew?"

"Yes, I have no wish to offend you or Elizabeth but I do think we should discourage the children's friendship. It is not that I do not like Matthew, on the contrary, I like him very much but, well, Matilda is thirteen now and I do not think it proper that they should be seen wandering the countryside and disappearing into the woods together unchaperoned. Also I think it would be healthier if they were encouraged to spend time with other young people of their own age, form other friendships. Louisa tells me they have begun holding hands in public. Perhaps we could manage to keep them apart for a year or two to take the heat out of the situation. They are far too young to be involved romantically and you would not want all this to interfere with Matthew's studies would you?"

"I understand how you feel, Daniel, children grow up so quickly one is hardly aware of it. You are right of course, I should have been more observant."

"I take it then that I can count on your support and that you will familiarise Elizabeth with our conversation?"

"Yes, I will give the matter some thought and keep you informed."

"Thank you, Richard, I will get back to my work."

The two men shook hands again and Daniel took his leave.

Richard returned to his study to think about what Daniel had said. He should have noticed himself that the children were growing too old to be left alone so much. He had been congratulating himself that he had managed to bring Elizabeth round to his way of thinking. He was not totally unsympathetic to her feelings. One of the reasons he had chosen the school in Kent was because of its proximity to London.

Elizabeth's own family was from London – her father had been a goldsmith who had owned a jewellery shop in London when Richard met her. Elizabeth had a brother – who had inherited the business – and a sister, in the city. Elizabeth and her sister had both inherited a considerable amount of money from their father in lieu of the business, together with some very good pieces of jewellery.

Richard had always been very aware that the life he offered, when they first married, had been a far cry from what she had been used to, but they had been very much in love – still were in fact – and Elizabeth had never complained. Richard had persuaded her that, with Matthew at school in Kent, she could make regular visits to stay with her sister in London. She could visit Matthew at the same time. These suggestions had gradually won Elizabeth over; at least they were preferable to Matthew going to sea.

Richard now began wondering if he could suggest that Christmas should be spent in London, it would be nice for Elizabeth to see her family at Christmas…

Daniel was feeling very guilty about his visit to the Vicarage, which he had not discussed with Louisa. He knew that she would have a very low opinion of him if he prevented Matilda from seeing Matthew, but if it appeared that the initiative came from the Vicarage…well, that would make life much easier at Uphall Farm. He did not much like the person he was becoming. He told himself that he was acting in the best interests of his family, but there was a gnawing at his insides just the same. He was very worried indeed that Matilda and Matthew had become young sweethearts. He had to put a stop to it somehow, however much he had to hurt Matilda. He could not possibly allow them to grow up and marry one day.

What would he do if his initial plan did not work? What if they spent a few years apart and still felt the same about each other? The whole situation was beginning to make him quite sick with worry. What very good reason could he give for keeping them apart without divulging his secret? He would have to make sure that Matilda lived a full and varied life and that she met plenty of other young men. Perhaps they should entertain a bit more, bring some new people into the house. It would help to cheer up Matilda, he was quite concerned about her low spirits, it was very unlike her to be so quiet and withdrawn. She was in the habit of disappearing for hours with her sketchpad. Mostly to Clancy's Wood. Hardly anybody went into Clancy's because it was on private property. Daniel himself only took the occasional walk through. Matilda had always had a fascination for the place, ever since she had been taken there as a young child. She liked to draw the trees and birds and listen to the sound of the wood. She never tired of it. The rest of the family tended to walk in the meadows, fields and by the stream. Matilda liked these areas too, but Clancy's remained her favourite.

Now as Daniel drew nearer to home he wondered how it would all end.

Matilda had developed the habit of calling at the Vicarage on the off chance that Elizabeth had had a letter from Matthew. She herself received a letter every month but she was always happy to hear extra news.

Elizabeth was pleased about the girl's visits, they helped to alleviate the loneliness she had felt since Matthew's departure. She had always wanted a daughter so she encouraged Matilda's visits, much to the consternation of her husband.

"Do you think you should encourage Matilda to call so much?" inquired the Vicar gently one evening.

"I like her company, I miss Matthew so much. Matilda and I both get great comfort from our meetings. Surely, after insisting that Matthew go away to school, you are not going to prevent me from seeing Matilda too. You have had your own way on most issues."

Richard knew that Elizabeth was speaking the truth. He also knew that Daniel would not be very happy to learn that Matilda called on them most afternoons after school.

Elizabeth was dreading having to tell Matilda that Matthew would not be coming home for Christmas. It would be the first time since her marriage to Richard that she would spend the holiday with her own family and she was looking forward to it, but she had grown very fond of Matilda, she did not want to cause her any unhappiness.

As Matilda left the school house – later than usual due to her piano lesson – she met old Walter Fennell the undertaker, he was now sixty-nine years old but remarkably sprightly for his age.

"Hello, Mr Fennell, have you heard from Matthew?"

"I have had one letter but I expect he would rather write to a pretty young lady like you than to an old man," he smiled at her, "I expect you miss him."

"Yes, but he writes to me every month and he always asks me to give you his regards if I see you."

"He says that every time?"

"He does – every month without fail – he is immensely grateful to you for teaching him the violin and carpentry."

"It was a pleasure. I am always happy to teach a willing pupil and he was that alright. How is he settlin'?"

"He wishes he were at home but his mother is going to visit every six weeks or so, she misses him too."

"Oh yes, I'm aware of it. I've just come from the Vicarage, they are lookin' forward to goin' up for Christmas."

"But Matthew is coming home for Christmas, he has just

written to tell me how happy he is to be coming back."

"That's not the impression I got from the Vicar just now."

Matilda attempted to keep her voice cheery. "Well goodbye, Mr Fennell, it is nice to see you, Happy Christmas."

"Goodbye, young lady, Happy Christmas."

Matilda was heartbroken; she would not have a happy Christmas if Matthew did not come home. She had lived for Christmas. She was supposed to wait for her father to collect her – the nights were dark now – but she would have to go to the Vicarage, she doubted that Mr Fennell had misunderstood.

"Is it true that Matthew is not coming home for Christmas?" she blurted out when Elizabeth answered the door.

"Come in, Matilda, yes I am sorry. My husband has arranged for us to spend Christmas in London with my sister, so naturally Matthew will be with us."

"But he is looking forward to coming home. Tears were streaming down her face but she did not care. "I must see him, Mrs Johnson, I miss him so."

"I am very sorry, I know how upset you must be." Elizabeth put her arms around the girl in a motherly fashion. "I will give him your love. His father thinks it is character building to be away from home. I have to support my husband, dear. Please try to understand."

"I do not blame you. I know you did not want him to go either." She hesitated then said, "will you take him a present from me?"

"Yes, dear, bring it round tomorrow."

Matilda went outside to wait for her father.

"Did I see you come from the Vicarage?" asked Daniel as he walked towards her.

"Yes, Father."

"Is anything wrong?" he asked holding his lantern nearer to his daughter's face and detecting her tears.

"Yes, Matthew is not coming home for Christmas and I cannot bear it. His parents are going to London instead."

Daniel put his arm around his daughter's shoulders as they began their walk home. He did not know what to say to cheer

81

her, he would leave that to Louisa, she was better at that sort of thing. Secretly he was relieved that the boy was not coming home but he did not like to see his daughter unhappy.

They walked the mile home with hardly an exchange of words. It was a very cold night, they were both wrapped up in their coats with scarves around their faces. Daniel was aware that his daughter was crying softly and he felt a lump in his own throat at the knowledge he was to blame. He had never intended to cause his family any unhappiness. Matilda had always been such a happy child. He did not know what he could do to improve the situation. He was not happy either – relieved maybe – but not happy.

When they arrived home, Matilda went straight to her room and sadly removed another Cornelian from the little box. She sat for a while studying the little stones as she thought of their happy day on the beach, she then took a brown paper parcel from the drawer and laid it on her dressing table. It contained a linen handkerchief that she had sewn herself, with an 'M' embroidered in one corner. She would take it to the Vicarage tomorrow.

Richard conducted the Christmas morning church service. The church was decorated with holly and other winter greenery. Flinton's little band of fiddlers were playing in the gallery. Matilda looked at all the happy glowing faces but her heart was heavy. The family had walked down from the farm through two inches of snow that had fallen overnight and, although the sun was shining brilliantly, it was still freezing. It was a truly beautiful Christmas Day – if Matthew had been here it would be perfect.

Richard went home with them for Christmas lunch. He would normally have gone to the Vicarage, but since his parents were in London, Louisa had invited him to join the family.

They had all helped to decorate the house the previous evening. There were bunches of holly and mistletoe hanging from all the ceiling beams in the kitchen and sitting room, and two huge bunches at either end of the chimney breastsummer.

The hall was adorned in a like manner and, through every window; a snowy wonderland was shimmering in the winter sun.

How happy I would be if Matthew were here, thought Matilda. We could have gone to Clancy's house for a walk in the snow, and to see the frozen pond that the ducks were having difficulty understanding – sliding about like Christmas skaters – so comical to look upon with company, but sad to observe alone.

After lunch was the present opening. Matilda imagined Matthew unwrapping his handkerchief.

Richard crossed the room to where she was sitting and handed her a brown paper parcel. "This is from Matthew," he said gently, "I have had it ever since he left in September."

Matilda smiled at Richard; he was such a nice man. He had lost his wife and child but he could still be considerate of her own pain. She cheered up a little, Richard could not have his wife and child back ever, but she *would* see Matthew again.

She unwrapped the parcel and found a wooden model of Clancy's house.

"Would you like to go for a walk?" asked Richard.

"I would like that very much, thank you."

"Will anybody join us for a walk?" shouted Richard above the merry making. But nobody else wanted to leave the roaring log fire in the inglenook.

"You miss him a lot, don't you, Matilda?" they were walking down Mill Stream Lane.

"I cannot describe how much, it is as if a part of me is missing."

"The time will fly, you will see. Think how quickly three months has passed, he will be home for good before you know it."

"But he will probably leave again, he says he must see the world, I thought I would bear it so long as he was well and happy, but I know he is *not* happy."

"He will be, and so will you."

"You are always so kind, Richard, even to silly little girls," she smiled up at him, then, her voice brightening, "I will race you to the stream."

By the time they reached the stream they were both out of breath, but their moods were a little brighter and their cheeks were rosy.

On their way back they laughed at the ducks.

Part Two

Broken Promises

Chapter One

"Well here we are again," said old Amos, settling himself in the chimney corner of the Village Maid. "Another day, another dinner. How's the world bin treatin' all of you then?"

Amos mostly had the chimney settle to himself these days, Diggory having shocked everybody by marrying a girl from Winford within three months of meeting her.

When he married, Diggory had been forty-two. The general consensus of opinion, in the Village Maid, had been that he would remain a confirmed bachelor, carrying a torch for Penelope Wyn-Jones for the rest of his life. But that was before he was bowled over by Clara. Now he was a family man, rarely accompanying his father to the alehouse.

"I see you're alone again tonight, Amos, the novelty of marriage and fatherhood hasn't rubbed off yet then for young Diggory? My, he's been a surprise to us hasn't he? I never thought he'd give up on Penelope." Fingal Pardoe took out his watch and checked it with the longcase on the wall. "It's a bit late for Shuffley isn't it, he's usually the first to arrive."

"That's because he's got no one nagging at him to stay at home," said Eli Penny, who was known to be henpecked.

"I think I'd rather put up with a bit of nagging than have no one to warm me bed," muttered Martin Partridge. "If I time it just right the chill's nicely off by eleven."

"We're all gettin' old, thass the trouble," complained old Walter. "Time was I didn't mind a nice cool bed."

"My missus is quite happy to get rid of me for a couple of hours," said Darcy, "she says I bring an 'aroma' into the house."

"Well now, would that be a pleasant aroma or an offensive aroma?" inquired Martin.

"I shouldn't think you need to ask that if she's pleased to get rid of him," said old Walter, and they all laughed heartily and leaned forward in their seats to familiarise their olfactory senses with Darcy's aroma.

"Maybe it's the wood; my missus says I allust smell of wood," offered Fergus Tooley. "Fortunately she like the smell, she says she'd rather I smelt like a good bit of mahogany than a sty full of pigs."

"Pigs don't smell," said Amos, indignantly. "Thass a myth, pigs are clean little critters, why I spend half my life in a pig sty."

"An' I reckon your missus'd like to know where you spend the other half," said Fergus playfully amid more chuckling.

"She allust know where I am," said Amos, "have no fear o' that."

"Well, she would if you allust smell of the pig sty, wouldn't she? She can sniff you out." They all laughed merrily, sniffing at the air surrounding Amos, as they did so!

"I sometimes wonder why I struggle down here every night, only to be insulted," grumbled old Amos good-naturedly. "I think we should have a bit of respect at our age, don't you, Walter?"

"If we got a bit of respect, Amos, these young uns wouldn't git their mile of mirth out of us now would they? We'd all be sittin' here like we'd lost a shillin' and found sixpence."

"Thass true I 'spose," agreed Amos, "I reckon they're probably keepin' us young at heart, an' thass the next best thing to actually bein' young."

"Talkin' of youngsters, I hear young Matthew Johnson is coming home in a couple of months," said Walter. "That young lass up at Uphall Farm will be mighty pleased to hear the news."

"Yes, I wouldn't be surprised to hear weddin' bells in that direction," said Amos, "they were never apart at one time."

"We never did git to the bottom of that one, did we?" said Darcy. "And I don't suppose we ever will."

"Don't be so sure of that," said old Walter. "Folk have been known to make startlin' confessions on their death beds, I reckon all will be revealed one day, you mark my words."

"I don't think he's keen to go in to the Church from what I hear," said Darcy, "I think he's got a bit of a wanderlust hasn,t he, Walter?"

"Aye he has," agreed Walter. "I must say I'm lookin' forward to seein' him again. You'd have to go along way to meet such a nice young man as that. He has a rare talent for the fiddle. Easiest pupil I've ever had the pleasure to teach, yes, I'm lookin' forward to his homecoming."

"Do you think he'll go into the Church, despite how he feels, Walter?"

"I wouldn't be surprised if he do as his father wants, but I'll tell you this much, he could make a good livin' as a carpenter. You'll have to watch it you two, else he'll take all your trade." As Walter said this he nodded in the direction of Darcy and Fergus.

"I don't think he has been back since he first went away to school has he, Walter?"

"Not to my knowledge, no, thass a bit funny really when you come to think of it, the Vicar and his missus always visit him down south. They go down for Christmas every year as well, stay with Mrs Johnson's sister in London. The Vicar hasn't taken a Christmas service in Flinton in six years. He allust leave it to young Richard. Mind you, I like young Richard; don't say a lot, but preach a good sermon. He's a nice chap is young Richard."

Walter nodded his head as if agreeing with himself.

"A lot of folk thought he'd marry the schoolmistress you know," added Randolph Clarke, "when it all fell through with Diggory." Randolph did not usually say much; he was a bit like Shuffley in that way. He said it was because his shop got so full of gossiping women that he could not get a word in edgeways, even if he wanted to. "Women are always matchmaking," he said now, "you only have to say 'Good-day' to a lady and they have you promised, married and a father in the twinkling of an eye. I can't understand it really, they get all dewy eyed over affairs of the heart, as if marriage is the most perfect state on earth, yet they're always complaining about their other halves. You'd be surprised what I know about you lot just by keeping an open ear and a closed mouth in that shop," and he too started nodding his head. "There's not much go on in this village that I don't hear about, what with the women all day and seeing you all at night, but even I don't know what's going on at that vicarage."

"Have they ever told the boy he's adopted?" asked Darcy of them all generally.

"Oh yes," said Walter. "They told him, before he went away, and I hear tell he took it badly, very badly."

"Well he would, he would; wouldn't we all?"

The assemblage fell into a reverie, no doubt trying to imagine how it would feel to be abandoned at birth.

"Where's old Tom tonight?" asked Darcy, changing the subject, "He hasn't been through for a mardle yet, thass not like him is it?"

Tom Foley, who was now in his seventies, had handed over the running of the pub to his son, young Tom. Although he did not do much serving behind the bar, he did usually wander through for a bit of easy conversation with his old contemporaries in the chimney corner, of an evening.

"Where's Father tonight, Tom?" asked Darcy of the landlord.

"He's walked up to see old Shuffley, he's a bit poorly today."

Concerned looks passed among the regulars.

"I thought somethin' was up," said Amos. "I'll take a walk to see 'im in the mornin', I don't much like lookin' at that empty chair, it gives me a weird feelin'."

"My father made that chair," said Fergus. " he made two for old Shuffley. They used to stand one each side of his fireplace. He made them to Shuffley's own requirements on account of his spinal condition. Shuffley asked old Tom if he could bring one down here. He never could sit on these wooden seats for long."

"Your father could make a comfortable chair, Fergus," said Reuben Healey joining the group. "I've still got one at home he made for *my* father. Like an old glove it is, still my favourite."

"Well I like to think my furniture will last as long," said Fergus proudly, "I've had no complaints yet."

Again their eyes drifted towards Shuffley's empty chair.

"Have you finished my new boots yet, Reuben?" asked Amos, winking at Fergus and Darcy, "I need to get them broken in afore the warmer weather."

"Why do you think I'm so late in tonight, I've been workin' on them all day and you know they won't want breakin' in, Amos. My, you need a thick skin to come in here of an evening."

"Thass just what I was sayin' earlier," rejoined Amos, "it make a change for me to do some teasin', I usually git it all directed toward me."

"Thass 'cause we know you're such a good-natured old codger," said Darcy, giving Amos an affectionate pat on the arm.

And so another evening of gentle banter and conversation passed between the locals, no matter how often they met, they still enjoyed each other's company.

Chapter Two

It was on a beautiful Sunday afternoon in April that Matilda walked through the village with her friend Verity Miles. She had seen a lot of Verity since Matthew's departure. The two had always been great friends.

Matilda had grown quieter and a little more withdrawn year by year. She knew there was a conspiracy in operation to keep her and Matthew apart. She had often asked Louisa if she could have the money to visit Matthew, but Louisa had sadly told her each time that Daniel would not allow it.

"I cannot go against your father," Louisa would say. "Although I have no objection to the two of you meeting."

The mere fact that Louisa did not oppose their friendship enhanced the relationship between mother and daughter.

Matthew still wrote every month. Matilda did not know if her father was aware of this fact. She rarely mentioned Matthew's name in her father's company, but she knew that his efforts to obtain the necessary finance to return home for a visit had also been thwarted; by Reverend Johnson. Like her, Matthew had the support of only his mother.

During the time that Matthew had been away Matilda had made it her business to ask discreet questions of Louisa and Elizabeth in an attempt to discover the identity of Matthew's real parents. Occasionally she had inquired of other villagers she felt she could trust. One of these had been old Walter Fennell, whom she knew was very fond of Matthew. She had written the information she had gathered, in a book, together with relevant dates. It had given her satisfaction through the long years to feel she was doing something for Matthew. It must have been very frustrating for him, she reasoned, to be given such shocking news and then removed from the area. She had not made any obvious headway on the subject but she was becoming more and more certain that the Reverend Johnson at least, knew more than he admitted to. Perhaps somebody had confessed to him in his official capacity of Vicar. He would then be duty bound to keep the confidence, even from his wife. Matilda was sure that Mrs Johnson was not keeping anything from her, they were more like friends now.

Matilda had no doubt that Matthew had been loved and wanted very much by the Vicar's wife. She could reassure him on that point if nothing else.

"You are very quiet," said Verity looking sideways at her friend as they neared the Village Green, "I thought that you would be overjoyed at Matthew's return."

"I am, Verity, really, but it is still two months away and I have raised my hopes in the past only to be disappointed."

"Have you never been even slightly interested in any other young man?"

"No, I have suffered so many boring evenings when Father has insisted I display my talents at the piano and by sketching. It is so humiliating, it is as if he is in a hurry to marry me off to anybody – so long as it is not Matthew. I have met more distant relatives in the last two years than I was aware existed. We constantly have house guests now and one feels obliged to remain at home with them. I am looking forward to the Summer, praying that Father will realize that I love Matthew and that our friendship has stood the test of time and separation. There is no valid reason for him to object to us seeing each other."

"What will you do if he *does* still oppose?"

"I cannot see how he can, I would have to defy him, unless he can furnish me with very good reason."

"You will hardly recognize Matthew after such a long time, I wonder if he has changed much."

"I do not care how much he has changed as long as he comes home this time."

"Do you think Reverend Johnson knows who Matthew's parents are?"

"I am beginning to think so, but Mrs Johnson does not know,

of that I am certain. She is always happy to talk about him with me, she said it was an answer to her prayer when he was left on her doorstep. She remembers the day as if it were yesterday."

"But still you cannot glean any clues from her?"

"No, but I would like to talk to Daisy Cartwright about it all. She was housemaid at the time. Do you fancy she would think it odd if I called on her?"

"Well, I would not think it had anything to do with Daisy if she worked there. Mrs Johnson would have known if her housemaid was with child."

"I did not mean that it might have been her baby, but if I heard her side of the story I might get a clue about the matter...oh, I do not know, Verity, I am clutching at straws."

The two young ladies had now reached the Village Green, where they sat on a bench in the sunshine.

"What about you, Verity, do you have your eye on any young, unsuspecting male in the area?"

"I quite like Robert Flowerdew, he has joined his father's practice in Winford. He has taken to walking past the house every evening, he then returns about twenty minutes later. He has said Good-evening on the last two occasions."

"He was very bright at school, you could do a lot worse and no doubt he and Leo will become partners in their father's firm in due course."

"I like Leo too, but he is walking out with Charlotte Worthdale – did you know?"

"No, I did not, I have lost touch with the village romances in my quest to unravel the mystery of Matthew's parents. Perhaps you should bring me up to date with all I have been missing." She looked eagerly at Verity.

The two girls spent an enjoyable hour talking and laughing in the spring sunshine, exchanging information on current village gossip.

During the course of the conversation Matilda's mood lightened considerably, she gradually felt the stresses and strains of the past six years begin to ease slightly. Perhaps it was the optimism of Spring in conjunction with the lovely day and the knowledge that Matthew should soon be returning. Whatever the reason Matilda felt more light-hearted than she had for some considerable time.

At seven o'clock the following evening, Matilda made her way to Daisy Cartwright's cottage. She was in pensive mood. She had only a nodding acquaintance with Daisy and was feeling a certain amount of nervousness.

The cottage was in Holly Lane, at the opposite end from the Flowerdews' house. It was a pretty abode with a thatched roof and tiny dormer windows, which gave it a sleepy appearance. It was in a row of similar cottages, their front gardens being separated by picket fences. They were all exceptionally neat and tidy. Matilda fancied they were Church properties, of which there were quite a number in the village.

Walking up the front path she became aware that she had not formulated an opening conversation piece. She was in two minds whether to knock at the door or retrace her steps down the front path. Before she had made her final decision, the front door was opened by Daisy, who wore an inquiring expression of surprise.

"Hello, Mrs Cartwright," said Matilda hesitantly. "I am not really sure why I am here, perhaps I should not be. I am sorry." Matilda turned away visibly embarrassed.

"Wait a minnut, is it Miss Canham?"

"Yes, yes but please call me Matilda."

"How can I help you?"

"Well, I do not know if you can but, may I have a private word with you?"

"Come in, the children are in bed and Sidney can find a job to do outside on a fine evening, can't you Sidney?"

As Daisy spoke she ushered her husband toward the kitchen. He nodded at Matilda and left the house.

"I do not want to intrude upon your evening, Mrs Cartwright."

"Daisy, call me Daisy, take a seat and tell me what's troublin' you."

"Thank you er…Daisy. I have been trying to pluck up courage to visit you for some time."

"I can't think what for," said Daisy pleasantly, smiling at Matilda to put her at her ease.

"It is a delicate subject, I do not know how to begin, I think perhaps I should leave before I embarrass us both further."

"If you have been wanting to see me for some time it must be quite an important matter. You might as well tell me what's on your mind."

Matilda proceeded to explain to Daisy the nature of her visit, she was obviously nervous and asked Daisy if the matter could remain of a confidential nature. Matilda explained that Matthew had taken the news of his adoption quite badly and she wanted to help him uncover the truth without offending the Reverend and Mrs Johnson.

Daisy, who was now thirty-five years old and a mother to four young children, was sympathetic to Matilda's plight. She related the whole story of the abandoned baby to Matilda, who realized that Daisy knew no more than Mrs Johnson did, but it was satisfying to have the story confirmed.

"You should have seen the Vicar's wife, Matilda, like the cat that got the cream, she was so happy. She love that boy as a mother would, no doubt about it."

"I had been hoping you could shed more light on the situation, but thank you anyway, Daisy, you have been very kind."

"I'm sorry I can't help more. If I hear anythin' round about I'll let you know, but thass not likely after all this time is it?"

"No, probably not, but I appreciate you talking to me."

"Thass bin a pleasure, I am looking forward to seeing the lad again, I was always fond of 'im."

"Thank you, I will leave now so that your husband can return to his house. Thank him for me please."

"Goodnight, miss, feel free to call again anytime."

"Goodnight, Daisy and thank you again. If ever I can be of assistance to you, please let me know."

Daisy returned to her sitting room reflecting on how nice

Matilda was and that she and Matthew would make an ideal pair. She would tell Sidney the nature of Matilda's visit was 'women's business'. She did not want the young girl's confidences bandied about the village and, as the Vicar employed Sidney, it was best to keep the details of the recent conversation to herself.

As Matilda walked home she mentally went over Daisy's story again and again, making sure she had not missed anything of relevance. She would write it all down in her book anyway when she arrived home. It saddened her considerably that she had found out nothing of any great importance since Matthew left. She would have liked to have some good news for him on his return.

She felt particularly bad that she was, in some small way, deceiving her father. She knew he did not want her to associate with Matthew yet she had been corresponding with him for six years. She tried to convince herself that she was not deceiving him because she had not lied to him. Had he asked her, she would have had to admit that she was still in regular contact. But he had not asked. Matthew for some mysterious reason had become something of a taboo subject in the household. Richard only mentioned him if he was sure they were not being overheard.

But now, thought Matilda, all that would be in the past. Matthew would come home and her father would have to accept their courtship. They had respected their respective fathers' wishes for six years.

Matilda had continued to visit the little house in the woods by herself. She had taken some old milking stools and a lantern to the place, and one or two other necessities. She had made it quite cosy over the years. She loved to go there to sketch, to be alone with her thoughts. She kept the place clean and tidy as if it were her own home. Fortunately there were four years between herself and her next eldest sibling. Loveday was nearer to Edward in age, so had never really been a playmate to Matilda. Anyway her younger brother and sister were not keen on the woods.

Matilda found herself becoming increasingly nervous about Matthew's imminent return. She wanted him back but would everything be the same? They had been children when they parted; now they were adults. Would they still be soul mates? What would he look like? Would he still think she was beautiful? A few Cornelians had been transferred back and forth between handkerchief and box over the years, mostly when she thought he would be coming home and then the visit had not materialized. Nothing major had happened since he had left but, to Matilda, the disappointments themselves had been of sufficient magnitude to warrant transferring one of her coloured stones. When she had suggested the childish game she had not realized just how much it would hurt her to be apart, the Cornelians had definitely helped. She looked at them every night before she went to sleep and her mind would drift back to their day on Winford beach. She knew too that Matthew still partook of the unusual little game, despite his growing up, for he told her frequently in his letters. It gave her a warm feeling. It was their own secret, special game. Her father and the Vicar could not rob them of everything.

The Vicar obviously thought that Daniel would agree to the young sweethearts' courtship now that they were older and Matthew had completed his studies, for he was in an exceptionally good mood when Matilda called on the eve of Matthew's homecoming.

"Hello, young lady, I assume we will have the pleasure of your company when we meet Matthew at the railway station tomorrow."

"You will indeed, I can hardly believe that he is coming home at last, I keep thinking I am dreaming, you have no idea how happy the news makes me."

"I think I have a good idea, I have not seen you looking so radiant in years. Your father did not want you getting too serious about each other when you were young – before Matthew had completed his studies – but I am sure he will have no objection now."

"Pardon me, Sir but I thought it was *you* who objected most to our friendship."

"Well, er, of course I was concerned too," blustered Richard, "but well, it seemed to be important to your father for you to both have a few years apart, to meet other young people. It was not a bad idea I have to agree. Romance can play havoc with studies, affects the concentration."

The Vicar realized he had made a misjudgement and was somewhat concerned at the girl's change of mood. In an attempt to recover the situation he now said jovially. "Do not be late tomorrow, we will leave at eleven o'clock. We will luncheon at Winford before coming home. Richard is going to meet us at the railway station."

Elizabeth now entered the room, she crossed to Matilda, put her arms around her warmly and said, "Isn't it wonderful, Matilda, home at last, I cannot believe it, can you?"

"I will not believe it until I see him, Mrs Johnson."

Chapter Three

Matilda strained to catch sight of Matthew as the passengers began alighting from the London train. She moved her head from side to side as first one person then another obscured her view. Then she saw him, unloading his suitcases from the carriage. She stood as if rooted to the spot, her breath coming in short gasps, her heart racing, she was so happy.

Matthew turned and began walking down the platform. He was tall... big... he was a *man*. For a fleeting moment she thought there was something familiar about his walk, some little facet of his gait that reminded her of someone. It kept flitting across her mind as an aggravating fly flits across one's vision; then he began to run, she found her own legs and began running too, faster and faster until they were in each others arms oblivious to everything except that they were together at last.

"Tilly, oh Tilly," Matthew whispered, "how I have dreamt of this moment." He did not want to let go of her but his parents and Richard were waiting to greet him. He hugged his mother who, like Matilda, was crying unashamedly, then his father and Richard.

The men walked back the short distance to retrieve the forgotten luggage before they left the railway station for luncheon at The Royal Hotel.

During the meal Matilda and Matthew hardly took their eyes off each other. They did not eat much, their hearts were too full. Matilda need not have worried, she could see that Matthew still thought she was beautiful. He was so handsome and grown up. Everything would be perfect from now on.

Matthew held her hand all the way home, where she was invited to stay for tea.

This is the most perfect day of my life, thought Matilda as she prepared to leave the Vicarage. Matthew was going to walk her home.

"I hardly dare offer," said Matthew's brother, "but can I offer you a lift?"

Matilda laughed. "No thank you, Richard. Matthew is going to walk with me."

Richard smiled; it was good to see them happy – so young and so happy.

"How does your father feel about my return?" asked Matthew as they walked up Hill Road en route for Uphall Farm.

"I have not told him. I could not risk him spoiling my day so I did not tell him. Mother knows of course. Father probably thinks I am with Verity."

"Well nobody can have any objection to us seeing each other now can they? I have carried out my father's wishes."

Matilda suddenly shuddered.

"Is anything wrong, darling?"

"I have just realized what this means; now you will go on your travels."

"Dearest, I did not realize how difficult it would be to be apart from you, I still like the *idea* of travelling but I could not leave you again."

Matilda was ecstatic; it had been worth the six years of separation just to hear him say that.

It was a beautiful evening in more ways than the obvious. She was glad Matthew had suggested walking

Hardly a breath of wind disturbed the high summer hedgerows, where wild flowers grew abundantly; poppies, cornflowers and buttercups to name but a few, while wild roses and honeysuckle added to the evening scents. Way in the distance, the poppy field appeared like a ribbon of crimson on the horizon.

Matthew took a long, satisfying deep breath, tightening his arm around his sweetheart's waist as he did so. She snuggled closer as he whispered huskily, "How I have longed for this day, just we two, walking in the countryside around all our old haunts."

She felt his arm tighten more as he continued, "Most of all I have longed to feel you close to me, to smell the freshness of you, to bury my face in your hair…"

She turned to face him as his other arm encircled her, her face was pressed hard against his chest – they did not speak, just stood and savoured the moment they had both longed for, for six long years.

That night she took one of the larger Cornelians from the handkerchief and placed it lovingly in her little painted box. She then closed her eyes and took some deep breaths, imagining herself breathing in the clean salty air of Winford beach. It was good to have Matthew home.

Chapter Four

"I heard in the village that Matthew Johnson is home." Daniel was evidently disturbed. "Did you know?" he looked at Louisa inquiringly.

"Yes, I knew."

"You have not mentioned it."

"I did not want you to get agitated."

"Does Matilda know?"

"Of course she does."

"Has she seen him?"

"Yes, she has seen him, she met him off the train when he arrived yesterday."

"You allowed her to meet him?"

"Yes, I allowed her to meet him, of course I did. He has been away for six years, they are friends, of course I allowed her to meet him."

"Even though you know I am against it, how dare you go against my wishes?"

"You are my husband, Daniel, not my keeper, am I not allowed an opinion on the matter?"

"I specifically stated that I do not want them to become serious about each other."

"That was when they were thirteen and fourteen years old. Have you not noticed that they are now adults? Matthew has finished his studies. Matilda has done your bidding for six years. She has worked hard at her painting, piano playing, sewing and household duties. She has also been courteous and charming to all the young men you have insisted she meet. I can understand you not wanting her to run around the woods and countryside with Matthew un-chaperoned, but you will surely now allow them to meet under suitable conditions?"

"No, I will not, she is not yet twenty-one, she must do as I say and I say that she must not see him – under any circumstances."

"You are being unreasonable, and you know it. I cannot support you on this matter any more, what better husband could she possibly have?"

"You mean he has proposed?" Daniel turned white.

"No, he has not proposed but I thought it was obvious that they would eventually marry."

"I do not agree, why is it obvious?"

"Because, Daniel, they are perfect for each other. Penelope is right, they are soul mates. Nobody could be more suitable for Matilda than Matthew. What do you have against him? I cannot understand you, I was always of the opinion you thought him a fine young man."

"I did – he is, but he is not for Matilda."

"Richard and Elizabeth are happy about the situation."

"How do you know that?"

"They would hardly have invited Matilda to accompany them to meet the train if they did not approve."

"So they are actively encouraging the courtship?"

"Of course and why not? You are the only one objecting."

"Please ask Matilda to come here at once?"

"I cannot, she is not here."

Daniel stood up and started to pace the room. How could he possibly keep his eyes on his children twenty-four hours a day when he had a farm to run? He should be able to rely on his wife to carry out his wishes.

Be reasonable man, he told himself, be reasonable, stay calm, think this through. He had hardly mentioned Matthew during the past six years; his name had gradually fallen into disuse. He had not liked to broach the subject because he had thought the friendship had come to a natural end and he had not wanted to resurrect old feelings that may have died. The Reverend had done a magnificent job keeping them apart. He had also managed to keep his wife happy with visits to London.

You are a fool man, he admonished himself, you have deluded yourself, you have buried your head in the sand, telling yourself it was all over when all the time they were keeping in touch.

"Have they been writing to each other?" Daniel now swung round on Louisa as if the idea had just occurred to him.

"Of course, why shouldn't they?"

"Why didn't you tell me what was going on?"

"You never asked if they wrote, your objection was that they were running around unchaperoned, you never said they could not stay in contact by letter, where is the harm in that?"

Daniel knew he was on dangerous ground here with Louisa. It was true, he had said his objection was that they were too old to be left to their own devices. Any reasonable man would have allowed them to write to each other. He decided to back off on that issue, but how was he going to address this pressing problem? He was worrying himself sick. He was going to have to confess but then that would lose the respect of Louisa, possibly even her love. Matilda was probably with Matthew at this very moment, where were they? What were they doing and why were Richard and Elizabeth encouraging them? Why shouldn't they? replied his alter ego, Matthew had been a model son, Matilda was perfect for him, why shouldn't they encourage them?

But I cannot allow it to continue, I must do something. How can I do something without losing the love of my wife and daughter?

He reflected on how quiet Matilda had become since Matthew's departure. How unhappy she had been every holiday and each Christmas when he had not come home. He had felt guilty, time after time, but he had pushed those guilty thoughts to the back of his mind telling himself he was doing the right thing, that he was thinking of what was best for his beloved daughter, and that one day she would thank him. *How could she thank him when she was not aware of the facts,* he screamed at himself. No, she would never thank him, she would blame him, blame him forever, for ruining her life. He would have to give in. *No he could not, how could he?*

"Please stop pacing, Daniel, sit down I am worried about you," Louisa said lightly touching him on his arm, trying to usher him to a chair.

Daniel shook himself free of her, painfully aware of her hurt expression. "I do not want to sit down, I cannot *think* sitting down."

"But what is there to think about? Tell me what is worrying you, I may be able to understand. As it is I am bewildered and becoming frightened of your mood. You have become obsessive about this matter. If you would calm yourself and think clearly, you would realize there is nothing at all to worry about. Our daughter is in love with a respectable, handsome young man who idolises her. We know his family well. They know us well. It is a perfect situation, we should think ourselves lucky and be happy for Matilda. We could not have chosen anyone better for her ourselves."

Daniel suddenly stopped pacing and slumped into an easy chair. He sat very still, his head in his hands. He would never have Louisa's understanding unless he confessed to her. He could see no other way out. His whole family was going to be lost to him. He would lose the respect of his friends, his standing in the Church and the village. Everybody would remember the day in church twenty years ago when the Vicar had pleaded from the pulpit for information about the abandoned baby. Every one would know he had been present and had ignored the Vicar's beseeching. He could not face the humiliation. He would have to leave his family, his farm and the village. He would be an outcast. What was he to do?

Matilda and Matthew met on Flintknappers corner as arranged the previous night. It was a beautiful evening as they wandered hand in hand towards Common Lane. When they reached the crossroads they turned left towards the Common itself. There was a new, unexpected shyness between them. It was strange considering how well they knew each other, but they had parted as children, now they were adults. Whenever Matthew reached for Matilda's hand he felt slightly shy. Before, Matilda would have grabbed his arm in excitement at a new idea or just to get his attention. Now, he noticed, she waited for him to make the initial physical contact. She was more demure, she was a young lady and acted accordingly. She was still very beautiful. He could not believe that she had waited for him all this time. He felt so proud of her. He wanted to be close to her, to hold her as he had the previous evening. He moved closer, so that their bodies touched, then they were in each other's arms again, clinging together as if somebody was waiting nearby to wrench them apart.

Matilda's thoughts were running parallel to his own. He must have met many other young ladies while away but he had returned to her.

She slackened her arms around him and gently pushed him slightly away. She looked up at him in the soft evening sunshine and smiled, he smiled back lovingly then crushed her to him again as the poem came to his mind.

> *The sun on her face*
> *And the wind in her hair,*
> *Golden as it dances*
> *Dances on the air...*

"You have beautiful hair, darling," he murmured huskily.

"You always did say that, but thank you."

"I always said it because it is true. I am so happy to be home again, home with you."

"I am ecstatic that you are here," she whispered.

"How could I ever have thought I could leave you to travel? All I want is right beside me. I must have been mad."

"You were a child, it was a romantic dream."

"I somehow thought I could travel without leaving you. How silly it all seems now. I must have bored you rigid with my boyish ambitions."

"You never bored me, you never could," and then she said changing the subject. "Do you know where we are going?"

"Of course."

They smiled.

"It is more cosy now, I have taken quite a lot of bits and pieces there."

"Good," he said as they began walking again.

"Are we silly?"

"Why do you say that?"

"We are going to our childhood haunts."

"You forget, I have not seen our childhood haunts for six years, I have craved for them, anyway they are now our adult haunts. He gave her an intimate look, his gaze lingering as his eyes travelled hungrily over her face.

"Look, the gypsies are here again. I hope they are not going to rekindle your desire for travel."

"Nothing will do that, not even a romantic gypsy caravan and fire."

They turned left at the top of the road and made their way to Clancy's.

As they pushed their way into the little house, Matilda looked at Matthew to judge his reaction. He stood in the middle of the house and looked round approvingly. Suddenly the room seemed smaller. Matilda was surprised at just how small. There were two of them taking up the space now and Matthew was a full-grown man.

"You have no idea how many times I have dreamed of this place, darling. Many times in the early days I thought of running away and coming back here. I wish we had found it earlier."

"We would not have found it at all had it not been for the Jackdaw."

"Did you ever see it again?"

"Many times, year after year. It always had a droopy wing, but it seemed happy enough."

"It all seems such a long time ago."

"Yes, but our game was effective. I looked at the Cornelians every night and felt very close to you. I am glad we collected them. Just think, I could have walked on the shingle a thousand times not knowing they were there. I have a lot to thank Walter Fennell for. He is such a nice man."

"He is, but then, so is everybody, I love them all, my world is perfect, it is such a joy to be alive."

They laughed, then went shy as their arms crept round one another once again...

"You know, don't you, that I am going to ask your father for your hand in marriage, just as soon as I have a stipend?"

"You have not yet asked *me* if I will marry you, just why are you taking it for granted, Matthew Johnson?" said Tilly with mock sternness, trying to take the intensity out of their conversation.

The two young sweethearts chuckled at the joke and then Matthew dropped down on one knee, took Matilda's hand in his, and said, rather solemnly. "Darling Tilly, will you please do me the honour of becoming my wife?"

"Yes, Matthew, yes, a thousand times yes."

They stood in Clancy's house holding each other tightly as the evening sun shone warmly through the shutters, making shadowy patterns of the leaves and trees on the inside walls and floors. They did not say much. There was no need. They could feel the heat of each other's bodies through their thin summer clothing. She could smell the maleness of him, feel his taut muscles as his arms held her close. He fought hard to control the needing of her as he buried his head in her neck, murmuring muffled endearments...

He pulled himself reluctantly from her, but his eyes did not leave her face. "I think perhaps we should go home."

"Yes – I suppose," she agreed.

They walked home to the farm via the poppy field, which was in full bloom.

Such a lovely month to return home, thought Matthew, as they sauntered through the flowers. His homecoming had been perfect.

In the distance over the meadow was Uphall Farm looking welcoming in the mellow evening sunshine...

> *Strolling through the poppy field*
> *With neither haste nor care,*
> *Watching brilliance dancing*
> *Dancing on the air...*

They climbed over the stile, with slightly more decorum than they had on the last occasion, as Matthew went first and then held out his hand to assist Matilda. He is so handsome and well mannered, thought Matilda. I am the luckiest woman in the world.

They crossed the meadow, stopping to fuss the horses, which were still grazing. Then passed through the gate and over the road to the farmyard.

Matthew savoured all the familiar sights that he had not seen in years. He loved the farm almost as much as Matilda did, they had had so many happy times around the place. The pair turned right and made their way past the sheds, hearing shuffles and lows that betokened the cows, contented after their last milking of the day. Then up through the garden, past the well and so to the dairy, which in turn led to the kitchen.

"You must come in and see Mother and Father before you go home." Matilda pulled Matthew through the kitchen as she spoke. "They will be so pleased to see you again."

"Mother, Father, look who is here."

Louisa was the first to rise from her chair to greet Matthew. She had seen the pair as they walked across the meadow and had pleaded with Daniel not to cause a scene the first time he saw Matthew after such a long time.

"Hello, Matthew, it is really lovely to see you again," she said as she put her hands on his arms and kissed him warmly on the cheek. "How you have grown, I hardly recognize you. Come and sit down."

"Thank you, Mrs Canham." Matthew turned and spoke to Daniel who was rising from his chair. "Hello, Sir, it is good to see you both again. I trust I find you in good health?" There was a query to his tone.

"Yes, very much so thank you, are you well yourself?"

"Yes thank you, Sir."

For all Daniel's misgivings about the young couple's courtship, he found himself looking at Matthew with pride. My son, he acknowledged privately, has grown into a fine young man, handsome, tall, dark, and swarthy. How can I not be fond of him? There is nothing to dislike. The very fact that he is so charming and presentable makes it impossible to find plausible reasons for objecting to him as a son-in-law. What young woman *would not* find him attractive? His daughter was alive again, visibly glowing with happiness. How could he hurt her? But hurt her he must.

"Tell us all about Kent and London, I understand you spent a considerable amount of time in the city with your mother's family. It must have been wonderful to have the opportunity of getting to know them all so well."

Louisa did her best to keep the conversation on a non-personal level.

"I grew very fond of Kent, it is now my second home. I have met so many new people there and have made good friends among my contemporaries. I cannot wait to introduce Matilda to them all, I am sure they will love her. As for London, well yes, it was good to meet Mother's family and to visit all the historical, political and social attractions but I would not wish to live there permanently. I would however love to give Matilda a guided tour now that I am so familiar with the place." He smiled in Matilda's direction, indicating how much he was relishing the thought of taking her to London to see the sights. His eyes were still telling her how much he loved her.

"If I am totally honest," he continued, "I have seen nowhere that compares more favourably with Norfolk and Suffolk. We are very lucky to live in such a lovely area I think you will agree. I have no great desire to move too far away."

Matthew thought this last remark might please Daniel and Louisa, had they been worried that he might take Matilda to the south of England to live.

It is obvious they are in love, thought Louisa looking lovingly at her eldest daughter's happy countenance. How can Daniel even consider separating them? They are so perfect for one another.

The conversation and catching up of the missing years went on for the best part of an hour. Matilda was glad to see the people that she loved getting on so well, but then, there it was again, something about Matthew that was reminding her of someone else. A frown appeared on her forehead as she tried to decipher of whom it was that Matthew was reminding her. They are probably fleeting expressions I observed when he was a boy, she thought, it was so long ago, and he had matured so much that it was almost like thinking of another person. But something kept niggling at her thoughts all the same.

"Well what do you think of him?" Matilda asked excitedly of her parents after Matthew left.

Louisa took her daughter in her arms. "I agree with you, he has grown into a fine young man. His parents must be very proud of him."

" 'Fine', Mother, what do you mean 'fine', said Matilda laughing. "Do you not think that he is the most handsome, most charming, most eligible young bachelor in the whole of England?" She whirled dreamily around the room holding out one side of her frock as she lightly touched items of furniture in passing, as if she were spreading a magical stardust around.

"What did you think, Father?" she now asked.

"Yes, I agree with your Mother, he is a fine young man."

Matilda did not seem to notice her father's flat tone, she was in a world of her own as she kissed her parents goodnight and floated happily out of the room.

"Thank you for being courteous to Matthew." Louisa murmured as she cleared away the crockery that had held their refreshments.

"It is not difficult to be civil to the boy."

"Of course it is not. I told you, you would see sense if you gave the matter due consideration."

"You misunderstand me, Louisa, I have not changed my mind about anything. I was just stating a fact that he is a very presentable young man. Now I am tired and must go to bed."

As he left the room Louisa noticed how troubled and sad her husband appeared, he had even developed a slight stoop. She could not understand him. She was concerned about his mental health. He was behaving very inconsistently. On the one hand he was agreeing that Matthew was ideal husband material and yet he was vehemently opposed to the couple's eventual union. What was she to do? She shuddered; it appeared that she could only have the happiness of *either* her husband or her daughter, that she would never have the happiness of both, yet she did not know why. Daniel was either unable or unwilling to share his worries with her. What had gone wrong between them? They had always been so close. There had never been secrets between them and now it appeared that there were. She had thought his recent behaviour could be linked to his father's death – Dan had died of a heart attack two years previously – but she had to admit that Daniel was acting very strangely long before his father died. Perhaps it is the added responsibility of running the farm; he had taken on extra work long before his father's death. She tried to remember the exact time that Daniel's behaviour changed. He had always welcomed Matthew into the house in the early days of the children's friendship, when did he alter his opinion of him, and why? She would have to resolve this situation one way or another. If she did not her family would be rent asunder.

She took the dirty crockery to the kitchen, extinguished the lamps and prepared to join her husband in the bedroom.

Chapter Five

The next morning, as Matilda approached the kitchen door, she was halted in her tracks by her father's voice. He did not sound very happy or reasonable.

Her step faltered as she wondered whether or not to enter the kitchen. She did not want to intrude if her parents were having an altercation.

She was on the point of turning away when she was, again, brought to a halt by her father's raised voice, but this time she heard clearly as he said, "I tell you Louisa I will not allow it. I will go myself to the Vicarage this afternoon to put a stop to the matter once and for all."

Matilda fled back to her bedroom. What had her father meant? He could not be referring to herself and Matthew. Why, only last night he had enjoyed a convivial evening with him. What was going on?

A worried feeling crept into her lower stomach; she trembled slightly. Nothing can go wrong now surely, she told herself. She had probably misinterpreted her father. But what else could he be going to the Vicarage to put a stop to?

She decided to go back downstairs to breakfast. If her father was going to the Vicarage this afternoon then she herself would go this morning.

Matilda was half expecting to find that all was not well at the Vicarage, but Elizabeth was her usual self when she answered the knock at the door.

"Come in, Matilda, Matthew is out with his father at the moment but they will be home for lunch. Can I give him a message or would you like to wait?"

"Would you ask him to meet me at half past two this afternoon please? He will know where."

"Yes of course, are you alright, dear? You look a little pale."

"No, no, I'm fine thank you, Mrs Johnson, I will see you again soon, I must get back now to help Mother."

As Matilda walked home she told herself not to be silly. She had probably jumped to conclusions due to hearing only half a conversation. She thought of the way she and Matthew had been kept apart for the past six years. That was no accident she knew. She was fearful, she was experiencing a sensation of impending doom. It had been a cloudy morning but the sun was now breaking through, promising another lovely day...she shuddered all the same.

Matilda looked at her watch for the umpteenth time; it was five and twenty to three. She had been at the clearing for fifteen minutes. She had brought the notebook with her to give to Matthew. It contained all the information she had collected about his abandonment.

Where was he? Perhaps his mother had forgotten to give him the message. She wrung her hands. Maybe her father had arrived at the Vicarage before Matthew left.

She paced back and forth in the clearing. Twenty to three – where was he? No – stop it, she told herself, he is only ten minutes late, anything at all could have held him up. He had not been expecting to meet her this afternoon, perhaps he had arranged other things to do that could not be avoided.

Then suddenly he was there. "Oh Matthew," she flung herself at him, "what is happening?"

He pulled her close before holding her at arm's length. "What is the matter, Tilly?"

"Is my father at the Vicarage?" Her voice contained mild panic.

"No, should he be?"

"I heard him telling Mother this morning that he was going to the Vicarage to put a stop to it once and for all."

"A stop to what?"

"I do not know. I can only guess that he means us."

"Us? But why would he want to do that?"

"I do not know. I cannot think straight; I only know what I heard. What else could he have meant?"

"But I was talking to him last night. He was very pleasant to me, you were there. He gave no indication that he does not approve of me."

Matilda put her head in her hands and began to cry. "I have a feeling, Matthew, that something is dreadfully wrong."

"Nothing is wrong, dearest, nothing will ever part us again, of that you can be sure."

He put his arms around her and began to kiss away her tears, holding her close to him.

"Promise me, please promise me."

"I promise you, darling, I do not intend to leave you ever again."

Matilda relaxed, comforted by his strength. Gradually her fears subsided as she lost herself in his embrace. It was a beautiful day; she was in her favourite place with the man she loved. She was vaguely aware that somewhere overhead, in the thick leafy branches, a blackbird was singing.

Matthew continued kissing her, reassuring her, holding her closer and closer as his need of her intensified. More and more passionately he kissed her and she responded to him hungrily.

Common sense evaporated along with their problems as he pulled her down onto the cool fresh grass of the clearing, his hands moving... searching... caressing...

"I love you, sweetheart," he murmured almost unintelligibly, "I love you so much, I have missed you so much, I will never leave you again."

"I love you too, with all my heart," she murmured softly.

They did not want to talk, only to love, with a passion and urgency that took away their breath and reasoning...

They removed their clothes – slowly at first as their eyes took over the caressing – then more and more quickly as Matthew buried his face in his darling's beautiful hair... moving his head down... flicking his tongue across her neck...her breasts... her body; savouring the sweet taste and aroma of her young skin...

burying his head deeper and deeper, pausing only to inhale great lungfuls of her – absorbing the very scent of her soul... and then more and more urgently as – for the first time – he tasted the exhilarating sweetness of the forbidden fruit that was his darling sweetheart.

They were, for once, oblivious to everything in their beautiful, natural world, save the beating of their hearts, the coursing of their blood and the heady spiralling senses that took them ever closer to their own heaven on earth, surrendering, with total abandonment, to perfect, unadulterated, young love...

Matthew looked across at Tilly lying by his side, lightly covered now by her previously discarded clothing. He could still see the curve of her young, white breast, partly visible under the covering. He gently traced the shape with a finger, then leant down to kiss the soft mound. Her eyes were closed and there was a slight smile playing on her lips, a smile of contentment and happiness. Her hair, that was spread wide over the grass, was occasionally being lifted by the breeze, making it flutter and dance around her face – sparkling in the sun. One arm was raised and bent at the elbow, allowing the back of her hand to rest gently at the side of her forehead.

He lay beside her, resting on his elbow, drinking in her beauty...

> *All at one with nature,*
> *'Neath her golden hair,*
> *That's dancing in the sunshine,*
> *Dancing on the air...*

He moved closer, putting one arm gently across her, laid his head beside hers and joined her in sleep...in the sunshine...in the clearing...beside the walnut tree... in Clancy's wood...as somewhere overhead the blackbird continued his song.

When they awoke it was half past four but they were in no hurry to disentangle themselves from each other's arms.

"Now you are mine forever, my sweetheart."

"I did not know I could be so happy, everything is now in perspective. If Father continues to disapprove we will wait until we are both of age. I will not let him part us again."

"It will be nothing compared to the last six years. We will see each other often. If I have to accept a curacy further afield I will have the finance to visit you, even if it is in secret. Which reminds me. We must have a contingency plan in case you are right about your father's intentions. We will leave notes here if we need to contact each other."

They held each other close and kissed again before, very reluctantly, replacing their clothing – shy again now, despite their new intimacy.

Before leaving the clearing a suitable hiding place was found along one of the walls in which to leave their letters.

Matthew returned home at half past five to find Elizabeth distraught.

"Your father wants to see you at once in his study, Matthew."

"What is wrong? You look ill."

"I am ill with worry, I do not know what is going on."

"What has happened?"

"Daniel Canham has been to see your father."

Matthew knocked on the study door and entered. Richard sat at his desk but now rose to greet his son. "Sit down, Matthew I must talk to you." He looked very worried.

"Mother says Mr Canham has been to see you."

"Yes he has. He does not want you to see his daughter again."

"He cannot do this, Father, we love each other, I intend to marry Tilly just as soon as I have a stipend."

"You cannot marry her, Matthew, ever."

"I can and I will."

"No, Matthew, you must never marry Matilda."

"Tilly will not always need her father's permission. When she is twenty-one we can marry anyway. You and Mother have no objection do you?"

"This morning, I had no objection. This evening I do."

"But why?"

"I cannot give you explicit reasons. It is a matter of confidentiality. If it is any consolation I am unhappy too, and so is your mother."

"Help me, Father. You cannot forbid me to marry Tilly without giving me a reason."

"You must trust me, Matthew. You can never marry her."

"Unless you give me very good grounds for not doing so, I will marry her just as soon as I am twenty-one. No one, not even Mr Canham, will stop me."

"*No, Matthew, you will not*" Richard raised his voice considerably.

Matthew's throat felt constricted, he was remembering another time he had stood in this study just as bewildered. He tried to control his anger, taking long deep breaths. "What reason can Mr Canham possibly have for refusing to let me see Tilly? I am trying to remain calm, Father, please help me understand."

"As I said before, you must trust me, there is a very valid reason, please believe me."

"Are you telling me that Mr Canham knows who my real parents are? Is my father a murderer? Or perhaps my mother is a whore. Am I nearer the truth now?" His voice had risen uncharacteristically.

"I cannot say. It grieves me very much but I cannot say. I cannot break a confidence. I think you should go again to stay with your mother's family in London."

"No, I will not, I am sorry."

"I too am sorry, I really am."

Matthew left the study and found Elizabeth crying in the sitting room. "What is going on, Mother, do you know?"

"No, Matthew, your father says it is a confidential matter between himself and Mr Canham."

"I will get to the bottom of this, if it is the last thing I do. I am not giving up without a fight."

"You know, don't you, that Daniel Canham will prevent you

119

seeing his daughter at all now? I am so sad for you."

Matthew sat with his head in his hands, the events of the day going round in his head. Is it not strange, he thought, that one could wake in the morning feeling at peace with the world but by nightfall find one's whole life in turmoil?

"I wish," he said now, "that I could give Tilly a ring, something tangible to show her that I intend to marry her, no matter how long it takes to resolve the problems."

"Come with me, Matthew." Elizabeth caught hold of his arm in a sudden display of positivity, and pulled him toward her bedroom.

She opened a drawer in her dresser and took out a large leather-covered box. She opened it. Inside were smaller boxes all containing beautiful items of jewellery, made by her father and left to her in his Will.

"Take your pick, Matthew, you can give Tilly any piece you choose, I have no daughters or granddaughters to leave them to at present. I gave Richard a piece for Jane, so you must have one for Tilly."

Matthew could not believe it; it was like having the choice from a jeweller's shop. He did not know whether to choose a ring or a locket. There were two lockets – one square, one oval. The latter was engraved with flowers, which were studded in the centres with tiny diamonds.

He chose the oval locket. It was in a grey box, lined with dark blue velvet.

Matilda also arrived home to find her mother distressed, but doing her best to hide it. Loveday was now fifteen and Edward thirteen and they shot sympathetic glances in the direction of their older sister as she entered the kitchen. Mother and children had congregated in one room as if their combined strength could permeate Daniel's bad temper and bring peace and happiness back to the household – a valiant but futile notion.

"I sense a troubled atmosphere," ventured Matilda looking from one to the other apprehensively.

"Your father is not in the best of moods, he wants to talk to you after dinner."

"Do you know the essence of what he has to say to me?"

"Yes," replied Louisa, "but I am not at liberty to tell you."

Matilda went to her room and transferred a Cornelian to her 'happy' box, it was the largest she could find, for nothing could compare to the happiness of the afternoon. Her father could not take that away from her, whatever the nature of his talk tonight.

The evening meal was eaten in virtual silence with the two younger children casting furtive glances every now and again in the direction of their father, who was displaying such a dark countenance that they wanted to escape as soon as possible from the heavy brooding atmosphere.

After dinner Daniel directed a stern glance towards the two younger children. "I would like you both to retire to your rooms and stay there until told otherwise."

They scuttled off at once, pleased to be removed from the situation at last.

Matilda had not eaten much; such was the churning of her stomach. She watched apprehensively as her mother also made a hasty departure.

"I will come straight to the point," said her father, taking his place in one of the chairs alongside the hearth and gesturing for her to take the other. "You will not be seeing young Matthew again unless it is unavoidable in a social situation."

She went weak and begin to tremble. "I do not know why you are saying this, Father," her voice was unsteady. "What do you have against Matthew?"

"I have nothing against him as young men go, but he is not for you."

"I am sorry, Father, I cannot comply with your wishes, I love Matthew and he loves me."

"*Love*, what do you know of love? He has been home a matter of days, that is all, you cannot know whether or not you are in love."

"I have known him for fifteen years, I think *that* is long enough."

"You were but children then, you have known him as an adult for only a few days."

"You will not dissuade me, Father, I am nineteen, you cannot keep me from him forever. In two years time I can marry without your consent. If I have to wait that long then I will, but I would rather have your blessing."

"YOU WILL NEVER HAVE MY BLESSING, do you hear girl? YOU – WILL – NEVER – HAVE – MY – BLESSING." Daniel's face had taken on a purple hue, he had risen from his chair and now stood towering above Matilda, he too was shaking. "In future you will not leave this house without my permission."

"You cannot keep me locked up forever," whispered Matilda, frightened half to death.

"I WILL IF I HAVE TO," thundered her father. "YOU WILL NOT MARRY HIM. NOW GO TO YOUR ROOM."

But, as she turned to leave – her breath coming in short gasps – she saw her father clutch at his head with one hand, as he stumbled, putting out his other hand in a futile attempt to steady himself as he crashed down onto a side table, sending its contents flying in all directions.

"MOTHER," screamed Matilda but Louisa was already running into the room having heard the commotion.

Louisa bent down beside her husband on the floor trying to soothe him as he spluttered unintelligibly.

"Tell your brother to ride for the Doctor as quickly as possible," she said without taking her eyes from Daniel. "Hurry."

Matilda was rooted to the spot in horror. I have killed my father, she thought, and I do not know how it all came about.

She suddenly found her breath and her strength as she ran to the door calling for Edward.

"EDWARD, EDWARD."

Edward appeared at the top of the stairs looking frightened. "What is all the noise about, what…?"

Matilda interrupted him. "You must ride for a doctor, Edward, hurry, Father has collapsed."

Loveday, who by now had also emerged from her room, came downstairs too, whimpering as she did so. "Will Father die,

Matilda? Please do not let him die."

Matilda put an arm around her younger sister, leading her to the kitchen. "I do not know what happened, stay here and try not to cry, I must help Mother."

As Matilda re-entered the sitting room, Louisa was putting a cushion under Daniel's head. "We had better not move him," she said now in a small voice, then, "has Edward gone?"

"Yes, he went straight away, I doubt he stopped to saddle her. Oh, Mother what have I done, I did not mean to…"

"It was not your fault, I have been worried about him for some time, he has been acting very inconsistently. Try not to blame yourself."

"But I must blame myself. It was because of me he was so angry."

"Yes, Matilda but it was unprovoked, it was unreasonable behaviour – we both know that."

Matilda was pleased to have her mother's support but it did not make her feel much better. If her father died, she told herself, she would be to blame.

It seemed like hours before Edward arrived back with Doctor Henry Miles – or Dr Henry as they called him; to differentiate from his brother Dr Benjamin.

Louisa, Matilda and Edward stood motionless as the Doctor examined Daniel on the floor.

"We thought it best not to move him," whispered Louisa.

"You did right, Louisa. He has had a slight stroke."

Louisa gasped in disbelief, covering her mouth with her hand. "But he is only forty-two."

"I am afraid illness is no respecter of age." He turned now to Edward. "Could you help me carry your father to his bedroom, Edward?"

"Is he going to be alright?" asked Louisa anxiously.

"With bed rest and quiet he should make a full recovery but keep him very calm."

The two carried Daniel up the stairs to his room, where Louisa helped the Doctor undress him and put him to bed.

"Do you know what brought it on, Louisa? I mean, has he had any worries or problems?"

"He had got himself worked up into a frenzy over Matilda's friendship with Matthew Johnson. For some reason he is opposed to him. It is all very confusing, he has been acting so strangely lately. He likes Matthew but objects to Matilda walking out with him. I dread to think where it will all end."

"I think it would be best to humour him, for the time being at least. Perhaps you could convince Matilda of that."

"She loves her father, I am sure she would not knowingly put him in danger."

"I will call on him again tomorrow."

"Thank you, Henry, I am much indebted to you."

The Doctor took his leave.

Louisa returned downstairs to find her three children sitting quietly in the kitchen, their visible stillness belying their churning emotions. "The Doctor thinks your father will make a complete recovery if he has rest and peace." She now put her arm around Matilda, saying. "I know this is a lot to ask but will you please respect his wishes, at least until he is better?"

"Of course, Mother, you know I wish Father no harm, I am just so unhappy."

Matilda went upstairs to her room and removed a stone from her 'happy' box. Never before had she transferred a Cornelian in opposite directions twice in the same day. Her heart was heavy. She would never dare defy her father now; she did not want to be responsible for his untimely demise.

Having written a letter to Tilly, Matthew prepared to take it – with the wrapped locket – to the clearing. He walked up Common Lane and skirted the Common. Had he chosen to go the alternative route – by the way of Hill Road – he might have been surprised to encounter Edward, riding bare back, posthaste for the Doctor...

As it was, Matthew found the clearing deserted, apart from the wildlife. He had not, in truth, expected to find Tilly there this evening after her father's conversation with the Vicar, but, nevertheless he had hoped. He now found the ledge where they had agreed to leave their letters and inserted the little parcel and correspondence. He placed a stool in front, although he knew nobody ever came here except himself and Tilly. The locket is so valuable, he thought, I should not really leave it in the middle of a wood. But he did not have much choice.

He laid down in the clearing for about an hour and a half, going over recent events. It had been a long day, one of many emotions. He was so glad that Tilly had asked him to meet her this afternoon and he had made her his own. He had scaled undreamed of heights of happiness this afternoon and been plummeted to the depths of despair this evening. All the same he would put a Cornelian into his painted box tonight to represent their lovemaking. Nothing could detract from that. He would resolve the other problems somehow, he vowed.

The following afternoon Matilda asked Louisa if she could go for a walk. They had all been taking turns to sit with Daniel. The atmosphere in the house was suffocating in more ways than one. Matilda felt that everyone must be blaming her, although she was assured that this was not the case. The guilt she felt on the one hand was crushing, but on the other hand she knew there had been no good reason for his outburst. They had been taking turns to go out in the air for an hour at a time. Matilda had insisted on going last.

She went to her room to collect her writing materials. She would go to Clancy's Wood and leave Matthew a letter acquainting him fully with the unhappy situation at home. She knew he would understand if she did not meet him for a while.

It took some time to write the events of the previous evening. She finished by writing:

I know you will understand, Matthew, that I cannot meet you in the foreseeable future, I am therefore even happier that we gave such expression to our love this afternoon. I will love you forever.

Please join me in trying to remain optimistic for our future.
Ever yours,
Tilly.

She then folded the letter in preparation for leaving it in their pre-arranged hiding place.

She was surprised to find the space already filled. She carefully removed the parcel and letter. She read:

My Darling Tilly,
I have had the most horrendous time since leaving you this afternoon. Your fears proved correct. Your father visited the Vicarage this afternoon to inform my father that he no longer wanted you to associate with me. I have no idea why. I have had an awful argument with Father although I do not hold him to blame. I even suggested that maybe your father knew something about my origins, that maybe I was from 'bad stock', a murderer or a whore perhaps. But still he would not break your father's confidence. He did however appear to be genuinely unhappy about the situation but, he says, he has to comply with your father's wishes.

I feel so frustrated. If I knew why your father was acting in this way I would, at least, be at liberty to make judgement, as it is I am stymied.

I expressed a wish to Mother that I would like to give you a present – a symbol of my everlasting love for you. She quite surprised me by offering me a choice from a considerable collection of jewellery, which was left to her by her father – he was a goldsmith and a jeweller you may remember. So, darling Tilly I am able to give you the present I have left with this letter.

We will stay in touch as arranged. That failing, I will send messages by way of brother Richard, who I know is sympathetic to our cause. Try to be brave, darling.
Love always,
Matthew.

Matilda unwrapped the parcel. She could not believe what she found inside. She had never before been given anything to match it. She knew it was very valuable, but it was the fact that it was from Matthew that meant the most. Dear Mrs Johnson, she thought, how understanding she is. She unfolded her own letter and added a post script:

I have just found my present, Matthew. How can I ever thank you enough? It is beautiful, you have excellent taste, I will treasure it for as long as I live. Thank you again, T.

Having secured her note in the hiding place she collected her writing materials, together with Matthew's letter and gift, and headed back to her duties at the farmhouse. She knew that Matthew would find her letter – he would no doubt check that she had collected the parcel.

Matthew found Tilly's correspondence that same evening, although his mother had already told him of Daniel's illness. It was, apparently, the talk of the village. The news put a whole new dimension to the argument of fighting their parents. Matthew knew he could not make Matilda choose between himself and her father. If she defied her father he would become worse. He could even die. Tilly would not be able to live with that, Matthew knew he had to take the decision out of her hands. He went to his own father to tell him of his plans.

"I think that is the gentlemanly thing to do," said Richard. "I am very proud of you, son, I know it cannot have been easy for you. We will help financially until you get settled."

"Thank you, Father. It is the hardest decision I have ever made but I cannot risk Mr Canham's health, he is obviously set in his opinion of me. I would like to think, however, that one day you may find it possible to tell me the reason I am such a bad choice as a son-in-law."

"It is nothing like that, Daniel is very fond of you, you must know that."

"All I know is that I am confused, I just want to do right by Matilda. I have promised to marry her one day, I have given my word."

"You cannot do that, you must set her right, so that she has the opportunity of marriage to someone else – and children. Most women want children."

"But I am hoping to resolve the problems."

"You never will. It grieves me greatly to tell you this, but I feel I have to. It would be *unlawful* for you to marry Matilda. You must set her free."

"*Unlawful?* How could it be unlawful? You are worrying me, Father. You must tell me what you mean. I am not a child any more."

"I know you are not a child, even so, I cannot explain. You must trust me on this matter. You have made the right decision, son, but be careful in your choice of words to Matilda. Go and find yourself a wife and enjoy life, put all this behind you, I beg of you."

Matthew could tell, from his father's manner, that he was beaten, he therefore prepared to write the most heart-rending letter of his life. How could it be unlawful to marry Tilly? The only people you cannot marry are your...

Oh God no she cannot be my sister *no, no, no.* The realization was too awful to bear. Louisa was quite happy about their romantic inclinations so it must be Daniel who was his parent. *What had he done? He had lain with his sister, no, no he could not have done. He would have known. The love he had for Tilly was no brotherly love. He would have known, he would have known.*

Matthew was sobbing now, great, body-shaking sobs that tore at his heart and his throat. He was trying to make sense of what his father had told him. He knew he had told him more than he thought wise in the circumstances. He was relying on him not to tell Tilly. Daniel must have kept it from his family – *Tilly did not know – Louisa did not know. Only his father knew, and now him.* But Father did not actually say that, he reminded himself, he only said it would be unlawful to marry Tilly. *But what else could it be?* he screamed at himself, *they must be related. No, no, no,* he could not believe it. It sullied their love. He would allow nothing to do that, ever. He was not related he told himself. He would have to lose Tilly but he would never believe they were related. There would be an explanation, somewhere, sometime there would have to be an explanation. If Daniel were not ill he would confront him now but he knew it was not possible – Daniel *was* ill.

Matthew knew he could never tell Tilly of his fears. It would destroy her. She would lose respect for her father and she would be as horrified as he was at their lovemaking being incestuous. He could not do that to her. He would have to word his letter very carefully. But one thing he was sure of – rightly or wrongly he would always love Tilly.

Matthew composed the letter to Tilly very carefully.

My Darling Tilly, he wrote,

Thank you for your letter, I am very glad you like your present. I know I was optimistic when I wrote to you yesterday but I did not then know about your father's condition. I have now had time to think in depth about the situation. Tilly, darling, I cannot put you in the position of having to choose between your father and myself. If your father died it would be on our consciences forever. I have therefore made the most difficult decision of my life; I am going away again.

Never, ever, doubt my love for you, darling, I will hold in my heart forever, the memories of our last afternoon together, as I am sure you will too. You are beautiful, and I want you to have a beautiful life. I am not asking you to forget me. I could not bear it. Please try to be brave but above all try to be happy, be happy for me, darling – it is so important to me.

I will go off and do some travelling, giving your father the opportunity of a complete recovery. I know how much you love him. We will never lose touch, especially as we have the Cornelians, it was a wonderful idea of yours. The next time we meet I want to see your 'happy' box full to the brim.

Until then, I remain forever yours,

Matthew.

Once again he made the journey to Clancy's house where he found Tilly's own correspondence to him. After exchanging the notes he took a good look round the house and clearing. These memories would have to last for a long time. He then went home to pack his belongings once again. He had been home for such a short time – just five days.

He passed his fingers lovingly over the painting of the little ship as he sadly removed yet another Cornelian from the box.

Chapter Six

Matilda found the letter the next afternoon. She knew in her heart that Matthew had already left, but that did not stop her running all the way to the Vicarage. She was, of course, too late.

Elizabeth did her best to comfort the girl. Even the Vicar fussed around her in a fatherly fashion. They were very fond of her. They assured her that she would always be welcome in their home, even told her that she must visit often. She promised, between sobs, that she would. They had become like second parents to her – especially Elizabeth. "I will always be here for you, Matilda, you know that, you have become like my own daughter. One day, no doubt, we will look back on all this and make some sense of it. But for now we must be strong and help one another, for I will miss him too, though he has promised to write."

Matilda dragged herself back to the farm. When would she see Matthew again? How could she be happy without him? He had asked her to be happy for *him*. He had asked the impossible, he must have known that. However long it took she would wait for him. Of one thing she was sure – he would always love her. She would take comfort from that while she helped to nurse her father. He at least was returning to health under the guidance of Doctor Henry and the loving care of his family. He was returning to health, but he did not appear too happy. He looked older than his years. Matilda had very mixed feelings about her father. She loved him deeply and she knew that he loved her, but he was the one who was ruining her life, how could he do that if he truly loved her? There were so many questions she wanted to ask him. Did he for instance know who Matthew's parents were? Were they 'undesirables'? How could they be, they would never have produced a son like him if they were criminals or some such.

Her head ached with all the weeping and the questions going round and round her brain. She felt as if she were going crazy. She would have to be careful; otherwise her mother would have another patient to nurse.

She would have to cling to the fact that Matthew loved her. He would always love her. She became a little calmer as she neared the farm, but her head still ached and her heart was heavy. Five days, just five days they had had together.

She wondered how long that five days would have to last her.

When Matthew left Flinton he headed for Winford and went straight to his brother Richard, to whom he related the events of the previous five days. "I am going away, Richard, I may as well get the wanderlust out of my system. I will write to you, now and again, to keep you informed of my whereabouts. Please keep an eye on Tilly for me, I am so worried about her."

The brothers hugged one another warmly before walking to the railway station where Matthew caught a train to Illingham. It was the first leg of a journey that was to take him many miles, for at Illingham he obtained work on a cargo ship, bound for South Africa...

Chapter Seven

"Well here we are again," said Amos making himself comfortable on the settle, "and how are all my beauties tonight?"

"We're still a bit dumbfounded from all the goin's on of the last few days," replied Silas who did not frequent the Village Maid quite as often as some of the others did. "It's a sad old do about young Daniel, he can't be more than forty-five."

"I don't think he's that," said Zackery. "He's about the same age as the young Vicar. They're the best of friends you know."

"Well, whatever he is, he is too young to have a stroke, even a mild one, added Fingal. "He's always been fit and well hasn't he? It makes you wonder what's goin' to happen next in this 'ere village."

"I wonder what caused it, somethin' must have caused it, young folk don't go havin' strokes for no good reason now do they?" said Amos concerned.

"Well, you know I don't like spreadin' gossip," said old Walter, " but I think it's got somethin' to do with the young Miss and the Vicar's son, thass what I hear tell anyway."

"Which son do you mean?" asked Martin.

"Young Matthew, thass who I mean," replied Walter. I think a lot of that young boy and I know he thinks a lot of that young gel."

"Well, why do you think it's got somethin' to do with him?" asked Martin.

" 'Cause he's gone off agin. Only home for five days and now he's gone agin," said Walter sadly.

"Dint he tell you why? You're great friends with the lad aren't you?" asked Fingal.

"He's bin to see me twice in the last five days," replied Walter, "once to say hello, and once to say good bye. He was as happy as a sand boy the fust time, but he was in a terrible bad way the last time. I thought he might pipe a tear or two. He put his arms around me and told me to take care now. He thanked me for all I'd done for him with the fiddle and the carpentry and everythin'. An' then he said somethin' really strange, he said, 'Thank you for introducing me to the Cornelians.' "

"What did that mean, Walter?"

"Well, I showed him some Cornelians one day, that I collected from Winford beach. He was right taken with 'em. Said he was goin' to tell Tilly; thass what he call the young Miss – Tilly."

"Well thass a strange tale, Walter, if ever I heard one," said Fingal.

"He said to take care 'til he saw me agin. But I got the feelin' it would be a long time afore he was home agin, I felt like howlin' meself."

"Well, I can't think what to make of that," said Amos. Did he take the young gel with him?"

"I don't know, I didn't ask. He took me a bit by surprise like. I should've asked, shouldn't I?"

"Does anybody know how Daniel is?" asked Zackery.

"He's makin' headway," said Silas, "I saw his head cowman this mornin', you know, young Albert Clarke, Randolph's son"

"Randolph hasn't bin in lately, I s'pose he's busy now the light nights are here agin," said Amos. "I reckon he'd know what was goin' on. He hears all the gossip in that shop of his. Not much git past Randolph."

"I think I'll ride up and see Daniel tomorrow evening if he's on the mend," said Zackery Renawden. "He gives me a lot of business you know with all the farm horses."

"He's a nice chap, couldn't meet better," said Martin. "He never miss Church on a Sunday, not unless he's ill, an' I hear he's very generous to the collection box."

"I heard that young Edward Canham was so frightened that his father was goin' to die, he rode bare back for the Doctor," said Amos draining his mug. "Aye it's a shocking do, it must have been a shock for them all."

"Well you're not sayin' much tonight, Shuffley. You usually

have a fair inklin' of what's goin' on."

"I'm savin' me breath," said Shuffley. "That bout of flu took it out of me this time, I must be gettin' old."

"Aye, we're all gettin' old Shuffley," said Amos. "Time 'n' tide wait for no man."

"Talkin' of waitin', where's Reuben Healey tonight?" added Amos.

"Oh, Reuben *H*ealey," mimicked Darcy joining the group. "You said that very poshly tonight, Amos. I thought you usually dropped your aitches."

"You'll cut yourself one o' these days Darcy Worthdale on that sharp tongue o' yours, I'll have you know I don't often drop my aitches."

"Well, thass just as well," replied Darcy. " 'Cause with a name like Farthing you've got to be mighty careful about dropping your aitches."

They all roared with laughter at Darcy's latest joke.

"Cheeky young beggar," muttered Amos. "I'll git my own back on him one o' these days, you mark my words."

"You've got to admit he's comical, Amos, say what you like, he's comical. You'll be a long while livin' that one down." And they all chuckled again into their mugs of ale.

And so the evening wore on in the usual fashion of banter and convivial conversation in the chimney corner. Amos did not mind being the butt of Darcy's jokes. He was actually quite fond of him; he gave them all a good laugh.

Chapter Eight

"Where is Matilda?" Daniel asked of his wife.

"Now you must not fret about things, she is downstairs."

"Do not let her meet Matthew. Promise me."

"Matthew has left the village, he does not want to give you anything to worry about, so he has left."

"How is Matilda?" Daniel inquired, hating the fact that he was responsible for the renewed unhappiness of his daughter.

"She is bearing up. Of course she is not happy about the situation but her first concern is your health. She has sat with you a lot these last two days. You have slept most of the time."

"I am going to try not to worry about things so much, I thought I was going to die. I do not want to leave you to fend for yourself too early."

"I am glad to hear it. Try to accept the vagaries of life. We do not want anymore frights like this one."

"Yes, I must not get so anxious, nothing is worth dying for is it, not at forty-two? I must put things more into perspective in future. I will make myself a promise here and now."

"Our Edward wants to become a doctor now. He said he felt so useless, but he got Henry here quickly, you have him to thank for that."

"I am thankful for all my family, Louisa. I do not deserve you all, I wish I were more worthy, of you in particular."

"What a strange thing to say, you have always put your family first, of course you are worthy of us. I cannot make you out sometimes."

"I will try to make it up to Matilda, I love her so much, I do not want her to be unhappy."

"I know, dear, you must relax a bit more about her. She will want to get married one day. You cannot keep her at home forever Daniel. Maybe it will all come right in the end."

"I hope so, I truly hope so, for it would break my heart to see her unhappy all her life."

Louisa was a bit confused by what Daniel was saying but she thought it best not to question him in his present state of health. Henry said he should make a complete recovery, it would not hurt to humour him, until then at least. "Do you feel up to having visitors? Richard has called to see you," said Louisa.

"I will see him for a short while, I still feel so tired."

Louisa left the room to go in search of Richard whom she found in the sitting room with Matilda.

Richard had been acquainting Matilda with Matthew's visit to him, assuring her that he would keep her informed of his whereabouts, but of course he could not tell her all of Matthew's fears. Some things were better left unsaid. He would not give her anything else to worry about; anyway, Matthew had asked him to keep certain facts to himself. It was an awkward situation, he acknowledged. Being Matthew's brother and Daniel's best friend put him in a very difficult position, but Matthew had confided in him, and, to date, Daniel had not. Richard found it very difficult to believe that Daniel was Matthew's father and he had told Matthew this. He had known both Daniel and Louisa for many years. Matthew had been conceived around the same time as Daniel's wedding. Richard knew that, at that time, Daniel had been completely smitten with Louisa. It was just not possible. He had managed to put considerable doubt into Matthew's mind on the subject. He thought he had sent him on his way a little more relieved than when he had entered his house. He had assured Matthew that, in his opinion, Daniel was not his father, perhaps, he had said, Daniel was ill and confused. He now rose to go upstairs to see his friend.

As he left he kissed Matilda on the cheek and gave her hand a reassuring squeeze.

Matilda was grateful for Richard's support. Although he was her father's age she thought of him as younger. That was probably because he was Matthew's brother. Whatever the reason she was glad she had him as a friend. He was a direct link with Matthew and she knew she could trust him. She was aware that the next few weeks were going to be difficult. She would be thinking of Matthew all the time but she must keep the fact from her father. She did so want him to get better. Life is hard, she thought. When she was a child she had had no idea how difficult it was to become. All those idyllic days with Matthew, making their plans, talking about their future – it had seemed so simple somehow. How had it all gone so wrong?

Three weeks later Matilda began to worry about another matter. She checked her calendar again and again. It must be all the worry, she thought. What with her father being ill and Matthew away it was no wonder her body had gone haywire. She would try not to worry, after all she was only one week late, she was very unhappy but her physical health was good, she had not felt sick or dizzy. No, it was just worry. But she half hoped it was not. She would be so proud to have Matthew's baby. It was just the circumstances that made it difficult.

Her father was back at work, the household had returned to normal. Matthew's name was never mentioned – unless her father was out of earshot.

One morning in September Matilda was leaving the general store when she heard her name called. "Miss Canham, it *is* Miss Canham isn't it?"

Matilda turned to see a woman about fifty years of age who was familiar by sight but not of her acquaintance. "Yes, I am Matilda Canham," she answered.

"Well, Miss, it's just that I've often seen you about an' I thought that as you had such an affection for young Matthew, well, I'd say 'Hello'."

"You know Matthew?"

"Yes, I'm Maggie Osbourne, I was his wet nurse, he was a lovely baby I grew to think of him as me own. He's a fine man now, isn't he?"

"I am very pleased to meet you, Maggie, which way are you walking?"

"I live in Fishers Row on the Green, would you like to come an' have a cuppa tea with me, Miss?"

"I would like that very much, and do please call me Matilda, my, it is muggy today, isn't it?"

The two women made their way to Fishers Row where Maggie brewed a pot of tea in her kitchen. "Come through to the other room, Miss, it's a bit more comfy."

"No, really the kitchen suits me very well, I like kitchens. It is probably the food smells and the fact that most people have their back doors open. I like fresh air, don't you?"

"Yes, I suppose I do, Jack – me husband – he don't like to be shut in either, he's a farm worker."

"Yes, one gets used to being out of doors, I have always spent a lot of time walking out of doors myself."

"It's very nice to meet you at last, I've said to Jack many times I'd like to say hello."

"I am very glad you did. Mrs Johnson has told me how good you were to her and the baby during a difficult time."

"Poor little mite, who do y' think could leave a bairn like that?"

"It does seem unthinkable, was there no village gossip on the subject?"

"Oh yes, there was plenty of that at the time but no one ever got to the bottom of it did they? Funny that, you'd think that someone would have an inklin' about it. Oh I'm sorry, I probably shouldn't be sayin' all this to you should I?"

Matilda dropped her gaze sadly and studied the mug that held her tea, she then looked back at Maggie and said quietly. "I am always happy to talk about Matthew and I love meeting people who know him. It would be lovely to find out who his real parents are." She checked herself hurriedly. "Oh, he thinks the world of the Johnsons, as far as he is concerned they are his real parents."

"Yes, I know he do but I know what you mean all the same. Do you think he'll be home again soon?"

"I really do not know, Maggie, but I would like to think so."

"Is your father completely recovered now?"

"Yes thank you, he is as good as new."

Matilda sensed that her father's illness had sparked a considerable amount of village gossip – and that it had been connected with Matthew's departure. She saw little sense in denying it, especially as Maggie kept in contact with Elizabeth at the Vicarage. She said now, "I suppose you have heard that my father opposes my friendship with Matthew?"

Maggie looked embarrassed. "I didn't mean to pry…"

"No, of course not, these things have a habit of getting about but, perhaps you could be discreet…" Matilda began to cry, she felt very silly but she could not help it. She liked Maggie, she was motherly. "I am so sorry I do not know what is the matter with me."

"Don't you worry, it will do you good to have a good cry, you'll feel better for it. We'll have another cuppa tea shall we? I won't say nothin' to nobody. Some things are best left between women." Like most of the villagers Maggie regularly doubled her negatives.

"Thank you, I am glad to have met you, I called on Daisy Cartwright a few months ago to make her acquaintance, now I know you both."

"Oh you mean Daisy Drew. I can't git used to her bein' Cartwright. She's a dark un, she never said."

Matilda smiled, "I asked her to be discreet too."

The two women chuckled; a bond had been forged between them. Matilda rose from the table to take Maggie's hand. I should go now before the storm breaks. I will see you again, thank you for the tea. Goodbye, Maggie, goodbye."

"G' bye, Miss. Call again, anytime now."

Matilda decided to go home via Common Lane rather than walk back through the village. Her face was a bit puffy from crying. What was the matter with her, breaking down like that in public? My condition I suppose, she thought. But I am happy about my condition; it is everything else that is wrong. Oh, where was Matthew, she needed to talk to him. She would go to Winford on a shopping trip and call in on Richard. He might have had a letter. She felt a bit cheerier, but then it began to rain. She started running for the woods, thinking she could shelter in Clancy's house, but she did not feel very well, a bit light-headed. She would have to walk after all.

By the time she reached her shelter she was soaked through. The rain was coming down in torrents but the thunder was limited to a few rumbles in the distance. She opened the shutters, on the opposite side of the house to where the rain was driving, and opened a window. It was so airless. She sat on one of the stools with her back resting against the wall, watching the relentless rain as it drove past the window. She felt very lonely, it was not like her to feel so depressed, everything has its beauty and normally she would have taken pleasure even in the rain. But today it seemed more like a burden, beating down on her as she fought, but failed, to raise her spirits.

Eventually the thunder reached Flinton.

She wondered whether to remove some of her wet clothing but thought better of it, she was not cold, just drenched. She must look a sorry sight, in the middle of a wood, in a hut – well more of a rough-hewn cabin really – in the torrential rain, with the thunder and lightening raging overhead. Her hair was beginning to dry a little now. At least she would have the storm to blame for her sorry appearance when she arrived home. If she were lucky her sodden state might detract from her general worried demeanour.

She wondered where Matthew was. She suspected Kent. He had said it was like his second home now. Yes, no doubt he was in Kent and, as she had reminded him one day, it did not take long on the railway. She toyed with the idea of going to find him, she knew where his old school was, and the college, he was probably in the same area, he would not want her to face this problem alone. But always her thoughts returned to her father and what this latest turn of events would do to him. She sighed deeply, whichever way she turned she would hurt somebody. Round and round went her thoughts until her head ached again. Then she realized that the rain had stopped, that the sun was breaking through and, as it did so, she felt surprisingly more optimistic. She rested her hand on her stomach, which was still very flat. My baby, she thought, this is my baby. This is the most important person in the world to me. I must nurture him and care for him, for no one else will. I cannot worry about everybody else, I will put my baby first, no, she corrected herself, I will put *our* baby above everything else. For the first time in twelve weeks she felt there was a purpose to her life. *She was carrying Matthew's child; she would have a part of him forever.* She would not allow her condition to be a problem it was a blessing. She realized she had only thought it a problem because of her father.

Instead of despairing she must make plans. *This* child would never be abandoned. *This* child would always know who its parents were.

Her father had invited numerous people to the house over the previous six years in order to keep Matilda's thoughts occupied. Two of these had been her Aunt Laura and Uncle Jack from North Norfolk. Matilda had taken an instant liking to her Aunt and Uncle and they to her. Each time they left, they invited her to stay with them. Now was the time to take them up on their offer. She would write to them as soon as she had changed her clothes. Not only that, but she would go into Winford tomorrow to buy material for two new dresses. Ones that she could let out as required. There, she was making plans; far better to have a positive approach to the whole situation instead of worrying. If she could manage to hide her condition from her father until Christmas, he would not be suspicious of her going away. The biggest immediate decision she had to make was whether or not to tell her mother. After much soul searching she decided she would – but not just yet.

The following morning Matilda caught an early train to Winford. She had a list of shopping to do for Louisa but her biggest purchase would be the material.

She reached Winford at half past nine. It was a sunny day but much cooler now that the storm had cleared the air. She alighted from the carriage outside the railway station, the huge, ornate, brick building that witnessed so much of Winford's bustle. She was about to walk to the shops when she changed her mind and headed for the beach.

As she crossed the bridge her attention was brought to the Royal Hotel. Was it only three months ago that she had sat in the hotel dining room with Matthew and his family? She smiled at the thought of that happy day, when they had not been able to take their eyes off one another. She walked slowly past the hotel, making her way toward the promenade. The sea looked beautiful, quite calm, little waves were breaking and running up the shore as if they were whispering, so as not to infringe too much on the beauty of it all. The beach was very sandy here. She turned her head right to look at the grand houses lining the way and the impressive carriages going back and forth. She remembered the day on the beach when Matthew had told her that they would, one day, have a large house. If she could have him back she would very happily live in Clancy's House with him in the woods.

She kept on walking until the shore became stonier, where she took the steps down to the beach, until she found the spot where they had collected the Cornelians.

She was walking along as if in a dream, but vividly remembering their day long ago. She wondered if the dreams of the children, playing on the sands today, would come true. She hoped they would. Shattered dreams were so hard to bear. She bent down and hunted for a Cornelian. She found several. On her way back she gave them to the children playing on the sands, holding them up to reveal their translucency. She watched as they ran excitedly to show their parents. Tears began to well in her eyes and trickle down her cheeks. She was so emotional these days but she was glad she had walked with their child on the Cornelian beach. Matthew's poem came to mind...

> *Walking by the sea shore*
> *Sun is glinting there,*
> *Glinting on the sea spray*
> *That's dancing on the air...*

She tossed her head as if displaying her lovely hair to an

imaginary Matthew by her side. *You see, Matthew, I am not going to hang my head in shame, I am proud to be carrying your child and I shall hold my head up high.*

She had reached the Royal Hotel once again. She felt in her pocket for a handkerchief to wipe away the remainder of her tears before she reached the shops.

She chose blue and green material. She would make a dress in each colour. The material was very heavy, she was glad she had left it as her last purchase. As she was about to leave the shop she realized she was rather hungry. She had been out longer than she had intended. Matilda arranged with the assistant to collect her parcel later and made her way to the Tea Shop. About to enter, she turned at the sound of her name being called. Richard was walking briskly towards her.

"I thought it was you, Matilda, are you alone?"

"Yes, I was just about to have a cup of tea and a cake. Will you join me?"

"I would be delighted, it is not often that I have the company of a beautiful young lady."

Matilda smiled; Richard always said the right thing. "Have you heard from Matthew?" she asked hopefully when he had ordered for them.

"No, I am sorry. I have not heard a word since he left. Perhaps he is very busy getting established somewhere," he offered lamely.

"I wonder what he will do, I would not be surprised if he set up a business as a carpenter and joiner."

"Well at least he has a few options. I am sure it will not be difficult for him to earn a living."

They fell into a companionable silence as they sipped their tea and ate their cakes.

"And how are you, Matilda? Are you taking good care of yourself?" Richard looked at her intently.

"Yes, I have decided to be more positive, I thought I might go and stay with my Aunt and Uncle in North Norfolk for a while."

"Will you go soon?" Richard had difficulty hiding his

disappointment.

"I thought perhaps straight after Christmas, but maybe before. I have not quite made up my mind."

"Will you be gone long?"

"I am not sure." Matilda was not looking directly at Richard, a fact that he noted with concern.

"I will not be able to tell you if I hear from Matthew."

No, that is the only drawback, would you write to me if I give you the address?"

He smiled, "Of course Matilda, anyway I expect I will see you lots of times before then."

"Richard…"

"Yes."

"No, I am sorry, it does not matter," she gave him a little smile.

She had been about to tell him she was with child. It was all too easy to talk to Richard.

"I am going to Flinton this afternoon to have dinner with Mother and Father. You will let me drive you?"

"Thank you, yes, but I have a parcel to collect from the drapers first."

They left the Tea Shop and collected the parcel.

"My, this is heavy," said Richard, "did you intend carrying this yourself?"

"Only as far as the railway station."

"I think that would have been far enough, you must be stronger than you look."

I hope I am, she thought, I will have need to be.

As the pair walked up the Vicarage path Matilda felt unsteady and reached for Richard to steady herself. "I think I am going to…"

Richard dropped the parcels and was just in time to catch her as she fainted. He carried her to his front porch, where he had quite a job unlocking the door. Once inside he laid her on the couch. By this time she was coming round.

"I am sorry, Richard, I do not mean to be so much trouble." She began to get up.

"No, lie still, you must lie there for an hour or so. Has this happened before?"

"Of course, it is not unusual for a young lady to faint."

"But it is unusual for a young lady to faint for no good reason." He looked at her worriedly.

Matilda began again to weep. "I am sorry, I am so emotional these days, take no notice of me."

"I could never do that, Matilda, is anything wrong? It sometimes helps to tell somebody."

She dropped her head and studied her lap, before she said quietly, "I am with child."

"I thought that might be the case." He covered her hand with his own.

"Are you ashamed of me?"

"I could never be ashamed of you."

"I am proud to be carrying Matthew's baby but I am afraid of how Father will react. I do not want to make him ill again."

"Have you told anybody?"

"No."

"Not even a doctor?"

"No."

"Do you think that is wise?"

"Probably not, but what can I do?"

"Will you let me call a doctor to you now?"

"I cannot put you to that trouble."

"It is no trouble. Do not move until I get back, I only have to go a few doors down the road."

The Doctor came and examined Matilda. He confirmed the pregnancy and pronounced her fit and well but advised her to rest as much as possible and visit him in a month's time.

"But I cannot...."

"It is alright," said Richard, "I will attend to it. After all, Matthew is my brother and I promised I would keep an eye on you. Anyway I want to. I can collect you now and again on one pretence or another, but I think you should tell your mother of your condition. Just in case of emergencies."

Matilda reluctantly agreed. "Oh, she said, feeling inside her purse. "I almost forgot to post my letter."

The journey back to Flinton was a serious affair. Richard was at pains to reassure Matilda that the matter would stay between themselves. If nobody knew, nobody could tell her father. But he urged her to tell her mother as soon as possible.

"Do you think you will be able to keep it from your father until Christmas?"

"I do not know. I hope so; Mother and Father will not want me to be away then. You do understand I have to put my baby first, don't you, Richard? Even before Father if necessary."

"Yes, of course I understand. I am wondering just how long you can keep Daniel in the dark. He will have to know sometime. It may upset him more if he is the last to be told."

"I will discuss it with Mother. It will probably be better if she tells him after I have gone. He does not get so irate with her."

"What about Matthew?" Richard asked tentatively.

"I would naturally like to tell Matthew myself if possible, but I need an address. There is only one place I can leave a letter but he may not get it for years." She looked wistfully into the middle distance, her mind somewhere in a hazy future with Matthew.

Matilda waited another four weeks before she found the courage and opportunity to tell her mother. They were in the dairy, alone, one morning in late October. "Mother I need to talk to you," ventured Matilda hesitantly.

"You sound very serious, dear."

"I am very serious, I am sorry but I am about to give you a shock." She sat down on a stool and began to cry, knowing how disappointed in her, her mother would be, but she carried on, whispering now. "I am going to have a child."

"Matilda! Are you sure?" Louisa too sat down with an expression of disbelief on her face.

"I am very sure, I have seen a doctor twice now."

"But it is so long since…"

"Yes, it is four months since Matthew was at home. Please do not be angry with me. It would probably never have happened if

Father had not been so opposed to our courtship. Anyway I am not sorry; it is all I have of Matthew now. I am proud to be carrying his baby."

Louisa was trying to come to terms with this latest bolt from the blue. She gazed at her daughter, who appeared so forlorn on the little stool in the dairy, that her heart went out to her. She crossed the short distance between them, pulled Matilda to her feet and put her arms around her. "It is your father I am worrying about."

"Yes, Mother I am concerned too. I wrote to Aunt Laura and Uncle Jack to ask if I could visit them. They said I could stay as long as I liked. I only have to let them know when I will be arriving. I thought," she hesitated here, "I thought it might be better if you told Father after I have gone."

"You are probably right, dear, I will choose the time carefully."

"I think it might be better if I found my own way of earning a living. I do not think Father will welcome me back, do you?"

"We must hope for the best, but I will help you anyway, my paintings sell quite well locally as you know. Perhaps I should take some to London. I do not want you to settle far away Matilda, promise me you will not lose touch."

"I will never do that."

"Have you told anybody else? Verity or…"

"I had to tell Richard, I fainted when visiting him one day, he got concerned about my health. It was he who called a doctor. But no, I have told nobody else. Richard has promised to keep it to himself. He has not heard from Matthew and neither have the Johnsons. They are all quite concerned."

"Your father will be disappointed if you are not here for Christmas."

"I thought I would try and stay until the day after Boxing Day. I am not showing at all yet, do you think that will be possible?"

"I think you may just get away with it, you are young and fit, thanks to all your walking, we will hope for the best."

On Christmas Eve morning Matilda made up two extra baskets

of festive fare. She and Louisa were in the habit of making up baskets for each of their farm workers. This year she asked if she could include Daisy Cartwright and Maggie Osbourne. Edward offered to drive the trap into the village to deliver the baskets to the cottages, as was the custom. Matilda went with him to call on Maggie and Daisy, and to do some shopping.

Having made the deliveries to her two friends, Matilda called on Elizabeth and Richard Johnson to tell them of her plans to go away.

"I will miss you," said Elizabeth hugging her tightly. "Do not stay away too long will you?"

"I hope not but my aunt is very keen to have company. Although they are only about two miles from a town, their cottage is quite isolated." Matilda hesitated then added. "I do not suppose you have heard anything?"

"No, dear, I am sorry, I am disappointed too. Do not give up hope, Matthew is not the type to forget us all. He is probably worried about your father and thinks the longer he waits the better."

"Richard has kindly offered to accompany me to North Norfolk, he says he needs a break but I think he is just being gentlemanly."

"It is probably a bit of both, he *does* get lonely, I wish he would consider re-marrying. It is nine years now since he lost Jane."

Matilda then went to say goodbye to the Vicar who was working on his Christmas Morning service. After that she left the Vicarage. She would see them both in church the next morning but she had wanted to say goodbye properly, in private. She felt a little as if she were deceiving them by not mentioning the baby. She really did want to tell them about their expected grandchild.

Chapter Nine

The journey to Beeton in North Norfolk turned out to be an enjoyable experience for Matilda. The weather had remained remarkably mild. She had not enjoyed saying goodbye to her family, for she did not know when she would see them again, especially if her father refused to have her back, but she had tried to be positive. The best way to view the situation, she had decided, was as a new phase of her life. A new year, a new start.

She had taken an early carriage into Winford, with her luggage, Richard had met her. They had taken the train to Norford then had an hour's wait for a connection to Beeton. Richard is an excellent travelling companion, thought Matilda, as they settled themselves in their carriage for the second leg of their journey. She had not realized he could be quite so entertaining. He is probably trying to keep my spirits up, she decided.

"It is very good of you to escort me all this way, Richard."

"Not at all, I am quite enjoying myself, anyway, I could not risk you fainting again and my not being here to catch you. You never know whose arms you could fall into."

"I am glad you accepted my aunt and uncle's invitation to stay a day or two. It will make me feel more at home to have you there, I do appreciate all you have done for me I assure you."

"I know, Matilda, but it has been a pleasure, so do not worry your pretty head."

"I have never been away from home on my own before."

"Would you like me to visit you once a month?"

"I would love it. Would you really do that?"

"So long as your aunt and uncle agrees."

"I know they will."

"Then that is settled, I shall look forward to it."

Two days later Matilda found it as difficult to say goodbye to Richard as she had to her family, but at least she would see him again soon.

Life at Beeton turned out to be extremely pleasant. The nearest town, Bramfield, was on the coast and within walking distance so, in that respect, it was quite like being at home. Laura introduced Matilda as her niece, who was staying with her while her husband was away on business overseas. It was not far removed from the truth, although the two women did not know it. Laura was very sympathetic to Matilda's situation and was happy to help.

Matilda went walking in the woods with Jack whenever possible and to town with Laura. The evenings were spent sewing, preparing for the baby. With two of them at work for three months they would have more than enough.

The first month flew by and Matilda found herself looking forward to Richard's first visit. She had had a letter from her mother who told her that she had not yet found the right moment to speak to her father. At this rate, thought Matilda, the baby will be born before Father knows anything about it.

It was now the end of January and Richard was due to arrive that afternoon, it was Tuesday. Laura went with her to meet the train and, as they waited on the platform, Matilda was again reminded of the day that she met Matthew when he came home from Kent. Life is just a series of the same events with different people, she mused. She was surprised at just how much she wanted to see him again. She put that down to him being a direct link with Matthew.

As the train came into view, Matilda grabbed Laura by the arm excitedly. "It is here at last."

"You like Richard a lot, don't you, Matilda?"

"Of course, he is such a nice man, you like him too, don't you?"

"Most certainly, and if Matthew is anything at all like his brother I can understand why you are in love with him."

"Well, as you know, they are not blood brothers, but yes,

come to think of it, they are quite alike. Maybe because they were brought up by the same people."

The train drew to a noisy, hissing stop, Richard alighted and was surprised when Matilda threw her arms around him.

"It is so good to see you again, are you well?"

He returned her warm embrace and smiled. "I am very well and I do not have to ask if you are, you look positively blooming."

Matilda blushed visibly. "That is probably due to the cold wind," she said a little too quickly, for she knew it was because of the excitement she felt at seeing him again.

"Have you heard from…?"

"No, I am sorry I have not. I wish I had."

Matilda smiled; she did not want to spoil the happy mood. "Well, no news is better than bad news is it not? At least you are here, that is very good news indeed," and she hugged the arm she was holding.

After dinner that evening Richard asked if Matilda would like to take a short walk with him. She sensed he had a good reason for wanting to go out on a cold, January night.

Once in the garden he turned and said, "I saw your parents on Sunday, I have a letter for you from Louisa." He passed her the envelope, which she put into her pocket to read later.

"Are they both well?" She wanted to ask if her father knew about the pregnancy but she had a feeling that Richard was about to raise that subject himself.

"Your father knows you are with child, Louisa told him on Sunday evening, just before I called."

"How did he take it?" Matilda whispered.

"Surprisingly well, considering. Apparently he had told Louisa that the stroke had frightened him, that he would try not to worry about things he could not change. She told him that she had something to tell him that would upset him. He knew at once that it concerned you and Matthew. He sat down and prepared himself. She told him very gently why you had gone away. He held his head and began to tremble then he reached for Louisa's hands and said. 'This is all my fault'. He broke down and cried in Louisa's arms then said he must go for a long walk. He was still out when I arrived. That was how your mother was able to tell me."

"Do Loveday and Edward know?"

"Yes, your mother told them while your father was out. They are all on your side. They both think it was unfair of your father to part you. They are too young of course to understand all the social implications."

"Do you think Father will be alright? You are his best friend, you know him well."

"I think the fact that you were away helped to a degree. He misses you so much that I think he would have forgiven you *anything*."

"I will write a letter to them before you leave. Would you take it next time you visit?"

"Of course. I am happy to help in anyway I can. I love you all, you know that."

"Dear Richard, I wish you did not have to be dragged into the midst of our problems."

"Everyone has problems, it is just that we do not always hear about them. Now I had better get you indoors by the fire."

They had not walked far, just around the house really, but Matilda felt better for the air and the fact that her father had accepted her position.

The letter from her mother more or less told the same story that Richard had.

Once indoors the news was related to Laura and Jack. The next two days could now be enjoyed to the full.

Daniel had recently taken to going for an after dinner walk, even in inclement conditions. When Louisa had broken the news about Matilda's baby, he had gone for a particularly long walk and found that it had helped to concentrate his mind. He discovered that he was able to stay calmer if he was exerting himself out of doors. Rather like while he was at work during the day. Sitting in front of the fire tended to make him dwell on his problems. He had done his utmost to prevent a romance and marriage between the young couple but had inadvertently pushed them closer together – and now this. He had prayed to God every night to forgive him his sins. How could he be such a hypocrite as to banish his daughter from her home when he was a hopeless sinner himself? Alternatively how could he welcome her home accompanied by a child, which had been fathered by her brother; a living reminder of his own sins? It would be unbearable torture to him, he would go mad. He was already spending great portions of each day in isolation, and then, when he should have been with his family in the evening, he was again choosing to be by himself. He was becoming a hermit but he found it unbearable to be in the company of his innocent wife and children. Their very innocence had the effect of exacerbating his guilt. What story was he to tell their friends and acquaintances? Could he convince the whole family to pretend the child belonged to his sister-in-law from Beeton? It would save Matilda's reputation. More lies. More deception. More sin. Where would it all end? What about Richard and Elizabeth Johnson? They were not aware of the situation yet. How would the Vicar react to this news so soon after his confession? The infant would be their grandchild too. In name, if not biologically.

Each evening in the blackness of the night Daniel walked and worried. Each evening likewise he came to no conclusion. He would go home, spend an hour or so with Louisa, then take to his bed.

Louisa was so relieved that Daniel had appeared to take the news well, that she overlooked the fact that she hardly ever saw him. He will settle down again, she told herself. A few long walks will do him good. He misses Matilda, he will welcome her home again eventually. He is a Christian man; he will do the right thing by his daughter.

Although Louisa was on tenterhooks in Daniel's company, and Daniel spent ninety per cent of his waking hours, racked with guilt, the subject causing the consternation was rarely mentioned, except by their two younger children, when they were sure they could not be overheard.

And so the Winter wore on in a kind of peaceful fragility.

The season had been exceptionally mild, but on the third day of February it changed quite suddenly and drastically. The inhabitants of GameKeeper Cottage awoke to find a white world with strong winds battering the house. As the day wore on the winds gathered strength. Jack instructed the two women to remain inside the house all day. It was too dangerous for them to venture abroad, especially Matilda. The temperature did not rise above freezing at all. The snow fell so heavily that visibility was restricted to a few feet.

The cottage was sheltered on two sides by the dense woods of the estate but was quite exposed at the front, which faced south, and also on the west side. Jack had difficulty keeping the paths round the cottage clear of snow. He was particularly worried that the baby might want to make an early appearance, in which case he would have to walk a mile into the village and hope that the midwife was of sturdy stock. He had urged Matilda to rest as much as possible in the hope that the weather would improve before they had need of outside assistance.

The weather did not improve and it became impossible to keep the gale force winds out of the cottage. After three weeks of relentless snow and gales, Jack and Laura were exhausted. Matilda was despondent. She had not been out of doors since the snow arrived; a state of affairs she found hard to bear. In addition to that, she knew that Richard would not be able to make his end of month visit.

As she stared out at the blanket of whiteness she wondered where Matthew was, and if he were thinking of her. Never a day passed that she did think of him and wonder why he had not written to her or his family. She was very concerned that he had met with an accident.

Four weeks earlier she had written to the Reverend and Mrs Johnson, informing them of the coming baby. She had been as careful as possible, taking great trouble to use fitting words. She did not want them to think badly of her and she certainly did not want them to think that Matthew had deserted her. She explained that Matthew did not know of her condition. She had heard nothing from them. She told herself that the weather was to blame for post not getting through, she desperately hoped that were the case, she could not bear it if they thought so ill of her that they could not maintain relations.

She had explained her worry over her father's health and that she could not risk making her condition public until he had been informed by her mother. She hoped they understood. But did they? Elizabeth would probably be hurt that she had not confided in her. Matilda loved the Johnsons, they were like family to her. Oh, why cannot it stop snowing, she thought, she would go mad if it did not ease soon. She now had to wait another month for a visit from Richard, her link with her family. He would know how his parents had taken the news. She could do little except sew, read and help with light household duties. There was no piano to play. She would go out soon, she told herself, snow or no snow.

And then, two weeks into March, a thaw set in.

Richard put down his book and laid his head back on his chair. His surroundings looked cosy. The fire was casting a warm glow over the room and the flickering lamp lent a comforting ambience to his home, as the light played on his books and on the oil painting above the hearth. Louisa had painted the picture; it was of Jane and himself. On the table beside his chair was a lace cloth that Jane had made in the months prior to their wedding. On the cloth stood the lamp with a small statuette of a caroller under a street light. They had bought the ornament on their one and only excursion to London together, a souvenir of a happy day.

Richard sighed deeply. He wanted for nothing materially, although he was far from wealthy. He was happy in his vocation, he had loving parents, but increasingly now, he felt lonely. More and more he had the need for company in the evening. He supposed it was the weather that had brought on his low spirits. He had not seen his parents for six weeks or his friends Daniel and Louisa. But the thought that troubled him most was how much he had missed his trip to North Norfolk and he knew it was not the two day break he missed, so much as Matilda herself. It had perturbed him more than a little of late to realise just how much she meant to him. It was pertinent that he should see her – Matthew had particularly asked him to look after her – but therein lay the problem. He was no longer keeping an eye on Matilda for Matthew; he was doing it because he wanted to see her himself. He loved Matthew, he would do nothing to cause him distress, but he had grown to love Matilda. The more he acknowledged, to himself, his love for her, the more he realized it was hopeless. Just how much more complicated could the situation get, he wondered. Matilda was having a child that Matthew knew nothing about. Matthew had the notion that he could be related to Matilda, while she herself had no knowledge of this notion at all and was wondering why he had not corresponded with her. For that matter Richard was surprised that he himself had received no communication. He had half-expected Matthew to write to him requesting secrecy but no, not even that. This morning he had received a letter from his parents asking that he go to Flinton Vicarage as soon as the weather allowed. He could guess why they wanted to see him; they had probably received a letter from Matilda. He would have to confess to them that he knew about the pregnancy. They would be hurt that he had known for so long and not mentioned it. He would have to explain that it was a confidence he had been unable to break. How would his father react he wondered, not only to his grandchild being conceived and born out of wedlock, but that the union itself was of an unlawful nature? The most amazing aspect of the whole state of affairs was that all parties pertaining to the present situation had acted in innocence – with the exception of maybe one person – Daniel. He still found the likelihood of Daniel being Matthew's father, extremely slim. And here was another complication for he could not raise the subject with Daniel since his friend had not confided in him. And why, pondered Richard, had he not done so? They were best friends, always had been. No, he did not believe Daniel was Matthew's father but why else would Matilda and Mathew's wedding be unlawful? Nothing made sense. Perhaps his father had mis-understood Daniel's reasons for opposing the union or, and this seemed a far more likely scenario, perhaps Daniel himself was confused – he had acted quite out of character on many occasions of late.

Richard picked up his book again but found he could not concentrate. Tomorrow he would go to Flinton, then in two week's time he would go to Beeton…and try to remember that Matilda looked on him as her brother-in-law.

The trees around the cottage had dripped water incessantly for two days but Matilda did not care. The sun was shining and she could walk outdoors. Richard would visit in less than a fortnight but, most importantly of all, she would soon give birth to Matthew's baby.

She had a book full of sketches she had made since arriving in Beeton, a lasting memento of her visit. She had made drawings of her aunt and uncle, the cottage, the views from the windows and of the deer that roamed in the forest that often came quite close to the house before bounding off at the slightest noise.

She had remained quite slim for the first six months of her pregnancy and then put on considerable weight during the next three months. She began to wonder if the new dresses she had made would be big enough after all! On the whole, she decided, she had enjoyed her stay in Norfolk, she could have done without the snow, but it had been a relaxing period and she had felt free. She would not have enjoyed that same freedom at Flinton, where she was well known. She would have been stared at and gossiped about. Here she had felt respectable, and proud to be carrying Matthew's child.

She had also had the opportunity of getting to know her aunt and uncle. They were more like friends now. She and Laura enjoyed each others company so much that she would be loth to leave her.

One evening as they sat sewing Laura broached a delicate

subject. "What will you do if you cannot return home?"

"I have tried not to think about that but I suppose I should."

"You are very welcome to remain here. I have discussed the matter with Jack, he is in full agreement."

"Matilda got up from her chair, bent toward Laura, and kissed her. "You are both so good to me but I would not want to be a burden."

"There is something else I want you to know," she hesitated. "If you are not allowed to take the child home, I would be honoured to take care of it for you. You could visit as often as you wished of course. I – er – I just thought you should know that you have support. I hope I have not offended you."

"Oh, Laura of course you have not offended me. I am so sorry you cannot have your own children but I could not leave my baby, even temporarily. I hope you understand."

"Of course I do. I myself would not be able to. You did not mind me offering?"

"It is so good of you to offer. We will stay in touch whatever happens, won't we?"

"You just try to keep me away from my new niece or nephew."

The two women smiled warmly at each other, knowing their friendship was of an enduring nature.

Chapter Ten

Richard tapped on his parents' back door and entered their kitchen for the second time in two weeks. The previous week's visit had been a nightmare. He hoped they had now had time to reflect and calm down a little. Elizabeth was the first to welcome her son.

"Oh Richard, thank goodness you are here, what is to be done?"

"Hello, Mother, to what are you referring? Do we have yet more problems?"

"I would have thought we have enough. Are you sure you have not heard from Matthew?"

"I have not heard a word, I promise you."

"But you knew about the baby and did not tell us. How do I know you are not keeping other facts from us?"

"I told you last week," said Richard patiently, "I could not break a confidence. Matilda felt very isolated, she had to talk to somebody, and anyway, she fainted, so I guessed something was wrong. I am a vicar, I cannot tell my mother confidences that have been entrusted to me, please try to understand."

"I am distraught, your father is too. We must find Matthew before the baby is born so that they can marry."

"But, Mother, they cannot marry. Daniel Canham would not permit it, and neither would Father."

"But I do not understand why, they are perfect for one another, we must make our grandchild legitimate."

"I am afraid Father would not agree."

"He of all people *should* agree. He is beside himself with worry about the situation but will not agree to the obvious solution. I despair of him."

"So you may, so you may," said her husband, entering the room, "but I have very good reasons for opposing the union and so does Daniel Canham, you will have to trust us."

"I am surrounded by secrets and conspiracy," said Elizabeth, looking beseechingly at her son. "Please, somebody enlighten me, I am becoming ill with the worry of it all. What are we to do when Matilda brings the baby home? The villagers will suspect – and with good reason – that the child belongs to Matthew. We are supposed to set a moral example but I for one do not want to ostracise my own grandchild. How can I fraternise with Matilda without seeming to condone illegitimacy?"

"Perhaps we could pretend that Matilda has married somebody else," ventured her husband, very shamefacedly.

"Apart from it being a flagrant lie that nobody would believe, and having to coerce Matilda, and her entire family, into the deception as well, I am ashamed of you for even suggesting the idea," exclaimed Elizabeth haughtily.

"Now please do not let matters get out of hand again, we discussed all this last week," pleaded their son. "It does no good at all to get so agitated and upset. We may, as Churchmen, be expected to set good examples but we, and our families are only human, we are bound to have domestic problems like anybody else. Your parishioners will sympathise with you, not condemn you. I am sure no one will want you to ostracise Matilda or her child. They would probably think you a poor Christian if you did. We must show some humility."

"You are quite right, my dear, I am so glad you are here, we must all calm down before dinner."

With tbat Elizabeth left the room.

Richard and his father sat in silence for several minutes following Elizabeth's departure. It would seem that everything had been said several times over. It was doing no good whatsoever going round and round in circles. Eventually young Richard said, "Perhaps I should go and have a talk with Louisa and Daniel, after all, we do not know for certain that Matilda is coming home, she may choose to remain where she is."

"Do you think that is likely?"

"No doubt that will depend on Daniel, the problem is, he is fairly inconsistent nowadays. He could tell me one thing tonight and change his mind completely by tomorrow. But I will go up after dinner anyway. They may have letters for me to take to Beeton tomorrow."

"Does the lass keep well?"

"Very well, Father."

"She is a lovely girl, it is a crying shame she cannot marry."

"*I* still do not know why they cannot."

"No, it is a heavy burden I carry there, a very heavy burden indeed." The old man studied his shoes carefully as he sat beside the fireplace, his face troubled. Richard did not like to see his father so wearied by worry. "I have left you a letter Richard, it is with my private papers, it explains things a little more fully. You must read it in the event of my death."

"You do not feel able to confide in me before you die?"

"Unfortunately not, not on this matter."

Richard cast his eyes about the room. He always felt so at home at Flinton Vicarage, but then he would, he had grown up here. "Is that letter for Matilda?" he said now, espying the envelope on the top of the piano.

"Yes, your mother and I had difficulty finding the right words, but we are very fond of Matilda, we do not want her to think we blame her in any way. They would have married had they been allowed to. Their courtship would no doubt have remained less intense had it been allowed to progress in the normal manner."

"Yes, no doubt," replied Richard, as he pocketed the letter.

The walk to Uphall Farm seemed shorter than usual, but that was probably due to the fact that Richard was not completely relishing the visit. Daniel was more withdrawn of late; conversation was not as easy as in the past. But, Richard told himself, he must try to get some idea of whether Matilda was going to be welcomed home. She would expect him to know when he visited tomorrow. He was looking forward to his visit; the baby was due.

"Daniel is out walking," Louisa informed him as she welcomed him into the farmhouse. "He has been gone an hour,

I expect him home any minute."

Did Richard imagine it, or was Louisa's voice falsely bright? "I thought I had allowed plenty of time for Daniel's walk, is he going further nowadays?"

"I think that may be the case, I am quite concerned about him, he appears to prefer to be out of doors. I am beginning to think it is my company he avoids."

"I am sure that is not the case, Louisa. It often takes a while to come to terms with unexpected events. Things will settle down, you will see."

"He talks sometimes of Matilda coming home."

"He will allow it then?"

"I am not sure. I am of the opinion that he wants his daughter back but not with the child. That would cause too many problems. I think he intends to ask Matilda to leave the child with Jack and Laura. They would dearly love a baby but are unable to have any. How do you think she would respond to that idea, Richard?"

"I do not think Matilda would give up Matthew's child without a fight. She is very proud to be having his baby. It is all she has left of him."

Richard waited a further hour for Daniel to return home, but when his friend did not return he said goodbye to Louisa and began to walk home.

As he skirted the Common, he espied a lone figure standing at the edge of Clancy's Wood. The sky was not clear, the moon intermittently disappeared behind clouds, but Richard was sure he had seen somebody. He called out, "Is that you, Daniel?"

"Yes it is me," came a voice out of the darkness, "I was hoping you had not seen me."

"That is no way to treat your oldest friend." Richard's voice contained disappointment and hurt.

"I am sorry, Richard, I did not mean to offend. It is just that lately I have preferred my own company. It gives me time to reflect on my misdemeanours and plan my future."

"I am going to see Matilda tomorrow, do you have a message for her?"

"Please tell her I miss her and hope she is well."

"The child is due at any time."

"I pray that all goes well, she is so young."

"She looks in excellent health, you will be happy to know. I am sure she will not have any problems."

"I hope not."

Richard detected despondency in Daniel's voice and he asked his next question with a certain amount of trepidation, "I expect you will be glad to have her home again?"

"I will, Richard, I will."

Well, he had his answer. He could honestly tell Matilda that her father wanted her home. The question was, would she be allowed to bring her child? He dared to go further, "I expect you will enjoy having a youngster around again."

"We will see. I had better return home before they send out a search party. Goodnight to you and, er, please give Matilda my love tomorrow."

"I surely will, and I will tell her you are looking forward to her return. Goodnight, my friend, take good care of yourself."

Daniel continued on his way to the farm. He had done a lot of thinking lately. He would ask Matilda to leave the baby with his brother and sister-in-law. He would explain to her that she stood a better chance of eventual marriage if she did not have a child. It would be best all round. And now, he thought, I had better start spending more time at home in the evenings. I am becoming odd in my quest for solitude. It is time life returned to normal.

As the train pulled in to Bramfield railway station Richard looked out eagerly from the window. He then realized that he could not expect Matilda to meet him this time. The platform was deserted as he picked up his luggage and proceeded to the gate leading out to the road. It was only three miles to Beeton but he felt a little downcast that *nobody* had come to meet him. Had they forgotten he was arriving today? He had so looked forward to seeing Matilda but it would seem that *he* was not so important to *her*.

He walked along the country road at a good pace, trying not

to feel sorry for himself. Presently he became aware of a horse and trap approaching. As it got closer it slowed to reveal Jack in a state of agitation.

"I am sorry I am late, Richard, we are all at sixes and sevens. I was about to leave when Laura asked me to fetch the midwife."

"You mean..."

"Yes, any time now. I hope you are used to looking after yourself for I fear we men will get little attention for a few days yet." He chuckled good-naturedly.

Richard found himself growing alarmed. Over and over he had told himself that Matilda would be alright, but then he would remind himself that Jane had died in childbirth. He had felt useless then, and he felt useless now.

"Has she a doctor with her?"

"No, I understand the women like to cope on their own."

"There *is* a doctor in the village?"

"Oh yes, we have an excellent doctor, do not worry, I will soon fetch him if he is needed."

On arrival at the cottage, Laura met the two men at the back door. "She is not having an easy time, if it is not all over within the hour she will need a doctor." Laura paused then asked, "Would you make us some tea, please Jack?"

"Can I see her?" Richard asked worriedly.

"It is best you stay downstairs, she will not want you to see her at the moment."

"Will you tell her I am here please, Laura?"

Laura returned to her delivery room duties. "Richard has arrived Matilda, he is asking after you."

"I am so glad. I was afraid he would not come again. I feel better now that he is here. Oh Laura..." As another contraction gripped Matilda's body she held tightly to her aunt's hand. "I did not know it would be so painful, Laura, I am worn out, help me please." Then she remembered Richard and how he had lost Jane. He must be so worried about her. "Please would you go downstairs and tell Richard how well I am, and give him my love?"

Laura returned downstairs to give Richard the message and

to collect two cups of tea.

The baby still refused to be born. When another thirty minutes had elapsed, Jack was sent to fetch the Doctor.

Richard paced back and forth across the parlour floor praying for Matilda. He could hear her screams overhead. "Please God," he prayed, "keep her safe. I could not bear to lose her." Back and forth, back and forth, until at last Jack returned with Doctor Spence.

"Hurry, help her please," Richard implored the Doctor as he ushered him up the stairs. He then started pacing again. Anybody would think I was the father, he thought, I *feel* like the father.

Why don't you go for a walk, Richard?" Jack asked, "I'll join you if you like."

"No, I do not think I want to leave the house; Matilda might need me."

"It could be quite a time yet."

"No, I would rather stay."

If I did not know differently, thought Jack, I would say Richard was the father in waiting.

Richard caught Jack observing him. "I have known Matilda all her life," he explained. "When Matthew left, he asked me to look after her."

The two men sat, one each side of the fire, saying little. Each time a noise was heard overhead, they put their heads to one side, to strain their hearing for a baby's cry – none was forthcoming. "Do you think everything is alright?" asked Richard. "Shall I go up and find out?"

"Best leave it to the experts, I will make you some more tea."

And then they heard the cry.

Richard bounded up the stairs two at a time to find Laura coming out of the bedroom.

"It is a girl," she said, "a lovely healthy girl, but a little on the small side."

Richard put his arms around Laura and hugged her tightly; tears were running down his face. "How is Matilda?" he asked tremulously, as Jack joined them.

"Matilda is…"

She was cut short by the midwife calling her. "Excuse me please."

Within a few minutes she was back with them, "You will never guess what has happened, it is twins!"

"Twins!" they repeated in unison.

"Yes, twins, a girl and a boy. The boy is smaller but they are both well."

Richard sat down on a chair in the corner of the landing. It was all right, it was over, Matilda was well and she had twins – a boy and a girl. He was so relieved. He smiled happily at Jack. It was only then that he realized just *how* worried he had been.

Matilda awoke at eight o'clock to find Laura sitting by her bedside. She smiled sleepily across at her. "I still cannot believe it, two babies, I wish Matthew were here." Her voice broke, "I miss him so, Laura. I do not even know where he is." She was crying softly, "I am sorry, I am always in tears lately."

"It is perfectly natural to be emotional, dear, think nothing of it, we are just so happy that you are all well. The babies are beautiful. I took them to the door to show Jack and Richard. Richard cried unashamedly, he really is very fond of you, Matilda. He is so relieved it is all over. He is eager to see you."

"He can come in now, Laura, I do not know what I would have done without him. Matthew would be proud of him."

"I will make some tea and send him upstairs with it."

"Thank you. Before you go, would you open the top drawer of the dresser and pass me the little painted box and the knotted handkerchief that you will find there?"

Laura did as she was asked; she looked at Matilda with a puzzled expression as she handed her the two items.

"You will think us very childish, but Matthew and I have a way of helping us to cope with our separations." She then proceeded to enlighten her aunt on the subject of the Cornelians, she had never told anybody else, she felt a little silly, but she was not allowed out of bed.

Laura did not laugh; she left the room quietly.

Matilda caressed the little box for several minutes, running her thumb lovingly over the painted flowers that she had put there when she was ten. She then untied the handkerchief and selected the two prettiest stones, which she laid gently in the box. Twins merited two Cornelians she decided. Then she put the box and handkerchief under her pillows and prepared to see Richard.

Far away from England, in a South African harbour, a young man was entertaining his shipmates with his violin playing. It was a beautiful evening. The moonlight was playing on the water, as it lapped gently at the sides of the boat. He laid his violin to one side as he came to the end of his song. But his friends were not going to let him go so easily. "Play it again, Matt," they implored, "You always sing that one with such feeling, it reminds us of home."

And so he began again:

> *The sun on her face*
> *And the wind in her hair,*
> *Golden as it dances*
> *Dances on the air...*

...and, in no time at all, he was back in Clancy's Wood with his sweetheart.

He was happy tonight, he realized, as he prepared for bed, happier than he had been for a long time. It was a hard life on board ship, but it did not leave a lot of time for maudlin thoughts. Yes, tonight he felt happy for the first time in months.

He opened his little wooden box and gazed at the Cornelians, remembering another sea so far away; another sea and another beach...and a little girl in a green frock and a straw hat, with a ribbon that tied under her chin.

He dropped a stone into the box... and then, he knew not why, he smiled and added another one.

Chapter Eleven

After much deliberation and discussion, Matilda named her children Sebastian Matthew and Sarah Matilda. The infants were of a contented nature, providing they were close together but when one was taken up to be attended to, the other would become fretful.

Jack had made Matilda a wooden crib that could be rocked from side to side. When Matilda fed one child she would be able to rock the crib with her foot in order to keep the other happy.

Within a short time she discovered that the children had distinct personalities of their own. Sarah was most demanding and, as a consequence, was usually fed first; she was also bigger and more robust than her brother. Sebastian was placid, of a more delicate build and not quite so vocal as his sister.

Richard remained at the cottage for three days and took great delight in the babies. He would sit beside Matilda's bed for hours talking to her and holding the children.

He looks so at ease, thought Matilda, as she observed him with her babies. They must remind him of his own dear child, and of Jane, yet he does not mention either. Matilda's heart went out to him; she had grown very fond of him.

"I wish you could stay longer," she said now, "have you noticed how you are always around just when I need you?"

"I am very pleased you think that, I hear most women think just the opposite of their husbands."

He immediately realized how his words must have sounded, and added quickly, "I speak in my position of surrogate father of course." He smiled to cover his embarrassment at the subconscious *faux-pas*. He would have to be more careful. He was beginning to look on Matilda and the children as his own personal family. Oh that that could be, he thought wistfully, he would be the happiest man on earth.

Richard began to feel anger at Matthew, surely he could have written to one of them, he should have settled somewhere by now. He must be aware of the anxiety he was causing Matilda.

"Perhaps I could visit a little more often until you return home."

"Dear Richard, that would be wonderful but I could not put you to that trouble or expense. Anyway, I do not know if I will be returning home."

"Your parents are looking forward to your return."

"Has my father actually said that?"

"He has indeed."

"I cannot understand it. He was most emphatic that I had nothing at all to do with Matthew and now he wants to welcome me home with his children."

"It does seem odd I grant you."

"Are you absolutely sure?"

"Absolutely, in fact I have some letters for you, one from my parents and one from yours. I am sorry. I forgot about them in all the excitement."

He now handed both envelopes to Matilda and watched her facial expressions as she read. He was surprised at how downcast she appeared when she finished.

"Is anything wrong?"

"You may have misunderstood my father, Richard. Whilst you are correct that he wants me home, they make no mention of wanting my children too."

"Matilda I am so sorry, I automatically assumed he was including your child, your children," he corrected himself. "It did not cross my mind to think otherwise. He had been walking and sorting out his thoughts."

"I will not leave them. I know Laura would gladly have them; she has always wanted children. To tell you the truth she has offered, but I could not do it."

"Of course you could not leave them."

"Apart from anything it would be repeating history. Matthew would not want me to abandon his children as he himself was abandoned. I have first hand knowledge of the distress such action causes."

"I have difficulty understanding Daniel myself these days but I thought he was much better on Monday evening when I saw him. He gave no indication that he would not welcome your child." Richard was remembering Louisa's fears.

"I will have to put my mind to earning a living, perhaps I could teach the piano or sell some paintings. I will take in washing if I need to." She began to cry.

Richard took her hand in his. "Do not distress yourself, I am sure your father will welcome his grandchildren. If he does not we will think again."

"If I refuse to go home alone he will probably stop my allowance, oh Richard, I am such a trouble to everybody."

"You are no trouble to me and you are the whole world to your children. You have just given birth; you are bound to be emotional. I will go to see your parents again, I will tell them you could not possibly leave your babies. Now cheer yourself up; Spring is here. The garden is full of flowers, I will go and gather some primroses for your room."

Matilda smiled, what would she have done without Richard? Then, with no warning, she began to cry again. Where was Matthew she could not bear not knowing how or where he was.

Richard returned with the promised flowers and a cup of tea.

"They are beautiful, thank you. I do not know how I will ever be able to repay you, Laura and Jack; you have all been so kind to me."

"That is because we all love you. Now, try to be optimistic, just because your parents did not actually mention a baby does not mean they do not want it. Do not forget, when they wrote that letter, the babies had not arrived. Once they see them, they will love them."

"I have a horrible notion that they want me to leave them with Jack and Laura. I do not know where else they would expect me to leave them."

"Enough of all this talk. You are keeping your babies with you whatever happens."

Richard was pondering the situation. Could he offer Matilda a position as his housekeeper? She was very young of course and not exactly related to him so it could cause gossip; in his profession he had to be careful. She was his Goddaughter, he reminded himself, he had a moral obligation toward her. Perhaps he should discuss the matter with his father. He said now to Matilda, "As soon as I return home tomorrow I shall go and tell your parents that you have been safely delivered of twins. Would you like to write to them?"

"I will write, thank you, I shall tell them what wonderful grandchildren they have." She smiled; she had so much for which to be thankful. "And now, Richard Johnson, we shall all remain cheerful for the remainder of your visit, otherwise I fear you may desert me, then where would I be?"

"*Twins!*" Despite the circumstances Louisa could not contain her happiness. "Are you sure she is well?"

"Extremely well, Laura is fussing over them all like a mother hen, she is in her element. Jack is enjoying himself too. They have both grown very fond of Matilda."

"I must go to see her."

"She would like that."

"I am sure I would not be missed for one day, perhaps we could all go." Louisa was already making plans in her mind's eye.

"Is Daniel out walking?" asked Richard cautiously.

"No he is just doing his evening rounds on the farm. He has taken to staying in lately. Ever since your last visit in fact."

Louisa looks much happier, thought Richard. He was glad; it grieved him considerably to witness discord in their family; they were all so dear to him.

"What is all the excitement about?" asked Daniel, entering the kitchen. The two younger children ran to him eagerly.

"Matilda has had twins," enthused Loveday, "Is it not exciting?"

"Twins!" Daniel sat down heavily on a wooden kitchen chair and turned his gaze to Richard, who was entering the room.

"How is she?" he asked a little dazed.

"I have been telling your wife, she is in excellent health."

"Has she chosen names?" asked Louisa joining the assemblage.

"Sebastian Matthew and Sarah Matilda."

"Sebastian and Sarah," she repeated. "Those are lovely names. Can we all go and visit, Daniel?"

"Oh yes, let us, please," implored the children in unison.

Daniel felt decidedly outnumbered, he did not see how he could refuse, after all, Matilda was their kin, they had all been concerned for her. He looked around at the three expectant faces waiting for his reply and then said slowly, "I do not see why not."

They all hugged him and he had to admit to himself that he enjoyed being back in the bosom of his family. He had felt apart from them for so long. He had not liked being so. He must not make them all pay for his sins. Even Matilda was not aware of her relationship to Matthew. They were all innocent. All except himself; he should show a little more Christian attitude to his family or he could find himself being alienated all over again.

"Has Matilda mentioned the Christening?" asked Louisa.

There was an awkward silence.

"She has not said anything, perhaps she will wait until she comes home,"

Richard was aware he was being presumptuous, but he felt the atmosphere to be such, that he could risk it. "I am visiting again next week," he continued, "I could make arrangements for a night at a hostelry, or would you be returning the same day?"

"Probably the latter," said Louisa feeling it unwise to pressure her husband too much. She had not expected him to agree to the outing at all; she had been very pleasantly surprised.

Chapter Twelve

Matildada looked nervously at the parlour clock for the umpteenth time that morning.

She had decided to have the babies christened in a private service at the village church to coincide with the visit of her family and the Reverend and Mrs Johnson. Richard had arranged for them all to stay the night at the King's Head hostelry in Bramfield, because her aunt and uncle did not have sufficient room.

Richard, Laura and Jack were to be godparents. Considering the circumstances Matilda was overjoyed that the Johnsons had agreed to attend. It would be a real family occasion, with the exception of Matthew. After the service they would all go back to the cottage for a Christening luncheon. Matilda knew that her father would not cause any unpleasantness today; if *that* were forthcoming, it would be later; today was a celebration.

As Jack brought the horse to a halt at the church gate Matilda scanned the area for a glimpse of her family, she had not seen them since Christmas, it was now late April.

"Do you think they are already in church?" she inquired of Richard.

"You worry too much, Matilda, we are early, perhaps they have not arrived yet." He smiled down at her, then at Sebastian who was in his arms, "I have arranged a surprise for you after the Christening."

"A surprise! What is it?"

Richard chuckled, "If I tell you that it will not be a surprise."

"You are very clever, Richard Johnson, you told me that so that I would stop my worrying."

"Was it effective?"

She nodded up at him. "I am intrigued, I cannot think what it might be."

"Good," was all he would say; he was enjoying keeping her guessing.

Laura and Jack were following behind with Sarah. Matilda turned her head toward them, "I suppose you are both in on this secret that Richard is keeping from me?"

"Our lips are sealed," said Jack as he turned his twinkling eyes toward Laura, "you will have to be patient, young lady."

It was then that Matilda caught sight of her parents coming through the lych gate, Richard and Elizabeth Johnson followed them, behind them were Loveday and Edward.

"They are here," she cried happily, and then she was running back down the church path to greet them.

Louisa put her arms round her daughter and held her close, "You look so well, dear."

"I am, Mother, and I am so happy to see you all." In turn she hugged and kissed each member of the party. Elizabeth too held her tightly.

"Now where are our grandchildren?" she said warmly.

Matilda felt so proud of her babies as she showed them off to everyone. Only her father appeared reticent, but that was to be expected, she would not let it spoil the day, he had hugged her warmly, so warmly in fact that her fears for the future had all but melted away. She had noticed that he looked lovingly at both infants.

Loveday and Edward were both delighted with their niece and nephew and went to great lengths to inform their sister so.

Eventually the door was reached and the gathering ceased their chattering as they passed through the porch and into the hallowed confines of the country church.

As they neared the cottage on the return journey, Matilda could see that a horse and carriage had lately arrived. A man had climbed down from the driving seat and stood waiting to greet them.

"Who is that?" asked Matilda of her companions.

"That," said Richard, "is your surprise."

"But who is it?"

"It is Mr Price from Bramfield, he is here to take some photographs."

"Photographs! Oh Richard what a lovely idea. How do you manage to always think of just the right thing to say and do?"

The photographic session was a great success. The babies were taken individually, then together with Matilda. Next, Richard joined the group – standing in for Matthew. Each set of grandparents were photographed with the infants, then Jack and Laura, then Loveday and Edward. Lastly the whole group were photographed together.

After a late luncheon everyone went for an afternoon walk, except Laura, who volunteered to look after the babies, a task she never tired of. She was still hoping that Matilda would decide to stay in North Norfolk, but she had noticed how happy the young mother was to be amongst her family again; a fact that did not augur well for her remaining in Beeton.

Matilda read and re-read the letter from her mother. It was as she had feared. They were asking her to leave the infants with Laura and Jack, and return home.

...your father thinks it would be best for everyone. Your chances of marriage will be considerably reduced if you have two children...

They had not written the word 'illegitimate', but Matilda realized it was conspicuous by its absence, she also realized that the feelings expressed in the letter were not those of her mother or brother and sister.

At the Christening Matilda had been pleased to notice the attention Daniel had given to the babies, he had gazed on them at length, seeming to search their little faces, rather like Matthew said he searched his own. That is strange, she thought as the realization came to her, I now know what he meant, I wonder why Father does that.

She sat down on a kitchen chair, resting her arms on the table, she stared at the letter, as if by this action she could change the wording. "How can he expect this of me, Laura?"

Laura had to choose her words carefully. She desperately wanted the babies to remain with her but, in Matilda's position, she knew she would not be able to part with them either and she did love Matilda, she had become almost like a daughter.

"I suppose we must try to see the situation from his perspective. There will undoubtedly be gossip, especially as the children belong to Matthew, who is a vicar's son. It was a well-known fact that you and Matthew were sweethearts, the villagers will know he is the father; it will not be easy for you."

"Then I will not return home, I will be twenty-one in eleven months time, perhaps by then I will have heard from Matthew."

"You can stay here as I have said before."

"Thank you, you have both been so kind to me, but I think I must take control of my own life, the problem is, I do not yet know how."

Jack was in a hurry when he came in for his lunch, "We are felling a huge oak today. Would you like to see it come down?"

"Oh no," said Matilda, horrified, "I hate trees being felled, why must you do it?"

"I suppose it will end up as a magnificent piece of furniture in the Hall. Sir Wainwright takes such family pride in the place. To know that his furniture is made from estate trees pleases him immensely. It is a sight to behold, you should come and watch."

Laura and Matilda looked at each other with some doubt.

"You go," said Laura, "I will look after the babies. I may not have them here for much longer. Let me have them all to myself for the afternoon."

"Alright, I will come, but I do not think I will enjoy it. At least it is not going to be burned."

Although it was now early May the weather was still quite inclement. There was a stiff breeze blowing as Matilda and Jack made their way back to the felling site.

"Obviously you will have to stand well clear," Jack told her as they hurried along. "Do not move closer whatever happens."

Matilda laughed at Jack's concern for her; he was quite fatherly sometimes. "I will definitely stand clear, I have no intention of being flattened by an oak tree."

Matilda watched the men at work for a good hour before she signalled to Jack that she was going for a walk to keep warm. They had obviously been working on the tree for most of the morning and keeping warm in the process – just *standing* was a different matter.

As she walked, she reflected on the letter from her parents. She wanted to go home, but not without her babies. There must be some way she could earn a living, but, she acknowledged, it would probably necessitate leaving her children with a nursemaid during the day. Who better than Laura, who had grown very fond of them? Perhaps after all she should consider remaining here.

As she walked back toward the felling site, she heard the massive tree creaking as if in protest. She was just in time to see the magnificent oak sway and begin to fall.

All at once she saw something run into its path. She put her hand to her mouth and gasped as she realized it was a fawn. She wanted to run forward to save the creature but realized the foolhardiness of her thoughts and stood rooted to the spot, willing the little animal to run. With the noise, and combined shouting of all watching, the little animal appeared to become disorientated…the huge tree fell, trapping the fawn amongst its branches.

Matilda watched as it disappeared from view under a myriad of branches. She could visualize it struggling, fighting to free itself. She wished she had not come to watch the felling.

After what seemed an eternity the workmen found the fawn and brought it out. It was no longer alive. The poor little thing had died from fear and exhaustion. Matilda wept as she turned and headed for the cottage, she could not get it out of her mind. Had it relaxed and waited to be rescued it would still be alive. She felt an empathy with the little animal, likening it to her own dilemma, she was struggling with her problems, going over and over them in her head and making herself weary with it all. The weight of the crushing oak was on her, she could not see a way out, but if she relaxed, would someone come to her rescue? Who could? Matthew was ignorant of her situation.

She reached the cottage at last, cold and weary. After tearfully relating the afternoon's events to Laura she went to her room and removed a Cornelian from her box. 'For the fawn', she whispered, 'for everyone who feels trapped and frightened that they are essentially alone.'

Matilda felt slightly guilty for feeling lonely, especially when Richard, Laura and Jack had done so much for her. But she *did* feel alone; nobody could make her decisions for her. She was responsible for two more human beings now. Any solution she found would affect them too. She must learn from the fawn and not act too hastily.

She replaced the painted lid and hugged the little box to her chest, willing Matthew to get in touch with her. Her eyes were tightly closed as she brought to mind a picture of him. 'Please come home, darling, I feel much stronger when you are with me. I want you to meet your children'.

With a heavy heart she replaced the box in the drawer and sat on the side of her bed. Tonight she would write to her parents, telling them she could not leave her children. She felt certain that that would result in her allowance being stopped. She got up wearily from the bed as Sarah's hungry cry floated upstairs.

Chapter Thirteen

The letter lay on the table between them like a piece of hot coal that had burned them, making them reluctant to touch it again.

"I am sorry, Daniel but I am glad she will not leave them. She would be miserable for the rest of her life. As for marriage, it is of no consequence to her unless she were marrying Matthew. You will never win her round to your way of thinking. Please let her bring the children home ," Louisa implored.

"I have made my decision and it stands."

"You have become stubborn, if you are not very careful you will lose your daughter and grandchildren. Is that what you want? Can you imagine how you would have felt if your parents had made you give Matilda away as a baby?"

"That is completely different."

"Oh, why?"

"Because we were married, we did not bring shame on our parents."

"Matilda and Matthew would have been married had you allowed it. They *will* be married just as soon as she reaches twenty-one. You might just as well accept the situation now, and allow her to return. You have two other children to consider. Loveday and Edward will not respect you for treating Matilda so shabbily. How do you expect her to earn her own living and support two children without the help of her family?"

"I am going for a walk."

"That is your answer to everything, but it solves nothing."

Daniel knew that Louisa was right but how could he allow the babies to live here; a daily reminder to him of his own sins? How could he look on the children without remembering they were the product of an incestuous union, albeit an innocent one? He would go mad. He would be looking for signs of abnormality – waiting for divine retribution. However far he walked and however much he ruminated, he would not be able to change the situation. He mentally weighed his options; he could stick to his guns, so to speak, but that would alienate his whole family, or, he could allow Matilda to bring home the babies. That would keep the majority of the family happy, but he would never be able to escape from the consequences of his guilty secret.

On balance he knew he had to relent. It was all his fault anyway. He would return home and eat humble pie.

Matilda took her babies home at the end of May. She knew it would be difficult, especially the gossip.

As usual it was Richard who accompanied her. He had arrived at the cottage the previous night so that they could get an early start. The ensemble rested at Winford Vicarage where the infants were fed and prepared for the carriage ride to Flinton. Richard prepared a light lunch for himself and Matilda. He enjoyed having them all in his house; it gave him a warm feeling.

Matilda was very apprehensive about returning home, she knew that her father had acted under duress. It would be much easier having Richard with her; being Matthew's brother and her father's best friend, he was a natural intermediary between herself and her parents.

On the approach to the farm Matilda asked Richard if they could stop for a while. "You cannot imagine how nervous I feel," she said tremulously, "I have dreamt of this day, but now that it is here I am frightened that I am going to wish I were still in Beeton. Laura was so unhappy when we left wasn't she? I wonder if I have done the right thing, taking my children away from someone who wanted them, to bring them to somebody who obviously does not. I am so unsure of myself nowadays, Richard. Do you think I have changed?"

"You are bound to have changed considering the circumstances, I have noticed you are much quieter, by that I mean you are not so talkative," he smiled at her.

"I *think* more."

"You *have* had a lot to endure."

"I think about Matthew mostly – where he is, what he is doing, why he does not write. It is so frustrating not being able to contact him."

"I am sorry, I wish I could help."

"You *do* help; I could not have managed without you, I will be eternally grateful."

Richard was pleased that Matilda would now be only four miles distant from him. He could visit often, especially through the Summer. He thought of the three of them as his own family. Sometimes he had difficulty keeping his feelings to himself. Oh that *I* were the constant subject of her thoughts, he wished silently. I would not leave her for anything. But even as he thought it, he knew he was being unfair to Matthew, who had done the honourable thing in going away to give Daniel the best chance of recovery. He had now been gone for eleven months and no one had heard a word from him, that in itself was very strange, especially considering his feelings for Matilda. Richard knew that he did not stand a chance with the young mother – nobody did, so long as there was the slightest chance of Matthew returning. He now shook himself out of his reverie, "I think we should continue or we shall be late for dinner."

"Of course, I am sorry."

Richard returned to the driving position and set the horse in motion.

Louisa was overjoyed at having her daughter and grandchildren home. She had been preparing for them all day with Loveday's help.

Richard, Daniel and Edward unloaded the luggage, which was considerably more than when Matilda had left.

Dinner was quite a joyous occasion although Daniel did not say much. He had to agree that the babies were delightful, and it pleased him to see Louisa so happy. Babies always seemed to make women bloom, he thought, watching his wife fussing over the infants. He could see that she was going to be in her element. I have made the right decision, he decided as he watched his family. I must not make them pay for my wrongdoings. The children are not the first illegitimate babies to be born to a local girl and they will not be the last. I must keep things in perspective and try to forget the other more regrettable details surrounding the babies' birth.

Life gradually settled down at the farmhouse, with Richard visiting every week, after having dinner with his parents.

Mr and Mrs Johnson also called to see their grandchildren regularly.

Sarah thrived, putting on weight at quite an alarming rate; Sebastian however remained of a more delicate constitution. He caught several colds throughout the Summer, which he did not shake off so easily as his sister did, often causing Matilda to worry over him. She tended to cuddle him for a bit longer after his feeds, she told herself it was to compensate for Sarah always insisting on being the first to get attention. Whatever the reason she felt very protective of him, he had such a sweet nature; he was no trouble at all.

One Tuesday evening, in early August, Richard was late for his usual visit. Matilda decided that she would walk down the road to meet him. She had been very busy all Summer with the children, so had not been out walking as much as she would have liked. As she rounded the bend of Hill Road she caught sight of him leaning on a field gate, staring out over the ripening corn. She called to him – he turned his head as if in a dream and began walking toward her.

"You look very thoughtful," she said as he kissed her on the cheek. "We feared you had deserted us."

"Sorry, I have been lost in thought, I did not realize how late it was getting."

"Is anything wrong?"

"No...yes... well...er...I have some news for you."

She looked at him inquiringly. "Good or bad?"

"We have at last had word from Matthew."

Matilda's heart began to thud; her legs went weak beneath

her, so that she reached for Richard's arm for support.

He handed her a letter on which was written her name. Part of her wanted to tear it open on the spot, but another part of her wanted to take it somewhere private to savour every word.

"Do you mind if I go for a walk and read it alone?"

"Of course not, but do not be too long, it is coming in damp."

Richard made his way toward the farmhouse while Matilda walked down to the gate where, a few moments earlier, he had been leaning. Her hands were shaking as she opened the long awaited letter.

My Darling Tilly, she read,

I hope this letter finds you in good health. Please forgive me for not writing. I wanted to give your father every chance of recovery. I hope he is completely well again.

Not a day goes by that I do not think of you, it has been a difficult year. I felt dreadfully guilty for leaving you so soon again, but I considered I had no choice. I am glad you liked your locket.

When I left you I went to Illingham and obtained work on a cargo ship bound for South Africa. It is a very hard life but that is what I need, otherwise, darling Tilly, I will die of a broken heart. I know you will understand. Nobody will ever be able to destroy our love, what we have is very special, never forget that, my dearest.

I take my Cornelians and poppy field picture with me where ever I go and I have set our poem to music, it is a favourite amongst my ship mates when I sing it, although they do not know why it is so dear to me.

I have asked one of my friends to deliver my letters to Richard, by hand, when he returns to Illingham. I myself have travelled on to America, and who knows where else. Please try to be happy, darling and understand why I cannot take you away from your family. I love you too much to make you unhappy. We must accept that we cannot marry, considering how much distress it would cause to your father. We would never forgive ourselves if we were responsible for his untimely death.

I know you will find somebody else who will love you because you are so special. Take your chances of happiness, my love and, as I said before, make sure your little box is always full to the brim.

I will never ever forget you; you have a permanent place in my heart.

I love you,

Matthew.

Tears were streaming down Matilda's face and dropping on to the letter making the ink run. She tried to dry the page with her frock. She had waited so long for a letter only to get one that made her even more unhappy. For so many months she had looked on a letter as the answer to her problems – and now this.

It was dark when Matilda returned home. She knew Richard had not left, she would have met him on the road. She let herself into the kitchen quietly, passed though the hall, up the stairs, and so to her bedroom, where she collapsed on to her bed and cried her heart out.

She was not allowed to indulge in tears for long, the babies began to make hungry noises.

An hour later she again laid on her bed, staring up at the ceiling, dry-eyed now, but her chest felt as though her heart had been torn out.

Presently she heard a tap at her door.

"Can I come in?" it was Richard having to say goodbye.

She rose wearily to open the door and then fell sobbing into his arms. He led her back into her room and sat beside her on the bed as she tried to regain her composure.

"Matthew will not marry me while it makes Father ill. He is urging me to find happiness with someone else."

Richard did not speak but kept his arm around her shoulders.

"How can I be happy without him? He does not even know he is a father. Surely that would make a difference to him."

Still Richard did not speak, he was thinking of his own letter from Matthew in which he had said he could not risk marrying Matilda while there was any chance that Daniel was his father. He had urged Richard to encourage Matilda to look elsewhere for a husband. How would Matthew feel if he himself married Matilda, he pondered, but that would be foolish, knowing how much she loved Matthew. It would break *his* heart every day knowing *her* heart was somewhere over the sea with Matthew. No, he must not entertain the idea.

"I am sorry, you are always mopping up my tears."

"I wish I could solve all your problems, but you know I cannot. I am, however, your friend, even if I am your father's age. I hope you will call on me at any time if you need somebody to talk to. I am not far away and I am sure Louisa will take care of your babies for a few hours now and again. Promise me you will let me help."

"If you are not careful you will have me permanently at the Vicarage."

Nothing would have pleased Richard more but he could not say that, instead he squeezed her hand, kissed her on the cheek and took his leave... leaving Matilda to remove yet another Cornelian from her 'happy' box.

Chapter Fourteen

"I'm sure they belong to Matilda," said Randolph seriously to his companions in the chimney corner of the Village Maid. "My Albert would stake his life on it, he's been their cowman for years. Not much gets past him."

"I know it looks that way," offered Walter, "but I can't see young Matthew leavin' her in the lurch like that, he's a well brought up youngster an' he thinks the world of her, I know that for sure."

"You did say he was unhappy when he visited you last, Walter, perhaps she had met somebody else while he was away. He wasn't home for more than a week before he left again," Eli reminded him.

"No, I don't believe it. She was smitten with him, she wouldn't have bin interested in nobody else." Walter assured them, doubling his negatives like most of the villagers. "And anyway, why would the Vicar and his wife visit the farm so often if it wasn't to see their grandchildren? I've said afore and I'll say agin, there's somethin' very peculiar going on at that Vicarage."

"My Albert says the young Vicar is a frequent visitor to the farm," said Randolph, "Do you think *he* could be the father?"

"Never," said Old Walter, "the young Vicar has always bin a regular up there, he's Daniel's best friend. No they're nothing to do with him, he's old enough to be her *father*."

"Stranger things happen at sea," Amos said, joining the conversation, "affairs of the heart can be very complicated."

"You'd know all about them wouldn't you, Amos?" said Darcy. "Affairs of the heart, why I bet Noah was still a lad when you last had one of those."

"You're a cheeky young beggar, Darcy, allust have bin, I'll have you know that there might be snow on the roof," he pointed to his white hair as he said this, " but there's still fire in the grate." Amos nodded his head in a self-satisfied manner as he spoke.

"I wonder," said Old Shuffley thoughtfully, "Do you think thass what caused Daniel to have that stroke so young last year?"

The whole group now went very quiet, trying to remember just when Daniel had had the stroke.

"You could have somethin' there, Shuffley," agreed Amos.

"No, it couldn't have bin that," rejoined Walter, "I'm sure Daniel had that stroke while young Matthew was at home. He was only home for five days so the young gel wouldn't have known herself if she was expectin' let alone Daniel knowin'."

"Ah, but," said Shuffley, "you're assuming young Matthew is the father."

"He's right, Shuffley's right. I bet thass the crux of the matter," agreed Amos, "Why else would Matthew leave again so suddenly and Daniel have a stroke all in the same week?"

"I won't have it," declared Walter, "I know both them youngsters an' I know they're devoted to each other, no, I can't agree with you there."

For once the chimney corner assemblage was split down the middle.

"I s'pose thass another mystery we'll never solve," said Amos, "I don't know wass wrong with us all, it must be somethin' in this here ale addlin' our brains."

"Of course we may all be barking up the wrong tree," suggested Eli, "maybe the children don't belong to the young lass, she went away to stay with her aunt; maybe the babies belong to her."

"Then why all the secrecy?" asked Darcy. "No, I think we were right in the first place, it makes more sense."

"Eli may have somethin'," said Amos. "I'm sure young Matilda was at the Christmas mornin' church service. I remember thinkin' how peaky she looked. Now if she'd bin six months gone with twins I think somebody would've noticed."

Again there was silence as they tried to remember the previous Christmas.

"She delivered Albert's Christmas basket," offered Randolph, screwing up his face as he tried to bring the occasion to mind. "Yes, she definitely did the deliveries as usual. Amos is right she could never have been six months with twins."

"Well we'll have to agree to differ on that one," said Randolph, "but I can assure you all, them that work at the farm say the bairns belong to Matilda – and I believe them; you'll see."

Mid-way through September, Sebastian was ill again. It began with a cold which, as usual, lingered. Matilda did not worry too much at first having grown accustomed to his delicate constitution, but, when his little body became racked with coughing, she called in Dr. Henry, who diagnosed bronchitis. Louisa took over caring for Sarah while Matilda devoted all her time to Sebastian. She willed him to get better, prayed for his recovery but still he did not improve. Dr Henry visited every day, eventually telling her she must expect the worst.

He cannot die, she screamed in her head, he is only six months old, his father has never seen him.

She ate only sparse meals as she sat beside him, leaving him only to attend to her basic requirements. The family grew concerned for *her* health as well.

Richard began visiting every evening, he loved Matilda but he also loved the children, he prayed long and hard for little Sebastian.

Three weeks after he had first become ill, Sebastian began to rally. Matilda felt sure he was improving, he even gave her a little smile. When Richard arrived that evening he was relieved to find the situation more hopeful. He persuaded Matilda to walk in the garden for ten minutes while Louisa watched the baby, so they were surprised when she called them from the bedroom window.

As she ran indoors and up the stairs Matilda could not forgive herself for leaving her little son.

"He does not look at all well, Matilda, we must call Dr Henry again," said Louisa worriedly.

"I will fetch him at once," said Richard.

The Doctor arrived and gave Matilda the sad news that Sebastian was unlikely to live more than twenty-four hours. She sat in a chair and nursed him all night long, regretting leaving him for a walk in the garden. Richard and Louisa stayed up as well, frequently sitting with her and making her cups of tea, but for the most part she wanted to be alone with her little boy. Her head ached with tiredness, her arms were numb due to sitting in one position, but she could not disturb him.

At five minutes past six in the morning little Sebastian died in her arms – it was a full twenty minutes before she called her mother and Richard. Never in her life before had Matilda felt so desolate.

Dr. Henry was called for the last time, he gave Matilda something to make her sleep, she did not protest, she was numb with shock.

As if in a dream she went to the top drawer of her dresser and opened the little painted box. She searched through the stones to find the largest and prettiest one. She slowly lifted it out and held it up to the light, but she did not transfer it to the handkerchief, instead she laid it on the luxurious blue velvet of the little grey box, which had held her locket.

This Cornelian, she knew, would never go back into her 'happy' box.

The funeral was a small private affair, even so it left the villagers in no doubt as to the parents of the twins. Richard had difficulty conducting the service, he was so emotionally involved, but he wanted to do it for Matilda.

Afterwards little Sebastian was laid to rest in Flinton churchyard, where a yew tree afforded the tiny grave some dappled sunshine.

Chapter Fifteen

Daniel sank into depression once again. He alone was responsible for the little boy's death; he was convinced it was a punishment for his sins. Not only had he witnessed the passing of his grandson, but he also had to endure the heart-rending sight of his grieving daughter, as she lost weight and walked a tightrope of harrowing emotions, struggling to keep balanced enough to care for her little girl – who fretted for her lost brother – but always close to toppling over the edge into an abyss of despair, self-reproachment and misery. Nothing had the ability to lift her spirits. If she thought of Matthew she became angry with him for leaving her alone in her desolation. He knew where she was but had deserted her. Being in the company of others irritated her, especially if they professed to understand how she felt. Nobody could possibly know how difficult it was for her to continue living. Sometimes the weight on her chest was so heavy and painful, that she knew not how to take another breath. At these times she would snatch her daughter up and run to Flinton churchyard, where she would sit for hours by Sebastian's little grave, losing track of time and often feeling she was losing touch with reality. It was only her little girl moving in her arms, or the booming of the church clock, that reminded her she was still alive. It was often dark and chilly when she reluctantly left her little son. The ensuing journeys home were made slowly and sadly, as if every step were an effort. Every now and again she would turn and direct her eyes to the foot of the yew tree, where her baby rested. Each time she had to fight an overwhelming compulsion to run back to him, only the baby in her arms kept her trudging on to the warmth of the farmhouse, a warmth she herself did not want. Her heart was too cold, her feelings numb, a mere log fire could not warm or salve her wretchedness.

Christmas that year was a very subdued occasion. There had been an aura of great sadness over the house since Sebastian's death. He had been of such a sweet nature that he had endeared himself to everyone.

Matilda still obtained great comfort from Sarah. She seemed to get strength from nursing the little girl. She would find herself talking to her about her brother, trying to make sure he would not be forgotten. Matilda knew that Sarah missed him, although she had never been as placid as her brother had, she was even more fretful now that he was gone.

Mr and Mrs Johnson were invited for Christmas lunch. It made more sense, since Richard always divided his spare time between the two families.

Matilda made it known that she would walk down to the churchyard in the afternoon. She had put holly and other seasonal greenery on Sebastian's grave the previous day and had paused there that morning on her way to Church, but she wanted to stay a while alone with him on Christmas Day. Richard offered to walk down with her but she expressed the wish to go alone. He was so worried about her, she was quieter than ever these days.

"Perhaps I could walk part way with you," he suggested hopefully, "I could do with some air."

"Yes of course, I am sorry, I did not mean to be rude it is just that I will want to stay a while…be alone with my thoughts…and my little son."

"I understand, I will come as far as the church gate with you, I want to give you a present."

Matilda was not really interested in Christmas gifts. All she could think about was that this should have been her children's first Christmas. Her hand went instinctively to her neck to finger the gold locket as she thought of Matthew. He would never see his son. It made her sad to think of that. She had worn the locket every day since he had given it, it was strange how she felt herself touching it as she thought of him, she did it without knowing. The anger she had felt toward him had subsided a little, he did not know of her predicament.

She and Richard walked to the church in relative silence. She was glad he had offered to accompany her, but she did not feel like talking. She knew if she did, she would cry. As they neared the gate Richard put his hand into his inside pocket and brought out a small envelope, which he handed to her. On it was written '*With love from Richard, you will have happier Christmases than this one*'.

"Open it with Sebastian," he said, "it will be appropriate." Matilda reached up and kissed him on the cheek before making her way to the tiny grave. There were only two or three people in the churchyard – in the same situation as myself, she thought, facing Christmas without a loved one.

She came to a stop at the yew tree, leaning against it, as she stared at the ground covering her little boy. Her small offering of the previous day looked meagre compared to the gifts at home for Sarah.

As she knelt down to tidy the grave and touch the ground she realized she was still holding the envelope from Richard. She opened it slowly and saw a printed note, it simply said '*For your locket*'. Underneath were two miniature photographs of her babies.

As soon as she saw them she burst into tears. Richard could not have given her a better present. He must have returned to North Norfolk to arrange them. She fell back against the trunk of the yew tree, she slid down to the earth in a crumpled, dejected heap, she was sitting on the cold, hard ground of December but she did not care. Her tears fell copiously; she did nothing to stem them. She cried for Sebastian and for herself, she cried for Sarah who would grow up without her brother, she cried for Matthew wherever he was – trying hard to live without her, she even cried for the little fawn she had never forgotten, that had died under the crushing oak.

As it began to grow dusk she dragged herself up from the ground and made her way to the lych gate, decorated today with holly. As she passed through she looked back in the direction of the tiny grave – "I will be back soon," she whispered, "I will never forget you."

Since Matilda's return home with the babies she had spent more and more time in the company of old Rose, her grandmother. Rose had taken Dan's death very badly, they had been together for over half a century but she had cheered a little of late. The babies had given her a new lease of life.

So it was Rose's company that Matilda sought out when she returned from the churchyard. She knew, out of all her family, her grandmother would best understand how she felt.

As she watched the old lady cradling her daughter by the fire, Matilda's thoughts were with her little boy lying alone in the large family plot in Flinton churchyard. She could not shake herself out of her sombre mood, her depression still had a hold of her, she wanted to run back to the church to be with him. She kept seeing her little bunch of greenery lying on the grave, dwarfed by the yew tree.

As if reading her thoughts Rose said, "You will be able to put up a memorial stone soon, it will make you feel better. It is because the grave is unmarked you feel so sad."

Matilda raised her eyes to look at the old lady, "You are very comforting, Grandma, I doubt anyone else in the house knows how I am feeling."

"They are probably trying to cheer you by not mentioning Sebastian. They are not being unthoughtful."

"But I need to talk about him, I need to know he is not forgotten, especially at Christmas."

"I understand, dear, but I can assure you he is not forgotten – by any of us."

"Richard does not avoid the subject, look what he has given me for Christmas." Matilda removed her locket to show Rose the miniatures. "He always does the right thing, Grandma, it is uncanny how in tune he is with people's feelings."

"It was a lovely gesture, dear. His ability to care so genuinely is probably why he makes such a good Churchman. But remember, he too has lost a child."

Yes, thought Matilda, remembering his shaking shoulders in

Winford church ten years earlier, we all tend to forget that. He never talks of his own sadness.

As she replaced the locket round her neck she said a silent prayer for Richard – that he should find happiness.

Chapter Sixteen

Fingal Pardoe brushed the loose dust from his latest work and stood back to survey the newly lettered stone.

> In Loving Memory of
> Sebastian Matthew Canham
> Beloved son of Matilda and Matthew
> Twin Brother of Sarah Matilda
> Aged 6 Months.
> Born March 22nd 1868
> Died September 28th 1868
> Until We Meet Again

Well, thought Fingal, Walter was right, there's no doubt about that now.

He and Barnabas carefully lifted the gravestone onto the cart and set the horse in motion toward Flinton church.

Early the next morning, a young mother and her one year old daughter sat for an hour by the newest memorial stone in the churchyard, watching the dappled rays play on the pristine lettering.

"Now your father will be able to find you," whispered the woman as she hugged her daughter tightly. Then, her eyes returning to the gravestone, "God bless you and keep you, my darling."

Part Three

Lives and Loves

Chapter One

Matthew sat on an upturned fishing boat staring out to sea. The September sun was playing on the water as it crashed ashore sending the spray heavenward. A woman came into his line of vision, a solitary soul, walking with her head down studying the sand. Every now and again she would stop to pick up something, then turn to look out to sea. He began singing softly...

> *Walking by the sea shore*
> *Sun is glinting there,*
> *Glinting on the sea spray*
> *That's dancing on the air...*

He watched as the woman walked on for maybe two hundred yards. She reminded him of Tilly somehow. Although her hair was dark it was blowing in the wind in a wild fashion.

After stopping and staring out to sea again, she turned and made her way back toward him. He tried not to stare at her but his gaze kept returning all the same. He pushed himself off the boat and walked toward the sea hoping to strike up a conversation with her.

"It is a lovely evening for a walk," he said simply.

"I come here whatever the weather," she answered with a brief smile. "I have not seen you here before have I?" She blushed shyly as she spoke.

"No," said Matthew, "I am new to the area." He fell into step beside her as if it were the most natural thing to do. "Do you live locally?" he asked bravely.

"I live in one of those cottages." She pointed to a row of houses in the distance, wondering why she was telling a stranger where she lived.

"It is a lovely spot, so near to the sea."

"Yes," she agreed, "I like it."

They carried on walking in the direction of the cottages, walking along and up the beach at the same time.

"Am I going too fast?" she asked, suddenly noticing that Matthew was limping.

"No, it is an old wound."

"How did you do it?" She surprised herself asking the question, she did not normally talk easily to strangers.

"An accident at sea, I broke my leg in several places one night during a storm, the ship's doctor did his best but conditions were bad, it did not heal properly."

"My husband went to sea, he was a fisherman. He died five years ago."

"I am sorry, he must have been young." Matthew judged the woman to be about thirty -four.

"He was forty- six, he was fifteen years my senior."

Matthew did a quick calculation to find she was now thirty-six.

"You have not told me your name," she said as they approached her garden gate.

"Matthew, Matthew Johnson," he said extending his hand to her "and you are…?"

"Rhea Taylor," she said shyly, looking away quickly.

"That is a very pretty name." He was going to add 'for a very pretty lady' but thought better of it, instead he said, "Being local you may be able to help me, I am looking for somewhere to live, do you know of anywhere?"

The woman looked him up and down wondering whether to offer him her own spare room. The money would be useful, and he looked respectable, but common sense prevailed as she answered. "There is a seamen's mission in the town, you may have some luck there."

"Thank you very much, it will do until I find something more permanent."

"If you are looking for a permanent house I understand the end cottage is available. I can give you the landlord's address."

She hesitated then said shyly, "Perhaps you would like to come in while I look for it."

She led the way to her front door, which she unlocked and passed through. Matthew followed behind.

Rhea suddenly looked at him suspiciously, "Have you no belongings?"

He smiled at her to put her at her ease, "I took a room at an inn last night – The King's Head – my luggage is there."

Rhea wrote down the address and passed it to Matthew saying as she did so, "Perhaps I will see you again – if we are to be neighbours."

"I hope so. By the way I am hoping to earn my living as a carpenter and cabinet maker, the more people that know, the better."

"I will bear that in mind," she murmured, again looking away in shyness. "Good luck."

Matthew nodded, "Good evening to you, Rhea, and thank you for your help." He turned toward her door; Rhea gave him another of her brief smiles as she held it open for him, then he was gone.

Matthew moved into the end cottage the following day. He had few possessions, but that did not worry him. Since leaving Flinton he had found he did not need material belongings. He preferred to travel light. He looked out of his front window; he could just see the sea. Yes, this would suit him down to the ground, he thought, putting a Cornelian into his little box. He gazed at the painting of the ship and thought of Tilly. Little did they think their game would have to stand the test of time. It was part of his life now, transferring the stones back and forth. He did not need to count the Cornelians in the box – he could see that there were four.

Several times during the following months Matthew saw Rhea on the beach and stopped to chat to her. She was very quiet and shy, often appearing to be walking in a dream. He thought of Tilly, vibrant and talkative, always aware of her surroundings.

It was strange he could be attracted to two such different women. His thoughts surprised him – attracted? Was he attracted to Rhea? Yes he was, he admitted, he enjoyed her company, it was relaxing.

Matthew had found work with a local undertaker, his days of watching Walter making the coffins had paid off. It was a twenty-minute walk to work but he had found a short cut through the churchyard bringing it down to about fifteen minutes. All things considered he was content with his new life except for being a bit lonely. Often in the evening he considered knocking on Rhea's door but always changed his mind, not wanting to intrude. She appeared a very private person. Most of what he knew of her had been learnt on their first meeting. He had discovered that her late husband's name was Albert – but she had called him Bert – and that she had longed for a child.

One night as he walked home through the churchyard he saw the shadowy figure of a woman ahead of him. She was walking quite fast as if she were trying to gain ground. He realized she was probably nervous that a man was following so was about to stop, to allow her to make headway, when she turned her head – it was Rhea.

"Oh it is you, Matthew," she said relieved, "I thought somebody was following me."

"I was following you, but not intentionally, I usually cut through here to save time," and then noticing that her face was tear stained he asked, "Are you alright, Rhea?"

"Yes, I am sorry, I have been to Bert's grave. I miss him so, especially at Christmas. You see my parents were opposed to us marrying, I had to choose between them and him, so now I have nobody."

"I understand what a difficult choice it must have been," he said thinking of Tilly and her father's opposition to their own courtship.

"It did not seem too difficult at the time, we were so much in love nothing else mattered but I have missed them," Rhea continued.

"You could make contact with them now, are they local people?"

"They live about five miles away in Stoneham."

"Would you like to have some dinner with me tonight?"

Matthew had asked the question without thinking. He had surprised himself. He had nothing special to cook.

Rhea brightened up a bit, "That is very kind of you but why not come to my house?"

That evening was to set a precedent for the future. Matthew asked Rhea if she would like to spend Christmas Day with him. He suggested they attend Church in the morning, have lunch then walk along the beach in the afternoon. He had missed traditional Christmases, he thought of home too much around this time; it tended to induce maudlinism.

He felt guilty that he did not write home more often. The first letters to his parents, Richard and Tilly had preceded two years of silence, he had written sparsely since then, just to let them all know he was alive and well. Matthew knew he should let his family know that he now had a permanent address but he was afraid that Tilly would write to him or even come to see him. They could not possibly get on with their respective lives if they stayed in touch; it would start up all the old problems all over again. Tilly thought the only hindrance to their marriage was her father. But what if her father had died during the last six years? How could he tell her his suspicions about his parentage without tearing her family apart? No, it would be better if they did not know of his whereabouts, but, he decided, he would write to them for Christmas.

The three letters more or less told the same story. That he was well, settled and had given up the sea after an accident had left him lame. He wished them all a happy Christmas and said he would now write more often.

Very early the next morning, before work, he walked the five miles into Stoneham to post the letters. Being a city he knew no one was likely to come looking for him there.

Matthew spent Christmas Day with Rhea as planned. After tea

they sat by the fire and became really well acquainted although he was aware that he was being selective. He did not tell her the strange circumstances of his birth, nor about Tilly. Those were very private things.

As the evening wore on the atmosphere became more relaxed. Matthew played his violin as they sung carols together and chuckled when they sang different words. They roasted chestnuts in the fire and played parlour games. He entertained her with stories of his sea- going days. They both laughed more than they had in years.

They fell quiet watching the logs burning low in the grate as they cast a warm glow all round the little room, Matthew's thoughts turned to the day on Winford beach with Tilly. He remembered telling her they would have a big house and grand carriages, and that he would entertain her on winter nights by playing his violin and telling stories of his travels to her and their children. Their dreams had come to nothing. Here he was, in front of the fire, playing his violin, but there were no children, no grand house and no Tilly. Strange how he did not hanker after riches any more. This little house is quite adequate, he thought, letting his gaze travel round the room. It does not matter where you live so long as you live with the right person – so long as you are content.

Matthew looked sideways at Rhea, she too was in her own world probably thinking of Bert and *their* past Christmases.

He began to play the carols again very softly as if in accompaniment to her thoughts. She appeared oblivious to his music – until he stopped.

"I was enjoying that", she said lazily. She wore a dreamy look.

"Good, that was the intention." His smile lit up his handsome, dark face.

"I have had a lovely day."

"Me too, you are an excellent cook." He meant it; the meal had been superb.

He leaned forward and covered her hand with his own, then found himself unexpectedly saying, "I have grown very fond of you, Rhea, I would be very honoured if you would consider becoming my wife."

"Matthew I..."

"It is alright, you do not need to answer now, but please give it careful thought. I know you still love Bert very much, I respect that, I understand and I will not pressure you."

"I did not think I would ever be happy again but you have made me so, however, I was not expecting a proposal."

"I too have loved before, I would not expect you to forget Bert or to neglect his grave, it would make you unhappy, he is part of your life and I would be happy for him to remain so." He smiled at her worried face. "We might even have that baby you long for." He felt a little guilty as he uttered the last sentence, but he thought it might sway her decision.

"Oh, Matthew you are so understanding, how could I possibly refuse to marry you."

"You mean you are willing?" he could not believe she had given him an immediate answer.

"Yes, I am willing, *very* willing." She laughed happily at his surprised countenance.

Matthew gently pulled her to her feet and took her in his arms. His traditional Christmas had not been a disappointment. He hoped it was the first of many. He could see a happy family life stretching way ahead of them.

Chapter Two

Matthew and Rhea were married at Easter in Thimblethorpe parish church. He knew that she still loved Bert and that he still loved Tilly but that did not prevent them from loving one another. Love takes many forms, he reasoned, as he headed for London on the train with Rhea after the ceremony, and he *did* love Rhea. Had she resembled Tilly in looks or nature, he may have suspected his motives, but she was completely different, very self-effacing, he felt comfortable with her – content. Yes, he loved her very much and, with her, there were no complications.

They spent two days in London seeing the sights, but he did not visit his mother's family, he thought it best. They might ask him where he lived; he did not want any awkwardness.

On his last night there, he wrote to his parents and to Richard to inform them of his marriage. He asked Richard to gently break the news to Tilly. He hoped she too had found happiness, if she had not, his own marriage might encourage her to do so, he reasoned.

Rhea celebrated her thirty-seventh birthday in May still hoping for a child. "I should be satisfied, I know, I have so much but a child would make it perfect."

Matthew held her close, "It will happen Rhea I am certain; we must be patient."

They were very happy. She still visited Bert's grave regularly; she went alone, by choice. Matthew had told her how he was abandoned as a child. He had also told her of his love for Tilly and why he could not marry her. He was happy there were no secrets between them anymore, but in fairness to Rhea he decided not to correspond with Tilly in the future. He knew Richard would give her news of him. He was determined that his marriage would be a new beginning. He wanted it to be successful.

Louisa said goodbye to Doctor Henry at Robert Taylor's front door.

"I do not think it will be long now," he said softly, "she has put up a good fight, Robert is exhausted."

"We will keep an eye on them both, one of us will be here all the while," Louisa assured him.

She went back through to the kitchen to make Robert and Sally a cup of tea. Why do these awful things happen to the nicest people, she thought sadly. Sally had never had her longed-for children. She had given most of her baby clothes to Matilda for the twins. She had become ill a year ago, suffering headaches and dizziness. When she had not improved Robert had taken her to London to see a specialist. A brain tumour had been diagnosed. She had now been bedridden for eight weeks. Matilda helped out through the day while Sarah was at school. Louisa took over through the evening and Daniel slept at Robert's at night. They did not like to leave him alone at all.

This was the situation at Uphall Farm when Richard received the news of Matthew's marriage. He did not know whether to inform Matilda or not. He was still in the habit of visiting on Tuesday evenings and, because of Louisa's enforced absence, he had plenty of private, conversational time with Matilda.

Loveday had married a farmer ten years her senior and gone to live near Denham. Edward was away studying medicine. As Richard approached the farm he was still trying to decide what he should do, but his mind was to be made up for him.

"I am alone tonight, Richard," said Matilda wearily as she ushered him into the kitchen. "Mother and Father are both at Meadow Farm, it will not be much longer now."

"You have all been invaluable to Robert, he could not have coped without you."

"I do not know what will happen to him without Sally, they are so devoted to one another." She was close to tears as she spoke.

"God gives us the strength, as you well know, although I

agree he will take it badly."

"I will understand how he feels, I still miss Sebastian."

"I know, I know." He put his arm around her shoulders and led her to a chair. "You are tired, let me make you some tea."

"Whenever things go wrong I *will* Matthew to come home. I always feel he would make everything all right, but if he walked through the door right now he could not make Sally better. It is so silly of me to feel like that. I know he will never marry me while Father is alive, but if he were nearby it would help. I have been thinking of going to Kent to try and find him, he cannot be happy never hearing from his family. I am sure he would not willingly stay away, if he knew he had a daughter. I have been thinking of him a great deal lately while I tend to Sally, life is so short, we must do what we want to while we can."

"Matilda I..."

"You see, Richard I find it very strange that Matthew does not give us his address. For all he knows Father could have changed his mind about our marrying, so why does he not want to stay abreast of the situation here at home? Why does he seem to have given up hope of us ever marrying?" She searched his face as if it could give her the answer.

"Matilda," he said again gently. "I have had another letter from Matthew, I do not know how to tell you this, but I must."

"Is he ill?" She had jumped to her feet as if ready to go to his aid.

"No, he is not ill," he hesitated before saying, "He is married." Richard hardly dared breathe as he waited for her reaction.

"*Married!* No, Richard you are mistaken, he would not marry anyone else, he cannot, *I* love him." She sat down again forlornly, staring ahead as if in a trance, "He must marry *me*, he is Sarah's father."

"He cannot marry you, he is married already," he gently impressed upon her.

She felt as if something heavy were pressing on her chest

again, making it difficult to breathe, her head was spinning. She got up on her feet, in a daze, as if to run from this terrible news – Richard caught her, as – for the second time – she fainted in his arms.

When she came round she was lying on the couch, in the sitting room, with Richard beside her. She put out her hand to him as if to gain strength from him. He took it and held it tightly between the two of his own.

"Your father is still a young man, Matilda, Matthew would not wish him dead so that he could marry you. Do you not understand, dear; he is setting you free, free to find your own happiness without him. He urged you long ago to do just that."

"But I always thought he would wait for me."

"I have no doubt he still loves you dearly, but he has obviously found someone he can love as well. Love is not rationed. In setting you free he is loving you very much." He did not like to see her so distraught. *Her* pain was *his* pain.

"Do you know her name?"

"It is Rhea, she is a widow."

"Does she have any children?" Matilda asked desperately, as if the answer would somehow make a difference.

"He has not mentioned any." He waited patiently for her to absorb this before he spoke again.

"So you see, dear, it would be futile to search for him."

"He would not have married had he known of Sarah and Sebastian." Saying Sebastian's name made her dissolve into tears. Richard helped her to a sitting position and sat down beside her.

"It will do you good to have a good cry." He remained quiet until her sobbing had subsided then he went to the kitchen to make the over-due tea.

When Louisa returned home she found Richard alone. Matilda had gone to bed. He told her the news.

"It never rains but it pours," she said tiredly. "Do you remember how happy and vibrant she was as a child? I thought her life was mapped out for her with Mathhew. It would not do for us to be able to see the future, would it?"

"I think I will call again on Friday night if that is alright with you?"

"That is a good idea, with Sally ill I will not have much time for anything else. When I am here, Matilda is at Meadow Farm, this could not have come at a worse time."

Sally died early on the Thursday morning. The funeral was held on the following Monday. As Matilda sat in the church she felt as if she were mourning two loved ones. In one week she had removed two Cornelians from her little box. There were only two left in it. Strangely, those two stones kept her going. She would be alright she told herself, so long as the box held at least *one* Cornelian. It was absurd she knew, but she had become obsessed with the ritual of the stones. They seemed to give her life purpose.

It was four months later, in August, that Richard plucked up the courage to ask Matilda to marry him. They had been to Meadow Farm to call on Robert then decided to go for a walk.

"He is coping much better than I thought he would," Matilda said, "He has immersed himself in hard work all Summer. I have always liked Robert; he is very kind in his quiet way. He always had time for me when I was a child."

"He counts his blessings, they may not have had children but they had an extremely happy marriage for over thirty years. That is something to be grateful for."

"Oh, Richard," she stopped and put a hand on his arm. "You are always helping people through their troubles, I want you to know that I *do* think of your own sadness. Just this morning I was thinking that your child would be eighteen now had he lived."

"Thank you, Matilda."

They walked on in silence then turned left into Poachers Way, but they did not enter Clancy's Wood, instead they walked back through the poppy field.

When they reached the stile Richard stopped. "There is something I want to ask you, but I am half afraid to do so."

"That sounds very intriguing, what are you scared of?"

"Losing your friendship."

Matilda laughed, closing her eyes against the brilliance of the setting sun but when she next looked at him she saw he was deadly serious. "You will never lose my friendship. Who else is there every time I faint?"

"Will you sit down, Matilda?"

They sat on the step of the stile. She looked at him puzzled.

"Matilda...would you please consider becoming my wife?"

To say that she was taken by surprise would be putting it mildly, she was speechless, she had never dreamed that Richard was in love with her.

"Richard I – I do not know what to say, I had no idea..."

"If you want to say no, please just say it and then forget I ever asked you – but if you will consider it, if you think there is any chance you will say yes, you will make me the happiest man on earth."

She was twenty-eight, she had a daughter of seven. She could never marry Matthew. Sarah needed a father, she remembered how Richard had always been there for her, helping her, comforting her, never judgmental, always supportive, only ever caring about her happiness. Tears welled up into her eyes as she realized how long he must have loved her and all the way through she had reminded him how much she loved Matthew. All her tears had been for herself and Matthew and then for Sebastian. How could she have been so blind?

"Please do not cry, Matilda, forget I asked, it is alright, I am just a silly old man to ever think you might consider..."

"Ssshhh," she put her finger to his lips. "I would be honoured to be your wife."

He jumped up and pulled her to her feet, and there, by the stile, between the poppy field and the meadow, as the sun went down, he held her tightly to him, unable to believe his good fortune.

Chapter Three

Matilda had half expected her father to object to the wedding – after all, Richard was twenty-two years her senior, but amazingly, after the initial shock, her parents were extremely pleased.

The wedding was set for December, just before Christmas.

"We will tell Mother and Father tomorrow," said Richard draining his celebratory glass of wine. "It is too late to disturb them tonight."

Elizabeth and Richard still lived at the Vicarage but they now shared it with their son who had taken his father's place in Flinton now that he had retired.

"Where will you live?" asked Louisa excitedly.

Matilda suddenly became worried, she had not thought she would have to leave the farm. Richard noted her concern. "Where ever we live will be here in Flinton. I suppose at the Vicarage. Do you have any objection to that Matilda?"

"I had not thought about it." She brightened up. The farm would not be far way, after all, at one time she had considered living in Beeton. She thought of her two lonely Cornelians –tonight they would become three.

It was on the anniversary of their first meeting, as they walked by the sea, that Rhea told Matthew she was with child.

"What a wonderful anniversary present for us," Matthew cried as he lifted Rhea off her feet and spun her round.

He stopped suddenly, "I should not have done that now that you are a lady in waiting." His eyes twinkled at her.

"April seems a long way away doesn't it?" she said smiling happily.

"It will soon be here, think of all we have to do in preparation."

As they walked along the beach they made their plans.

212

Matthew would make a cradle, fit for a prince, he said. An onlooker would have thought they were sweethearts, they were oblivious to everything except each other. He had a feeling his 'happy' box was going to be much fuller from now on.

September in Flinton proved hot and sultry. Matilda had got into the habit of walking up to the river in the early evening. It was always cooler there under the oak trees and it would be much further to walk when she moved to the Vicarage. It would be a wrench to leave the farm.

She was lost in thought on this matter one evening as she sat on the bank of the river, cooling down. She was vaguely aware of the birds singing and the tumbling of the waterfall a few yards to her right, when to her horror something was thrown over her head, pitching her into blackness. Then she was being pushed backward as her assailant held her tightly. She struggled, trying to tear the covering from her face. *I am going to be raped*, she screamed in her head. *God, no, please help me.* But as she struggled and fought for breath she gradually realized she was just being held tightly. She was not being raped, and the person holding her was sobbing audibly, great body shaking sobs that made her rigid with fear, not knowing what was going to happen next. She lay there terrified, wondering if she would live to see her wedding day. And then after what seemed an eternity the weight was lifted from her, the covering whipped from her face and her attacker was gone, fleeing behind her. She dared not turn round; she was shaking like a leaf. Her fists were clenched, one of them round a piece of material. She suddenly opened her hand as an audible 'aarrh' escaped from her mouth. Out of her hand fell a button attached to a piece of cloth. She sat staring at it as if it, too, might jump up and attack her.

At last she looked behind her, there was no one around. She got unsteadily to her feet then bent down again, she knew not why, to pick up the button. At first she moved very slowly keeping her eyes fixed on the hedge behind her that ran along the side of Mill Stream Lane. She kept close to the river as she moved faster and faster towards the gap in the hedge of Hill

Road. Out on the road at last she ran toward the farmhouse, as if her life depended on it, and, for all she knew, it did.

Her heart was thudding and her breath coming in short gasps as she ran through the dairy and slammed the kitchen door behind her then drew the bolt across.

"Matilda whatever is wrong?" Louisa watched as her ashen daughter stumbled across the room toward a chair.

"Mother, I have just been attacked."

"By whom, are you hurt?"

"I do not know – no – I am scared." As she spoke she shot terrified glances toward the kitchen door expecting it to burst open at any minute.

Louisa called Daniel. He had just entered the kitchen from the hall when there was a loud knock on the back door. "Do not open it" Matilda cried to her father as he walked forward, "Please do not open it."

"She has been attacked," Louisa informed her husband, "she is terrified."

Again the knocking came at the door. "Hello, anyone at home?"

"It is Richard," said Daniel, again going toward the door, but Matilda shrank back toward the hall in a state of shock.

Richard wanted to go for a doctor but Matilda would not hear of it. She wanted them all to stay with her, she felt safer that way. All of a sudden she did not mind the thought of leaving the farm to go to the Vicarage.

As the night wore on she began to relax. She went over and over the incident in her head. He had not hurt her. She had been terrified but he had not hurt her. Daniel and Richard had wanted to go and search the area but she had begged them not to leave the house.

That night she awoke several times feeling she could not breathe. After each nightmare she would lay awake unable to sleep.

She dared not leave the farm alone from that day until her marriage on December the twentieth.

Matilda and Richard had a truly beautiful white wedding. It had snowed for two days making the Church and countryside as pretty as a picture. Their families and friends were all present. Even Laura and Jack were there. Afterwards they all went back to the farm to celebrate.

Christmas too was a joyous occasion. It had become a tradition for the two families to celebrate Christmas at Uphall farm, this year they had naturally invited Robert as well.

At first he had declined their invitation but they would not take 'no' for an answer, saying they would worry about him if he spent the day alone. And so, with the exception maybe of Robert, the house was full of happy people.

In the afternoon Matilda and Richard walked down to the church where Matilda visited Sebastian's grave. She had always gone down on Christmas Day. He was part of her family. She stayed about half an hour, talking to him as if he were with her. She went to the grave every week but Christmas Day was special. As always, when leaving, she paused at the lych-gate and looked back to the yew tree, as always she whispered her intention of returning soon.

On their return they found Robert in the farmyard. Matilda urged Richard to go into the house so that she could talk to Robert alone.

"I came out for some air," he said apologetically.

Matilda remembered the note that Richard had given her the Christmas after Sebastian had died. She said now, "Things *will* improve Robert, I know you do not think so, but you will have better Christmases than this one."

"I do not know which is worse, being alone, or feeling lonely in a crowd."

"It *will* get better," she impressed upon him. But he seemed not to hear her as he stared out over the meadow.

"I do not think I can carry on one more day, let alone one more year. I know you mean well but it seems to get harder rather than easier."

Matilda realized he had not been coping as well as they had thought. "You must not stay alone so much in the evenings. You are always welcome at the Vicarage and here as well." She put her arms around him in comfort.

"I am so sorry, Matilda, so very sorry."

"For what? It is not a crime to be sad."

"I am sorry for everything, for not giving Sally a child when she wanted one so much…"

"You are not to blame for that."

"I am sorry for not having your faith in the future, for not being stronger."

"You are no weaker than anyone else in the same situation."

"You know that Sally and I loved you as a daughter, you were like a little ray of sunshine when you visited us, remember how you loved the pigs?" He smiled and screwed up his eyes as if peering into the distant past. "Life was full of hope in those days, how quickly it all dissolves."

"I think we should go indoors, it is getting very chilly."

She steered him out of the farmyard, past the cowsheds and so up the garden path toward the back door from where happy chatter floated out onto the cold December air. "Let us try to rouse our spirits a little."

Once inside Matilda was coerced into playing the piano so that some carolling could be enjoyed. How wonderful it would be if Matthew were here too, she thought. All my loved ones are in this house today. All except Matthew and our little son – but they are not forgotten.

That night Richard surprised her by telling her that they were going to Europe for a holiday.

"Europe! When?"

"I thought in two months time. It is a wedding present from my parents, your mother and father have agreed to look after Sarah."

"You are all very devious," she said prodding him playfully. "I had no idea of your plans."

"That, Mrs Johnson, was the whole idea."

Mrs Johnson, he had not called her that before. She suddenly realized she had always expected to be Mrs Johnson one day – Mrs Matthew Johnson.

It was the first day of the New Year, early in the morning that Robert Taylor's pigman, young Sid Sheldrake, ran through Uphall Farm gates calling for Daniel. He did not stop calling as he ran to the back door, hammering on it loudly.

"What is going …"Daniel began.

"Help me, it's Mr Taylor, I need help to…" the man did not finish, instead he turned and ran off the way he had come.

"What has happened?" Daniel shouted as he followed the distraught man back to Meadow Farm. But the pigman just kept running as fast as he could until he came to the door of Robert's hayloft. Daniel was close behind. He stared in horror at the scene before him. Robert's body was hanging by the neck from the rafters of the loft. Daniel suddenly sprung into action "Cut him down man, cut him down."

Between them they brought the body down. They were far too late, Robert was already dead – probably since the night before.

"I should have done something," Matilda wept when she heard the news.

"We could not watch him twenty-four hours a day. He wanted to be on his own."

Richard did his best to comfort his wife but Matilda blamed herself. "He told me he could not carry on."

"And you told me, so am I to blame also? No-one is at fault, we all tried our hardest, it is seven months since Sally died, none of us thought it would come to this."

Robert was laid to rest in Flinton churchyard with his wife. In the absence of a family his funeral was arranged by his friends, who gathered together at Meadow Farm to pay their last respects.

Nicholas Flowerdew solemnly read Robert's Will. Everything had been left to Matilda.

"We should not be surprised," said Daniel to no-one in particular. "Sally and Robert always did think the world of Matilda."

Matilda walked out of the house in a daze. It would appear that she was the only one who *was* surprised at the contents of the Will.

She was now Mistress of Meadow Farm.

Chapter Four

Matilda and Louisa spent the following two weeks sorting out the contents of Meadow Farmhouse. There were many good pieces of furniture, which Matilda decided to keep. Clothes could be given to the poor, she decided, as for personal effects well, they could be put together and a decision made later. She had always liked Meadow Farm, it was on high ground so the views were spectacular, and it was no further from Clancy's Wood than Uphall Farm, which was its nearest neighbour.

As she packed clothes into boxes there was a knock at the door. It was Ambrose Fennell, the undertaker. "I have brought Mr Taylor's personal effects," he said solemnly, "the things he was wearing when he died."

"Thank you, Mr Fennell, it was very kind of you, I should have remembered to collect them."

"Actually, Mrs Johnson, they are very old clothes, a bit raggedy in fact, but I thought you should have them."

Matilda did not know whether to open the parcel or not. If the clothes were old they could be burned. She doubted if anyone would feel comfortable wearing the clothes that a man had been wearing when he committed suicide. She decided she should at least go through the pockets before destroying them.

The clothes were indeed tatty. She felt a bit strange as she went though the pockets. She wondered why he had put on such worn things. She examined the trousers, shirt and shoes and put them to one side to burn, then picked up the jacket. Having checked the inside pocket she suddenly dropped the garment as if it had burnt her fingers. She stared at the item of clothing as it lay on the kitchen table. One of the buttons was missing – it had not just fallen off. A large portion of fabric was missing too. This button had been *torn* off and she was almost certain it matched the button and material she still had at home. Her legs had turned to jelly, she could hear her blood pounding through her temples as the realization hit her that her assailant in September had been Robert – dear Robert whom she had liked and respected – loved even.

Matilda heard her Mother coming down the stairs and quickly threw the jacket on the other clothing. When Louisa entered the kitchen she found Matilda seated on a chair looking pale and upset.

"Is anything wrong, dear?"

Matilda did not want to tell anyone about her discovery, not yet anyway. Not until she had compared the button at home with the jacket.

"I felt a bit strange," she informed her mother. "Perhaps we should stop for a snack and cup of tea."

"Do you think you could be with child? Oh, Matilda that would be such good news."

"No, I do not think so, I am just a little tired."

"Sit still, I'll make the tea."

Matilda had no option than to sit still, her legs were in no position to take her weight. Her brain was working overtime – trying to understand why Robert would terrify her.

She went over and over the incident by the river, he had not really hurt her, he had held her tightly and he had sobbed. She remembered the terrible body-racking sobs. Gradually she relaxed.

She recalled how she had felt after Sebastian had died, how she had held Sarah so tightly – and Richard. She remembered the all-consuming need for human contact and the anger she had felt toward Matthew – Matthew whom she loved with all her heart. Grief does strange things, especially grief for one who is loved deeply. Poor Robert – he had been so devoid of human contact – no parents, no children, that he had hurt somebody he loved merely by holding them tightly. That must have made him feel ten times worse, she thought sadly. And he had apologised. At Christmas he had impressed his apologies upon her – over and over again. He had also told her that they had both loved her. "I forgive you Robert, I understand," she whispered staring at the pathetic little pile of tatty clothes.

"What did you say, dear?" Louisa asked gently. Her daughter had been staring into nothingness for at least fifteen minutes, but she had a little more colour.

"I am feeling much better now. One thing I am certain of – it is definitely not the heat causing my problem."

The kitchen was the warmest room in the house. They had not bothered to light fires in the sitting room or the bedrooms so the house was quite cold. Louisa chuckled at Matilda's joke.

"No, but it may be the cold."

The button *did* match the jacket. Matilda decided not to tell anyone about her discovery. She did not want to sully Robert's memory; instead she disposed of both items together and laid the matter to rest. At least she would not now be nervous of going out alone.

She had inherited a considerable amount of money along with the farm. She would now be able to repay her parents, and Laura and Jack. She had felt indebted to them for so long.

Her first job on inheriting the farm had been to transfer everything from the hayloft, where Robert had died, to the building next door. The farm workers had declared a strong aversion to entering the place. When it had been cleared, Matilda had arranged for the door to be nailed up. She did not think the men unreasonable; she felt the same way herself.

In early March Matilda and Richard left for Europe.

Louisa and Daniel cared for Sarah at the farm. She was now nearly eight years old. She was a robust, solidly built child with dark hair and complexion, she was also a bit of a tomboy, preferring outdoor pursuits, she was very like her father. Daniel loved his granddaughter but he often wished she did not remind him so much of Matthew.

One evening as Louisa sat with her husband by the fire she looked across to where he was dozing in a chair. He is very much more content these days, she thought, watching the firelight flicker across his features. He stirred, subconsciously feeling her gaze upon him.

"Am I falling asleep again?" he said apologetically, "I must be getting old."

"I do not think fifty-two is old."

"It is a lot older than forty-two." I did not think I would still be here ten years later."

"I think our daughter is very happy at last."

"Yes, everything has turned out for the best, she will be well looked after by Richard."

"I wonder if they will have children. I would like to have some more grandchildren. It would be especially nice for Richard before he gets too old to enjoy them. He is your age don't forget."

Daniel had not forgotten. It had eased his conscience somewhat when Matilda and Richard had married and he was pleased they appeared so content. He had not enjoyed being responsible for his daughter's unhappiness. He was particularly pleased that Sarah had a father at last, but – and it was an important but – he realized that Matilda could eventually be a very young widow. Something else he would, no doubt, feel responsible for.

"Perhaps they will have some news for us when they return, Matilda needs a good rest after the events of the past year."

The atmosphere was so relaxed between them that Louisa dared to mention Matthew's name.

"I was very surprised to hear of Matthew's wedding. I am not sure if Matilda would have married if there had been a chance of him returning. What I mean is, I am not sure that Richard would have asked her to marry him."

"I just hope he is happy as well."

Daniel sounded so sincere that Louisa felt compelled to question him.

"Would it really have been so bad if they had married? You seem so fond of him sometimes."

"I *am* fond of him, it is difficult to explain how I feel, it distresses me to talk of it. Let us just be thankful that Matilda is happy at last."

Louisa could see that the contented atmosphere was being strained. She dropped the subject. Daniel's happiness and health were very important to her. He had been a good husband and excellent father to her children. He had been exemplary in every area, except the one relating to Matthew. It was strange, she would never understand him on that subject, and she could never pressure him for an explanation because he became unreasonably agitated, and then the whole family suffered. Life had returned to some semblance of normality of late, for which she was grateful. All her children were happy and she had a beautiful little granddaughter. She had no wish to rock the boat.

Chapter Five

Matthew and Rhea's son was born at the beginning of April. It was not an easy birth. Although the child was fit and healthy, Rhea was exhausted. Matthew worried about her, so much so that he wrote to her parents, telling them of the marriage, their grandson's birth and their daughter's weakness.

Margaret and Henry Harkness visited their daughter the following week. The re-union was very emotional, there were regrets on both sides. Margaret offered to stay to help out. Henry said he would visit often.

Matthew was pleased to have brought about a family re-union but he wished the circumstances were different. He doted on his little son whom they had named Matthew Henry. He had added a Cornelian to his box the night his son was born. He felt compelled to continue playing the childish game, in fact it had become a tradition. He was happy to play it. It was a link with home, with his family and with Tilly whom he felt he had deserted. He hoped she was happy.

Gradually Rhea gained strength and was able to enjoy her longed-for baby. She and her parents became close again due to the daily contact in the little house and Henry's regular visits.

"You have totally changed my life, Matthew," she said to him one evening as they all sat round the fire listening to his music. "Next Christmas will be the best ever." She smiled at her parents, wondering how she had coped with the estrangement, but she knew it was out of loyalty for Bert. They had not accepted him, because they had not deemed him good enough for their only daughter. She gazed down at her little son. She wanted the best for him too but she hoped it would not be at the expense of his happiness. She looked at her parents. They had grown old during the intervening years. Pride is a destructive force and life is short. She knew there would be no more separations.

Matthew's family flourished along with his business, he was making quite a name for himself in the community. He had a workshop in the back garden and a plate by the front door; he had been able to give up working for the undertaker. Life was good at last; he had a family again. He liked Margaret and Henry. No one was all bad or all good, most folk were a mix, and circumstances often dictated actions. If somebody asked to borrow a shilling when one was in a good mood they stood a good chance of getting it. It would be a different story if one had just lost a guinea! His workshop was conducive to philosophical thought!

"I know now why Matthew wanted to travel."

Matilda was enthusing about her wonderful four weeks in Europe. She found it easier now to mention Matthew's name without hurting quite so much.

"We have seen so many wonderful places, Mother. We went to the Louvre in Paris and Notre Dame Cathedral, we saw all the artists in Montmartre, they live such an exciting life, so different from ours, at times we felt quite naughty. I am not sure it is a seemly area for a vicar." She gave her husband a twinkly look. "I will never be able to paint again without remembering them. And at night, the views of the Seine were beautiful. I have made many sketches. We will have to go back one day with Sarah. If ever I run away from home that is where I will go," she joked.

Matilda was hugging her daughter as if she had been away for a year; she had missed her so much.

Four weeks after they had returned home Richard had a letter from Matthew.

"Matthew and Rhea have a son," Richard said gently, " they have named him Matthew Henry".

Matilda was experiencing weird sensations, she automatically thought of Sebastian, *he* was Matthew's son. She felt herself becoming angry and jealous of this unknown woman who had Matthew's constant company, and now had his son. He had presumably been with her through her pregnancy, cared for her, loved her, and now she was witnessing him holding their son. Matthew had never held Sebastian, he had never seen him and now, their poor little boy, who had lived such a short time, was lying in Flinton churchyard, while Rhea's son was alive and well. She could not bear it. She went into the kitchen to sit by herself.

Matthew had not known of her pregnancy, she reminded herself, he would have come home had he known. And she could not blame Rhea for anything. She knew also that she wished their son no harm, she was *glad* he was alive and well, he was an innocent little baby. She felt privileged to have known Sebastian. Matthew would never know his eldest son. She should feel sympathy for him – not anger.

Richard joined her. "I am sorry if it has upset you."

"I am happy for him, honestly I am, he deserves happiness. I just sometimes feel angry that I do not have my own son. I am truly sorry, Richard, I know you must feel exactly the same. You are a much nicer person than I am."

"You are a wonderful person, and I love you very much. It is natural for you to feel bitter at times but you *do* have a beautiful daughter."

"Yes, I have so much to be grateful for, especially you, I do not deserve you."

They held each other tightly both thinking of their lost children. They parted and smiled at each other. It really was wonderful news that Matthew had a new family.

"Let us drink to their health," said Richard finding some glasses. "And may they be as happy as we are."

But Richard was perturbed at Matilda's reaction to the news; one could almost be forgiven for thinking she was still in love with him. Would Matthew always be a ghost between them, he wondered. What if he decided to come back to Flinton? He felt ashamed of himself for even beginning to doubt Matilda's love for him. All the same he had been her second choice of husband. Matthew had been her first; he could not forget that – however much he tried.

Chapter Six

The following two Christmases in Flinton and Thimblethorpe were happy occasions. Both Matthew and Matilda were content in their respective marriages.

In the middle of January an influenza epidemic began to sweep the country. Few people escaped it but the elderly and the very young fared worse. Many schools were closed and doctors worked overtime.

Among Flinton's victims were Amos Farthing and Old Shuffley, who died within a fortnight of each other. The church was packed on both occasions; they had both been well-loved members of the community.

At Old Shuffley's funeral most villagers realized that, though they had known and respected him for years, they had not known his name. It was strange to listen to Richard referring to Shuffley as, Edward John Maddon. Even some of the chimney corner regulars had not known it.

Just as the group were coming to terms with the deaths of Amos and Shuffley, Old Walter had a heart attack and joined his friends in Flinton churchyard.

By the middle of March the worst of the epidemic was over though few people took chances. Both Matthew and his son were ill and had just recovered when Rhea fell victim. But Rhea did *not* get well; she died very early one morning after a harrowing week of fighting.

Matthew was broken hearted. He buried Rhea in Thimblethorpe churchyard with her first husband, Bert.

The following nine months were a blur of working hard, caring for little Matthew and consoling her parents. Rhea had left her house to Matthew but, although he now had a permanent home of his own, he found it difficult to settle there without his wife. Margaret and Henry pressed him to move in with them but even that did not appeal. He did, however, agree to spend Christmas with them. It would be too painful in his own house.

Early on Christmas Eve Matthew and his son visited Rhea's grave. He wept openly as he laid his small offering on her resting-place. After sitting for a while and praying with his son he picked up his luggage and walked slowly to the town centre where they caught a carriage into Stoneham. He had not looked forward to Christmas but he knew he should make an effort for little Matthew.

Matthew had grown very fond of his mother and father-in-law; they doted on their only grandson.

It was a freezing cold day, although there was, as yet, no snow. As he turned from the carriage, the imposing building of Stoneham Cathedral stood before them. He felt drawn toward the huge arched doors. There were several street traders outside the gates, selling their Christmas wares. As he made his way toward the Cathedral gates, several tried to attract his attention but he was not in festive mood.

He felt a hand on his arm as he passed through the milling throng. "Buy some ribbons for the girlie's hair, Sir," He turned to see a gypsy woman tugging at his sleeve.

"Actually it is a little boy, he has no need of ribbons."

He tried to carry on but the woman was persistent, "For your lady love then, for Christmas."

The pleading in her eyes won Matthew over. "I have an abundance of ribbons bought over the years, I do not know how you manage to persuade me," he smiled at the woman, she looked familiar, I think I have bought them from you before, are you here every Christmas?"

"I am often here at this time of year. Thank you, Sir, Merry Christmas to you and the child."

"Merry Christmas."

As usual Matthew had been over generous to the gypsy, probably because she reminded him of Flinton Common, and Tilly. But she had improved his mood. He put the ribbons into his pocket and made his way through the Cathedral gardens, holding little Matthew close to him against the freezing wind.

As always, when he entered the building, he felt at peace. Was it because of his boyhood days at the Vicarage? Should he have gone into the Church after all? It was not too late, he was only thirty-three.

Today the Cathedral was quiet and peaceful, tomorrow, when he came back for the Christmas morning service it would be packed with worshippers.

Today he needed peace.

Chapter Seven

More and more Matthew began to think of home, it had been such a long time since he had seen his parents. They were growing old; they did not even know where he lived. He felt very guilty about that. He loved them both very much. He did not even know if his letters were getting through. His parents could have moved.

One morning, therefore, in early July, he decided to visit home.

Matthew and his son arrived at Winford railway station very late at night. He decided to stay at a hostelry overnight and travel to Flinton the following morning.

As he and his son boarded a carriage to Flinton the following day, Matilda was making her way to Meadow Farm as she did most days. She was determined to run the farm herself while she could. When Sarah was not at school she accompanied her mother, running backward and forward between the two neighbouring farms all day, much as Matilda had done when she was young, taking great delight in the animals.

Matthew and his son alighted from the carriage and made their way to the Vicarage.

The village looked much the same as when he had left twelve years ago.

As they walked down the street, passers-by looked at them curiously, some nodding in greeting. He nodded back wondering if they recognised him, and if so, how long it would be before Tilly knew he had returned.

He stopped, suddenly realizing he was passsing the old schoolhouse. A sad smile played around his mouth as he stared at the familiar building.

He raised his eyes to look at the red roof and the chimney

pots. He felt tears well up in his eyes. He was amazed that the roof of his old school could evoke such emotion, but it was dear to his heart, imprinted on his mind...it could be seen from Uphall farm...where Tilly had lived.

Tllly...was she still in Flinton? If so, would she be happy to see him. He felt his courage fail him, he wondered if he should have come back.

He suddenly realized he was still staring at the school. He could see movement inside. He looked down to where his little son stood patiently waiting, his hand within that of his own.

"This is where I went to school, Matty," he said huskily, "We are in Flinton, where it all began."

Matty looked at his father in puzzlement

"I will tell you all about it one day," he said softly to his son.

Matthew set down his luggage and brushed the tears from his face, then began walking the last few hundred yards to his former home.

He noticed the rhododendrons were much higher and thicker.

He hesitated with his hand on the wicket, staring ahead at the house where he had been abandoned.

He took a deep breath, smiled at his son, and pushed open the gate.

He hesitated again as he approached the front door. Should he ring the bell and wait as a stranger would, or should he go round to the kitchen door...where he had been left under the porch when he was one day old?

He decided to ring the bell in case his parents had moved.

Richard junior answered the door and stared in disbelief. "Matthew? Matthew, how good to see you." He put his arms round his young brother and nephew then ushered them through to the sitting room.

"I cannot believe you are here, you should have let us know, we could have met you. Wait here while I go and prepare Mother and Father for a surprise, they are sitting in the garden."

Richard's head was whirling, Matthew was home. How would

Matilda react? And what about Sarah? Matthew did not know she existed. He had better tell his parents to be careful until Matilda had told Matthew about his children.

"Mother, Father," he said carefully when he reached them, "I want you to prepare yourself for some wonderful news."

His mother stood up excitedly, "Richard are you going to be a father?"

He gently sat her down again. "No, Mother, that is not the surprise, but it is just as good."

"What could be as good as that?"

"Your young son has returned home."

"My young son? You mean Matthew? Matthew has returned?"

"Yes, he and your grandson are waiting indoors for you, but," he checked them, "we must not mention Sarah until Matilda has told him about her. I will go up shortly and inform her that he has returned."

Elizabeth and Richard almost ran indoors, such was their excitement. They did not wait to speak, just took Matthew into their arms and hugged him, then his little boy. Elizabeth was crying with happiness, Richard was having trouble controlling his own emotions.

"Have you brought Rhea?" Elizabeth asked when she could talk, looking around as she did so.

Matthew explained briefly about Rhea's death, and how he had longed lately to see them all again. "It was sixteen months ago, I miss her dreadfully, but I have come to terms with it."

Matthew could not believe that he was in the sitting room of his old home. His parents looked well – older maybe – but well. But what was wrong with his brother? He had seemed overjoyed when he had opened the door to them – surprised maybe – but overjoyed. Now he appeared edgy – quite willing to let everyone else do the talking.

Gradually Matthew relaxed; taking great pleasure in the happiness his return had generated. Little Matty was enjoying all the attention he was getting from his grandparents and uncle.

Two hours flew by as Matthew filled in the details of the

missing years.

Nobody had mentioned Matilda – it was like an unwritten law between them – until Richard dared to broach the subject.

"As you can imagine, much has happened here since you left. Your old brother has even married." He sounded nervous.

"You have married? I cannot believe it. Where is the lucky lady?"

"I would have written to you if I could, you know that." Richard sounded serious; he looked at Matthew as if asking his forgiveness.

"Of course you would," he said puzzled. "Am I going to meet your wife?"

"She is Matilda."

"Matilda?"

"Yes."

He sat down in a fireside chair in a state of shock; it was a few moments before he spoke. "Do you mean *Tilly*?"

"Yes."

A silence pervaded the room, the clock ticked loudly as if urging somebody to speak but no one knew what to say. Eventually Richard said, "I will leave you all to have lunch while I go and inform Matilda that you are home. She will be overjoyed."

Richard left the house to go to the farm. He could have taken his horse but he needed time to decide how he would break the news. He was feeling very insecure. Matthew was young, handsome and swarthy while he himself was fifty-three years old. How could he compete? Do not be foolish, man, he admonished himself, you do not have to compete, Matilda loves you, you are her husband. But still he worried. He was glad Matthew was here, he loved him, he was his brother and it had made his parents so happy, but, he felt frightened, more frightened than he wanted to admit.

He arrived at Uphall Farm first but, upon inquiry, learned that Matilda was still at Meadow.

"Is anything wrong?" asked Louisa.

"Matthew is home. He arrived this morning. We have not

mentioned Sarah. We thought Matilda should tell him about his daughter."

Louisa sat down; she was clearly surprised to hear the unexpected news.

"Shall I keep Sarah here tonight?"

"That is a good idea. I will go and see what Matilda thinks, we will be back shortly."

He found Matilda pouring over the farm accounts in a little office housed by the back door.

"Hello," she said, getting up and kissing Richard, "It is unusual to see you at this time of day, are you checking up on me?" she smiled at him and at the thought, Richard doing anything devious was inconceivable.

"I have some very good news for you."

"It must be good if you have walked up here especially to tell me."

"Matthew is home." Richard felt just the same as he had when he had imparted the news of his brother's marriage. He waited for Matilda's response.

Matilda looked more shocked than surprised. Her face had drained of colour as she sat down heavily onto her chair. She had dreamt of this day, now it was here she was not sure how she felt, relieved, happy, surprised, even frightened, worried that her father might start acting strange again. She was experiencing all these feelings. Above all she was wondering how he would take the news that he was a father. And what of Rhea? How would *she* take the news that her son was not Matthew's first born?

"Where is he?" she asked breathlessly.

"At the Vicarage." Richard did not take his eyes off his wife's face.

"Does he know of Sebastian and Sarah?"

"No, we thought you should tell him, perhaps you should go somewhere private and break it to him gently. Your mother has offered to keep Sarah at the farm overnight, I think that would be a good idea."

"Yes, it is. We will do as you say." Matilda spoke quickly. "I could go for a walk with Matthew after dinner this evening. Are you agreeable to that?"

"Yes, of course." What else could he say?

Although Richard agreed he did not feel easy about the situation. He would have preferred Matilda and Matthew to have stayed at home to have their private talk. He did not like feeling so insecure. He was ashamed of himself. Was he doubting Matilda's love? However he felt, he knew he would have to control his emotions. Matthew had to be told about his children.

"I will come home now." Matilda tidied the desk unnecessarily, wanting to hurry but actually moving very slowly indeed. She did not want Richard to know how keen she was to see Matthew again.

They walked back to Uphall Farm to tell Louisa they would accept her offer. After telling Sarah she could stay with her grandparents as a treat, they walked back to the Vicarage.

"How does he look?"

"Very well apart from a limp, he had an accident at sea you remember."

"I presume Rhea and the child are with him."

"No, Matilda, Rhea died sixteen months ago. I think he has been missing his family since he lost her."

The news stunned Matilda. Matthew was here and he was free to marry her but *she was not free*. Did she wish she were? Her head was spinning, trying to take in all the news of the day and at the same time wondering how to break her own news to her erstwhile lover.

She stood facing him at last. Her heart was thudding in her chest, her legs felt too weak to support her. She was vaguely aware that there were other people in the room but she could not take her eyes from him to look at them.

He was looking at her strangely, a mixture of love and apology in his eyes.

The silence was deafening.

Twelve years...they were not in private...neither knew quite how to behave. Although their hearts were racing and they longed to embrace, they were inhibited by the presence of the family.

Eventually – after what seemed like an eternity, but could only have been seconds – Matilda walked toward him in greeting. They lightly held each other and kissed on the cheek as any other sister and brother-in-law would, but both knew the old magic was still there.

"It is *so* good to see you, Matthew." Matilda's voice was tremulous as she tried to stay in control, but her eyes told him everything.

"You look extremely well, Tilly, it is wonderful to see you again."

They were being polite, saying all the right things but their inner emotions were running riot. Matilda tore her eyes away from his face to pay attention to his son.

"You are such a handsome young man," she said quietly holding him at arms length as if surveying him thoroughly. Then she pulled him to her and gave him a long, warm hug. He stared at her intently, neither overly responding nor seemingly objecting.

There was an awkwardness in the house, though everyone was trying their best to overcome it. Richard came to the rescue. He said to Matthew, "Perhaps when the little chap is in bed you and Matilda should go for a long walk to catch up on all your news."

Matthew looked at his brother astounded, "You would not mind?"

"On the contrary, I think it a good idea."

And so it was that Matilda and Matthew found themselves alone at last as they closed the front door behind them. Matilda was surprised to see that Matthew carried a bag with him.

They automatically turned left at the wicket and then right into Hill Road. They did not speak until they had done so. It was as if they would be overheard. Having turned the corner they stopped and turned toward one another.

"Oh, Matthew, it has been unbearable not knowing where you were, never do that to me again, promise me now." There was such urgency and pleading in her voice that he felt ashamed.

"It was not what I wanted, I was terrified of causing your father harm and, in so doing, hurting you. Is he well, Tilly?"

"Yes, completely recovered. He has been for years but he would never have allowed our marriage."

"This is not the way we planned it, is it? I do not know what to call you. I want to say 'Darling' but you are my brother's wife. Oh, Tilly, how I have longed to talk to you."

"I was very sorry to hear of your wife's death." Matthew knew that she was sincere.

They walked on for a while in silence then, "You would have liked Rhea, I know you would."

Again they continued in silence until Matilda said. "Do you think I could hold your arm?"

"Dear Tilly," he smiled sadly down at her. "If Richard does not mind us taking a walk together I am sure he will not mind you taking my arm."

Richard had left the Vicarage shortly after his wife and brother. He was a safe distance behind them, anxious not to be seen. He had tried not to follow them, he did not like doing so, but he could not help himself. He was sure they were walking too close together, he could not make out if they were holding hands – the evening sun was playing cruel tricks with his eyesight. If he was seen he would say he was calling on Louisa and Daniel, perhaps he should do that anyway, he told himself. They could not be holding hands, it was too intimate a gesture, but they were very close, he was sure of it. This is agony, he thought, pure agony, why do I subject myself to it? Even so, he walked on.

Matilda and Matthew turned right into Poacher's Way as they headed for Clancy's Wood.

They are going to Clancy's, observed Richard, their old haunt. What had he become, following his wife in such a fashion? But still he did not turn back.

"Do you still come here regularly?" Matthew inquired of Matilda as they entered the wood.

"Nowhere near as often as I used to. But it is still my favourite place."

It was very strange, but as they entered Clancy's house the erstwhile lovers were transported back in time. The polite conversation gave way to heartrending confessions of unhappiness and heartbreak of their early years apart.

"I do not know how I bore it, Tilly. I had constant pain in my chest, I felt I had deserted you."

"I have something to tell you, Matthew. It is the reason Richard suggested we take a walk."

He looked at her serious face, she was biting her bottom lip, struggling to find the right words. At last she said carefully, "You were not to know, but you left me with child."

He stared at her, shocked, he put his hand to his head as if his neck was too weak to support it with this new knowledge. "Tilly I…I am sorry, what have I done to you? I should have thought – checked – I have ruined your reputation. *Oh God what have I done?*"

He took hold of her and held her close, trying, by this action, to erase his wrongdoing from her life. She dissolved into tears at last against his strong body, crying for all the times she had needed him and could not have him. She sobbed until she ached, releasing at last all the pent up emotion of twelve years.

As her tears subsided she began telling of her pregnancy, her time with Laura and Jack, and the birth of their twins. At this point she stopped and looked at him, plainly distressed, "Our little boy died when he was six months old, Matthew. I needed you so much and did not know where to look for you. I have needed to tell you all this for twelve years.

Matthew stared at her, the pain in his face was clearly visible. He could not come to terms with the trouble and problems he had caused her, or the knowledge he had children he had never seen – one whom he would never see.

They sat holding on to one another looking deep into each

others faces, the magnitude of the events of twelve years, rendering them speechless.

As the night wore on they brought each other up to date with their respective lives. Matthew told Matilda of his love for, and his life with, Rhea. She told him how she came to rely on, and grow to love, Richard. The only thing Matthew did not tell her was his fears that they shared the same father. He could not cause her further pain. Especially now they had a child.

"Tomorrow I shall introduce you to your daughter and show you where Sebastian is buried, but tonight I can show you their photographs. She took off the locket she was wearing and handed it to Matthew. It was growing dark as he looked, for the first time, on his children. There were tears in his eyes and his face was contorted with the effort of keeping his composure, as he handed the locket back.

Matilda explained that Sarah did not know who her father was. "She accepts Richard as her father now, I will explain one day but for now it might be better if she knows you as Uncle Matthew, at least until she is a little older. Could you accept that?"

He assured her he could, for now anyway.

Suddenly he remembered the bag he had brought with him. He handed it to Matilda.

"What is in here?" she asked puzzled.

"From the time I left, until I married Rhea, I gave you a present each birthday and Christmas. Some of them are just interesting stones from an exotic beach or a shell that you would not find in England; for sometimes I had no money," he explained. "There are ribbons and scarves and a shawl from Africa. They are all labelled with each occasion and where they came from. And one day I *will* tell you all the stories of my travelling."

She smiled at him, overcome by his thoughtfulness. "Thank you so much, Matthew. It is nice to know you were thinking of me while you were away. Do you still play our Cornelian game?" She was overcome with emotion at being given the presents, and knew she would cry unless she changed the subject.

"I know it sounds childish but yes, I do. It is not a game anymore, it is a way of life and always will be."

"It is the same with me, so long as I have one Cornelian in my happy box, I have hope."

It was nearly dark when they left Clancy's Wood.

As they stepped out into open ground Richard concealed himself behind a tree... He had been watching for nearly three hours.

"Did you see something move over there?" asked Matilda, "I thought it was a man."

"I cannot see anything now, do you want me to investigate?"

"No, no, it does not matter, I expect it is somebody out for a walk."

When they returned home they were surprised to find Richard was out.

"Do you know where he has gone?" inquired Matilda.

"I assumed it was Church business, dear, he has been gone since just after you left."

Matilda thought of the man she had seen. Could it have been Richard? Was he following them? What an absurd thought, why would he do that? But the possibility lingered with her just the same.

The Johnson family talked late, well into the early hours of the next morning. There was so much to discuss, consciences to clear, misunderstandings to clarify. Richard had returned home about an hour after Matilda and Matthew. He had called to see Louisa and Daniel, he said.

Uphall Farm was not far from Clancy's Wood, thought Matilda. Why did it unnerve her to think of Richard watching her? No, it could not have been him; it was alien to his nature.

Matilda and Matthew decided to go to Winford the following day so that Matthew could get to know his daughter. The village was already rife with gossip about Matthew's return. They needed to be somewhere public but away from prying eyes. Winford was a comfortable distance. Matilda planned to collect her daughter from Uphall Farm and walk down to Flintknapper Corner where Matthew would meet them with the pony and trap. By cutting through Fletcher's Loke and Sycamore Lane they would be out on the Winford Road well away from the village. But first she wanted to take him to Sebastian's grave.

"We have bought a family plot," Matilda explained as Matthew stared at the headstone of the tiny grave. "I want to be buried here with him."

"I never saw him, I was not aware he existed. How can that be?" There were tears in his eyes. "You would think I would have known. But then maybe I did in a way."

He remembered how he had often felt happy or very sad for no apparent reason. There had been times when he had felt weighted down with grief, he had not known why. It suddenly dawned on him that only once had he transferred two Cornelians, to his box, together; only once in twelve years. He would look at his diary when he returned to Thimblethorpe but he was almost certain that he would find that it was the night of his children's birth. He ran his fingers over the lettering of Sebastian's memorial stone as if he were caressing his son's face.

"Thank you for putting my name on here, Tilly, I am glad it is here for all the world to see."

"I knew it would be important to you in view of your own situation. It is strange, I always vowed that my children would know who their parents were but I have one who does not know and one lying here, too young to have been told before his death."

"We must tell Sarah, we should not wait."

A decision had been made.

"Where are we going?" Sarah asked when Matilda collected her.

"We are going to Winford so that you can get to know your Uncle Matthew and your cousin Matthew."

"Why can't I meet them at the Vicarage?"

"You could, but it will be more exciting if we go to Winford, it is a lovely day. You can play with little Matthew on the sands."

"But he is only three, I am eleven."

"He has lost his mother, dear, we must be especially nice to him."

"Do you think I will like Uncle Matthew?"

"I am sure you will, he is very much like your father, but younger."

"Why have I not met him before?"

"Because he went to sea for many years, but now he is back so we will see more of him."

The pony and trap was waiting at the corner. Matthew watched in awe as Matilda and Sarah approached. They were so alike yet totally different. Sarah was almost as tall as her mother but she had black hair and a dark complexion whereas Matilda was pale with golden hair. Sarah had a slightly heavier build but was not unfeminine. Today she wore a blue frock and straw hat. She reminded Matthew of Tilly, the day they had gone to Winford beach; except that Tilly had worn green.

He could not believe that this lovely child was his daughter.

He jumped down from the trap.

"Sarah, this is your Uncle Matthew and Cousin Matthew and this," Matilda said proudly, gently pushing Sarah ahead of her, "is Sarah."

Matthew took Sarah's hand and kissed her on the cheek. "I am very pleased to meet you," he said quietly. Again he was having trouble keeping his emotions in check. "And this Sarah, is your," he hesitated here, he had been about to say 'your brother Matthew' but he corrected himself just in time and said "your cousin Matthew. His grandparents call him Matty, it would probably be less confusing if we did likewise." He hugged young Matty and smiled at Sarah.

She liked him already. "Well," he continued, "shall we make for the seaside before it gets dark?" The children laughed at his joke although it was questionable that Matty understood it.

"Oh, Sarah before we forget, we have a present for you, don't we, Matty?" The little boy nodded his head as Matthew handed Sarah a small parcel.

She opened it at once. "Ribbons," she cried, "lots of ribbons for my hair, look, Mother, all different colours."

Matthew smiled, he was glad he had stopped to buy them from the gypsy woman.

The journey to Winford was made in high spirits with Matthew often breaking out into song. The last song he sang, as they approached the town, was 'their' song. He sang it with feeling and Matilda knew he was singing it for her. It was the first time she had heard the tune that Matthew had composed for their poem – she liked it, she would be able to sing it herself now.

On arrival at Winford the family group – for that is what they were- lunched at the Royal Hotel. Again it was reminiscent of their past, making the two adults lapse into silence more than once. They were not, however, allowed to remain silent for long, with two such happy children in their midst. Little Matty was such an endearing child that Matilda had loved him on sight. How could she *not* love Matthew's child? He was adorable.

After a walk along the pier the family headed for the sands which were, today, being enjoyed by a considerable number of holidaymakers.

The children had fun paddling in the sea, where Sarah discovered that she *did* like playing with a three-year-old after all. She was acting quite the little mother.

This is how I always imagined it, thought Matilda, as she sat with Matthew watching the children, how did it all go wrong? Perhaps it had just taken a different route. She was not unhappy with Richard, in fact she was very contented, it was a different sort of love, difficult to explain. She knew she would be able to rely on Richard until they were parted by death. The only surprises would be planned, pleasant ones – he liked to plan surprises for her. And Matthew had been happy with Rhea, he had told her so, they had produced a delightful child. Matty would not be Matty if he had belonged to her. He was Rhea's child, she reminded herself. The more she dwelt on the subject the more sure she became that she would have liked Rhea. Strange how she had felt jealous of her when she had heard of Matty's birth.

"I was sad to hear of old Walter's death," Matthew broke into her thoughts. "I had hoped to see him again when I came home."

Being on the beach had brought to Matthew's mind Old Walter and the Cornelians. "I am glad I called on him before I went away," he continued, "I thanked him for everything then, teaching me to play the violin and carpentry. Walter had nearly as much influence on my childhood as my father."

"Have you thought of returning here to live?" She hardly dared breathe while she waited for his answer.

"I think of little else nowadays, I thought myself settled in Thimblethorpe, it is a charming town, I felt at home there by the sea. Rather like Winford pushed South. And Stoneham is a lovely city, especially the Cathedral and gardens; I love strolling in the grounds. I visit quite often so that Matty can stay in touch with his grandparents. But it is people that matter and Thimblethorpe is not the same without Rhea. Having said that I would probably feel sad if I left. I have friends and family there now, as well as here. Life is not easy is it, Tilly? I feel dreadful that I deserted you when you were with child, but if I had not left, I would not have met Rhea and had Matty. I cannot imagine life without the little chap."

"I understand, he won my heart in minutes."

"I left because of your father, it is strange how he has had such an impact on my life. I hardly dare say this, darl... Tilly," he corrected himself quickly, "I do not know if I could bear living close to you knowing I can never have you. Oh, Tilly..." He held his head in his hands. A moment ago he had felt so buoyant sitting with her watching his children play, but now he was despairing again. How could he still feel so attracted to her when she was probably his sister? How would she feel if he told her his fears? How would Sarah feel if she ever found out? Was he unnatural to feel as he did? *'Your marriage would be unlawful'* he heard his father saying again. Oh, God, what had he done? How did Daniel look on Sarah? But she is so lovely, how can she be the product of an incestuous union? He must stop thinking about it, he would go mad. Is that what had happened to Daniel? Had he gone slightly mad worrying about what might happen if he and Tilly remained sweethearts? How could he ever face Daniel after what he had done, if he had given his sister a child? He did not see how he could come back to live here.

"Matthew…"

"Yes."

"No it is nothing. Yes, it is something I keep catching a fleeting expression that reminds me of *someone*. I noticed it when you were home twelve years ago, I keep seeing it again but I cannot quite think what it is or of whom it reminds me. It is so transient. I wish I could place it. It could tell us who one of your parents are."

Matthew began to panic; she was seeing her father in him. How long would it be before she began having her own suspicions?

"Perhaps you are seeing expressions I had as a boy."

"I thought that myself at first, but now I am not so sure."

"Perhaps the sun is addling our brains." He tried to make light of the situation.

"It is certainly addling yours if you have not noticed we are both wearing hats!" They laughed and caught each other's eyes. Their gazes held in mutual admiration. They were reluctant to look away.

"When will you tell Sarah that I am her father?"

"I will wait for the right moment, it will be easier now that she has met you. I can tell she likes you very much."

Matthew did not transfer any Cornelians that night – although he was overjoyed at having met his daughter he had also learned the details of his son's death.

Matilda however did put a stone into her happy box – Matthew had come home at last.

Chapter Eight

"You like Uncle Matthew don't you Sarah?" Matilda was walking by the mill stream with her daughter. She was no longer nervous in the area since discovering who had attacked her.

"He is nice, Mother, can we go out with him and Matty again?"

"Maybe before he goes home, but there is something I want to talk to you about, now."

"Have I done anything wrong?"

"No, why do you ask?"

"You look so serious."

"I want to tell you about your father, your *real* father. As you know, Richard is your stepfather."

Matilda hesitated, wondering how to phrase her next words, she glanced at her daughter who was staring at the ground. "Are you not curious about your real father, wouldn't you like to know his name?"

"I know who he is, Mother," Sarah looked at her mother as she said this but then looked quickly away again, worried what her reaction might be.

"*You know who your father is?*"

"Yes, I am sorry if I should not, Mother."

"How did you find out?"

"I asked Grandma Rose."

"You asked Grandma who your father is?"

"No, I asked Grandma who Matthew was?"

"I am a little confused, dear, why did you do that?"

"It was Sebastian's grave. I always read it when we go there. It says, 'Beloved son of Matilda and Matthew – Twin brother of Sarah Matilda,' you are always so sad and quiet when we visit, so, I asked Grandma Rose. I knew we had the same mother and father. If Sebastian's father is Matthew, then so is mine."

Matilda was dumbfounded, why had she not thought about

the grave, how thoughtless she had been, she should have realized that Sarah would read it, but it had never entered her head. How it must have troubled her young daughter and she had not felt able to ask her own mother about it. She looked at her little girl who appeared apprehensive.

"I am very sorry, Sarah, I feel I have let you down. You are quite right, I am always so preoccupied with thoughts of my little son when I go to the churchyard, that I have neglected your feelings." She put her arm around her daughter. "Please forgive me."

They walked on in silence for some time before Matilda asked, "What did Grandma Rose tell you?"

"I asked who Matthew was and she asked me how I knew of him. I told her that I had seen his name on Sebastian's grave so I knew he was our father. She said that Matthew is Father's brother. She told me that it is a private family matter and that you would explain everything to me when I am older."

"I *will* explain everything when I feel you are old enough to understand. Until then we will continue as we are. I am glad you know that Matthew is your *real* father but Richard loves you very much and would like you to continue calling him 'Father'. That is alright isn't it?"

"Yes." The child smiled at her mother, glad that the awkward conversation had come to an end. Now she would not feel guilty about her talk with Grandma Rose.

She was however very curious about why Matthew was her real father, quite what did 'real father' mean? According to her Grandma Rose, he was her 'biological' father. She had never heard of anyone else having a biological father. Everyone she knew had either a father or a stepfather. It was most confusing and obviously something that one did not talk about in polite company. Even so she was very glad that she was Uncle Matthew's daughter – he was nice, very nice. She hoped he and little Matty would stay in Flinton.

But Matthew decided it might be unwise to stay permanently.

"Why can't you stay?" asked Elizabeth when he informed her of his intentions.

"I think it best if I do not."

"I am always being fobbed off with inadequate answers, I see no reason why you should not stay. Carpenters are always in demand. You and Matilda have gone your separate ways, surely no-one can object to you staying." Her voice began to break as she continued, "Your father and I are getting older, Matthew, we have seen so little of you and we will miss little Matty."

Matthew put his arms around his mother, he did not like to see her so distressed, she had been good to him, she loved him as her own, and he did want to come home. He had missed so much of his daughter growing up. His mother was right. If he wanted to come back then he should – Daniel Canham, however, might object.

"I will give it some thought, Mother, you know I would love to stay with you but I have a house and family in Thimblethorpe now. But, as I said, I will think seriously about it. In the meantime we can write to each other and you could visit me."

Elizabeth brightened up a bit at his promise. "Thank you, dear, you have given me some hope, I wish I knew the reason for all the unpleasantness."

"You and me both, Mother, you and me both," he replied dejectedly.

That evening in the garden Matilda told Matthew of her conversation with Sarah. He was as surprised as she had been but was very glad that she had known who he was when they had gone to the beach.

"Will you consider coming home, Matthew? It would make us all very happy. We have worried about you for twelve years."

"I have promised Mother I will give it serious thought. If I decide to return here to live, how do you think you father would feel about it?"

"I do not think my father should influence your decision at all. You went away in the first place because of him. You should now consider your own feelings and those of *your* family. We have all experienced unhappiness in our quest to keep Father healthy. He must learn that he cannot control us forever."

"Since I spoke to Mother earlier today I have been toying with the idea of coming back, maybe to Illingworth or Winford but Margaret and Henry would miss us, we are their only family."

"You are right, it does need thought, they love you too. We have been a little selfish. If you do not come back to live perhaps you could visit more often, especially at Christmas?"

Matthew felt torn between Thimblethorpe and Flinton. It would not have been such a difficult decision if it were just himself. He felt mean at the thought of taking Matty away from Margaret and Henry. He was their only family now. Matilda was right about Daniel though, everyone had considered his health, now it was time to consider other people – his mother and father, his children and Tilly and Richard. Perhaps he could persuade Margaret and Henry to move north as well. That was not likely, he reasoned. Was there a way of keeping everyone happy?

"Please agree, Daniel," Louisa implored, "the past cannot be changed. You know very well that Matthew would have married Matilda, had you let him. You must take some of the blame yourself. We must make a gesture to assure all the family that we hold no grudges."

"You are right, as usual. Yes, alright, we will hold a dinner party for the two families. An early evening one so that the children can eat with us before their bedtime."

Daniel smiled lovingly at his wife. She would enjoy getting the families together. He knew she was eager to see Matthew again, she was very fond of him. She was also looking forward to meeting young Matty. Sarah had told them all about him.

Young Matty – his grandchild – it was important that he should meet him. He would make an effort to get to know the child. Would that please Louisa or make her suspicious? He must try to stop analysing everything. No one knew, or suspected, he was Matthew's father except Richard, whom he had told in confidence. As Louisa had reminded him, the past could not be changed. He must continue to make the most of the present and the future.

It was strange, he mused, how he had come to accept Sarah

as a normal child – she *was* a normal child, it had been in his own head that she might not be. He must not think about that, it was dwelling on *that* subject that made him feel ill, as if he might go mad. Matilda, Louisa and especially Sarah must never find out he was Matthew's father, the idea of them discovering his secret had been bad enough before, but now that Matilda and Matthew had had a child, well, they would all be horrified. He must now endeavour to act normally in Matthew's company so that, in his family's eyes at least, the past could be laid to rest, his guilt weighed heavily enough on his conscience as it was. He would go along with the dinner party on Saturday evening, he might even enjoy it, it would be good to see his son again, especially as he did not now have to worry about him marrying his daughter.

Nobody was more surprised to hear about the invitation than Matthew. It must be in his own honour, he reasoned, for the rest of them could have a dinner party when he had left. It would be nice to see Louisa and the farm again. He felt at home there. It would be true to say that he also liked Daniel. He did not, however, admire him for deceiving them all, if indeed he had, and he could see no other logical explanation for him refusing to let his daughter marry him. What he could not understand was that neither his mother, nor Matilda, nor Louisa had ever suspected Daniel of being his father. But then, he himself had not thought about it until his father had mentioned that it would be 'unlawful' for him to marry Tilly. Perhaps, he mused, they had thought about it but had been frightened to voice it. After all it was a very controversial subject.

At this point a more worrying thought entered his head. If Matilda saw him, as a grown man, in the company of her father, would she realize who she was being reminded of in those fleeting expressions? As usual his buoyant mood gave way to despair as the old worries played havoc with his emotions. Would this nightmare never end? If only he could discover who his biological parents were, but that was becoming more and more unlikely, he was now thirty-three, even if Daniel were not his father, one or both of them could be dead. He was very pleased that Sarah knew who *her* father was.

He decided to have a talk with his brother on the subject.

"So you see, Richard how important this matter is, apart from it haunting me, it could have tragic consequences for Sarah if she found out her parents were brother and sister."

Matthew had asked Richard to take an evening stroll with him in order to enlist his help. He continued, "You are a vicar, people confide in you. Some day someone may tell you something relating to my birth, if anyone *does* will you please tell me?"

"You know I cannot break a confidence."

"But I am your brother, surely it would be understandable for you to tell me. The situation is unbearable for me. It has had a profound effect on my life already. Who knows how else it will effect me, Sarah or Matty."

"I understand how difficult it is for you, I will do my best to help you discover who your parents are and if anybody confides in me I will ask them if I can tell you, I will impress upon them how important it is to you. I know you have good argument to suggest that Daniel is your father – sometimes you almost convince me – but I *knew* Daniel and Louisa at the time of their wedding. I cannot imagine that he would have been involved with anybody else and do not forget, you were born exactly nine months after they married. It is as much a mystery to me as it is to you."

"I am sorry to keep going on about the same old subject. I know you and Tilly are very happy together so you would not have wanted me to marry her anyway but, I think of how difficult it must have been for her after I left, I feel so guilty about it. But then I have to balance all that with Matty. He is very special to me. I could not be without him. Had I married Tilly – I would not have had Matty. I realize now I had a charmed existence as a boy. I have since found out that life is transient, fragile and something over which one has little control."

"We are becoming maudlin, Matthew, perhaps we should wend our way homeward."

Chapter Nine

The dinner party was a significant event for most of the assemblage. Of the nine people sitting round the dining table, only little Matty was oblivious to the undercurrent of emotions playing havoc with the digestive systems of the diners.

Matty was enjoying all the attention he was getting, especially from Daniel and Louisa. He was far too young, of course, to realize he was playing an important role at this occasion. It is easy to turn to a child in an embarrassing situation, or to relieve an awkward silence.

Daniel was secretly enjoying himself whilst being aware that most of the diners were of the opinion that he was suffering – as usual he felt a fraud. He had at his table his wife whom he adored; his eldest daughter, whom he loved beyond question; then there was his best friend Richard who, like a knight in shining armour, had come to his rescue by marrying Matilda; his beloved granddaughter Sarah, who in some strange way he felt responsible for – he must make sure she was happy to compensate for her incestuous conception. Also at his table tonight were his good friends Elizabeth and Richard – Richard who shared his secret and had helped to separate the erstwhile lovers. And then there was Matty, his newly acquired grandson, who was the image of his father, sturdy, of strong stock – a handsome little chap. And last but not least was this son of his, whom he accepted privately with pride, and rejected publicly with shame. Matthew was certainly a son to be proud of. He was well mannered, manly, good-looking but most of all he was honourable – far more honourable than he himself was. He had gone away and stayed away, giving up the woman he loved to protect the health of her father. Yes, he was certainly honourable. And so Daniel surveyed his guests with love and pride, his dinner table tonight presented a scene he never thought he would see.

Louisa was also happy. She felt this was the final hurdle in her battle to achieve a happy and united family. Matthew, as Sarah's father, was part of her family no matter how Daniel felt about him and if tonight went well it could set a precedent for the future – she must tread carefully but she would succeed, of that she was determined. She was very fond of Matthew. It was her husband's fault that he had been treated so unfairly and now here he was, a young widower with a child to raise alone. He had not deserved what fate had handed out to him. He deserved to be happy. At least she could make sure he had a family circle to return to whenever he wished.

Sarah was feeling very grown up being allowed to dine with the adults. She had taken charge of Matty, insisting he sat near her, he was her little brother, a fact not publicly acknowledged but she knew it to be true and she knew that everyone at the table was aware of it – everyone except Matty himself. One day she would get to the bottom of her strange family history but for now she would enjoy having all her parents and grandparents and her little brother together with her. She particularly liked her father Matthew – as she thought of him – sitting opposite her. He winked at her and made her blush on several occasions during the meal, as if they were sharing a secret, and maybe they were…

Elizabeth was happy because she felt her youngest son had at last been accepted back into the bosom of his family. Her husband and Daniel had treated him harshly for no obvious reason. He had fallen in love at a very young age, as far as she could see that was his only crime. If tonight went well, Matthew would feel able to return at any time, maybe permanently, but especially for holidays and Christmases.

The retired Vicar of Flinton was in an exceptionally good mood because all his loved ones looked happy – particularly his wife. He had not felt at ease at being unable to tell Elizabeth the real reason for keeping Matthew and Matilda apart. She must think him very harsh and he was not. He wished Daniel had not confided in him. He wished he had remained in ignorance of the situation, especially where young Sarah was concerned. She must never know the circumstances of her birth; it would destroy her. She was a lovely natured child; a granddaughter to be proud of; dark and strong, like her father.

Richard spent most of the meal wondering what impact Matthew's return would have on his marriage. Having seen him again, would Matilda realize she was still in love with him? Would she compare his dark, handsome physique to his own – he had to admit it – rather flaccid one? Would she regret marrying him? He could not bear to lose her, she was his life, he had waited so long for her knowing she would choose Matthew if she could. But she could not and he had won his prize at last, his beautiful, young, vibrant Matilda. But what had transpired in the woods? He had waited for nearly three hours. Matilda would not be unfaithful to him, would she? The answer to that was beyond his comprehension. There was still so much mystery surrounding his wife's relationship with his brother. They were uncannily in tune with each other and he felt there were areas of their friendship that she would never divulge to another living soul. Even so he knew she loved him. She had married him and he was sure it was not out of pity. She had truly grown to love him and depend on him. He liked that, but still the doubts niggled away. She loved him, but did she love Matthew more? It might have helped allay his fears if they had a child. She was a young fertile woman. He supposed it was his fault she had not conceived. He looked across at his wife's lovely face and smiled but, silently, he was praying that she would still love him when Matthew went home...

Matilda began her meal with trepidation, frightened that something would spoil this happy occasion for her. Her father looked calm enough but he had the habit of bubbling up and exploding for little or no reason, not so much recently, but she knew he was capable of it. The strange thing was she knew he liked Matthew, he always had. She watched as her father's eyes repeatedly sought out her ex-lover. Ex-lover – what an unusual term to use to describe Matthew – he was her everything: friend, ex-beau, confidant *and* erstwhile lover. Her father would stare at Matthew for an unusual length of time as if he were mesmerised. She remembered how Matthew had described it when he was a boy, '*searching my face as if looking for something.*' It was true, she realized, and the light was very good on this early summer evening. Why did he do that? He looked at Sarah in much the same way sometimes. And now, she noticed he was even searching Matty's face. Perhaps he looked at everyone like that. She thought about it and decided it was not true. Now what did Matthew, Sarah and Matty have in common? They were all related; that was all she could think of. She remembered something else Matthew had said a long time ago – that maybe her father knew who his parents were – that maybe they were undesirables. Perhaps he was looking to see if Matthew or his children resembled these 'undesirable' parents.

She looked around the table, her husband kept smiling at her, quietly reassuring her as he often did. That was one of the things she loved most about Richard. He cared about her so deeply but in a very quiet way. She knew he would never hurt her. She noticed too that Matthew was enjoying his daughter's company, he winked at her now and again; communicating secretly in a way that made her daughter blush. Matilda smiled at the sight of it all. Her family were all together at last. How she had dreamed of this night. Her gaze caught Matthew's and she knew he was reading her thoughts just as she was reading his. Their eyes held as if magnetic forces were at work, transporting messages back and forth between them, and they were helpless – unable to look away until all the messages had been sent and absorbed. She wondered if anybody had noticed the messages being sent but the easy conversation had flowed on regardless. Her insides and legs felt like jelly, nobody had made her feel that way except Matthew. The effect he had on her was way out of her control, it always had been. It probably always would be.

She noticed how happy Elizabeth and Richard were. Nobody could ask for better parents-in-law, she loved them almost as much as she did her own parents.

Matilda smiled at her mother. She had taken a gamble tonight but it had paid off. She could be proud of herself...

Matthew's feelings were very mixed. He had been away for so long it had taken a while to relax. Daniel had shaken his hand quite warmly and said it was good to see him. Louisa had hugged him as usual. Everyone seemed happy, except maybe, Richard. Did he think he was a threat to his marriage? No, Richard would not fear him. He looked at Matilda who was watching her father. She seemed content but he also knew she was still in love with him. Rightly or wrongly the attraction would be between them forever, they would have to be careful, work hard at keeping it under control. No one was mentioning the past. Unwritten laws decreed that conversation tonight would be unprovokingly diplomatic.

His glance travelled round the dining table. Daniel's behaviour was exemplary; he was even paying attention to Matty. Was that under orders from Louisa or did he think he might not see his grandson for some time? Only Daniel could answer that one and Daniel, he knew, would not. Next he observed Louisa, he liked her, always had, she was doing her utmost to make the evening a success and, amazingly, she was succeeding. His parents were seated on either side of he himself. He had spent the last three days in their company, he knew they were pleased he was being accepted back into the extended family – Richard marrying Matilda had joined the two families together – that old wounds were beginning to heal. Then there was his little son, being fussed over by everyone, especially Sarah, and thoroughly enjoying himself. That just left Tilly and Sarah. He was so proud of Sarah, she was like a female version of himself to look at, but with Matilda's femininity, she was going to be a strong, dark beauty in a few years time. He hoped he would always be able to put his children's happiness before his own. He wanted his children to love and respect him, not pussyfoot around him, as Daniel's tended to do.

Last, but not least, was Tilly, his school friend, confidante, sweetheart, lover and now, surprisingly, his sister-in-law. What was going on in that beautiful head of hers as she surveyed her family circle? He knew what was going on when she looked at him; he knew she was with him, in the clearing, in Clancy's

Wood. Oh, how he loved her, their love had withstood everything, but he had lost her – to his brother, to dear Richard whom he loved as well. If he had to lose her, it was fortunate he had lost her to someone he loved, it was more bearable, and this way he would always be able to keep in touch without arousing anyone's suspicions. As far as everyone else was concerned they were now related by marriage, the passion of their youth was quelled; it was all in the past. But their own minds and hearts knew different.

The dinner party had been a great success. Daniel had his arm draped lightly around Louisa's shoulders as they said goodbye to their guests then returned indoors and closed their front door.

"I think that went very well, Daniel. Matty is delightful isn't he?"

"He is certainly a little charmer, just like his father at the same age."

"Can you remember Matthew clearly at that age?"

"Yes. I suppose I saw him a bit more often than you did – when I called at the Vicarage."

"It is so sad that he has no mother."

"Yes indeed it is."

Daniel had hoped that Matilda and Matthew would both find happiness. He had been pleased when Matthew married Rhea, even more so when Matilda married Richard. His biggest fear now was that Matilda would be a young widow…before Matthew found a new bride…

That night two Cornelians were transferred into 'happy boxes' as two young people looked out from different, Vicarage bedroom windows in the direction of Clancy's Wood.

Chapter Ten

Matthew decided to go home on the Tuesday morning. He was finding it difficult living in the same house as Matilda and Richard. He would have departed on the Monday – but for a request from Sarah that they spend another day at the beach. This time however there was a difference – Richard accompanied them.

As the children frolicked on the sands again, the three intricately related adults sat and talked.

"You *will* come home for Christmas won't you, Matthew?" Matilda asked as if her life depended on his answer.

"I will do my best. As I said before I will feel mean leaving Margaret and Henry on their own at Christmas."

"I have a great idea, why didn't I think of it before? If you could persuade them to come with you, you could all stay at Meadow Farm; it is still empty. And if you returned permanently you could manage it for me. Margaret and Henry could spend months at a time in the countryside with their grandson." Matilda was showing signs of her youthful exuberance as she voiced her idea.

"That might be the solution." Matthew was toying with the notion quite seriously. "For Christmas at least. I will let you know what they say. Thank you, Tilly."

Richard was not quite as keen although he said nothing. Christmas was not so bad, he would like to see his brother again soon, he loved him dearly, but – and he hated to admit it – he was jealous of him, of his youth, his looks, but most especially, his hold over Matilda. In some ways he felt quite guilty at his jealous thoughts. He was insulting his wife by assuming she could be unfaithful to him but, as always, he remembered the unusual bond between the two…and the three hours he waited by Clancy's Wood.

Maybe if he told her about Matthew's fears, if he planted the notion in her head that she could be his sister...? No, he could not hurt her, or Sarah. They would not thank him, he would rather lose them than hurt them. Sexual jealousy is a terrible thing, it makes one think in ways one never would otherwise. All he wanted for his wife, his brother and his step-daughter was their happiness, and if that was at the expense of his own, well, so be it.

The day at the beach was tinged with a little sadness as they all came to terms with Matthew's and Matty's leaving the next day. Christmas was still so far away.

Matthew and Matty said their goodbyes to Elizabeth and Richard at the Vicarage but Richard, Matilda and Sarah went to Winford railway station to see them off. It was emotional; Sarah did not want them to go and saw no reason why they should. Her obvious distress upset Matthew. She was his child too, he knew he must consider her feelings when making his future plans.

The two men shook hands warmly but Matthew hugged his daughter and Matilda. She felt very frightened, as if she might not see him for another twelve years but she had his address now, she could write, she could even visit!

As she watched him walk to the train she saw it again, something about his walk that she had noticed on this same platform when he came home from theological college. Of whom did he remind her? She wished she could think. It would be such good news for Matthew. One day she would, she was sure. It was just a matter of time.

"Who would like to have lunch and a look around the shops?" asked Richard a little too brightly. But he got a result. Both Sarah and Matilda took him up on his offer.

By the time they returned home their spirits were a little better – maybe because they both had a new frock! They found Elizabeth already making plans to visit Thimblethorpe.

"I think we will go in about eight weeks time, before it gets too cold."

"You plan to take me along as well then," said Richard dryly from his armchair. "Am I not a bit old to go gallivanting?"

"Nonsense you are just a spring chicken."

"I do not call eighty-two anything but old," he grumbled good-naturedly, "and I am not sure you should go either, you are only four years younger."

Matilda left the elderly couple to their discussion. She did not think either of them should go but they would probably do as they pleased regardless of her advice. They were both strong willed.

The chimney corner at the Village Maid was once again buzzing with gossip.

Old Amos's place on the double settle was usually occupied these days by his grandson Amos, sometimes accompanied by his father Diggory.

Old Shuffley's chair had stood empty for a full year – like a monument to his memory – before anybody used it. There was talk of removing it altogether but nobody liked the idea. In the end it was agreed that Fergus should use the chair because his father had made it. Fergus was now sixty-two and getting to the stage where he appreciated a comfortable chair of an evening.

Reuben Healy, another old timer, was now sixty-eight. Darcy had reached sixty-five – the same as Zackery – so the senior member of the group was Fingal Pardoe, retired stone mason, at seventy-three with Eli and Randolph not far behind.

"I tell you he stayed at the Vicarage," said Darcy emphatically, "along with his brother."

"Thass a rummin that is," said Fingal, "when you think about it. The Vicar must've found it awkward, knowin' his brother is the father of his wife's daughter."

"I'm glad you said that at the beginnin' of the evenin', Fingal, I don't think you'd have managed it at the end," joked Darcy.

"Walter was right about who the twins belonged to, it's a shame he didn't live to find out who young Matthew's real parents are," said Fingal sadly, thinking of his friend.

"*We* still don't know, don't suppose we ever will. Thass still the biggest unsolved mystery of the village. Thirty-three years ago that was, and we're still no further forward."

"Somebody will confess on their death bed, just like Walter predicted," said Darcy, "I don't think I'll live to see the day though."

"You'll see us all out, Darcy, they say the good go first you know."

"Well that say a lot for us don't it? We're a sorry old bunch of sinners then," said Eli joining the conversation, "but then my wife's bin tellin' me that for years."

"I've never known a man so henpecked as you, Eli, perhaps thass because you ruffle your good lady's feathers, you should try a bit of charm, that work a treat on most women."

"If I tried charm she'd accuse me of bein' up to somethin', you don't realize how carefully I have to tread."

"Talkin' of treadin' carefully, there's a funny old smell in here tonight," said Darcy. "Did you clean your boots, young Amos, afore you came out?"

"Don't you start on me and my pigs agin, my grandfather put up with enough of that, poor old grandfather, you led him a merry dance."

"I kept him young, like I do all of you, I thought the world of old Amos, he knew that."

"Aye, I s'pose he did, I know he was fond of you."

"We miss the old timers – Walter, Amos and Shuffley. I wonder how many of us will still be here next year," said Fingal.

"None of us if we don't cheer up," replied Darcy, "I dread to think the state you'd all be in if I wasn't around. Now what were we talkin' about *before* we all got so miserable?"

"Young Matthew comin' home after twelve years," Fingal reminded them. "And he's a widower. If Matilda hadn't married the Vicar she could have had her childhood sweetheart back."

"She's very happy with the Vicar, you know what young blood's like – far too fiery – git you into all sorts of trouble," said Fingal knowledgeably.

"And what trouble did your fiery young blood get you into, Fingal?" asked Amos eagerly.

"Well I don't think it was anything to do with Matthew Johnson." said Darcy "*he's tall, dark, and handsome.*"

"I wasn't always short, fat and bald," grumbled Fingal.

"No, you used to be short, fat and hairy," quipped Darcy bravely.

But Fingal knew he was joking, he had never been particularly fat due to lifting gravestones around all his life.

"He's got a good lookin' littlun."

"Who has?" asked Amos.

"Matthew Johnson, lovely little fella, image of his father."

"Thass a very funny set up at the Vicarage if you ask me," said Eli. "I wonder if that young lass know who *her* father is."

"There's no doubt about that," replied Fingal, "it's on her brother's headstone, I put it there myself. There for all the world to see. Young Matilda was very insistent on it at the time. She made some remark about history not repeating itself. I like young Matilda, she makes a good vicar's wife."

Matilda and Richard were in the privacy of their bedroom when she told him her news. It was early September.

"Are you sure?"

"Very sure, I went to see a doctor at Winford today while you were about your business."

"Oh, Matilda, you have made me the happiest man on earth. I had almost given up hope."

"You should take your own advice, you must never give up hope."

He was holding her tightly, he could hardly believe that at last they were going to have a child. He loved Sarah, of course he did, but he had longed for a child with Matilda. His age was a worry. Would he see his child grow to adulthood? He must not think about that.

"We are going to have to wait until morning to tell Mother and Father."

"I am sorry but I wanted to tell you in complete privacy."

"Thank you, it will give me time to get used to it."

"I wonder how Sarah will take our news?"

"She will be overjoyed, think how she mothered Matty."

"Yes, she did rather enjoy herself."

"I am so happy, darling, for us all."

"I know how much this means to you, I was scared to tell you sooner in case I was wrong."

"You must look after yourself, and this time you will have no worries, and most importantly, you will stay at home."

"You have made me very happy, no one has a better husband than I. I do not deserve you."

Needless to say Elizabeth and Richard were ecstatic when told the news. So much so, that for one whole day she did not mention visiting Matthew. Her plans had been shelved because neither she nor Richard felt up to the journey, not yet anyway.

"When is it due, dear?" Elizabeth inquired of her daughter-in-law.

"Early April."

"That is a lovely time, all the Summer ahead for the baby to benefit from."

Matilda thought of Sebastian, he had only lived for one Summer. She still missed him so much. She would always miss him.

As Richard went about his church business that day there was a new spring to his step. A baby would cement their marriage, he reasoned. Not that their marriage needed cementing, the misgivings were all in his head. Matilda had given him no reason at all to doubt her love for him. She had treated him no differently during Matthew's visit home than she normally did – if anything, she had been more affectionate. But could that have been because she was happy – happy to have Matthew back, he worried; if a body was happy, it tended to respond with affection to the whole world!"

Why did he feel so insecure?

As he left one of the church cottages, after visiting Mr Stiles – who was housebound due to arthritis – he looked up at the clock on the tower opposite, nearly three o'clock it told him, nearly three o'clock, he repeated to himself, *nearly three –*

nearly three. The words screamed at him. *No it could not be so.* Life could not treat him so cruelly. He had stopped in his tracks, staring at the church clock. He stood as if transfixed until the clock had struck the hour ...boing ... boing ...boing...it told the whole village. But one man was getting an entirely different message than the mere hour of the day. One man had a cold fear in his heart as he walked slowly across the road and through the lych gate and made his way toward the coolness of the flint stone building. He paused in the porch, feeling ashamed of his thoughts. But had not the church just reminded him? *Nearly three hours* he had waited by Clancy's Wood for Matilda and Matthew to emerge, that was eight weeks ago – *and his wife was eight weeks pregnant!* Richard sat on the bench seat inside the porch unable to control his emotions. His head was in turmoil. He had waited so long to hear the news that Matilda was with child. For sixteen hours he had been ecstatically happy, he thought nothing could mar his joy, but the clock had managed to do just that.

Richard rose unsteadily from the porch seat and entered the church. He made his way to the front and fell on his knees, praying for forgiveness. Forgiveness for having such wicked thoughts regarding his wife. Even so he could not shake off the fear that he had been made a cuckold – by the brother he loved.

Richard sat in the church for over an hour, trying to rid himself of his wicked notions. He felt unworthy to return home to his wife – his lovely, young, innocent wife, who was expecting his love and support throughout her pregnancy, not the dark, suspicious thoughts he was harbouring at the moment. How could he go home in such a sombre mood when he had left her this morning so happy? He would have no explanation to give her. How would he ever be certain that it was *his* baby she was carrying? He could ask her! No, how could he ask her without admitting that he suspected her of infidelity? But if he did not ask her, he would never know. He would spend the rest of his life wondering if the child he was rearing was his own. If he *did* ask her, if he admitted that he doubted her faithfulness, it would drive a wedge between them, of that he was sure. There was nothing for it, he would have to keep his fears to himself. They were of his own making. They were of no real relevance. Neither his wife nor his brother would treat him so shabbily. This is what he told himself as he prayed for forgiveness and for the strength to put such destructive thoughts out of his head forever, for he knew that if he allowed them to remain, and to grow, they would ruin his marriage and his life. He must not let that happen.

"You are very quiet tonight, Richard, is Mr Stiles no better?" Matilda inquired of her husband, as she cleared the plates from the dining table.

"I was thinking we must write and tell Matthew our good news, in fact I want to tell everyone, I might even announce it in church on Sunday." He smiled at his wife, pleased that he was winning the war with his suspicions.

"I do not think it is necessary to go that far. News seems to spread like wildfire in this village with little or no help from anyone. It never fails to amaze me. However, I feel just the same, I want everyone to know. I am just so happy to have made *you* happy."

She is sincere, thought Richard, observing his wife. She obviously does not have a guilty conscience. Unless she is doing as I am, trying to make out nothing is wrong. Oh, this will not do. It will not do at all. The child is mine; I refuse to think otherwise.

Chapter Eleven

Matilda was determined that Christmas was going to be her best ever. She would have all her loved ones under one roof for the first time. Matthew was keeping his promise to come home.

Daisy Cartwright had accepted an offer of employment to housekeep at Meadow Farm. All week she had been busy cooking, cleaning and preparing beds. Hams and joints were ready to carve, mince pies, sausage rolls, cakes, puddings and pastries were made and decorations adorned the house. Being six months pregnant Matilda had to be content to supervise and perform only light duties but she wanted to be part of all the happy preparation. Sarah too was in her element as she helped in the house and waited for little Matty to arrive.

Similar activity was taking place at the Vicarage and Uphall Farm where they would all congregate on Christmas Day.

By four o'clock on the twenty-third of December all that could be done in advance had been completed. The three houses sparkled, their larders and pantries were full. Holly and Mistletoe hung from every available beam and stairway.

There was no snow but that did not matter, it would have hindered travelling.

Matilda, Richard and Sarah were at Meadow Farm waiting for their visitors to arrive. An evening meal was waiting, fires were spreading warm glows in every room, lamps flickered invitingly at the latticed windows. Albert had gone to meet the train at Winford. Sarah kept running outside to see if she could see the carriage lamps approaching.

"You will wear your boots out running back and forth," laughed Matilda. "it will not get them here any sooner," but her gentle chiding fell on deaf ears as her happy daughter continued to dart in and out, cheeks aglow from the winter winds.

"They are coming," Sarah called excitedly as she entered the kitchen for the umpteenth time, "I can see the lights coming up the hill."

The visitors arrived at last and were welcomed into the house. Sarah immediately took control of Matty who had not forgotten them. Margaret and Henry were made to feel very welcome.

Matthew hugged Matilda, Sarah and Richard. "Your condition suits you, Tilly, you are positively blooming." His face was hard and cold against her warm, soft cheek. She wanted to wrap her arms around him to warm him through... he wanted to press his lips to hers, hold her close and lose himself in her warmth. Instead they kissed politely and pulled away from each other... but not before he had felt her blossoming body against his own. His dark eyes seemed to penetrate hers and see clear into her head, as usual she felt weak at the knees and in her stomach. Richard dared not look at them, he was afraid of what he might see... afraid of what he could lose.

"You must all be ravenous after your cold journey," Matilda said as she ushered them to the dining table. "The food is all cooked and waiting."

It was a very happy group that shared the meal, catching up on news and getting to know each other.

"I am so glad you decided to spend Christmas with us," Matilda said to Margaret and Henry as they drank their after dinner coffee. "I hope you will visit us often, I am trying to persuade Matthew to come and manage the farm for me. I thought staying in the farmhouse might whet his, and your, appetites for country life, you see I am being very crafty." She smiled at the elderly couple, winning them over completely. "I also thought you would be more private here and have more room than if you stayed at the Vicarage with us, but please feel free to call in on us at any time."

"It was a lovely thought, wasn't it, Henry? said Margaret. "I am sure we will enjoy ourselves. You are making us very welcome and we can see that Matty is pleased to see his cousin."

"I nearly forgot," proclaimed Matthew going into the hall to search his overcoat pockets. "Ah here they are, ribbons for a lovely young lady's hair, the gypsies catch me every year outside Stoneham Cathedral." He handed his purchase to Sarah who kissed him shyly on the cheek thinking how nice it was to see her 'real' father again. She was so lucky to have two fathers that adored her, she felt very privileged.

Richard tried not to feel threatened by Matthew, he knew he should not, after all he had Matilda and Sarah all the year and he knew they loved him. He must be charitable while Matthew was at home; he loved his young brother too.

Matthew walked toward him. "Congratulations, Richard, you must be very happy, you will make an excellent father," he hesitated then added. "You are already an excellent father. He put his arms around his older brother, "You are a credit to us all, you deserve all the happiness in the world." The two men smiled warmly at one another then fell into conversation about their parents.

"Father has not been so well lately, he wanted to visit you but he has been so tired, we thought it would be too much for him. You have made their Christmas by coming home."

"I feel quite guilty about being so far away but if I came home I would be taking Matty away from his grandparents. They think the world of him as you can see."

"Perhaps you should consider Matilda's offer of the farm. You could continue your cabinet making from there; there is enough room. Margaret and Henry could stay as often as they wished."

"I thought it best to let them see the place before I broached the subject to them. One or two holidays here might convince them that it would be a fine place for Matty to grow up. I do not want to pressure them."

"Of course not, I am sure Mother and Father will understand. They are pleased to be in contact with you again, they love you very much."

"I'll call on them first thing tomorrow, I saw them very briefly on the way up tonight."

When Matilda, Sarah and Richard had left, Matthew settled himself in an easy chair and surveyed his surroundings. It was a charming farmhouse, very comfortable. The views were splendid, he would not mind living here, back with his family. He owed it to Sarah.

"Well, what do you think of my family?" he asked Margaret and Henry when Matty was in bed.

"They are all very charming, Matthew and this is a lovely house." Margaret looked around as she spoke.

"You must come again in the Summer, the countryside is beautiful then. There is a river nearby and woods and the sea is only a short distance."

"You obviously love the area," said Henry detecting a longing in Matthew's voice.

"Yes, I suppose I do, it is where I grew up, after all."

"When is Matilda's baby due?" asked Margaret.

"At the beginning of April."

"She is a lovely young woman."

"Yes, she has always been beautiful. Richard is very lucky, but then, he deserves to be."

He would like to come back here to live, thought Margaret, and there is nothing to stop him except us. He has not known us for long yet he is staying in Thimblethorpe for our benefit. Rhea was lucky to meet such a nice young man. What would we do without him?

On Christmas Eve Loveday and Edward, with their families, arrived to spend Christmas at Uphall Farm. Loveday and John arrived first with their two children Ellen and Joe who were now six and four years old respectively. Edward and his wife Mary arrived two hours later with their young son Edward Junior.

The rest of the day passed in happy anticipation and catching up on family news.

Christmas morning found the whole family in church. Richard conducted the service. Matilda was very proud as she watched him deliver his sermon. Out of the pulpit he was a very quiet unassuming person but once he stepped inside he became passionate and forceful; encouraging soul searching and provoking thought among his parishioners. Today's service naturally related to the birth of Christ and the gifts that were brought to him in the stable... He concluded by saying, "But the gifts you give to your loved ones today need not cost a fortune, you can give love and tolerance, happiness, care and devotion and you can give forgiveness..."

Was it just her imagination or did his eyes linger a little longer on her as his gaze swept over the congregation? For some reason she felt perturbed, her husband sounded so powerful in that pulpit. Most of the time she did not consider herself to be a sinner, but sometimes she remembered that she had defied her father and the consequences had been that she had given birth to two illegitimate children. Was everyone here today searching their consciences and thinking why they needed forgiveness? She looked behind her to where Matthew sat with Matty. Did he feel guilty too? Then there was her father, he must take some of the blame for what happened, and her mother, did she regret not standing up to her husband?

Matilda looked around the packed church. Did the villagers talk about her, she wondered. What did they think about Matthew coming home and spending so much time with her? They all knew he was Sarah's father. She began trying to imagine what they must think. Perhaps they thought that she, Richard and Matthew were a *ménage à trois*. She admonished herself mentally; what terrible notions to be having in church on Christmas Day and all because her husband's eyes had caught her own. She looked sideways at Sarah and smiled, then back to her husband as he announced the last hymn. For some peculiar reason, this morning she realized she was a woman with a past but she was also the Vicar's wife. What an intriguing combination that must be for the inhabitants of Flinton. Was she such an asset to her husband after all? Was he telling her this morning that he forgave her her girlhood waywardness? Strange, until this moment she thought he already had forgiven her and she had never thought he considered her particularly wayward!

After lunch the whole family apart from Rose, Elizabeth and Richard went for their usual Christmas afternoon walk.

Matilda and Matthew walked down to the churchyard. "I usually come down here by myself, it's nice to have company, what I mean is, it's nice to have *your* company. I prefer to be alone for half an hour with Sebastian on Christmas Day, give him my undivided attention, do you understand?"

"Yes, Tilly, I should have been here with you, how did it all go wrong?"

"You are here now, that is the main thing. We must not think of it as 'going wrong', we both found someone else to love. It did not go according to plan that is all."

"You have grown very wise, I will not ask if you are happy but I can see you are content. How could you not be – married to Richard? He is one of my favourite people."

"I cannot begin to tell you how good he is to me, I could not hurt him." Matilda looked deep into Matthew's eyes; he understood what she was saying or rather what she was *not* saying.

"I know, but I will always be available if you need me. I will never cut myself off again, I promise you." They walked on in silence, quite briskly to keep warm, until Matthew said, "Your father seems to have accepted me again. He did not appear to mind when I said I would accompany you."

"Father is a little easier to live with now, anyway he could hardly object to you visiting your son's grave, even *he* would not be *that* unreasonable."

"I have thought about coming back, but do not keep the farmhouse empty for me. It may be a while before I manage the move. But," he put an arm round her shoulders and pulled her briefly to him, "I will be here for the Christening," he hesitated before adding needlessly, "that is if I am invited." His dark eyes were merry as he smiled at her. "Oh, Tilly, this is going to be a good Christmas, one to remember when we are back at Thimblethorpe, one that merits a Cornelian." She smiled back at him, happy just to be in his company, it was like being in a time warp, they could be any age walking together toward the church, any age at all.

They placed their Christmas offering on their little son's grave and stood quietly, each in their own thoughts. Matilda as always could see his little face and feel his warm body in her arms. She remembered how she used to give him extra cuddles after his feeds to compensate him for always being last. She was glad now that she had done so. Oh, how she missed him. Part of herself was buried here under the yew tree; she always felt a pulling of her heart strings when she came here which made her reluctant to leave. Each time she turned her back to leave she felt as if she were deserting him afresh. Losing her son was her greatest sadness, she knew nothing could ever be worse.

Matthew was trying to imagine how it had been for her; he should not have cut himself off. Sebastian had been his own flesh and blood, as Matty was; yet he had not known him – would never know him. He took a step toward Matilda and put his arms around her. They stood silently as the wind whipped round them, howling round the near deserted churchyard, nipping at their faces.

They stood like a rock against the sadness of their loss then turned to begin their walk home.

That Christmas night surpassed all Matilda's imaginings. Matthew played the violin as she accompanied him on the piano for carol singing round the fire. The family laughed as they thought of another and yet another carol to sing, their faces aglow from the huge log fire and the flickering lamps. Matthew entertained them with stories of his travels abroad, just as he had forecast he would one day. The only difference was that he was not married to Matilda and *their* happy children's faces were but two – Matty's and Sarah's. Even so it was more than either of them had dared dream of during the preceding, difficult years and the other children – Edward, Ellen and Joe – made up the numbers anyway.

Next came parlour games as Matty drifted off to sleep and was eventually carried to a quiet room where he could continue slumbering in peace, Edward, Joe and Ellen following to their beds one by one.

Supper had been an ongoing event through the evening but when the clock struck twelve the furniture was moved to the edges of the room and the dancing began. Dancing was not deemed proper on Christmas Day. The first one was a particular favourite of the time, and as Matthew's music became faster and faster, waistcoat buttons and collars were loosened and windows flung open to keep the dancers in a fit state to continue the merrymaking. A barrel of cider was on the kitchen table, with an assortment of Louisa's home made wines and the remains of the supper. Matthew and Matilda took turns at providing the music until Louisa decided to help out when the dancing slowed down to a more genteel pace, thus allowing the pair the opportunity to dance together.

"Do you think you should be dancing, Tilly, it is very late, you have had a busy day?" Matthew whispered in her ear as they waltzed around the room.

"I would not miss the chance to dance with you at Christmas for anything, I have waited too long for this moment, and anyway, I have been sitting down all evening, one dance will not hurt me."

"One dance – is that all I am to be allowed?" She felt his hand more firmly on her back as he spoke.

She put her head back and watched the holly and the mistletoe as it quivered on the beams. She would not forget this day in a hurry; future years would be measured against it and found wanting. All her loved ones under one roof at last. All happy – even her father.

At around two o'clock in the morning the music ceased and the party began to break up. Tired but happy the merrymakers wended their ways home and sought out their beds, knowing that they would be late risers the following morning.

Boxing Day followed a very similar pattern to the previous day except that the dancing began a lot earlier and the singing was put off till later when they had all regained their breath. The songs were more varied and Matilda knew that Matthew wanted to sing 'their' song – but he did not, it would have been too obvious. Several times she felt his eyes on her and forced herself not to look at him. Was it normal to love two men at the same time, she wondered? Matthew's presence did weird things to her insides, especially when he danced with her and she could feel his lean, young body against her own. Richard did not have the same affect on her physically but she loved him deeply just the same and could not bear to be without him. It was a more comfortable love, she felt content with him and she knew he loved her deeply. He was proud of her. But however much they loved each other she knew there would always be a unique bond between herself and Matthew. Was it wrong? She did not fully understand it herself she just knew it existed as if it were natural and therefore acceptable. It did not affect her deep love for Richard, she felt honoured to be his wife, could not imagine life without him, and sometimes it frightened her when she thought of his age and the possibility of her being widowed. He was her rock against the world and all its cruelties. She was his treasure; he loved looking after her. They needed each other.

Matthew on the other hand could manage without her, for he felt close to her and she to him however many miles separated them and she knew it would always be so.

Chapter Twelve

On April 10th of the following year Matilda again gave birth to twins. She had sailed through her pregnancy, this time with an attentive husband by her side and with all her family around her.

The birth was an extremely happy occasion and much easier than Matilda's first confinement. It had been half expected that she would again have twins.

To keep everyone happy the children were each given three forenames, James Richard Daniel and Isobel Louisa Elizabeth. Matilda had laughed when naming James. "We cannot have another Richard it is confusing enough with two, I refuse to even contemplate it as a first name."

The names had been chosen jointly but Richard had to admit he was relieved that Matilda had not suggested one of Matthew's names – Luke for instance. She had named Sebastian after his father. If the twins belonged to Matthew, he consoled himself, would she not have wanted one to bear his father's name? It was small comfort in the circumstances but a scrap of hope at which to cling. Matilda and Matthew had produced twins before, had they produced them again? Richard wished he understood the biological intricacies of the situation. How could he ever be absolutely sure in the circumstances? He constantly found himself searching the twins for evidence of paternity. Isobel resembled Matilda with a down of pale gold covering her little head. James was dark as he himself was, but so was Matthew! In colouring they were the opposite of Sebastian and Sarah. He tried telling himself that James did not have *quite* such a dark skin as Sarah but was that a fact or a desperate conscious attempt at establishing his fatherhood once and for all? As always he resolved to stop worrying about it but he knew that he still would!

Matilda positively bloomed after the birth of her babies. Everything had been so perfect. The infants were both healthy. At first she had worried that one would be weak, as little Sebastian had been, but they both thrived, seeming to grow before her very eyes. She was busier than ever, trying to juggle motherhood with her duties as a vicar's wife and running Meadow Farm which she still insisted on doing alone. She had a reliable workforce that she grew to depend on, Albert Renawden especially. Albert was Zackery's son who lived in one of the farm cottages. She had considered offering him the job of Farm Manager but she was still hoping that Matthew would come home permanently and take her up on her offer. She did not keep a dairy herd like her father, preferring instead to continue keeping pigs as Robert had done.

It was a blustery day in October that same year that Elizabeth had a stroke. She was gathering some late-blooming flowers in the garden when her husband saw her slump over. He immediately rose from the dining room table – where he had been reading the paper – to call his son for assistance. At first it was thought that she had merely become dizzy and fallen but after examination by Doctor Henry the family were told it was a mild stroke and that a more severe one could follow.

As Elizabeth lay in her bed looking pale and tired her husband sat by her side, his hand covering her good one, the other laid limply on the cover. He was frightened; he and his wife had been together for over sixty years; he could not imagine life without her. How quickly their lives had passed by. It seemed but yesterday that they had married and then Richard had been born, their dear son of whom they were so proud. And then all those years later – out of the blue – they had been given Matthew, whose life had sadly been blighted by mystery and intrigue, in which he himself had unwittingly played a major part. But, could he have done otherwise? Poor Matthew, he wished with all his heart that he could have told him what he knew.

"Richard," Elizabeth's single word broke into his thoughts,

bringing him back to the present. He leaned closer to her so as to hear more clearly as she continued weakly, "I do not think I will be with you for much longer, I feel so tired…"

"No, no, my dear, please don't say such things, we will all help to nurse you back to health," but even as he said it he did not really think he would see his wife back to her old self, one of her arms was paralysed.

Tears welled up into his eyes, as he looked helplessly on this sweetest of women who he had always been so proud to call his wife. She smiled warmly at him, wishing she could ease his pain. He looked so forlorn and frail himself, how could he cope without her and she was about to cause him more consternation.

"Richard would you please do something for me?"

"Anything, my love, any thing at all, just ask."

"Please tell me why you forbade Matthew and Matilda to marry. You know I would not normally ask you to break a confidence but I cannot die without knowing, please do not make me."

Richard's troubled eyes travelled sadly over Elizabeth's face. She was going to die, would it be such a great sin to tell her what he knew? She would not divulge the secret to anyone else he felt sure but if that were so why had he not been able to confide in her years ago? He was aware of the answer to that one – a parishioner had entrusted the information to him. He studied Elizabeth's hand, still lying limply on his own, he gently lifted it to his lips as his gaze returned to her face. "As you know, my dear, it has always pained me that I could not confide in you about the matter. It is the one aspect of my vocation that I have had trouble coming to terms with but, you are right, you have been loyal to me on the subject for many years and you deserve to know the truth." He then told her the nature of that long ago visit by Daniel Canham, and the secret to which he wished he had never been privy.

Amazingly Elizabeth did not appear overly surprised but she withdrew her hand from his to wipe a tear from her eye before she said, "It is as I thought, it was the only logical explanation, and now I am going to ask you to do something else for me. Please do not let Matthew go to his grave in ignorance, he has a right to know of his origins. He has more right than any of us, promise me, Richard, please. I am sure you can think of a way."

"The secret was entrusted to *me*, Elizabeth. No one else has given Daniel their word, therefore rightly or wrongly I have left a letter for Richard. I could not risk Matthew and Matilda ever being allowed to marry, even after my own and Daniel's death. Richard, no doubt, will share the information with Matthew. It is all I could think to do."

"Thank you, dear, you are a good man."

She closed her eyes and appeared to fall asleep but presently asked, "Does Matthew know I am ill?"

Richard dispatched a telegram this morning, I know he will get here as soon as possible, try to rest, dear."

For the next two hours Elizabeth drifted in and out of sleep. Each time she awoke her eyes sought out her husband's face and she smiled at him. He would gently squeeze her hand and then she would drift off again. This pattern was repeated through the evening.

Around half past eight she awoke with a jolt. "Would you ask Matthew to come up please, Richard?"

Richard gently stroked her hair back from her face as he answered, "Matthew is not here yet, dear."

"But he carried me upstairs."

"No, dear, it was Richard who carried you upstairs, Richard and Doctor Henry. It is surprising how alike they are considering they are not blood brothers. You have raised two admirable sons, I am proud of you." Again he stroked her forehead as she stared at the ceiling with a puzzled expression on her face.

"I know Matthew was here, I saw him, I love him as my own."

"He knows that, dear, but I will tell him again when he arrives." Again she drifted off to sleep.

Through the night Matilda and her husband took turns to sit with Elizabeth, promising Richard they would wake him if her condition worsened; it did not.

At eleven o'clock the following morning Matthew and Matty arrived at Flinton having caught an early train.

"How is Mother?" asked Matthew, of his father.

"She is bearing up well but is a little confused. She thinks you were here yesterday so do not be surprised if she is a little muddled. Go on up, son, oh and before I forget, your mother was telling me last night how much she loves you – as her own, but then we all know that, don't we?" Richard smiled at his youngest son, then unexpectedly put his arms around him saying as he did so, "And *I* love you as my own too, never forget that, Matthew."

There were tears in the old man's eyes as he gently pushed him toward the stairs adding huskily, "Thank you for coming so quickly, you will make her very happy."

Matthew tapped on the door and entered his mother's room. She was asleep. He quietly positioned himself in the chair beside the bed, feasting his eyes on the woman who had raised him. How tired she looked. He should never have stayed away all those years. She had not deserved it, loving him as she did. But what else could he have done in the circumstances? He loved her so much; she had always been on his side – she and Tilly. How lucky he was to have the love of two such women. She stirred, her eyes flickered open for the umpteenth time that morning and focussed on his face.

"Matthew? Is it Matthew?"

"Yes, Mother, it's me." He leaned forward and kissed Elizabeth on the cheek, taking hold of her hand as he did so.

"I knew you were here, I told your father so, he is getting old now, so forgetful. How will he manage without me? You will all take care of him, won't you?"

"You are going to get well again, Mother, but, yes, while you are ill we will all take care of him so do not worry."

"I knew you would help me, Matthew, as soon as I fell there you were with your brother, you both mean the world to me, I am so lucky."

Matthew thought it best not to contradict the old lady. He smiled at her warmly saying "*I* am the lucky one – lucky to have found such wonderful people, I love you both very much, you *are* my real parents." As he put emphasis on the word 'are' he pressed her hand.

Her lips puckered and tears rolled down her cheeks as she gazed at him. Her voice was feeble and faltering as she continued. "Everything will turn out well for you, Matthew, please do not hold any grudges against my dear Richard, he loves you so much, he would never deliberately hurt you, but he is very principled; he has integrity."

As she said this she lifted her chin and stared into space in a proud fashion and then her eyes closed as she again fell asleep. Matthew continued to sit beside her thinking of all the times *she* had comforted *him*, then suddenly she was awake again.

"Have you seen her lately?"

Matthew assumed she meant Matilda, "Only briefly, I came straight up to see you."

"She loves you very much. I know she loves you."

"Yes, Tilly is very special."

"Tilly? Does she know Tilly?" Matthew realized his mother was very confused.

"Yes, of course, Mother." He stroked her hair back from her forehead gently as he spoke.

"Then I am sure everything will turn out well." The old lady smiled, then sighed deeply, "Be kind to her, Matthew, after all, she is your mother."

Those were the last words Elizabeth spoke. Her waking moments became shorter and twelve hours later she died in her sleep as she suffered a second stroke. Her husband was by her side.

Matthew was very perturbed by his mother's last words. Surely she would have told him if she knew the identity of his real mother, but then she had been confused – or had she? Elizabeth had always been very mentally alert. He wondered whether to mention the incident to his father. After the initial shock of Elizabeth's death had passed he would probably ask what his wife's last words had been. He would have to tell him then.

The question *was* asked and Matthew related the answer. Richard was puzzled. "Of course your mother did not know, she would have told you."

"Perhaps she had promised not to."

"No, no. I will not have it. Elizabeth would have told me, at least, if she had found anything out as important as that. She might not have told me the identity of the woman, but she would have said she knew."

Matthew conceded that, once again, he would have to let the matter drop. This secret had plagued him all his life and it looked as if it would plague him until he died.

Elizabeth had been greatly loved and admired. The entire family was grief stricken but the villagers were in mourning too. There was a constant stream of visitors to the Vicarage door, everybody wanted to pay their respects and give their condolences to the family. It was the end of an era, the end of a sixty-year reign by a gentle woman who influenced by example, and whose example had been exemplary.

Part Four

The Homecoming

Chapter One

Eight years later...

"Didn't she make a beautiful bride?" Daniel stood tall and straight as he remembered how his granddaughter had looked earlier that day. "I knew Sarah would be a beauty, just like her mother." He put his arm around Matilda's shoulders as he spoke.

"Sarah is nothing like me, she resembles her father," she looked across at Matthew who was still watching the carriage as it disappeared into the distance, taking Sarah and her new husband on the first leg of the journey to Scotland, for their honeymoon.

"She may have Matthew's colouring, but she has your beauty and bearing," Daniel insisted, looking lovingly at his daughter.

"I will second that," said Matthew joining the conversation, "I am just so grateful she did not inherit her looks the other way round, otherwise I may never have had the honour of walking her up the aisle."

Everyone smiled at Matthew's joke; it had been a perfect day. There had never been any question as to who would give Sarah away. Richard had insisted that Matthew should have that honour so that he himself could have the pleasure of conducting the ceremony!

On their return the newly weds would take up residence at Uphall Farm with Daniel and Louisa. Old Rose had died two years after Elizabeth and she was sorely missed, especially by Louisa. It would be good to have Sarah back at the farm. Apart from that it was Daniel's intention to eventually leave the farm to Sarah. It had eased his conscience somewhat to arrange his Will in this way. Louisa would have the farm for her lifetime, and then it would pass to Sarah. Edward had made London his home, Loveday and her husband would inherit their farm from John's parents, Matilda had Meadow Farm so Daniel reasoned that Uphall should go to Sarah, his way of atoning in some small, pathetic way for her incestuous conception, for which he held himself responsible.

He had grown to love Sarah in spite of himself. At first he was sure she would be taken from them as Sebastian had been, then he had looked for flaws in her personality and mentality, but none had materialised and he had gradually fallen under the spell of her delightful tomboyish nature.

He had spent countless happy years with her on the farm where she had loved to learn and participate in all the work. Nothing was too demanding for her, she was a strong, healthy girl who did not mind getting her hands dirty but, for all that, she was feminine, very feminine.

Her favourite time of year on the farm had always been the harvesting. She would spend long days out in the fields with the men, the horses and the dogs, coming in at close of day with wisps of corn and grass intermingled with her luxurious black glossy hair – the epitome of natural beauty, health and strength.

Oh, yes, he had many pictures of her in his head that would stay with him forever. Pictures of her drawing water from the well and gently coaxing a litter of nervous kittens to drink. Pictures of her sitting quietly with mares as they foaled and cows as they calved. Pictures of her climbing on to the haywain for a well-earned rest when the women brought out the baskets of refreshments. Playing with the dogs as they scampered off after rabbits and field mice who had just had their habitat removed. And the pictures of her today as she had walked up the aisle, radiant in an ivory wedding dress – made by Louisa and Matilda – on the arm of her handsome dark father – his son – as she took her vows with Alistair. Then, out into the sunshine of the churchyard with the church bells ringing over head and her dark eyes flashing and darting from one person to another who wished her well, but coming back time and again to rest happily on the face of her new husband.

Yes, Sarah had grown into a beautiful woman whose tomboyish nature had mellowed just enough to give her an air of dark feminine mystique; the same qualities that had beguiled him forty-three years ago. Qualities of another beautiful woman with black, glossy hair and flashing dark eyes who had captivated his senses and set him on a course of mental torture and guilt but without whom he would not have his beautiful granddaughter, Sarah.

Daniel was brought out of his reverie by his son-in-law's voice. "Our family is growing up, Matilda." Richard's voice sounded wistful as he watched the eight-year-old twins scampering about the Vicarage garden, reluctant to accept that the day was drawing to a close. "Look at them," he continued, "who would think that they could look as angelic as they did in church this afternoon?"

The children had acted as Sarah's attendants along with Matty who, at twelve, appeared very grown up of a sudden.

"Isobel will always behave well when Matty is around, he is her hero," replied Matilda, "she would follow him to the ends of the earth let alone up an aisle."

Sarah had met Alistair on the return journey of a family holiday to Europe two years previously, his family farmed in Scotland, he was the fourth child of six. Matilda and Richard had returned to France several times since their honeymoon, taking the children with then on most occasions.

Now Sarah was setting out on her own honeymoon, to Scotland, where she would be introduced to the rest of Alistair's family and see the farm on which he had been born.

Six months later saw another family milestone but one of a much sadder nature – Richard senior died in his sleep, he was ninety-one years of age.

On the evening of the funeral his two sons locked the door of the Vicarage study and opened the letter addressed to Richard.

My Dear Richard, they read,

It pains me greatly to burden you with this information but, I feel at least one person in the family should be familiar with the situation. Daniel Canham came to see me today and informed me that he is Matthew's natural father. He would not divulge the name of the mother, only that she was dark and beautiful, of good parentage and no longer lived in the area.

He implored me to assist him in preventing the marriage of Matthew to Matilda. For obvious reasons I agreed.

I pressed him to tell me the name of Matthew's mother but he was adamant that he could not – at her request. He did however say that a clue to her identity would be found among his personal possessions when he died.

I cannot imagine that he would confess to such a thing were it not true.

I wish he had not confided in me. It troubles me that I cannot tell Elizabeth about the confession but my biggest regret is that I will have to hurt Matthew —what will he think of me?

*Should I have taken Daniel's secret to my grave? I do not know. I have thought long and hard on the matter and have come to the conclusion that **somebody** should know in case Matthew's determination to marry Matilda ever looks like succeeding. I do not envy you this responsibility. I personally think Matthew has the right to know who his parents are but **I** have been made to promise I will not tell him. You have made no such promise Richard and I leave the whole matter in your capable hands.*

Your devoted father,

Richard William Johnson
6th July 1866

The brothers continued to stare at the letter long after they had finished reading, then sat down, both deep in their own thoughts. Eventually Richard broke the heavy silence, "It is as you suspected, Matthew, I cannot believe it, Daniel is my best friend, I thought I knew him."

Matthew was visibly shaking. "What have I done? What have I

done to Tilly? She has had my children. Sarah is so beautiful, what will it do to her if she ever finds out? It was bad enough to suspect he was my father but to have it confirmed – to see it written – I cannot bear it. I – can – not – bear – it."

Richard watched helplessly as great sobs racked Matthew's body – the big strong man was broken. In one day he had buried his father and had a nightmare confirmed.

"How can I live with this knowledge? How can I continue to look at Matilda and Sarah without feeling sick at what I have done to them? Help me, Richard for I am lost – lost."

Again great sobs shook his body, "Do you know what is the worst thing, Richard? I love her, I love her still, she is your wife and my sister but I do not love her as a sister Richard – I am a monster – *I do not love her as a sister, do you hear me?*" Without being aware of it Matthew had risen from his seat to grip Richard's shoulders, and he was shaking him as he spoke.

Gently Richard removed Matthew's hands and steered him back to his chair, where he slumped in a daze. His ravaged face was twisted in horror and self-hatred, his tortured eyes staring straight ahead but unseeing. He turned to his brother and continued in a small voice, "How you must hate me, Richard, how you must hate me and rue the day I was foisted upon you all."

"No, Matthew you are wrong I could never hate you, you are my young brother, you brought such joy to us all. We were honoured to welcome you into our family. You are a victim, not a sinner."

"But Matilda is your wife how…."

"I have always known you love Matilda and I know she loves you. The two of you will always be special to one another. I have learned to live with that. But I also know she loves me – in a different way perhaps – but she loves me just the same. I adore her, I will not think differently of her just because of this," he waved the letter about in the air then dropped it back onto the desk. "We are all the same people that we were yesterday, nothing has changed, we are all inextricably linked together, we cannot change the past, but we must learn to survive in the future. We cannot allow this matter to eat away at us and drive us all mad, as it almost did Daniel."

"Daniel – my father Daniel – no wonder he had a stroke when he learned of our intentions. How can I respect a man who cannot own up publicly to his wrongdoings? How can I ever sit at his Christmas table again?"

"Perhaps I should not have shown you the letter."

"I would never have forgiven you, you promised if you found out you would tell me."

"But having shared the information I have caused even more trouble. Matilda looks forward to the family reunions and so does Sarah. Please do not make them pay, Matthew. We are men we must be strong, we must put aside our own feelings for them."

Matthew held his head in his hands. He should go away again. He knew he should go away again, but he had promised Tilly he would never do that and how could he leave Sarah, his lovely daughter? He saw little enough of her as it was. He had missed her early years altogether. None of this was their fault. Richard was right, he should not make them pay. It would make him as bad as Daniel if he did. He sighed deeply, shaking his head violently as if trying to free his mind of the horror.

"You are right, Richard, you are a wise man. It will not be easy but I will have to bear this burden alone. Tilly and Sarah must never know, thank you."

Matthew rose unsteadily to his feet and put his arms around his brother, tears filled his eyes again as they stood together in their father's study. It had been a heartbreaking day but they were united as always. Nothing and no one would come between them, they both knew that.

Slowly they released their hold on each other. Matthew sat down again. Richard crossed the room to pour them each a brandy. They needed something to steady their nerves before they rejoined Matilda in the sitting room. They also needed each other... they would always need each other... they shared a terrible secret.

They were not blood brothers – they were closer than that.

"Do you know what I should do, Richard? I should go to Daniel and demand to know the name of my mother. I should shake him by the neck and force the information out of him."

"And do you think he would tell you? Do you think he would risk losing Louisa? He probably thinks his secret has died with our father. He is probably feeling more secure than he has for years. No, Matthew, I do not think it would be wise to confront him, it would only succeed in tearing the whole family apart again, is that what you want?"

"You know it is not."

"Then for Matilda's and Sarah's sake let it rest."

"He is the one person who knows the identity of my mother and I cannot ask him. I sometimes think I will go mad."

"According to Father's letter you will probably find out when Daniel dies." Even as he spoke he knew the words would afford little consolation to Matthew.

Me *and* everyone else, what will happen to the family then? Does Daniel think that when he is gone we will all be immune to hurt? Does he not realize that if he has left such information among his papers it will explode in our faces, tearing us all apart?"

"No doubt he will be discreet, he would not want to hurt his family. He has probably left you a private letter, as Father did me."

"I hope so, for all our sakes."

Again they fell quiet, each in their own thoughts, until Matthew continued vaguely, "I think it would be best if I limited my visits home to one a year. I do not think I can face Daniel too often without voicing something on the subject. Anyway Isobel and Matty are extremely close; we should not encourage history to repeat itself."

Richard went cold, the old fears stirred once more in the pit of his stomach, '*history to repeat itself*'. Did that mean that Isobel and Matty were half brother and sister too? Matthew was very upset, had he made a slip of the tongue while his defences were down. Would he ever be one hundred percent sure that his darling children were his own? He should ask Matthew outright, now, while they were discussing family relationships so candidly, but of course he could not. He could not risk Matilda finding out that he had doubted her fidelity. If the words were once uttered they would be between them forever. Did all families live their lives on a tightrope? Living whole existences in a carefully constructed cocoon of self-delusion? He had spent years convincing himself that the twins were his and he was not about to destroy his own fragile existence. Somewhere deep in his memory, where he tried not to look too often, was that shameful night he had followed his wife and his brother. He hated the shadowy memory of his furtive hiding behind the tree. He had sunk that night to a level he had not thought possible. He deserved to pay for it.

Chapter Two

For the following eight years Matthew and Matty returned to Flinton only for Christmases and for the Christenings of Sarah's two sons Luke Sebastian and Richard Daniel. For four of those years Margaret and Henry accompanied them, then after Henry's death, Margaret visited three more times until she joined her husband and daughter in Thimblethorpe churchyard. Matthew had never been happy about persuading the old couple to move to Flinton with him, so had let the matter rest. Events following his father's death had further deterred him, until he had eventually abandoned the idea altogether, especially as he found it uncomfortable to socialise with Daniel too often, also, he had opened a shop in Thimblethorpe and, with Matty as his understudy, had enjoyed such success that they had a comfortable lifestyle with money to spare.

Now there was nothing apart from the business to keep them in Thimblethorpe so, on their last visit home, Matilda had implored him to return to Flinton. His heart had always been in the village and he knew Matty loved it too so why should he not return? He weighed up the situation in his mind. His brother Richard was seventy-two years old and he did not see enough of him. How many more years would they have together? They should make the most of them. Many of the old-timers had already passed on. People like old Doctor Miles, Fingal Pardoe, Mother Cooper – the well known and loved mid-wife – Tom and Sadie Foley from the Village Maid, Reuben Healy the shoemaker who, like most of the others, had passed his business to his son, in this case Gideon.

Zackery Renawden the blacksmith had also died leaving the horses of Flinton in the capable hands of *his* sons Zackery and Ambrose. Then there was Darcy Worthdale, the well known wit of Flinton, who had passed on just last year at the age of eighty-one. His son Charles had now taken over the family tradition of providing the villagers with their furniture and raising spirits – in more ways than one – at the Village Maid.

Martin Partridge, the butcher, had also been succeeded by his son – young Martin who with *his* son, John, continued to supply the best meat, poultry and sausages for miles around.

Eli Penny and Randolph Clarke, two more familiar Flinton faces had both died during the preceding eight years leaving their respective namesakes to carry on their businesses.

Old Fergus Tooley, at seventy-nine, still liked to think that he did a days work but his boys Fergus and Hartley were the mainstays of that particular establishment, still enjoying a friendly rivalry with the Worthdales.

There would always be a Silas Twybar at Wood Farm but the present one was the grandson of Old Silas.

Diggory and Clara Farthing had raised three strong, healthy sons and a daughter to ensure the continuation of Farthing Farm – still the biggest pig breeders in the district.

Yes, the faces were changing but the village remained remarkably the same, he could walk through it and still feel he was twenty – twenty, that was a long time ago, the most traumatic of his life. Was it really thirty years ago he had said his goodbyes to Tilly, his parents, brother and old Walter Fennell and run off to sea? How time flies. He had not then been able to imagine himself at fifty, but here he was, fifty years old and considering returning to his roots. The more he thought about it the better he liked the idea. The only drawback, as usual, was Daniel. Would he want to be that close to Daniel? On the other hand did he enjoy being miles away from the rest of his family? Daniel always seemed to win in these mental arguments, a fact that was beginning to rankle Matthew considerably. He had seen little of his parents during their later years – because of Daniel. He had missed his daughter's formative years – because of Daniel. He had not known his parentage – because of Daniel, and even now, at fifty years old – he still did not know the identity of his mother – because of Daniel.

It was time he stopped considering Daniel.

Matthew looked across his workshop to where Matty was polishing a bureau. "I have been thinking of moving back Flinton way, how do you feel about it?"

"Are you serious, Father?" A broad beam had spread over Matty's face, putting a sparkle in his dark eyes. A damp black curl was clinging to his forehead as he stood, cloth in hand, waiting for Matthew's reply.

Matthew chuckled. "Well I think you have given me your answer and yes, I am serious, very serious. I have been giving it considerable thought lately. Our entire living family is up there. I can give a month's notice on the shop at any time."

"Would we live at the farm?"

"I do not think I should change professions at this late stage in life and there are already two cabinet makers in Flinton. I think three would stretch trade a little too far, don't you?" He smiled at his son, "We have got to think of your future, you have more of it than I. What do you think of setting up business in Winford? It is a thriving town with its fishing industry."

I should love it, Father, we would be only a few miles from Isobel..." he blushed self-consciously, "...and James of course."

Matty was extremely self-effacing, much like his mother had been, and very quiet. With his dark, good looks and gentle nature he made a very presentable young man. Matthew had taught him all he knew regarding woodwork, he had, naturally, also taught him the violin. But, reasoned Matthew, it would be some years before he felt confident to ask a young lady to walk out with him, he was painfully shy. All the same, if they were going to move to Winford it might be prudent to acquaint his son with the extraordinary details of their family history – and hope he did not lose his respect.

And so that very same evening Matthew told Matty about his early life, his love for Tilly, the ensuing parting, the heartbreak and how he found love again with Rhea only to have her too snatched away. Matty listened enthralled, to the whole story. He was amazed that his father had such a past and he was honoured and proud that he had entrusted him with the details. They had always been close, they lived together and worked together, but the story bound them even closer.

"So you see, Matt you are more closely related to your cousins than you may have thought. I thought you should be aware of the situation if we are going back to live near them. I would not want you to find yourself in the same situation as I did."

The fact that his father had called him 'Matt' had not gone unnoticed by the young man, it was a landmark in their relationship. He felt very mature of a sudden; he was his father's friend and confidant as well as his son.

"So only you, me and Uncle Richard are aware of the facts?"

"Well, Daniel is aware of course but he does not know that we know."

"It is very complicated."

"Yes it is. But our main objective must be to protect Tilly and Sarah from the awful truth. Whatever happens in the future, they must never find out. You do realize the importance of this, don't you?"

"Yes, Father."

"It is such a weight off my mind to have confided in you, Richard is getting old, it is important that a young member of the family is aware of the facts."

A silence descended on the room as the lamps burned low and the two men slipped into their own thoughts.

After a while Matthew tentatively broached the subject of Isobel. "You and Isobel get along quite well, don't you?"

"Yes, she interests me, she is so vibrant and full of life, she makes me and James appear quite dull by comparison."

"You and James dull? Never, you are quite alike it's true, but never dull. You must not confuse 'quiet' with 'dull'. Isobel is very much like her mother was at that age."

"Really? But Aunt Tilly is quite reserved."

"Maybe now, but not then."

Matthew's thoughts turned to Tilly. She was still beautiful. There were a few silver hairs among the gold and a few fine lines etched on her face but she had changed little in his eyes.

He could still close his eyes and see her in Clancy's house, or in the poppy field, and especially on Winford beach in her green frock and straw hat as she frolicked in the surf and sea spray, her sparkling eyes catching his with unspoken love and admiration. This was the way he saw her each time he transferred a Cornelian from or to his painted box.

Matt's thoughts were with Isobel. How did he think of her? She was definitely interesting, as he had told his father, but she was more than that. She had charisma, an aura of excitement, she was even, of late, a little flirtatious. But then, sixteen-year old girls did tend to dip their heads and flash coy smiles in the direction of young men. He would have to be careful not to fall completely under her spell. Especially after what his father had told him. Although, he mused, one was allowed to marry one's cousin!

The room continued to grow dim in the flickering lamplight, the fire had burned low with neither of them noticing, strange how thoughts can keep bodies warm.

Matthew's voice eventually broke the spell, "So that is settled then, we will make preparations to move. I do not think the house will take long to sell so I will give notice on the shop tomorrow and inquire of any premises to let in Winford. Isn't it exciting? I feel almost young again. Shall we keep it a secret until we are ready to go?"

Chapter Three

On a blustery day in late October Matthew returned home with his son.

He had found it more difficult than he had imagined to leave his house by the sea. He had grown very fond of it.

Until he moved he had thought of the house as Rhea's – after all, she had lived there with Bert – but when the time came to leave he realized it had become his home too, the only home his son had ever known.

He could remember, as if it were yesterday, the evening that Rhea had pointed out her house to him. He had thought then what a lovely position it held and it had continued to delight him. They had all been very happy by the beach.

"The family will be very surprised to see us so late in the day," commented Matthew to his son as they made the journey to Flinton on the evening after their move. "They will think we need a bed for the night." He turned and winked at Matt and they both smiled, they were in excellent spirits.

It was James who answered their knock at the front door and he was about to call his parents when Matthew raised a finger to his lips to indicate that he wanted to surprise his brother and Tilly. They therefore embraced in silence in the hall before entering the sitting room.

"Could you possibly spare a warm drink for two weary travellers?" asked Matthew, standing well behind the two easy chairs in which Richard and Matilda were sitting by the fire.

"Matthew! I cannot believe it," exclaimed Matilda jumping to her feet and rushing across the room to hug their visitors. She was crying with emotion as she held them both to her in turn, her eyes shut tightly, savouring the happiness of the moment, before releasing them to be welcomed by her husband who,

Matthew noticed, crossed the room at a much slower pace.

"We were just talking about you both and here you are, as if by magic." Matilda busied herself drawing up chairs as she spoke.

"I hope you were saying only nice things about us," joked Matthew, although he was concerned at the change in his older brother.

"Matilda and I have just decided I should retire at the end of the year," said Richard resuming his chair by the fire, "I am getting too old to do this work as it should be done. My parishioners will soon feel compelled to visit *me* and inquire after *my* health!" Richard smiled wryly at his joke but Matthew could see he was in earnest. His brother had lost considerable weight since last Christmas; he was stooped and seemed to be troubled by intermittent bouts of coughing.

Matt, as usual, had not spoken since the initial exchanges at meeting but he too was surprised at the change in his uncle.

The door suddenly burst open to reveal Isobel who ran across the room to greet the new arrivals. "I thought James was teasing me when he told me you were here, he has spent at least five minutes convincing me he was not joking." Her eyes sparkled as she looked from one to the other but her gaze dwelt longer on Matt. A fact that did not go unnoticed by all present. Matt could feel the blood rushing to his face as Isobel smiled at him. He wished he were not so tongue tied in social gatherings, but Isobel did not appear to notice as she grasped his hand saying, "Come into the kitchen with me and James and tell us all your news, oh, I cannot believe you are here."

"Well, you have certainly made someone very happy this evening," laughed Matilda, then added, "No that is not quite right, you have made us *all* very happy."

"I hope I am about to make you even happier," said Matthew savouring the moment before springing his surprise, as he glanced from one to the other impishly.

"What on earth could be better than you being here?" laughed Matilda intrigued.

"How about 'staying here'?" answered Matthew.

"*Staying here!*" Both Matilda and Richard were now staring in disbelief.

"Yes, staying here," repeated Matthew. "Matt and I moved yesterday to Winford, lock, stock and barrel."

Before either of them could respond to this marvellous piece of news, the door burst open a second time as Isobel exclaimed "Mother, Father have you heard the news?"

Matilda found her voice, "We have just this minute heard," she said incredulously, her voice breaking, "Oh, Matthew," and again she hugged him but this time her tears fell copiously and she did not care who witnessed it.

Richard and Matthew embraced emotionally and Matthew was once again reminded of how frail his brother had become. As he held him, he had an overwhelming desire to transfer some of his own bulk and strength to this man who had always been there for him through the whole of his life. I should have returned home before this, he silently admonished himself.

The rest of the evening passed in a happy haze amid promises to visit the new house and shop and plans for Matt, James and Isobel to do all sorts of things together. At nine o'clock, Matthew and Matt left the Vicarage to call at Uphall Farm to tell their news to Sarah.

One morning, about six weeks later, Matthew was surprised to receive a visit from James. He appeared much younger than his sixteen years as he told Matthew that Richard had taken to his bed with severe bronchitis and wished to see him. Matthew returned with the boy immediately, wishing their horses could cover the ground more quickly.

Sarah met them at the Vicarage door and took their coats, telling Matthew to go straight upstairs. He knocked gently at the bedroom door before entering to find Richard propped up in bed looking grey and tired. Matilida was sitting in a chair beside him, holding his hand. She crossed the room to greet him. " Thank you so much for coming, Matthew. I am so desperately frightened and I have to appear strong for the children," she whispered. "He has been asking for you."

"Go downstairs and have a rest, I will stay as long as necessary." He gently pushed her through the door and quietly closed it behind her.

"Is that you, Matthew?" Richard asked weakly, opening his eyes."

"Yes, Richard, it is me."

"I am so glad you are here, Matilda is wearing herself out looking after me, perhaps you could encourage her to rest." He raised himself slightly as a fit of coughing racked his frail body then fell back exhausted onto his pillows. After a while he said, "You will look after them all for me, won't you? If the worst comes to the worst?"

"You need have no worries on that score, just concentrate on getting better." Although he said this, he was very frightened that he might not have his brother for much longer.

For the next five days Richard fought to survive. Matilda allowed only family and very close friends to visit. Doctor Henry called several times a day being both friend and medical attendant. Each time he crossed the road from his home to the Vicarage he feared what he might find, but Richard fought on.

Sarah moved into the Vicarage to help her mother and her younger siblings.

On the sixth day, however, Matilda saw that Richard was failing fast, his breathing was noisy and his pallor very grey. After lighting the lamp by his bed Matilda went downstairs to talk to her children. She told them she feared that their father would not live very much longer.

"Will you do something for me, Isobel?"

"Anything, Mother."

"I would like you to go and put on your blue, summer frock, the one with the scoop neckline and short sleeves."

"But it is December."

"Yes I know, but your father loves to see you in that frock. The bedroom is very warm. Come," she extended her hand to her daughter, "let us go and find it."

Isobel agreed, "You are quite right, it is the least I can do for him when he is so ill."

At seven o'clock that same evening – after Matthew and Sarah had visited Richard – Matilda, James and Isobel took their turn at the bedside.

In due course Richard awoke from fitful sleep; he wore the same troubled, pained expression as he had all week. But when his eyes came to rest on his daughter his features relaxed slightly "Why, Isobel, you look lovely, dear," he said weakly, "I always loved to see you in that frock."

"Yes, Father, I know. We thought it might cheer you a little," her voice broke with emotion at the sadness of the situation.

"It – has – certainly – done – that," he managed at length, "and – James, – my – dear – son, Have – I – ever – told – you – how – much – I – love – you? We – men – tend – not – to – talk – of – these – things." He stopped to get his breath before saying. "Yes – I – love – you – all – very – much."

Matilda saw that her husband was very tired. "Isobel would you reach over and adjust your father's pillows, dear?" she asked.

The girl reached over her father's face, his eyes followed her movements until they halted at a point on the inside of her arm, just above her elbow. A look of pure joy swept over the old man's face, for there, as plain as day, was a small oval birth mark about half an inch long, similar to one he had himself in the very same area.

Why have I never noticed it before, thought Richard, as tears came to his eyes. For sixteen years I have fretted that the twins might not be mine. I have even doubted Matilda's faithfulness to me, how could I have thought she could be capable of such a thing. He looked at his beloved wife sitting by his side, she was all he could ever have wanted and she had hardly left his side during his illness. She looked so tired, but still beautiful – she would always be beautiful to him even when she was old and grey. He checked his thoughts; he would never see her when she was old and grey, he was dying, of that he was sure. He wished he could die knowing that she would eventually marry Matthew but that could not be. He hated the thought of leaving her such a young widow – and what of his children? They would be well taken care of by Matilda, he reasoned, his lovely Matilda who had remained faithful to him after all. He smiled as he looked up into her face, their eyes met and held, telling each other of their mutual love and admiration. His darling Matilda, the prize of his life.

At ten o'clock James, Isobel and Sarah retired to their rooms. It was essential that some of them should get some rest. Matilda and Matthew, however, resolved to sit with Richard through the night.

Isobel stood in front of her mirror, seeing herself as her father had seen her – it *was* a pretty frock, she was glad her mother had asked her to wear it, it had appeared to please her father. She then proceeded to wash off the mark on the inside of her arm that Matilda had painted there. Why on earth had she requested such a thing? Was the stress and strain of her husband's illness affecting her brain? She thought not, her mother was extremely level headed, even so it was a very strange thing to do, and why had she been asked to keep the matter private? Would she ever completely understand the enigma that was her mother? She was too tired to decipher it all, but she also knew that she would get little sleep – she was too worried about her father.

Matilda felt a hand on her arm, gently shaking her out of her shallow sleep. She opened her eyes to see Matthew kneeling in front of her, his face contorted with grief. Her eyes flew to her husband where he lay pale and still, as her hand went to her mouth in a vain attempt to stifle the terrible sobs escaping from her throat. She pushed Matthew to one side as she got unsteadily to her feet, then fell sobbing onto the bed.

Matthew left her for several minutes as she futilely called Richard's name – gently shaking him as she did so, then he took her by the shoulders, lifted her up and turned her towards him where she continued to sob into his chest. It was four o'clock in the morning.

Chapter Four

On the first of January, eighteen hundred and ninety-seven, Matilda moved, with her children, to Meadow Farm, the Vicarage was needed for the new incumbent – a Reverend John Patterson.

There was much to move. As well as their own belongings there were a number of boxes that Richard, senior, had packed up after his wife's death and still more that Richard, junior, had packed following his father's demise.

The boxes were put into a small spare room, together with other items not in general use. Matilda had lots of willing helpers, including Matthew and Matt. She had become withdrawn again, Richard had been her mainstay in life and she missed him dreadfully.

Isobel and James took to spending a considerable amount of time with Matt – Matt was easy to be with – quiet yet concerned.

Matilda found herself accompanied every day by Sarah and the children. They were a great comfort. She had always been very close to her eldest daughter and now she had her grandchildren to care for her as well.

The days, weeks and months passed in a haze for Matilda. She seemed to be carried along somehow by everyone else. She could not remember having to make decisions and she felt too weary to change the situation.

One day, in early April, Matilda awoke to the sun streaming in through her bedroom window. It seemed to give her a jolt, reminding her that there was a world outside her home and it was a *beautiful* world. She stood looking out over the spring countryside and experienced an overwhelming desire to start painting again. Yes, she thought, I will paint today.

Having made her first decision in months she washed and

dressed with much more purpose than she had of late.

And so began her slow recovery. She knew she must make an effort for her family's sake if not for herself. It gradually dawned on her that they had been very worried about her. It was as if something had been switched on inside her, re-awakening feelings that had lain dormant for four months. She thought back to Christmas and realized she could remember hardly anything about it, although it had been spent as usual at Uphall Farm with all her family. The only thing she *could* remember was Christmas night when she had taken a Cornelian from her box because she was so dejected. Oh Richard, she had thought longingly, did I always convey to you just how much I loved you? There is this big empty space in my very being, a space that only you could fill. She had taken the locket from the grey leather box, where it lay with the solitary Cornelian she had put there after Sebastian's death. She opened it to reveal the miniatures of her twins, she had never changed the photographs, a fact she felt a little guilty about considering she had other children. She had stopped wearing it every day when she married Richard. It had not seemed right somehow to wear Matthew's locket all the time, although, there were occasions when she wore it under her clothes, it having a much longer chain than most of her other necklaces. Of all the presents her husband had bought her these had remained her most precious. She had returned the locket to its box and unfolded the piece of paper that she kept with it. She had read: '*With love from Richard, you will have happier Christmases than this one.*' Yes, my darling, she had acknowledged to herself, I did have happier Christmases and it was all due to you, but *this* Christmas is my most wretched since then.

The rest of the religious celebration was a blur.

Matilda shook herself out of her thoughts, it was April and she, with the countryside, was slowly coming alive again.

One day in early July, Matilda took her sketchpad and went for a walk. She had not thought where she was going, but when she found herself on the edge of Clancy's wood she decided to visit the cabin. Part way there she hesitated, realizing she should have taken some clippers with her. She had not been to Clancy's house for at least a year and it would no doubt be overgrown with foliage. Nevertheless, having walked so far, she decided to continue.

The route to the clearing was not too bad, which surprised her because she was the only person to use it. After forcing her way through the dense bracken – of the first turn off to the left – she turned right and headed for the old oak. She climbed over the gnarled, exposed roots – which had appeared huge when she was a child – then covered the short distance to the clearing. She leant against the trunk of the walnut tree – which now towered above her – and experienced the usual feeling of peace that engulfed her each time she visited this lovely oasis of tranquillity. Her eyes travelled over the familiar surroundings. Was it her imagination or was it much tidier? The grass looked shorter, the bushes neater somehow. She took a closer look, yes, they had been pruned here and there. Did Matthew still visit the place? He had now been back in the area for nine months so it was quite possible, though he had never mentioned it to her. Perhaps, she thought, he did not think it seemly to mention their old haunts when she had so recently been widowed.

She pushed herself off the walnut tree with her hands and traversed the short distance to where they had made a way through to the log cabin. She had to crouch down and push branches out of way but she did not mind – they had never wanted the way through to appear too obvious, although they knew no one else ever came here. Funny, she thought, she had never told anybody else about this place, not even Richard, Verity or any of her children.

Having pushed her way through the branches she came to an abrupt halt. Clancy's house stood before her but it looked different. The whole building looked neater – as the clearing did – there were shutters beside the windows, the only shutters before had been *inside* the house. Here and there new wood had been cleverly spliced into the existing logs.

Matilda made her way cautiously to the door, even *that* looked different, there was a new handle and lock that did not give way when she tried to open the door. She took a step back. Had someone else found the house? She thought that unlikely. The only other explanation was that Matthew had made the repairs and tidied up outside. She tried the door again, in case it was just sticking, but it did not budge. Matthew would not put a new lock on the door without giving her a key, she reasoned, so began to hunt in likely hiding places around the door. She became a little irritated about the situation. This had always been *her* place – but then she checked herself. The *clearing* had been her place, the *house* had been their place and if Matthew wanted to make changes he was entitled to do so. Matilda sat down on an old tree stump, about twenty feet from the house, and began to sketch the scene in front of her. All of a sudden she stopped as if somebody had interrupted her. Of course, she thought, how stupid I am. She pushed her way back to the clearing and began to hunt around the foot of the walnut tree. There, under a large stone, she found a leather pouch – inside was a new key.

The key turned easily in the lock of the door. Once inside the house Matilda got even more of a surprise. The inside shutters had been removed and replaced with curtains. The walls had been lined so that they were now smooth. A wood burning stove with flue had been recessed along one wall with a cupboard and shelves on one side and a settle on the other. Logs were piled to one side. The bed had been repaired and held a new mattress. Two cushioned easy chairs stood one each side of the stove. A sturdy table and two chairs occupied the opposite side of the room. There was a lamp on the table and a kettle on the stove.

Matilda had been so surprised that she had forgotten to close the door. She turned now and did so. Next she opened the cupboard door and found mugs and a bowl with a few basic provisions; there was also a box. The top shelf held blankets and a towel. The bottom of the cupboard appeared empty until she knelt down and found bottles of home-made wine.

Matilda noted sadly that the cupboard covered their hiding

place in the wall where they had left their correspondence. A little smile played at the corner of her mouth as she realized that Matthew would not have done that. She removed the blankets and felt at the back of the cupboard. Sure enough there was a handle on a tiny door, which pushed to one side to reveal the hiding place. To her amazement she found a note.

Dear Tilly, she read,

I do not know how long it will be before you revisit Clancy's but I know someday, when you feel better, you will come back. Like me you will find the place invaluable as you come to terms with your bereavement.

I found working here very therapeutic. I limited my time here to two days a week – Mondays and Thursdays – otherwise I might have been in danger of becoming a recluse, like old Clancy. Having finished the work I missed it, so, I continued to come here on the same two afternoons to write. Do not laugh at me, but I am writing my life story so that one day you can read all about my travels and adventures. I also thought that Sarah might one day like to hear my side of the story – so that she knows she was very much a love child. I think I am getting sentimental in my old age!

Take good care of yourself, my dear Tilly,

Matthew.

P.S. You can keep the key – I have another.

Matilda began to cry. She had been so depressed since Richard's death, so wrapped up in her own misery that she had given little thought to everyone else's grief. She felt very ashamed as she remembered how much time Sarah had given her, how patient she had been. She realized that Isobel and James had sought out Matt, dear caring Matt. Had she shut them out? She could not really remember. She had not consciously done so, but the past few months were a blur. She *did* remember that Matthew had called every Monday and Thursday without fail, supporting her, doing odd jobs around the house for her and staying for supper. It was very remiss of her but she could not remember *one* of those visits clearly – or what they had talked about. It was as if she were awakening from a dream. He must have called on the way home from here, she realized now. "Oh Matthew, I should have helped you too. I am so, so sorry," she whispered.

Eventually she brought her head up from where it had been resting on her arms at the table and wiped away her tears. She collected together her sketching materials, picked up Matthew's note and made her way home.

Chapter Five

About 2 years later...

"Are you comfortable, dear?" Matilda was in her element taking care of her daughter Sarah who, one week earlier, had given birth to a little girl she had named Alice Rose.

As Matilda cradled the baby in her arms she talked to her gently. "Your Grandpa will be in to see you again tonight, no doubt. Are you not a lucky little girl to have so many people who love you?" Matilda's voice had taken on a wistfulness, which did not go unnoticed by Sarah.

"I suppose when I have my babies you think back to when you had yours," she ventured cautiously.

"Yes, I suppose I do, it is only natural."

Sarah reached out to take her mother's hand, "Was it awful when you discovered your first pregnancy? I have thought about it often and wanted to ask you but I have never plucked up the courage. There are so many things I do not understand, for instance, why you could not marry our father."

"Oh, Sarah, half of it is just as much a mystery to me as it is to you. Your grandfather would not allow us to wed so Matthew went away. He did not know he had left me with child. The next I heard he had married. In the meantime I had grown to love Richard and he, me. You more or less know the rest. We will talk some more another time, I am quite happy to tell you anything you would like to know. It was all such a long time ago now." Matilda suddenly remembered Matthew's book. "Actually your Father Matthew has written down his life story. He said we might like to read it someday, so there you are," she smiled at Sarah, "all your questions will be answered."

"That is wonderful, do you think I will have to wait years?"

"Well, whenever you read it, I would not reveal its contents to your grandfather if I were you. He has always been a bit strange where Matthew is concerned."

"I would still like to hear your side of the story one day, Mother, perhaps you should write it down for us too."

"Maybe I will," Matilda replied thoughtfully. "Yes, maybe I will."

She returned the baby to its mother and busied herself tidying the room unnecessarily. Daisy's granddaughter Lucy was their housekeeper now and she kept the house immaculate.

Matilda returned downstairs to make them all a cup of tea. As she waited for the kettle to boil she reflected on the past two years.

Matthew had continued to call on Mondays and Thursdays, she had told him how lovely he had made Clancy's house and how much she had appreciated what he had done there. He had not mentioned his writing again and she had not inquired about it. He must have realized that she now went regularly to the cabin – but never on a Monday or a Thursday. Their conversation was always on general subjects – children, outings they had been on with their respective families, the farm, Matthew's business, rising prices, the jobs he did for her around the house.

Occasionally they talked of Richard, who had been very dear to them both. But, on a personal level, they were each aware of how they tiptoed around each other – never bringing up intimate subjects, never getting too close. It was a habit they had got into following Richard's death. Matilda had felt a little uncomfortable in Matthew's company initially. As if she might in some way – by some people – be thought to be keeping another man's company when her husband had so recently been taken from her. On the other hand Matthew was her brother-in-law – to all intents and purposes – and it was natural that he should want to help her – Richard had asked him to do just that.

Matthew was keeping *his* distance for another reason. He was afraid that as time went on Matilda might come to think they could at last get married. He knew they could not but what reason would he be able to offer her? So the uneasy charade continued, because neither had any desire to stay away from the other, quite the contrary, they were inexplicably linked, so attuned to each other that each was acutely aware of what was being played out. Each knew it would be so easy to tip the scales of their finely balanced relationship. Matilda had begun to wonder a little of late why Matthew was still behaving as he had when she had been newly bereaved and Matthew *knew* she was wondering, but he could not change matters – and he could not stay away. Sometimes their eyes would meet and the old telepathy would convey their thoughts but nothing was voiced and life continued in a surprisingly relaxed way considering the underlying current of suppressed sexual attraction that still smouldered gently between them, despite their more mature years. Sometimes Matthew wondered what would happen if Daniel died and revealed, at last, his terrible secret. How would Matilda react? And Sarah? How would they feel towards him if he told them he had known for some time that he was Daniel's son? It did not bear thinking about.

Little did he realize that the explosion was more imminent than he thought, and even *he* could not have envisaged its amazing revelations or to what extent it would alter the courses of all their lives.

Chapter Six

"Happy New Year to you all," boomed Amos Farthing entering the Village Maid, "the beginning of a new century."

"Now thass not strictly true," said his brother Diggory, "the new century don't start 'til next year, or so I've bin told."

"Well you try tellin' that to all them revellers that have got sore heads today," retorted Amos, "mind you, they'll probably be easy enough to convince at the end o' the year – they'll have another excuse to celebrate!"

"Have you heard the latest?" asked old Fergus Tooley from his chair in the chimney corner. At eighty-two he was now the only one of the old timers left who still frequented the inn.

"What's that, Fergus? You're not getting married again are you?" quipped Charlie Worthdale."

"Cheeky young beggar, your father'd be proud of you, Charlie, keeping up the old traditions like you do," grumbled Fergus good-naturedly. "We took some stick from him, dint we, Amos, you can remember how your grandfather was the butt of Darcy's jokes, can't you?"

"Aye," said Amos "I remember, and when Grandfather passed away he started on me. There must be something about us Farthings that attract the wits of this 'ere village," he smiled wickedly in Charlie's direction, "and afore you say it, it's not the pig muck."

"Anyway," said Diggory, "What were you going to tell us, Fergus?"

"I was goin' to tell you that the schoolmistress died yesterday."

"No, not Miss Havers. She can't be more than thirty."

No, no of course not Miss Havers, I mean the *old* school mistress – Miss Penelope Wyn-Jones."

"Good heavens, but then, she must have been nigh on eighty," said Amos, "I saw her last week brushing the snow from her door. I offered to do it for her but she gave me one of her haughty looks and said, 'I have not needed a man thus far in life, Mr. Farthing, a little bit of snow is not going to change matters – but thank you all the same.'"

"She was always a proud woman," said Fergus. "Very independent. Mind you, Amos, we all thought at one time she might marry your father, he was mighty sweet on her. Yes", he reflected thoughtfully, "she was very proud but very likeable all the same, and well mannered. She might not have needed a man but she allowed Diggory to see her safely home many a time."

"How did she die, Fergus?" asked Amos's brother Diggory, interested because of the connection with his father.

"In bed, from old age," answered Fergus. "The postman was worried when she didn't answer his knock – she was always an early riser – so he went next door to Verity Flowerdew's house- Verity kept a spare key for old Miss Wyn-Jones, just in case of emergencies. She found her upstairs in bed, dead as a doornail. No pillows – she didn't believe in pillows – she said they bent the back. She never sat in an easy chair either for the same reason. Always used a hard backed upright chair."

"Well it worked, she was as straight as a ramrod till the day she went. I know women half her age that aren't so upright," stated Amos.

"There aren't many of us old uns left now," muttered Fergus sadly.

There followed a few minutes natural silence as each of them absorbed the sad news about the old lady who had been a well-respected inhabitant of Flinton for about fifty years.

"I expect you'll be called on soon to make a headstone," said old Fergus in the direction of Barnabas and Gabriel, who had hitherto sat in silence listening to the chimney corner conversation. They nodded their heads in unison and puckered their lips as their hands went round their ale mugs.

In the lull that followed a voice floated across from the other side of the bar, where a larger room afforded space to the majority of regular village drinkers. "I tell you it's true," said the voice to a hushed audience, "as true as I sit here."

"What's all this about then?" called Diggory in the direction of the lone speaker.

The young man, who turned out to be Arthur Sheldrake, made his way through the passage and under the low doorway into the small front room of the inn.

"Well, as you know, I work up at Meadow Farm for Mrs Johnson and this morning I arrived as usual just as it was gettin' light. I went through the gate and shut it behind me, just like I allust do. It was foggy early on, quite thick but that dint stop me seein' what I did."

Arthur paused to take a substantial amount from his ale mug before continuing. He looked straight ahead as if he was seeing again the events of the morning. "I was walking in the direction of the big barn – where I leave my coat if I'm workin' inside – when I heard one o' the dogs bark, I turned to see what was upsettin' her, as she's usually so placid, and that was when I saw it."

The small assemblage waited with baited breath as Arthur continued to stare ahead with a far away look on his face.

"Saw what?" asked Amos presently, being a little less patient than the others.

"The ghost," said Arthur quietly. "I saw a ghost."

There was silence while this piece of information was absorbed.

"Are you sure it wasn't just the fog playin' tricks?" suggested Diggory in a small voice.

"It was definitely a ghost," reiterated Arthur. "It came through the barn door where the old hay loft used to be and walked across the farmyard and through the closed gate. It was wearing tatty old clothes and a cap and the dog was barking at it. Just outside the gate it disappeared completely. I was scared witless. I went up to the farm to tell Mrs Johnson. She said I looked as though I had seen a ghost so I said I had, and she laughed, but my legs were shakin' so much she made me sit down and have a cup of tea while I told her about it. She wasn't laughing by the time I'd finished telling my tale I can tell you, she was as white as I was. Then she said, 'It is twenty-four years ago since Robert hanged himself in the hay loft and we nailed up the door, it has not been opened since. It was early the next morning, around this time, that your father, Sid, found him. He went straight up to Uphall Farm to fetch *my* father and together they cut him down'. Then she said 'You need have no fear, Arthur, Robert was the gentlest of men. He hurt nobody while he was alive so I am sure he will hurt nobody now.'

Well I tell you, if I didn't have a wife and four bairns to feed I would not go back there," said Arthur frowning deeply and shaking his head.

"Well, Arthur, I'm not going to say I don't believe you because I've seen some strange things in my time and it would take a lot to surprise me at this stage," said Old Fergus, but young Matilda's quite right. Robert Taylor was one of the nicest people around and I, for one, don't fear him, ghost or no ghost."

"Maybe you were thinkin' about him as it's the anniversary of his death," suggested Amos helpfully, "and with the fog and everythin'…"

"No, I never think about him, I didn't know him and the barn was nailed up long afore I went to work there, I've never bin inside it. Tis true I've heard Father talkin' about the time he found him, but I tell you I never think about it."

All this tale telling was making Arthur thirstier than usual but there were plenty of listeners interested enough to keep refilling his mug and plenty of newcomers who wanted the tale told all over again.

"This is a funny old start to the new year, isn't it," declared Charlie, "I think we ought to talk about somethin' a bit more cheery, else we'll be afraid to walk home in the dark tonight."

Again there was silence until Gabriel asked, "What do you think of the new Vicar now he's settled in, a bit different to Reverend Johnson int he?"

"Well, I've noticed old Dan Canham never doze off in church anymore, in fact he had cotton wool in his ears yesterday mornin'," Diggory chuckled. "No one will be able to complain about not hearing at the back of the church, I should think we could all lay at home in our beds and still hear his sermons."

"Thass a very good idea," smiled Fergus, "I'll hev to try it."

Chapter Seven

March the twenty-second nineteen hundred was the thirty-second anniversary of the birth of Sarah and Sebastian.

Soon after breakfast Matilda donned her outdoor clothes and walked as usual to the churchyard. It was a bright blustery day and she enjoyed the walk down Hill Road, across the Main Street and up the hill towards the church.

As she passed through the lych gate her eyes automatically sought out the yew tree. She paused, there was something a little different about it, something had been added to the familiar scene. She screwed up her eyes in an attempt to see more clearly as she followed the path round to the left and began the lengthy walk to the yew tree.

As she got nearer she could see that it was a double bench seat. She began to run, eager to reach her destination. Once there she stood admiring the beautiful seat. It was sturdy and smooth. It stood at an angle at the bottom of the family plot, following the bend in the path. It was like two bench seats back to back with one facing the grave and the other, the path. It was carved with flowers and leaves all along the top, on both sides and along the armrests. There was an inscription at the back of each seat; it read simply, 'IN LOVING MEMORY OF OUR SON SEBASTIAN'.

Matilda ran her hand gently over the inscription; it was beautifully carved. She sat on the seat, gingerly at first, then more relaxed, still clutching the bunch of spring flowers she had brought with her. She would normally have gone first to the water butt by the church but she had wanted to look at the bench. Matthew has been very busy, she thought, first with Clancy's house and now this. It was so beautifully made that she found herself touching it time and again. "Thank you so much Matthew," she whispered, then she turned to walk over to the church to collect some water for her flowers.

Having arranged her bouquet she tidied the grave then sat back again on the seat in the spring sunshine, oblivious to everything, save the small area around her. As usual when she came here she thought back over the years reflecting on how life never goes the way one expects it to. After she had the twins she had prayed for Matthew's return, convinced that, without him, she would have no life. But she *had* had a life, she had been very happy with Richard but now she was fifty-three years old and alone again. It did not look as if Matthew had any intention of putting their relationship back on a more intimate footing.

"Do you mind if I sit with you?"

Matilda was drawn out of her thoughts by the woman's voice; she looked sideways to see an old lady looking at her with an inquiring expression on her face. She could see she was a gypsy woman.

"No, no, of course I do not mind. I am so sorry, I was lost in thought." Matilda moved from where she had been sitting in the centre of the seat, to one side, so that the old lady could sit down.

"I cannot remember this seat being here before," said the woman, "but it's very welcome."

"Yes it is," agreed Matilda, "I have only just found it myself. As you say, very welcome. I wonder why I have not arranged one before, some of us have a long walk to the churchyard, don't we?"

A silence fell between them before Matilda, holding out her hand to the woman said, "I am Matilda, by the way, and I am very glad to meet you."

The woman grasped the proffered hand warmly. "And I am Rosa," she said with a smile, then, her eyes falling on the inscription on the grave in front of them she said, "it is hard to lose a child so young, isn't it?"

"Yes," whispered Matilda, tears springing suddenly to her eyes, "Yes, it is very hard," then, "I am so sorry I do not know why I am crying, I think it was the tone of your voice, you have lost a child too, have you not?"

"Yes, many years ago, but I still miss him."

"Is he here in the churchyard?"

"I don't think so but I always look, just in case."

Matilda looked into the old lady's face with a puzzled expression.

"I am sorry, I do not understand," she said gently.

The woman sighed deeply and Matilda saw that she too was crying, she automatically put her arm around the frail shoulders, which were covered by a thick woollen shawl. "Would you like to talk to me about it?" she offered, tentatively.

"It was all so long ago," she began, wiping the tears from her face, "I was young, just seventeen, we were here on the common." Rosa looked at Matilda, as if asking forgiveness.

"It is alright, you do not have to tell me if it upsets you."

"I want to tell someone, I am getting old and it is getting harder to keep it all to myself but Elizabeth has gone now. As I was saying, we were on the common, it was midsummer, I was young and pretty then." The old eyes stared ahead as the woman thought back to her girlhood. "The village boys used to come up to the common and loiter by the woods, trying to attract the attention of the young girls. I was one of them. One particular young man was frequently there, beckoning me to talk to him. Eventually I did. After that he came to the common every evening and I would secretly meet him. We fell in love but I knew my father would never agree to me marrying anybody but one of my own kind – and I loved my father very much. I didn't want to fall out with him, besides, I had not known the boy long. I sometimes thought about running away so that I could be with my sweetheart but it was just fanciful dreaming, I knew my father would find me, he was so strict you see. So four weeks later, when my family left the village, I said goodbye to the young man and moved on with my own people.

"Shortly afterwards I found I was with child, I was frightened of what my father would do so I did not tell him. Instead I told my grandmother. Fortunately, my father used to go away a lot – horse trading – so my grandmother and I were often left alone for months – my mother had died when I was very young. So you see, I was able to keep my condition a secret from everyone except Grandmother. I dreaded my father finding out.

"I told Grandmother all about my young man, she thought the best thing to do would be to let his family have the baby, but she worried that they might reject it so she made sure they would not be able to. I told her where my young man lived – on the left hand side of the High Street in a large house with Rhododendrons along the front..."

Matilda's heart was thumping in her chest as she listened to the old lady's story, realizing that Rosa was Matthew's mother. She wanted to interrupt but she sat spellbound, willing the old lady to continue.

Rosa collected her thoughts and went on. "My baby was born late one morning but when I saw him I did not want to part with him, I got very upset. Again I thought of running away, but I was young, I had no money and I knew in my heart that my child would have a better future with his father's family than with me alone. My sweetheart was going away to medical school and I was terrified of my own father finding out about him so, eventually, I agreed with my grandmother's plan.

"She took my baby and travelled through the night back to Flinton and left him, as I thought, on the doorstep of the Doctor's house."

By this time Matilda could not keep quiet any longer, she was very excited, she hugged the old lady tightly saying, "I know your son, I have known him nearly all my life but he was not left on the Doctor's doorstep."

"No, I realized that the next time we were here. I went into the village selling my wares, my grandmother was ill so I was alone. I was desperate to see my baby, I planned to visit as often as I could – while Henry, my former sweetheart, was away – so that I could watch him grow up – and I did for several years. I used to see him playing in the garden with the other children, I knew he was mine, he was dark like me and he had a little mark near his temple; it looks like a scar but it was there when he was born. It grew with him and was always visible unless he wore a hat. Anyway, as I said, I saw him for several years and then one day when I called he wasn't there. I asked the doctor's wife where her other little boy was and she said, 'Oh he's not my little boy, he belongs to the lady across the road – the vicar's wife – but he comes across here to play with my children.'

"I was confused because I had given Grandmother such clear instructions but I went across the road and saw my little boy there.

"The vicar's wife, Elizabeth, had always been very kind to me, she invited me in for a cup of tea as usual. She had often talked of her little son but I assumed he was her own and that he was at school, I had not connected him with *my* little boy across the road. I did not know what to think. I could see Matthew – I knew he had been named Matthew – was being well looked after and that he was happy.

"When I went home, I told my grandmother that she had left my baby at the wrong house, she went over with me what she had done and I realized she had approached the house from the opposite end of the village. Both the Vicarage and the doctor's house are large with Rhododendrons at the front. They are identical except for being on opposite sides of the road."

"Yes, that is true," agreed Matilda.

The old lady continued, "I had my own family by this time and I did not have the courage to confess my sins. I kept telling myself I would come back for him next year but, when the next year came round, I would lose my courage and so the time went on until I knew it was too late and I would have to live with what I had done." The old woman again began to cry. "I have been wicked haven't I? Leaving my child like that, you must think I am heartless."

"No, no, I do not, I know how difficult it can be in those circumstances I have been in them myself."

"You have?"

"Yes, I have, believe me, I do not think badly of you."

Matilda knew she should tell Rosa her own story but that would have to wait. She was so excited about what she had found out she just wanted to tell Matthew. Her head and heart were in turmoil.

"Have you seen Matthew lately?" she asked of Rosa.

"No, that is why I am here. When he was about fourteen he went away to school. I asked Mrs Johnson where he had gone and she told me, so I tried to see him when we were down there, but never did. Then on one or two occasions I saw him on Winford railway station, he had luggage with him so I knew he was going away. After that I did not see him for years, then I heard he was living in Thimblethorpe, but I never saw him there either. I had to be very careful with my questions at the Vicarage in case they suspected something and I was only here for a short time each Summer. But then one Christmas Eve, by chance, I thought I saw Matthew outside Stoneham Cathedral. I wasn't sure because being Winter he wore a hat, nevertheless after that I made sure I was there every year. But for the last four years I have not seen him so I began to wonder if he was dead. That is why I search the new graves each time I come back here."

Matilda held Rosa's hand tightly. "Matthew is certainly not dead so you can stop your searching, I know where he lives…"

"You do?" Rosa interrupted.

"Yes," laughed Matilda.

"So, do you know him well?"

"Extremely well, he will be overjoyed to meet you, he has been looking for you all his life."

"He has?" Rosa could not believe what she was hearing, "You mean he knows he does not belong to the vicar's wife?"

"Yes he knows, he has known since he was fourteen."

The old lady was overcome by emotion, "What will he think of me? I did not think he would know he was adopted, as time went on I was afraid to upset his ordered life."

"Do not worry, I will explain everything to him, he will be so happy to know you at last."

"You think I should meet him?"

"Of course," Matilda hesitated, as she looked into the old lady's eyes, she looked frightened. "You *will* meet him, won't you? Please?" She pressed Rosa's hand, "I assure you, you have nothing to fear and I know Matthew will understand if you do not want to tell your family about him. Is that it? Are you scared of what your family might say?"

"No, I don't suppose so, it would be nice to have everything out in the open. I was so grateful to Elizabeth Johnson for bringing up Matthew, and she was so fond of him, that I knew I could not say anything while she was still alive, but, now..." The old lady's voice trailed off as if she was searching her mind for any reason there might be for her to continue keeping quiet about her early life.

"You *are* on the common I presume?" Matilda asked.

"Yes, just a few of us."

Matilda suddenly realized that it was Thursday – a day that Matthew always visited her. She wondered if he still went to Clancy's house on Thursday afternoons to write. It was worth a try, she reasoned. If not she would see him this evening, she felt sure. She turned excitedly to the old lady. "Matthew always visits me on Thursday evenings. You could come too, and meet him. In the meantime I will try to find him and tell him the news. I could send a pony and trap for you," she added, her excited mind flitting from one thing to another.

"No, I prefer to walk, I've walked all my life, but you'll have to tell me where you live."

Matilda gave Rosa directions to call at her house at seven o'clock.

"You must be very close to my son if he calls on you every week," said Rosa curiously.

"Yes, we are close, I married his brother Richard who died just over three years ago, but when we were young, Matthew and I were sweethearts," she paused seeing that she had Rosa's full attention. "Unfortunately my father refused to let us marry – I have no idea why – he got so angry with me that he had a stroke at forty-two. Matthew decided he could not risk my father's health so he went away. My father recovered but I found I was with child. I had twins, Sarah and Sebastian. Sebastian lived only six months...this is his grave." Matilda pointed ahead of them, "He was your grandson, Rosa." She paused to give the old lady time to absorb this sad news. "Matthew made this seat, you see," she said as she turned on the seat and showed the old lady the inscription on the back, "I found it here today, the thirty-second anniversary of my twins' birth."

Rosa's eyes had misted over with tears again and Matilda realized she was rather old to cope with the day's events.

"I am sorry, Rosa, this is all too much for you, isn't it? Would you rather wait until tomorrow to meet Matthew?"

"No, I want to see him as soon as possible, I'll come to your house tonight as we arranged."

Matilda walked with Rosa as far as Clancy's wood. The old lady was sprightly and seemed to have no difficulty keeping up with her.

When they parted Matilda knew a moment of panic. She feared that Rosa might change her mind about visiting her that night. She was half-afraid to let her out of her sight. Then she remembered how much the old lady had wanted to meet her son, and relaxed.

Once alone Matilda felt like a young girl again as she ran through the wood toward the clearing, praying that Matthew would be there. He was, the door was open.

She was very out of breath as she burst through the doorway, calling his name, "Matthew, I have wonderful news," she gasped throwing her arms around him and holding him tightly.

"Tilly, what has happened, sit down and get your breath back." Matthew was somewhat taken aback by the sudden visit from Matilda.

But Matilda was shaking her head impatiently and laughing at the same time. "I know who your mother is, and your father, honestly, Matthew, I do, I have just left her."

"*My mother? My father?*" He stared at her, astonished, "What do you mean, Tilly? You have just left her where? Are you serious?"

"I am very serious and very excited for you, I have arranged for her to come to the farm tonight to meet you."

Matilda was ecstatic and tumbling over her words in her haste. "Oh, Matthew, I am so happy for you, I feel thirteen again."

Matthew stared at Matilda, wondering how she could be so happy at finding out her father's terrible secret.

"Are you *really* happy, Tilly?" he asked cautiously.

"Of course I am, it is what you have always wanted," she looked at him bewildered – he had not asked her their names. "Don't you want to know who they are?"

"Yes of course," he answered slowly, in a daze.

"They are Rosa and Henry."

"*Rosa and Henry?*" Matthew was in a state of shock, he slowly repeated "Rosa and *Henry?*"

Matilda was now standing in front of Matthew, holding both his hands. "Oh, Matthew, it is all so clear now."

"Is it?" he asked as if in a dream.

"Yes, your mother is a gypsy woman, she is lovely, I have been talking to her for hours. Do you not understand? That must be why you always wanted to travel – it was in your blood. And think how well the gypsies play their violins, we have always admired them, have we not?"

"Yes," Matthew agreed, stunned. "Yes, I see what you mean," he paused, "And my father?" He waited with baited breath.

"You have known your father all your life, you like him…"

Matthew stared at Matilda, he was sure his heart and lungs had all stopped functioning, "He is Doctor Henry," she continued, oblivious to his inner turmoil, that is who you have reminded me of, but I could not see it."

"*Doctor Henry?*" his heart was thudding again. "I cannot believe it". His voice was small.

"But, Matthew, he does not know he has a child."

Matthew hardly heard her, his head was spinning, his legs felt weak, he sat down heavily on a chair, staring ahead as if in a trance, the blood pounding through his head. *Daniel was not his father – Tilly was not his sister*. He did not know whether to laugh or to cry. He was ecstatic at the news but he was also bewildered and angry. He had been led to believe he could not marry Tilly and he could have done, *he could have done*. Why had Daniel told his father a lie?

Matthew sat staring ahead for so long that Matilda began to

get concerned.

"Are you alright, Matthew?" she said gently, touching him on his shoulder.

He looked up at her, a deep frown on his forehead, a worried look in his eyes. "Have you told your parents the news?"

"No of course not, I came straight to you. I wanted you to be the first to know. What is wrong, Matthew? I thought you would be overjoyed."

"I am, Tilly, I truly am and before you tell another soul I would like to ask you a question."

Matthew stood up and put his arms around Matilda, pulling her close to him and burying his face in her neck. "Will you marry me, Tilly?"

It was now Matilda's turned to be stunned, she gently pushed him to arms length and studied his face, the dear, familiar face that she had loved since she first started school nearly half a century ago. She could see he was serious.

She crept back into his arms. "Yes, Matthew," she whispered as the tears came easily to her eyes.

The evening went very well. After the initial, expected awkwardness, Matthew and Rosa slowly relaxed. Matilda made sure they had complete privacy in which to get to know each other.

It had been comforting for Matthew to know he had met Rosa at various times throughout his life. It made him feel a little less cheated, and of course he had known Doctor Henry all his life, having lived just across the road from him for many years.

"But why didn't you make yourself known to me?" asked Matthew of Rosa, "If you *knew* I was your son?"

"I did not know that *you* knew you were adopted, I felt I had no right to upset your life," the old lady told him almost apologetically. Her eyes were downcast, her voice flat, so much so that Matthew put his arm around her, assuring her that he understood. Rosa smiled at him so pleased that she had at last got to know her eldest child who had never been far from her thoughts. "You are more than I deserve," she told him tearfully, "after I did such a wicked thing."

"You must not think like that, we all make mistakes and do regretful things, I myself, unknowingly, left Tilly at a very vulnerable time in her life. I can hardly judge you and my father. I am only too aware of how these things can happen, and I cannot put into words the tremendous sense of relief I am feeling, and the happiness I know at having found you. Please do not reproach yourself at all," he said, holding her tightly, "I could not have wished for a lovelier mother, I am so proud of you."

It was a very emotional evening for everyone and, as it drew to a close, there was a distinct 'family' atmosphere pervading the house. Souls had been bared, tears shed, secrets shared and plans made.

Rosa was due to leave the Common the following day but, she assured Matthew that, before she returned in the Summer, she would tell her two daughters and six grandchildren all about him. She could not, she said, change her way of life at this late stage.

Although Matilda longed to tell her family all the good news, Matthew was more reticent, he was very worried about how Daniel would react and was in no hurry to witness the event. There was also the subject of his natural father. Matthew knew that he had to visit old Doctor Henry at Winford – where he was living in retirement – and acquaint him with the fact that he had a son. At the age of seventy-four this was bound to come as a shock. There was also a chance that he would not believe it.

On the Sunday, Matthew paid his visit to Dr Henry Miles. The old man remembered Rosa well, but was shocked to discover that he had a child and was worried about the damage the news could do to his reputation.

"We need not tell anyone," Matthew suggested helpfully.

The old man laughed ironically, "You forget I practised medicine in Flinton for nigh on fifty years, nothing gets by the village gossips and I can assure you that if I were still practising, my surgery would be unusually full on Monday morning. No, I am afraid this is a storm I will have to ride out. Anyway, I am not going to publicly disown you. We, neither of us, have behaved in a dishonourable fashion, we were both in complete ignorance of the matter, were we not?"

Matthew got the distinct feeling that Dr Henry was secretly quite pleased at having found he had a son. Although he refilled his glass many times though the evening – to steady his nerves, he said – he also beamed at Matthew frequently saying, "Well, well, well," and, "who would have thought it, me, a father. Well, well, well." Now and again he would chuckle. "Well, well, well," he'd say again "*and* a grandfather *and* a great grandfather *and* I helped bring most of them into the world, well, well, well."

By the time Matthew took his leave, a very mellow Dr Henry was making all sorts of plans for the future. In one evening he had progressed from being a solitary sort of serious, old gentleman, facing a lonely retirement —to the head of a considerable family and his newly acquired patriarchal status obviously suited him well.

Far from feeling that he had given him a shock, Matthew was quite certain he had given the old gentleman a new lease of life. As he sat opposite him in front of the log fire – slowly coming to terms with the fact that this man was his natural father – he began to notice all the little affectations that Matilda had seen fleetingly over the years.

Why have I never been aware of the similarities before? thought Matthew. But then, he reminded himself he had never spent whole evenings with the man in such a relaxed atmosphere and, more significantly, it had never once crossed his mind that he might be Dr Henry's son!

"Mother, Father, we have some fantastic news to tell you." Matilda was flushed with excitement and happiness. It was Sunday afternoon and Matthew had agreed that their news could be made public at last, although rather reluctantly, Matilda had thought.

No sooner had they arrived at Uphall Farm than Sarah

joined them. "I heard your voices," she said, "what is this wonderful news?"

"You appear very pleased with yourselves," Louisa said, smiling, "I am intrigued." She looked over to where her husband was reading by the fire. Although it was March, the days were still quite chilly and being in their seventies, they were feeling the cold more of late. Daniel was peering at the four of them over his paper, in anticipation of the news.

"The news is wonderful," Matilda continued, "Matthew has discovered the identity of his real parents."

She waited for the reaction of her parents, certain that they would be as excited as she was herself. Matthew, on the other hand, was watching Daniel, who had paled and let his paper drop. One of his hands had gone instinctively to his heart; the other was clutching the arm of the chair. He was looking at his wife, who, oblivious to his distress, was hugging both Matilda and Matthew in turn, anxious to hear, at long last, the names of his parents.

"Well who are they?" she implored impatiently. "Do not keep us in suspense…"

But Sarah's, Matilda's and Matthew's attention was now being held by Daniel, who had risen from his chair, his face deathly pale, his brows knitted tightly together as he stared, petrified, at his daughter, waiting for his world to come crashing down around him.

Louisa followed their gaze and was horrified to see her husband looking so ill. All else momentarily forgotten, she went to his side, "What is wrong, Daniel? Are you ill? Speak to me please, shall I fetch a doctor?"

Daniel did not speak but he shook his head slowly at his wife and allowed her and Sarah to help him back into his chair, from where he continued to stare at Matilda.

"Are you sure you are alright, Father?" she asked, concerned.

"Yes," he whispered in a voice that was barely audible. "Are *you* alright, Matilda?"

"Yes, I am *very* well," his daughter answered puzzled. "I was about to disclose to you who Matthew's parents are, you will never guess who is his father, he has known him all his life…it is Doctor Henry – and his mother is Rosa, a lovely lady I met quite by chance in the churchyard on Thursday."

Matthew rushed to Daniel's aid as, once again, he had tried to rise from his chair but had staggered back and was in danger of falling into the fire. As he steadied the old man he said jovially – attempting to take the intensity from the moment – "I am glad the news did not have quite such a damaging affect on Doctor Henry when I told him."

"You mean he did not know?" said Louisa, incredulously.

"Not until last night, but I think he is quite taken by the news, after the initial shock had worn off, he appeared to be in his element."

Daniel was indeed feeling ill. He felt as if he had been hit in the chest and whirled round and round at the same time until he was so dizzy, disorientated and short of breath that he knew not where he was. As a great wave of nausea engulfed him, he felt himself falling and falling, the room swayed hideously around him and the voices of his family faded away into the oblivion of the ensuing blackness.

When he came round he was lying on the chaise-longue with four anxious faces peering down at him.

"I think you fainted, dear," said Louisa comfortingly, rubbing his cold hands with her own. "I will get you a brandy, are you sure you do not want me to call Dr Miles?"

Daniel shook his head, staring straight ahead. His mind was in turmoil, he wanted to ask questions but he felt too weak and frightened —yes, frightened – terrified that he would have another stroke. He must try to calm down, he told himself over and over. His heart was racing, he was light headed, he must not lose control. *He* was Matthew's father, he knew he was, why had somebody told Matilda lies, nothing made any sense to him.

He drank the brandy and listened as Matilda told the story of Rosa to Louisa and Sarah, but he could not take it all in, he was confused. How could Rosa be Matthew's mother? Juanita was his mother, who was Rosa? He had never known a 'Rosa'. And what had all this to do with Dr Henry? He wished he could clear his head and think straight. Should he tell them they were wrong? No, no he must not do that, he told himself, they would know at once that he knew something about the matter.

The voices droned on around him as he struggled to regain his equilibrium. He was hearing the story as if through layers of muslin, the voices rising and falling around him, telling this strange tale about people who did not exist. What was wrong with him, he asked himself, was he going completely mad at last?

Louisa continued to sit by her husband, holding his hand and murmuring soothing words to him at intervals, as she listened, enthralled, to the story of Rosa.

When it was time for Matilda and Matthew to leave they both realized they had not broken the news of their intended marriage, but neither of them mentioned the subject. They were too concerned about Daniel. "Shall I help you up the stairs before I leave, Mr Canham?" Matthew offered as he rose from his chair.

"Oh please do," said Louisa as Daniel just stared ahead. "I still think I should have sent for the Doctor."

"Would you like me to stay the night?" asked Matthew helpfully.

"No, it is alright thank you," said Louisa "I have got Sarah and Alistair here if I need help." Then turning to her husband she said, "Let Matthew help you upstairs and I will bring your tea up to you a little later."

Daniel did not argue, perhaps, he reasoned, he would feel better if he had a sleep, then he could try to clear his head and sort out what to do about this puzzling turn of events.

Chapter Eight

"Daniel, what are you thinking of, you cannot possibly go to London." Louisa was distraught with worry at this latest display of odd behaviour from her husband who was getting into his best clothes.

"I can go to London if I choose to, good grief woman what are you saying to me? I am seventy-five years old not *five*."

"But why are you going, and why in such a hurry?"

"I have some business to attend to," Daniel answered his wife rather curtly.

"What business can you possibly have in London? Your solicitor is in Winford, your bank is in Winford. Answer me, Daniel, please."

"Stop questioning me, Louisa. Suffice to say I have to go to London and I have to catch the early train today, now please stop hindering my departure."

Louisa could see that nothing she said would make any difference to her husband's plans. "Very well, you need to go, but wait until tomorrow so that I can accompany you."

"I am going today and I am going alone."

"Have you forgotten how ill you were last night?" What will you do if you get to the City and faint again?"

Louisa knew that her arguments were falling on deaf ears but still she tried to reason with her husband. "You are worrying me sick, do you really want to do this to me?"

Daniel took a deep breath and turned to his wife, trying to sound calm and reasonable, "Louisa, my dear, I do not know why you are getting so distressed just because I need to go to London. I will see you again tonight, or at the latest tomorrow, please do not treat me like a child just because I fainted last night. At our ages we must expect a few dizzy turns but we must not let them rule our lives. I feel fine this morning, now, are you going to breakfast with me and bid me farewell with a smile?" He smiled benignly at his wife then added, "I promise I will bring you a present home."

Louisa relented, not because of the present but because her husband sounded so plausible. After all, she reasoned, she would not like him to prevent her from going anywhere on her own if she felt the need. All the same she did not feel easy about the situation.

"Be very careful dear," she pleaded as Daniel set forth to the railway station with a reluctant Alistair at the reins. "And do please see a doctor if you feel ill again, fortunately there are plenty in London." She kissed her husband warmly on the cheek but he could see she was still concerned.

Daniel's first port of call was to Matilda, to say goodbye and to assure her he was better after his dizzy turn. "Your mother is worrying needlessly about me, I just have some business to attend to, perhaps you could call on her sometime today and reassure her that I am fine."

"Yes, of course, Father, but I must admit I do not like the idea of you going all that way on our own either. We only have your best interests at heart, are you sure you do not want one of us to accompany you?"

"Quite sure, Matilda, I will see you soon."

The pair kissed each other goodbye and Daniel got back into the carriage as Alistair indicated, silently, to Matilda that he was not happy with the situation either.

About an hour later Matilda had her second surprise visitor of the day when Matthew called on her. "Is anything wrong?" she inquired, ushering him through to the kitchen. "You are my second visitor of the day and it is not yet nine o'clock!" she then preceded to tell him about her father's mysterious trip to London.

"And he would not tell you why he is going?"

"No."

"Has Louisa no idea what it might be about?"

"No, he would not tell her either, she is worried about him, especially since he felt ill last night."

Matthew's mind was working fast. Maybe Daniel's trip was connected to his finding out that he was not his father, but, he could not tell Matilda that, instead he suggested, "Maybe that is what it is about."

"What?"

"Well, think about it. Last night he was ill, today he is going to London, perhaps the two are connected – maybe he wants to see a specialist doctor but does not want to worry Louisa unnecessarily, at this stage, if there is nothing wrong with his health."

"Why didn't we think of that ourselves?"

"Dare I say because the male of the species is equipped with a superior brain?" he chuckled mischievously and ducked, as Matilda picked up a hand towel and threw it at him.

"You may certainly *not* dare say such a thing, especially if you want the owner of my brain to marry you in the near future."

She smiled happily as she put the kettle on to boil saying as she did so, "I will go and tell Mother your superior notions later, it may put her mind at rest."

Matilda realized that she still did not know the reason for Matthew's unexpected visit. "Anyway, you still have not told me why you are here today. I am intrigued."

Matthew's expression turned from being one of good-natured carelessness to a serious frown. "As you might have expected," he said carefully, I have had much on my mind recently, I have not slept well because my mind has been full of this new knowledge. I have been going over and over things in my mind. I have been trying to remember all the times I have bought ribbons from the gypsies and, it is true, it was nearly always Rosa that I bought them from. When you consider how many gypsies there are in the country, why did I not find it surprising that I met one particular one so often? There were others around of course on nearly every occasion especially on Christmas Eve outside the Cathedral so why did I not think it strange when it was always Rosa who pursued me, often putting her hand on my arm to get my attention? And I always felt a warmth towards her, usually paying far more than the goods were worth. I told myself it was because she was old and the weather was cold, but looking back it was more the way she looked at Matty and me. She must have been feasting her eyes on us knowing that what she saw would have to last her a long time. It is so sad, Tilly. I should have seen it. I should have realized she sought me out for a reason. All those wasted years yet I have known my parents all my life. There is still so much to talk about with her. Then there are the children – her grandchildren. She wants to get to know them all when she returns in the Summer. She said she would quite like to see Henry again. Do you think they will mind if I call them Rosa and Henry? Or do you think I should get used to calling them Mother and Father...?"

Matilda smiled, "Do you want me to answer any of your questions, darling?"

"Oh, I am sorry, I am rambling."

"I am perfectly happy for you to 'ramble' you have lots to 'ramble' about. Anyway, I want to hear all your thoughts on the subject, we have looked forward to this since we were children, have we not?"

"Dear Tilly, I think it has made you as happy as it has made me."

"It most certainly has. I cannot tell you how I felt when I realized Rosa was your mother, I was like a child with a new toy. I could not wait to tell you. If you had not been at Clancy's I do not know what I would have done – ran to Winford I think." Matilda laughed, "I would soon have realized I was no longer thirteen, I cannot run far at all these days."

"To me you will always be young, but the image that stayed with me most while I was away was of how you looked the last time I saw you."

Matilda blushed deeply at Matthew's mention of their lovemaking. He still had the ability to make her legs go weak and her senses reel, even though they were in their fifties.

"I thought our day on the beach might have been uppermost in your mind while you were away," she said trying to regain her composure.

"While I was at school yes, definitely. I only had to close my eyes and there you were in your green frock and straw hat with the sea spray sparkling around you. You have always looked lovely in green, Tilly."

There was a far away look in Matthew's eyes and she knew he was thinking back to when they were children and had not a care in the world. "We have a lot of making up to do, Tilly, I have so much to tell you and there is so much I want to know about you and the children. We are going to be a real family at last."

She handed him a cup of tea. "I have an idea we have strayed slightly from our original subject, I am sure you did not come here today to tell me how lovely I looked over forty years ago."

"You are quite right, as I was saying, I have been doing a lot of thinking and I was wondering if you would mind me spending a bit of time here going through Mother's and Father's belongings. When Mother died, Father just packed up her things in boxes. He said he would go through them later, but I do not know if he ever did. You see, Tilly, I think Mother knew that I belonged to Rosa and I think she knew that Henry was my father. Even if it was subconsciously."

"What ever makes you think that?"

"It was something she said the day she died. She was sure that I had carried her upstairs when she collapsed, but I was not at home then. It was Richard and Dr Henry that carried her. Father tried to explain to her that I was not at home but she said he was getting forgetful. So you see, she mistook Henry for me. There must have been something in him that reminded her of me even if it was subconsciously."

"That is extraordinary."

"Father and I assumed she was confusing *Richard* with me, but, she definitely said to me 'you were with your brother', so you see, she was confusing *Doctor Henry* with me. The clues were all there, Tilly, and I did not see them."

"But I *did* see them and still could not solve them. "I knew you reminded me of someone but the images were so fleeting I had never connected them with Dr Henry."

"There was something else. Mother's last words to me – or anybody else for that matter – were, ' Be kind to her, Matthew, after all, she is your mother.' She said *that* as if she knew the person concerned."

"I see what you mean, but do you not think she would have told you if she did know? She knew how much it upset you not knowing who your real parents were."

"That is what surprises me. If she knew, I am sure she would have told me, especially when she was dying, or maybe she just suspected and, if she did, she might have written something in her diary. I am sure she wrote one. That is why I would like to have a look through those boxes."

After Matilda had made a call on her mother, to tell her Matthew's views on the London trip, they started going through the boxes that had been brought from the Vicarage. There was much reminiscing as each item was lovingly examined.

"Here they are," exclaimed Matthew opening up yet another box. He looked at Matilda, "I am half afraid of reading them. It seems unethical somehow."

"Yes, I agree. It is almost as though we are snooping, but, look at it this way, if there is anything of relevance recorded here, it was probably done for your benefit; so that when Elizabeth died you would know at least as much as she did about the matter. Why else would she have written it down?"

"Put in that context I would be failing her if I did *not* read her diaries." With that Matthew began taking the books out of the box and they started the lengthy process of examining the journals. They sat in companionable silence in the little box room, oblivious to the time ticking by, until Isobel put her head round the door.

"Will we be having lunch today, Mother?" she smiled at Matilda.

"Oh, my word, is that the time?" said Matilda checking her watch.

"Have you found anything interesting?"

"It is all interesting, there is much question of who Matthew's parents might be, but so far your grandmother has not suggested that she has any inclination of their identity. We will continue after lunch."

"Carry on for a while, I will make lunch, James will be in soon, we can have it together. I am as eager as both of you to find out what Grandma knew. It is exciting, isn't it?"

"I suppose it must seem that way to the youngsters," said Matilda, gently, when they were alone again. "They did not see the heartache it caused, did they?"

"Don't worry, Tilly, I know they do not mean to be insensitive. To the generation after them, the human suffering it caused will be even more obscured. That is the way of life, is it not?"

The reading continued through the afternoon. Elizabeth wrote much on the subject of Matthew's parents during the early years of his life. It would seem that, initially, she looked upon everyone as a possible candidate. She had not written her diary every day, on the contrary, sometimes months had gone by with no entry, what had been written was made all the more interesting by the absence of the minutiae of life. What was very evident was her constant fear that the baby would be claimed, so she had had very mixed feelings about discovering Matthew's parentage. For the baby's sake, and to satisfy her own and everyone else's curiosity on the subject, she had wanted to solve the mystery – but she had also wanted to keep the child. Her hopes and fears were recorded heartrendingly through the journals.

"Look at this," Matilda suddenly exclaimed, "It is when you were sent away to school." She handed the book to Matthew who read:

I am absolutely heartbroken. Richard is insisting that Matthew goes away to school, I will not be able to bear it. As if that were not enough he also let it slip that we are not Matthew's real parents. Our son is devastated that we are sending him away against his wishes. He needs us more now than ever, his world has been torn apart and he will be too far away for me to comfort him. Men can be so obstinate sometimes. Richard insists it will be 'character building' and 'do the boy good' to be sent away.

Why are men ruled by their heads, instead of their hearts? I sometimes feel like rebelling against my 'dutiful wife' image, much as I love him.

The next entry in the diary dealt with the day that Elizabeth and Richard had taken Matthew to his new school:

I had the most terrible feelings when we left. The headmaster insisted on Matthew coming out to the carriage to see us off. I let Richard down by weeping in public, but I could do nothing about it, even though it upset Matthew more. As the carriage pulled away I turned around and saw Matthew standing dejectedly by a man he had known only an hour or so. I felt as if we were punishing him for a crime he had not committed. The sight will stay with me forever; I cannot get it out of my head.

The next entry read:

Daniel Canham visited the Vicarage this morning. He and Richard were ensconced in the study for some considerable time. Since then my husband has been insisting that we should spend Christmas in London with my family. Whilst I am always happy to see my sister and brother, and their families, I am at a loss to understand why we have to go at Christmas. I know for a fact – from his letters – that Matthew is counting the days until he can come home. He is longing to see Tilly again. I cannot help thinking that this latest request has something to do with Daniel Canham.

Why should Daniel have any influence over where we spend Christmas? I am extremely suspicious. I wish I had been privy to the study conversation. Richard has given me some lame explanation about the children being too old to keep so much company. I am sure he is hiding something from me. Why would Daniel want to keep the children apart? I have racked my brains and the only conclusion I can come to is that Daniel might be Matthew's father. It seems totally absurd, but why else would he have such influence over Richard? It is certainly a possibility, especially when one thinks of the children's natural affinity to one another. They are often referred to as 'soul mates'. I personally have never known two youngsters to be so in tune with one another unless they are twins.

Matilda looked at Matthew in amazement; "Do you think your mother *really* suspected my father of being *your* father?"

"It would seem she had thought seriously about the possibility."

"I cannot believe it, everyone knows how besotted my father is with my mother, he has never looked at another woman. How strange for Elizabeth to think such a thing."

"Well, with respect, she did have good reason, did she not? And do not forget, the question of my parentage was never far from her thoughts. It is obvious from these diaries that she lived in fear of somebody claiming me."

"Yes, you are right of course. It must have been terribly stressful for her. All the inner turmoil she must have suffered, and yet she always appeared so placid. I loved her very much, Matthew, and she could not have loved you more if you had been her own child. I loved her for that too."

"You have never let me down, Tilly, you make me feel very humble sometimes, when I think of how I deserted you, yet you remained loyal to me all the way through."

"You did what you thought was the honourable thing at the time. That is all any of us can do. Who knows what may have happened to Father if you had stayed."

"I wonder how he is getting on in London."

"No doubt we are worrying over nothing. All will be revealed tonight or tomorrow. At least Mother is feeling a little better since I called on her this morning."

The reading continued:

Matthew is coming home at last, I am so happy, for Matilda especially, at least I have seen him regularly during the past six years. Matilda has amazed me by her strength and devotion to him. I am so proud of her. I do not think I could have coped so well.

"Dear Elizabeth, I did not feel I was coping well, in fact sometimes I thought I would go mad especially at all those infernal social evenings that my father arranged. You would probably have laughed at some of the 'young' men he thought might interest me, I used to despair of him. Some of them were old enough to be my father; some were widowers, albeit *young* widowers, with children who needed a mother. Sometimes he sounded desperate when he introduced me, as if he were saying, 'please do not find fault with *this* charming young suitor.' Strange really how I scorned those older men, then married a widower my father's age, but, Richard did not seem old to me."

She lowered her gaze and stared into her lap where Elizabeth's diary lay open, her thoughts with her late husband.

After a while she resumed reading:

It has been a terrible day, where will it all end. Daniel Canham has again been to see Richard. They were closeted in the study for most of the afternoon after which Richard told me that Daniel forbade his daughter to see Matthew again, unless it were in mixed social circumstances. Matthew is distraught. He pleaded with his father to give him good reason for not seeing Tilly, but Richard refused on the grounds of confidentiality. To tell you the truth I am heartily sick of that word.

*Richard asked Matthew to go back to London to stay with my family but he refused, and quite honestly I do not blame him. Matthew is now convinced that Daniel knows his parentage and that he is from 'bad stock'. I myself am of the opinion, more than ever, that Daniel himself is Matthew's father. It makes sense. It is the **only** logical explanation unless Daniel has gone mad. I dare not make my thoughts known, if I am wrong it would cause more human suffering than I could bear, and I dread to think what it would do to Matthew and Matilda. I know they want to marry.*

Matthew expressed a wish to give Matilda something tangible as a token of his promise to marry her. I allowed him to choose a piece of jewellery from my father's collection, he chose a locket, but I have the awful feeling that it will never be the harbinger of marriage, however much I wish it could be. I pray every day that I am wrong about Daniel. The youngsters deserve to be together.

P.S. We have tonight learned that Daniel has suffered a stroke. Where will it all end. I am beside myself with worry and now Matthew is saying he will have to go away again to give Daniel the best possible chance of recovery. I cannot bear it; he has only been home a few days – not even a week.

Matthew and Matilda were now reading the diaries together, "I caused Mother so much pain, didn't I? Do you think I could have acted differently?"

"I know for a fact that Elizabeth never blamed you. The three of us were victims of circumstance. If anyone was to blame it was my father, for acting so unreasonably and we are still completely in the dark as to why he did it."

Matthew could not look at her. With a bit of luck she and Sarah would never have to know the whole truth of the matter. However one looked at it, if Daniel had been convinced he was his father, somewhere, sometime there *had* been another woman in his life.

It was late that evening when reference to Rosa was found:

Rosa, the gypsy, called today, she is a lovely person, I have never really talked in depth to a gypsy apart from Rosa. They lead very interesting lives but, at heart, they are just like us; the same hopes, dreams and family problems. During our conversation I became aware of just how often she inquired after Matthew. She has always been interested in where he is and what he is doing. In the past I put it down to friendliness – I have asked after her family in just the same way – but while I conversed with her today I had the overwhelming feeling that she really is interested in Matthew – very interested. My heart began to beat faster and louder as I gently tried to 'lead' the conversation. I even confessed to her that Matthew was adopted but that we loved him as our own. I told her that he had been abandoned on our doorstep and that somewhere there was a woman that loved and missed him very much. I tried not to let her know I thought she was the person in question, but I made sure she knew that I felt very deeply for whoever had found it necessary to give up a child and that her sacrifice had brought me immense happiness and fulfilment.

I have known Rosa for many years; she was very beautiful when she was young, with long, dark hair. I do not find it difficult to believe she is Matthew's natural mother – considering how dark and handsome he is. I cannot imagine why it has taken me this long to realize it. Many gypsies go round the village when they are up on the common, yet only one ever comes to the Vicarage, that cannot be by accident. The more I have thought about it today, the more I have become convinced. Daniel and Rosa! They must have had a love affair when she was here in midsummer. The dates are perfect – Matthew was born in March – exactly nine months later! I think I have solved the mystery at last but I cannot say anything until Rosa confesses to me.

"She *knew*, Matthew," Matilda said with a certain amount of relief apparent in her voice. "I am so glad she knew. Of everybody, she was the one who deserved to know your mother. I am so glad they were friends."

"Me too, and in the end she realized who my father was." Matthew was looking much more at peace with himself.

"It has been a long eventful day, darling, and I still have to go along the lane to see if Father is home."

"I will come with you, we both need some fresh air after spending all day in the box room."

But Daniel was not home.

"He said it might not be until tomorrow," Matilda reminded her mother, "So do not worry."

Louisa heard her daughter but she was concerned all the same. Was Daniel ill? Would he bring bad news home to her?

Chapter Nine

The nearer Daniel got to London the more misgivings he had. In the middle of the night when he had lain awake and troubled, he had resolved to go and see Juanita, it had seemed a good idea then. But now, in the cold light of day, as he neared the capital, he was not so sure. He had brought with him the embossed visiting card, which Juanita had given him at the midsummer ball all those years ago. Would she still be at the same address? Would she want to speak to him? Would she still be alive? She was not much younger than he himself.

Sometimes his head was perfectly clear, and he could remember the details of their last meeting with no trouble at all, but, at other times, his memory seemed to cloud over and, try as he might, he could not recall all that had passed between them. He would have to hope that, if he saw Juanita, his head would be clear and he did not make a complete idiot of himself.

He took the card from his pocket and studied it for the umpteenth time, as if it would give him the answers to his questions. He knew he had spent the night with Juanita. He knew she had a son – when he had questioned her she had replied, "*Our son is in good hands, Daniel.*" She had been quite sharp with him, as if she had not wanted to be reminded of her youthful misdemeanours now that she had married well. If she had not wanted to be reminded then, would she want to be reminded now? There was every chance she would not speak to him.

His memory was going cloudy again. Who was Rosa? Why was she pretending to be Matthew's mother? Was someone paying her to confess? *Was Juanita paying her so that her past would never catch up with her?* That is it, Daniel reasoned, it was the only explanation. All of a sudden his head felt clear again. He remembered how he and Juanita had stopped to look at the gypsy encampment on their way to Uphall Farm. She had said she envied the gypsies their freedom. He recalled how wild she had seemed, saying she often slept out under the stars and how she liked to talk to girls who had more interesting lives than her. It was very likely that she had made friends with the gypsy girls who visited the common every year. Juanita was rich; she had a powerful husband. She could easily afford to pay someone handsomely in order to keep her good name untarnished.

Daniel felt pleased that he had solved the mystery and that he was not going mad after all – but then he remembered Henry. Rosa had said that Matthew's father was Henry Miles. Why had she said that? Maybe Juanita had not wanted to cause him any trouble within the family, he told himself. Henry had no family so had no one to upset. But Henry would know who he had had love affairs with!

Daniel began to feel dizzy and ill again, maybe Louisa had been right. He was too old to go travelling on his own. His head was aching, he was confused again. Now where was he, ah, yes, Henry Miles. Matthew said that Henry had accepted he was his father so he must have had a love affair with Rosa – not Juanita. Yes that made sense. He himself had slept with Juanita and they had had a child. Rosa and Henry had had a love affair and had *not* had a child. Juanita and Rosa had become friends and confided in one another about their romantic liaisons. Now Henry thought he was a father and was very happy about the situation.

I might as well turn round and go home, thought Daniel. Juanita's obsession with her good name has inadvertently let me off the hook. Now that Rosa had confessed no one will be looking for Matthew's parents any more. Juanita and I will keep our good names and everyone will be happy.

Daniel had just about made up his mind to return straight home when a terrible reality hit him. Matilda was a widow, Matthew, a widower. They still saw each other regularly. There was every chance they would want to get married in the future;

it was three years now since Richard had died. Daniel accepted that he no longer had any influence over them. The only way to stop them marrying would be to tell Matthew that he was his father, and pray that he would be gentleman enough to – once more – do the honourable thing. It was a lot to ask…

"Are you alright, Sir?" Daniel was brought out of his reverie by a porter, "The train does not go any further, you are at Liverpool Street Station." Daniel looked around him to find that he alone occupied the carriage, his fellow travellers having alighted without him realizing.

He picked up his overcoat, got off the train and made his way down the platform. He would endeavour to call on Juanita – to tell her he knew of her ingenious deception.

The maid took Daniel's coat and laid his hat on the elegant hall table. He straightened his tie and ran his hand over his hair, with the help of the hall looking glass.

"I will tell Mrs Fellstock you are here, Sir. Perhaps you would like to take a seat in the drawing room," she indicated a door half way down the hall.

Daniel entered the room but he did not sit down, he felt quite nervous at the thought of confronting Juanita again. She could be so haughty; it made him feel uncomfortable.

"Daniel, how nice to see you."

He swung round to see a very elegant, but elderly, woman approaching him. She was very slim with white hair piled high on her head. She extended a pale, well-manicured hand, bedecked with very expensive looking rings. He took the hand and put it lightly to his lips.

"You look very well, Juanita, and still very beautiful."

"Why, thank you, Daniel, you were ever the gentleman."

Did he detect the old flirtatious teasing in her voice?

"I thought you must have resolved never to call on me, it must be all of fifty years since we last met and I gave you my card."

"Yes, yes it must be." Daniel was feeling slightly tongue-tied.

"So, to what do I owe this pleasure?"

"I came to talk about our son."

"Our son?" Two small furrows had appeared on Juanita's brow. "I am sorry I do not understand."

"I want to tell you I know what you have done, and I appreciate it."

Juanita sat down in one of the many chairs that occupied the room and indicated to Daniel to do the same. "What have I done to make you so appreciative?"

"I refer to your, hm, er, private arrangement with the gypsy woman."

Juanita looked even more puzzled. "Honestly, Daniel I have absolutely no idea to what you refer – I have asked the maid to bring us some tea – could you be a bit more enlightening?"

"How many private arrangements do you have with gypsies?"

Daniel knew he must sound irritated but he could not have put it more clearly. Why was she acting so innocently?

"I have *no* private arrangements with gypsies, I do not *know* any gypsies."

Daniel was beginning to lose patience with this beautiful poised woman. He knew that would get him nowhere – it never did with the fairer sex – no, women definitely preferred the gentle approach, so he said, "Juanita, there is only you and me here, I have not come to rebuke you, on the contrary, I must congratulate you heartily. You obviously thought the whole thing out very well." Daniel was not being wholly honest, it had not been an admirable thing to do at all, but he needed to keep Juanita 'on side' as it were.

The maid brought the tea and set it down, on a table, in front of the lady of the house, who was having difficulty understanding her unexpected visitor.

"Daniel," she began cautiously, "do you realize I hardly know you at all? I have only met you on three occasions in my entire life and yet I *feel* I have known you forever. I have often wondered how you are and what you are doing. The night I met you stands out like a beacon in my life," she handed Daniel his cup of tea, then continued, "It was *so* romantic, you were *such* a gentleman, you could not stop talking about your lovely Louisa and your wedding day – do you remember?" She looked at Daniel and smiled but did not expect, or wait for, an answer.

"Do you recall what a beautiful night it was? It was made for lovers. The countryside was bathed in moonlight and a million stars twinkled overhead." Juanita paused here with a far away look in her eyes as she gazed upwards. "You were such good company – and then we came to the common with the glowing embers of the fires...and the silhouettes of the gypsy caravans against the midnight blue of the sky... you let me flirt with you, I always enjoyed flirting," she shot him a wicked glance, "I still do. That night has stayed clearly in my mind ever since. It is a memory I bring to the fore if ever I am disillusioned with life – and there have been a few times, believe me. My late husband was prone to what he termed 'indiscretions', a word that is not in your personal dictionary, Daniel – being a gentleman, in love with your wife." Her voice and face had taken on a bitterness, which did not suit her elegant features. It was soon swept away as she continued, "Oh yes, you cannot imagine how many times I have thought of our evening together and how many times I have wondered what it would have been like to have married a farmer in sleepy Flinton. But to be honest I do not think it would have suited me. I am excited by London society. I enjoy my visits to our country house, but that is probably because I know I will be coming back here, to *life*." She spread her arms wide as she said this and her face did, indeed, come alive.

"I used to get so bored in Flinton so it seems strange to me that when I am bored now, I think of that very place – especially *our* night in Flinton."

Daniel had begun to relax. The tea and the charming company were like balm to his troubled soul. He could have gone on listening to her dulcet tones all night. But that, he reminded himself, was not why he was here.

"You do indeed flatter me with your recollections of our one night together. I am pleased I have inadvertently helped you through troubled times," he began, "but I cannot understand why you never mention our son, or enquire after him, or why you are denying knowing Rosa."

Juanita stared at Daniel as if he were speaking a foreign language. "What do you mean 'our son'?" she asked bewildered, "and who is Rosa?"

"Our son, Matthew," Daniel replied in a raised voice, again losing patience. "The result of our night of passion. The son you left on the Vicarage doorstep fifty-four years ago to save your damned fine name. There, now I have said it."

Juanita turned pale, "Please moderate your language whilst in my home, Daniel, I have staff to consider."

"I am sorry, I am sorry." Daniel held both hands up in front of him. He had not meant to lose his temper.

"I reiterate, I do not know what you are talking about, we had *no* night of passion and we certainly *did not* have a son, I think I would have known."

"What do you mean 'no night of passion'?"

"Exactly what I said. I do not deny I spent the night with you," her voice had fallen to a whisper, "and I do not deny I did not want the fact known locally, it would have done my reputation no good at all – even though you were a gentleman – you surely understand, Daniel? But I can assure you there was *no* night of passion. If you remember you were *slightly* inebriated, you fell asleep almost immediately. I was not long in following. In the morning I was woken at first light by the cock crowing. You looked so peaceful and I knew you had a big day ahead of you, so I just kissed you gently, wished you happiness, and crept out of the barn, so that I could get back home before I was missed. I have always remembered you with affection, Daniel. Please do not spoil things. You are one of my most precious memories."

Daniel was feeling ill again, his face had drained of colour, Juanita had *not* borne his child. He had *not* been unfaithful to Louisa. All his married life he had felt guilty for no reason, he had denied his darling daughter her happiness with her sweetheart. What had he done? He had even confessed his sins to the Vicar. *What sins?* There had been no sins. He put his hand up to his pounding head and tried to absorb the new knowledge. Was she telling the truth? He stared at the woman in front of him, "Are you telling me the truth?" he whispered.

"Yes, of course." She went over to him and laid a hand on his arm, he was worrying her, he looked terrible.

"But...the night of the Ball..."

"What about it?"

"I asked you then why you had left your son...I remember distinctly, you answered, 'Our son is in good hands, Daniel.' You said *our* son."

"I was referring to *our* son – mine and Alexander's – I thought you did not approve of me leaving such a young child in London while I went to country Balls."

"But you gave no indication of knowing me when Richard introduced us. I assumed you wanted to keep our friendship a secret because of embarrassment."

"I thought it might be awkward for you to explain to your wife – if you had not told her about me. After all we *did* spend the night together, albeit innocently. Some people might not have believed us."

Daniel felt dizzy and disorientated. It was all too much to come to terms with. He had made so many people unhappy, not least his darling wife and daughter. He was a fool. He had jumped to conclusions because of his guilt. He had never fathered an illegitimate child. Matthew was not his. He had been so proud of him in spite of everything and now, *he was not his*. How would he be able to explain his unreasonable behaviour to Louisa and Matilda. It had all been for nothing... nothing...noth...

The familiar black cloak engulfed him once more as he tried to get to his feet but sank, instead, to the floor...

When he came round Daniel was lying on a sofa in a small room where he had been carried by two of Juanita's staff. She herself was sitting beside him looking very worried. He tried to raise his body to a sitting position but Juanita stayed him with her hand, "No Daniel do not move, I have sent for a doctor."

"I do not need a doctor..."

"Yes, you do."

The Doctor examined Daniel and told him to remain quietly

where he was for at least two hours. Juanita sat with him.

"Would it help to talk about it?" she asked gently. "You obviously have a lot on your mind."

Daniel gazed up at her concerned face. "Yes, maybe it would," he conceded. "I have kept it all to myself for far too long and you deserve an explanation."

For the next two hours Daniel gradually told his story, ending with Rosa's confession.

Juanita listened sympathetically. When he had finished he felt drained.

"You poor dear, I feel so sad for you. You had my address, why did you not write to me to ascertain the matter?"

"I do not know. Yes, perhaps I do. I did not think you wanted reminding of the past. I thought you had abandoned your child. That fact alone spoke volumes. I had tried to raise the matter at the Ball and you cut me short...as if you wanted to put it all behind you."

"But I explained. I thought you were being disapproving of me for leaving my son in London. I thought it none of your business."

"Yes, my dear," he extended a hand feebly toward Juanita who covered it with her own, "you have done nothing wrong, but I have been a fool, and now I am a very *old* fool."

"We will have supper together and you must stay here tonight. You will feel better tomorrow."

"No, I have taken up enough of your time and I must get home to Louisa, she will be worried about me, but thank you, Juanita."

"Then let me arrange a carriage to take you to the railway station."

"I think it will do me more good to walk part of the way, I need the air. I will hail a hansom when I get tired."

"But it is coming in foggy."

"It will do me no harm, I have walked in fog before. But," he smiled at her, "I would love to have supper with you, you have been very kind."

"What are friends for, Daniel."

"I am sorry for shouting at you earlier."

"I forgive you."

She kissed her fingers and touched the back of his hand. "We must keep in touch."

Daniel kissed Juanita affectionately on the cheek and descended the steps from her front door to the pavement. He paused and turned to raise his hand to her, the fog swirling around him.

"Do not walk too far, it is an appalling evening," she called as she waved, turned and re entered her house, feeling disconcerted that he had refused her offer of a carriage.

Daniel's troubles had gradually receded to the back of his mind as he had dined with Juanita and, having got his problems out in the open at last, he had been able to relax slightly and conversation had drifted to more enjoyable subjects.

They had discussed their children and grandchildren and Juanita had entertained him with amusing stories of London society and brought him up to date with all the latest offerings of the theatres and opera houses, many of which she had attended.

He had enjoyed his supper and felt quite rested. Strange how they felt like old friends, but then, she had been on his mind all of his married life and, surprisingly, as he had learned today, he had occupied her thoughts quite often too.

Initially he walked quite briskly despite his age – farming had kept him physically fit – but after a while his pace slowed and his brief feeling of well being gave way to melancholy. He thought of Louisa and instinctively closed his hand around a small package in his pocket. It contained an oval brooch depicting a miniature painting of a lady in a garden, which was surrounded by tiny diamonds. He had asked the jeweller to wrap it, and had enclosed a card, which read, 'To Louisa, my one and only Love, Daniel.' He was pleased with the present, he knew his wife would like it but, as his thoughts turned to his family, and Flinton, he began to get agitated again, angry even.

He had been such a fool to jump to the conclusion that he was Matthew's father. He had carried guilt through all his married life. Why had he done it? *Because the baby was said to have a 'foreign look' about it.* Had it not been for that, he would never have thought he might be the father, but Juanita and her family were the only 'foreigners' in Flinton…and he had slept with her nine months earlier…

His pace increased as he got more and more angry at the cruel blow that fate had dealt him, what made it worse was that he had only himself to blame.

His head started aching again as he continued on his way like a man demented, his coat flapping wildly around his legs. He began not to notice his whereabouts as he marched ever forward, his head becoming more and more confused as his temples throbbed and the unfairness of his life swamped his reason. Several times he bumped into pedestrians seeming not to notice them. He crossed roads in front of horses and vehicles, totally oblivious to his whereabouts but pressing ever onwards like a man on a mission. The dark, fog-bound streets gave him an eerie anonymity, as he walked for the best part of an hour, getting more and more disorientated.

Gradually his pace slowed again as his aged body tired and he began staggering and lurching. Several times concerned walkers asked him, if he was feeling ill, but he did not hear. The noises in his head were deafening. He did not know where he was going – but he continued on.

Suddenly he came to a halt. Ahead of him was the river. He swayed on his feet and raised a hand to his pounding head. He looked to his left, there was nothing but fog and the ghostly shapes of trees lining the walkway. He turned his head to the right; there, not too far distant, under a street lamp, was a bench. He tried to focus on the seat, which appeared to him to be hovering, floating just above ground level. He tried to keep his gaze on it as he staggered forward. If he could get to the bench he would be all right, he told himself. The elaborate wrought iron end of the seat loomed ahead but he seemed not to be making any headway. He tried to focus on its ornate armrest – if he could just reach it he would be safe. His thick wool overcoat could have been muslin for all the warmth it was affording him, but this was of no consequence to him, as he strove to reach the bench.

"Are you alright, Sir?" came a voice from the mist, "do you need any help?" A hand reached towards Daniel's elbow but he shook it off as he single-mindedly reached his destination.

"Probably over indulgence," said the voice to its companion, "thinks he's still in his prime," and the shadowy figures disappeared into the enveloping fog.

Daniel's head became a little clearer as he rested, staring ahead of him at the river and the passing boats as they drifted eerily out of the fog on one side only to vanish silently back into the misty vapour on the other. I must get to Louisa, he thought, I must tell her everything, I must explain, she will know what to do...I must catch a train...where is the train?...I was on my way home...

But even as he said these things in his head, he was drifting off again into confusion.

Presently he looked ahead and, there was his beloved Louisa, just in front of him. He could see only her face but she was smiling at him. Now and again she would turn away and then back again as if beckoning to him to follow her. He felt himself relax as he realized how close he was to his darling, but then Louisa's face metamorphosed into his mother's and it was Rose beckoning to him to follow.

His freezing, fog drenched, facial features twisted into the semblance of a smile as he reached out a stiffened, gnarled hand toward his mother... while his top hat fell to the ground... and rolled unceremoniously into the murky Thames...

Daniel had suffered his second – and final – stroke.

Chapter Ten

It was seven o'clock the following morning that the policeman called and Sarah went to fetch Matilda from Meadow farm.

Two hours later, still in a state of shock, Louisa and her daughter, together with Matthew, were London bound. It was a difficult journey. Louisa wept off and on all the way. When she was not weeping she was blaming herself for letting Daniel go to London alone.

"You are not to blame," Matthew gently reminded her. "He was determined to go."

"But he had been ill the night before, I should have called a doctor." She twisted her handkerchief in her hands as she looked, unseeing, at the passing countryside, while Matilda sat by her side, numb with grief.

Matthew knew there would be a traumatic day ahead of them. The message had been to the point – that Daniel had died in London. The policeman either did not know, or was not telling them, any details. The London constabulary would inform them of all they wanted to know, he had assured them. But it was a long way to the capital and there were many questions going round in each of their heads, the biggest one being why Daniel had insisted on going alone. Matthew had a strong suspicion it had something to do with him – and Rosa's confession, but he had no idea what. It could not have been to alter his Will because Daniel had always dealt with Flowerdew and Flowerdew at Winford. Ahead of them too, was the unpleasant task of formally identifying the body. The policemen had not seemed in any doubt that it was Daniel. He supposed he must have been carrying some identification.

"Do you think you could manage just a light lunch before going to the police station?" Matthew asked the two ladies tentatively. "I know it is difficult for you but you will feel much worse if you eat nothing at all."

"Perhaps just a cup of tea and a sandwich, Matthew," Matilda whispered painfully, while Louisa just stared at him, unable to find room in her thoughts for food.

Having arrived at their destination they entered the building with trepidation. After the awful task of identification was over they were ushered into a tiny room and asked to wait. Presently a policeman arrived with Daniel's personal effects. He gently told them where the body had been found and that the Doctor was almost certain there had been no foul play. Most of what he said went unheard by Louisa, until the policeman passed over Daniel's belongings one by one.

It was at this point that she began taking notice. She took his coat and held it to her face as the tears ran unashamedly down her cheeks. She wanted to touch everything that was passed to them before Matthew put it in the bag that had been provided. Lastly, the policeman handed over Daniel's wallet and its contents, with the little package – still wrapped – from the jewellers.

"Mrs Fellstock *has* been informed," said the policeman, "It was she who told us who Mr Canham was, and where he lived."

Three faces stared blankly at the man, but it was Matthew who spoke.

"Mrs who?" he asked.

The policeman picked up the embossed card lying on top of the wallet on the table. "Mrs Fellstock," he said again. "It was the only clue we had to Mr Canham's identity. Incidentally she asked us to pass on her sincere condolences and an offer of accommodation, should you need to stay in the City tonight."

Matthew picked up the card and studied it, then passed it to Louisa. "Do you know this lady?" he asked gently.

"No, I do not think so," Louisa said, trying to clear her head, which ached relentlessly. "I cannot recall a Mrs Fellstock," she said very quietly and almost apologetically.

"Perhaps we should call on her," Matthew suggested, "she might be able to shed some light on why Daniel was in London."

"I think I agree," said Matilda bewildered.

Louisa was still holding the little package but she looked up at her daughter. "I do not know if I can face a social visit, and I am fearful of what might be revealed."

"I think you might regret it in the future, if we do not call on the lady, after all, she would not offer us accommodation if there had been anything unsavoury between herself and Daniel," Matthew offered helpfully.

"No, I suppose not," the newly widowed lady acknowledged.

"Then that is settled."

Louisa, Matilda and Matthew sat in silence as Juanita told them of Daniel's visit to her the previous day.

"It was as much of a shock to me as it is to you," she finished quietly. "I had no idea he thought we had had a child together."

No one spoke. The silence was suffocating – she continued cautiously, "I am sorry if I have upset you...but I am sure you would rather know the whole story...would you not?"

Matthew found his voice. "Yes, yes of course we would. We are just dumbfounded at hearing it."

Louisa stared ahead. This was one more shock she did not need. "I thought I knew my husband well," she whispered distraught, "but he lived with a secret for all our married life, a secret that he found necessary to keep even from me. It explains everything. I never once thought he could be Matthew's father. We had been childhood sweethearts. I was sure there had been no one else in his life...but I was wrong." She looked now at Juanita.

"No, no, you were *not* wrong, there was absolutely nothing between Daniel and myself except friendship."

"But it was a friendship he found necessary to hide." Louisa replied sadly.

"Only because he had this weird notion that we had done more than sleep in the barn. I can assure you, Louisa, he talked of nothing but you and your wedding, he was as besotted with you then as he was yesterday when he called. He had just bought you a present, he could not wait to get home to you. Please believe me. He was such a tortured soul. Thinking he had been unfaithful to you was too much for him to bear. He could not forgive himself for preventing the marriage between Matilda and Matthew. He lived all his married life with guilt and shame. I was as unaware of it as you were."

Matilda had not said a word. She felt she could quite easily become hysterical. Her misery...her illegitimate children... her shame...her loneliness...her heartbreak...it could all have been avoided. She had loved her father unconditionally... and he had betrayed her. He had not had the courage to tell her the truth. He had made them all pussyfoot around him, terrified of causing him a second stroke – and in the end he had caused it himself.

She sat rigid, oblivious to the conversation around her and for some unknown reason she thought of Richard – her rock against the world – was he here with her now; helping her through this madness? But as she reflected on him she became aware of her own guilt. She knew that Richard had followed her to Clancy's Wood when she went there with Matthew, shortly after his return to Flinton. This knowledge had always bothered her, for it showed that her husband had felt threatened and *she* had made him feel that way. She knew also – when the twins were born nine months later – that he was frightened that her children might again belong to Matthew. He had never voiced his fears, so she had kept silent on the issue. She had often wanted to bring the subject out into the open, especially when she had noticed her husband looking from James to Matthew, as if seeking a likeness. Why had she let him go on torturing himself? But she knew very well why. It was because, in a way, she felt she *had* been unfaithful. Unfaithful because she had always loved Matthew. Through everything he had been there – in person or in thought. If she had got into an open discussion with her husband, she knew she would not have been able to convince him that she did not love Matthew. The subject was just too dangerous to discuss. She had loved Richard and he had known she loved him, she had not wanted to upset the delicate balance of their happiness, besides, she did not want him to be aware that she knew he doubted her. She knew he was ashamed of it. And so the façade had continued, each aware of its existence and each too frightened to do anything about it – until he was dying. She had known she could not let him go while there was still the slightest amount of doubt in his mind. It had been too late to talk about it – he would have thought she was telling him anything he wanted to hear, in order that he could die in peace. She had realized she had to convince him without saying a word…

She was no better than her father.

This realization jolted her out of her righteous mood. Her father had not been wicked, he had been frightened, terrified even, of losing everything that he held dear, better to keep quiet than to risk not being believed. Would her mother have accepted that he had not intended to spend the night with another woman? And how would he have convinced her that it had meant nothing to him when he himself had been convinced that a child had been conceived? Yes, her father had caused untold suffering to a myriad of people, but the person who had suffered the most was himself – and now he was gone…

"Tilly, Tilly…" Matthew's voice penetrated her thoughts.

"Oh, I am sorry." Matilda shook her head in an attempt to clear it. "I was miles away, I am sorry…"

"Your mother and I have accepted Juanita's offer of hospitality – if that is acceptable to you."

"Yes, thank you, Juanita, it is very kind of you." Matilda could see that, while she had been lost in her own thoughts, the two older women had warmed to each other and were now united in grief.

"I forgive you, Father," she whispered, as her mind turned instinctively to the little painted box that held her Cornelians.

It had been a very sad day.

Chapter Eleven

The chimney corner assemblage was more subdued than usual.

"I wish the old uns were still here," said Fergus to no one in particular, "we never thought it would end like this. Old Walter used to say someone would confess on their death bed. Poor old Daniel too. Who'd have thought he'd die all alone in London. I've never known a week like this one."

"What was Daniel doin' in London? asked Gabriel, "Thass a funny old place to go alone at seventy-five."

"No one seems to know, an' if they do they're not a lettin' on, you don't like askin' questions when folk are newly bereaved, do you? I hear tell Mrs Canham's takin' it very bad."

"Well she would, they were childhood sweethearts you know," said Amos. "Grandfather'd tell us what's goin' on if he was still here. He used to keep us up to date with all the village news."

"Not much got past your grandfather, Amos. What with him, Shuffley, Old Walter and of course Randolph we used to hear most of what went on hereabouts."

"I wonder who'll take over the farm," said Diggory, "I can't see Edward giving up medicine to come home."

"No, you're right there, I hear he took to it like a duck to water. It was when Daniel had that first stroke that young Edward decided to be a doctor. Poor little beggar, rode down to the village bareback. He said he'd never want to be in that position again – feeling useless when someone was ill. The Doctor said he was as white as a sheet when he burst in. That must've bin over thirty years ago now. It seem like yisterdy," reflected Fergus sadly. "Where do all the time go, thass what I'd like t' know."

"Talkin' of doctors I hear old Henry Miles is like a dawg with two tails since discovering he's a father," Diggory stated gleefully. "Who'd have thought it? He was never considered to be the guilty party, was he?"

"Well thass 'cause he weren't here was he? We dint need three doctors now did we? He never came back until old Doctor Miles died," said Fergus. "Oh, I wish the old uns were still here. They were mighty interested in solving that mystery. 'The Mystery of Flinton' we used to call it. We spent many a night in here tryin' to fathom that one out. No one ever thought it might be young Henry Miles."

"Thass not surprisin' considerin' he dint know himself," said Amos Farthing, "That just go to show, they're no better than the likes of us, despite all their educairshun."

"Old Shuffley thought the baby's mother was that half-Spanish girl that used to live up on Winford Road, and it made a lot of sense at the time, we thought he'd cracked it, the mother anyway. We never even considered the gypsies," said Fergus, "Well they'd gone away agin by that time hant they? Mind you, some o' them are lovely lasses an' they do have a foreign look about them. We shoulda considered them."

"Where's Charlie tonight?" asked Amos, changing the subject.

"There you are," exclaimed Gabriel, "you're allust moaning about him but you miss him when he int here."

"Well when you spend a life time bein' made fun of you sorta miss it when it int around."

"You're just like your grandfather was with Darcy. I think you're quite fond of Charlie when all's said and done, aren't you?" asked old Fergus.

"Yes, but don't tell him I said it or his head won't git through that door."

"We're goin' to hev to find another mystery to solve now, aren't we?" said the old man. "We've gotta have somethin' to mardle about."

"Not if it's goin' to take fifty-four years – we'll all be long gone – six foot under and pushin' up daisies."

Chapter Twelve

Verity hugged her dearest and oldest friend. "I just *knew* you and Matthew would marry one day," she exclaimed, "you were made for one another. Do you remember how the subject dominated our girlhood conversations?"

"How could I ever forget?"

"It seems a long while ago, doesn't it?"

"It was a long time ago, it never crossed my mind then that I would marry Richard. I *did* love him, Verity."

"I *know* you did, I was there remember. Anyway I think it is quite possible to love two people at the same time. Love takes many forms."

"I sometimes feel wicked that I loved them both, I would find it difficult to explain to most people, but as you say, you were there, so you understand."

"Have you told anybody else your news?"

"We told the children soon after Matthew proposed. We were about to tell Mother and Father when he became ill – the night we told him about Rosa – and then, well, it did not seem right to talk about marriage after Father..." she trailed off, still not liking to say the actual word. "I have now told Mother, she is very pleased for us of course. It has been difficult for her to come to terms with the facts surrounding Father's death. Strangely though, she now writes regularly to Juanita, they are even going to visit one another."

It did not go unnoticed by Verity that Matilda had at last said the word 'death'. A good sign, she thought, that her friend was beginning to come to terms with her father's demise.

"Now tell me your news, Verity, did your Uncle Henry's newly acquired fatherhood rock the family to its foundations?" She was being a little mischievous now, due to the fact that Verity often complained that her family – full of doctors and solicitors

– was rather stuffy.

"They were all shocked, to say the least. I think, at first, Father felt that Uncle Henry had brought shame on us all but, Uncle Henry is so happy with his new found status that Father is gradually being won over." She paused then exclaimed, "I have just realized – when you marry Matthew, we will be related."

"So we will, it is such a complicated state of affairs, isn't it? I cannot get used to you being Matthew's cousin."

"Neither can I, but since I have known I have seen those similarities with my Uncle Henry – that you used to talk about."

"How are the rest of your family?"

"Susannah and Megan have decided to live together now that they are widowed, they both still sew, so they have a common interest."

"Lydia taught them well, my mother always said she was the best dressmaker for miles." Matilda paused, "And how is Robert?"

"You know Robert, he does not change much. Do you remember how many times he walked past our house before he plucked up courage to speak to me?"

"I began to think he never would."

"I found his shyness quite attractive."

"That is just as well considering you married him!"

"Yes, especially now that we are alone again, children soon grow up, do they not? I am lucky that Nicholas and John both live in Winford, it is not too far for me to visit my grandchildren."

"I am even luckier – mine live down the lane."

Chapter Thirteen

"Do you think it was a good idea to come to London for our honeymoon?" Matilda was in pensive mood as they peered through the railings of Buckingham Palace watching the Changing of the Guard.

"I think it was an excellent idea. I do not want our capital city to be only synonymous with your father's death. This way you will have happy memories of it as well."

Matilda squeezed the arm of her new husband. "I sometimes forget that you and Richard were not blood brothers, you are so like him in many ways, especially your thoughtful nature."

"He was probably a very good influence on me in my formative years."

"Look, the King is in residence," exclaimed Matilda, pointing to the Royal Standard fluttering in the breeze over the Palace. "I wonder if we will see him."

"I cannot get used to having a king can you?"

"No, but then that is not surprising, considering we have had only one queen for all of our lives. I wonder if there will ever be a longer reign than that of Victoria."

The pair strolled on down The Mall and entered St James Park where they found a vacant seat beside the lake. Matthew put a protective arm around Matilda, "Have I told you how beautiful you looked on Wednesday, darling?"

She laughed, "Many, many times. It is the general idea to look one's best on one's wedding day."

"Thank you for wearing a green frock and a straw hat."

"That 'straw' hat, as you put it, was very expensive. The milliner might take objection to you describing it so." She laughed gaily, "But it was money well spent if it made you happy."

"I cannot put into words how I felt that day, Tilly. To marry you and have my real parents witness the event was more than I have ever dared hope for, let alone to have my children present and meet a whole new family."

"It went well, did it not? You looked so at home with you new family, especially when you all got together with your violins, I felt very proud of you, darling, you make that instrument sing."

"Thank you, as far as I am concerned it was the best thirty shillings my parents spent on my education when they bought it for me. It is strange, but I used to feel so frustrated at not knowing my origins – now I feel privileged to have had *two* such wonderful sets of parents." He paused before saying with a chuckle, "I was about to say I feel I have known them all my life."

They sat in silent contentment, each in their own thoughts, as they watched the ducks at their antics – wagging their hindquarters in the air as they dived time and again.

Presently Matilda broke the silence by saying, "I hope Isobel and Matt will be as happy as we are. I was so relieved when he asked me for her hand in marriage. I do not think I could have coped with her waiting for him to propose for much longer, her excited expectation was so infectious it felt as if we were *all* waiting for a proposal."

"Matt has always been shy, but I must take some of the blame for his dithering."

"You? Why?"

"Because I told him several years ago about the family problem. I knew how keen he was on Isobel so I thought I should warn him that he was more closely related than he thought."

"But...you mean...you knew my father's secret all along?"

"Darling, I am so sorry. How could I possibly tell you about it. It would have destroyed your family. How would you have felt – thinking that your children belonged to your brother? How would Sarah have reacted?"

Matilda stared straight ahead at the ducks but she was no longer seeing them.

Matthew continued, gently, "I hated keeping something so

important from you. It tore me apart, but telling you would have destroyed you, I could not do that, darling."

"How long have you known?" she whispered tremulously.

"The day I left the locket for you at Clancy's…"

"*That* long…?"

"Not for sure. The night my father told me it would be *unlawful* to marry you. I could think of no other reason except that we were related. I could not let you go on hoping that we would marry one day so I wrote you the letter and went away to sea. What else could I have done?"

Matilda's brain was working overtime, " So my father had confessed to your father?"

"Yes, Tilly."

"Did you tell anyone your fears?"

Matthew hesitated; he was not enjoying this conversation, it was supposed to be a happy week. "I told Richard before I left."

"*Richard* knew? All our married life *Richard* knew?"

"I had to tell someone. Father would not discuss it. Mother was bewildered by the whole business. I could not just leave with no one understanding why I was going. Richard promised me he would tell me if he ever found out who my parents were. He understood how miserable I felt about the subject. *He* loved you too, Tilly. He probably loved you for years before he declared himself. Please understand that we had no option but to keep silent."

"So that is why you stayed away so long?" she whispered.

"Yes, if I had come home you would have expected me to ask you to marry me – and I would have wanted to – but how could I have done, suspecting I was your brother? Then when Father died he left Richard a letter telling him about Daniel's confession. We opened it together the night of Father's funeral. You cannot imagine how I felt to have my worst fears confirmed." He too now looked away and stared miserably at the lake. "The worst thing was, knowing that I still loved you, but not as a sister. I thought I must be some kind of monster."

Matilda turned and looked into her husband's troubled face. He had protected her. He had not abandoned her – he had

365

loved her too much to cause her suffering. He had borne all the worry, guilt and shame by himself. From the day he had left, until last year when her father had died, he had thought he was her brother and that they had had an incestuous love affair. What a terrible burden to bear alone. No wonder he had been so shocked to return home and find that they were the parents of twins. She remembered his sobbing in the clearing. '*What have I done to you?*' he had said. It now took on a completely different meaning.

"Oh, Matthew," she said choking on her words and taking him in her arms. I am so sorry, my father caused you so much unhappiness, how can you ever forgive him?"

"Because, like him, but for a different reason, I had to keep a secret from the woman I loved – or risk losing her forever."

"What made you decide to tell me all this?"

"I do not want us to have any secrets from one another. This is a new beginning and we have already waited far too long for it."

"Thank you, Matthew – for telling me, I mean."

"We have talked ourselves into a sombre mood, Tilly and we are on honeymoon."

"Then we will talk ourselves out of it post-haste. I wonder how they are coping at home?"

"I do not think you need worry. Isobel and James are quite competent."

"Dear James, there is another shy one, but I do not think it will be long before he plucks up courage to ask Eloise Miles to walk out with him. He does not say much but I can tell he is quite besotted. I have been so lucky with my children, I could not have asked for better. Sarah and Alistair are doing a wonderful job running Uphall."

"Did you mind very much not inheriting the farm?"

"Not at all, I have Meadow Farm, Father had obviously thought it out very carefully. I would have been surprised at the wording of his Will, had we not called on Juanita when he died. After all, '*I bequest my farm – lock, stock and barrel – to my wife, Louisa, for the rest of her natural life, thereon to pass to my granddaughter Sarah – in its entirety – in some small recompense for the abominable stigma I have had the misfortune of forcing upon her,*' did seem rather strong if it related only to her illegitimacy."

"Well, he did not have time to change the wording before he died. He would have left it to her anyway – he knew how much she loved it."

The Sunday morning was passing very quickly. Matthew took his watch from his pocket. "I think," he said, "we should make our way back for lunch, we must not be late, Juanita is a stickler for punctuality. Any way, you must put your feet up this afternoon we have a big night ahead of us."

"We do?"

"Yes, we do, it is a surprise?"

"What sort of a surprise?"

"A wedding present from Juanita."

"You have kept it to yourself, that is not fair," she pouted, playfully prodding him gently in his ribs with her finger. "Tell me what it is... please," she pleaded.

"Alright, you have won me over, it is a night out in London – first night tickets to see Lillie Langtry as Marie Antoinette in 'A Royal Necklace' at the Imperial Theatre." Matthew recited carefully.

Matilda laughed, "That is wonderful, I can tell you have been practising that. How generous of her."

"She is such an exciting lady, is she not? I can quite understand Daniel being fascinated with her when he was young."

"It was only one night."

"All the same she is the type of person that would stay in your mind even if you did not think you had good reason for it."

"I wish I were as haughty and elegant as Juanita."

"Well, I am glad you are *not*, I much prefer the natural look. I like to think of you sitting on the top of the stile, with a backdrop of the poppy field and your hair blowing wildly in the wind...or in Clancy's clearing, lying on the lush green grass after we have enjoyed…"

"*Matthew!*" she turned to him in mock horror, her eyes laughing merrily.

"I was going to say, ..after we have enjoyed a *picnic*."

"That is just as well."

He glanced sideways at her, a wicked grin on his dark, handsome face, "I was going to *say* a picnic…but, of course, I was *thinking* of something entirely different…"

Their eyes met and held in the old familiar way, as they walked on into the future.

The Epilogue

The old man rose feebly from the bed and, with the help of a stick, moved slowly to the window, where a chair afforded him rest, and a view of the meadows below the stream, which ran through his land at the back of his farm. To his right was the wood – Clancy's Wood.

It was a beautiful morning, bright and crisp, with a fresh wind blowing. The sort of weather he loved.

He had been out of his sick bed for only a week, after suffering bronchitis, which turned to pneumonia, from which he thought he would never recover. James and Eloise had looked after him admirably but he was tired...so tired. If he was going to die he was determined to do it with the sun and the wind on his face, not cooped up indoors – and certainly not in bed.

His whole family had visited him in twos and threes the previous day – to keep his spirits up they said – they knew how he hated being confined indoors. They seemed to have an inordinate amount of energy all of a sudden; just watching them tired him out.

He raised himself wearily and returned to the bed, which was now in one of the downstairs rooms, where he and Tilly had had their own quarters – much like Rose and Dan had enjoyed at Uphall Farm. Funny how life went full circle. The bed had been brought down two years earlier when Tilly had been so ill. Thinking of Tilly invariably made him cry these days. He wished she were still here with him.

He sat down again, his breathing shallow and laboured, and looked up to the wall on which the bed head stood. On one side – *his* side as he thought of it – was a small, battered frame, which held a child's simple watercolour of a young girl in a poppy field. The perspective was not quite as it should be, but that was of no consequence to him – he had taken that little painting all over the world.

On the other side of the bed – Tilly's side – was another frame, holding his poem to her. The paper was yellowed now and did not lie flat in the frame, some of the words were barely discernible but that did not bother him either – they had known the poem by heart.

He gathered his clothes around him and began to get dressed, taking his time, resting between donning each item, all the while looking towards the window and the sunshine. It had a magnetic effect on him.

Once dressed he shuffled through to the kitchen where Eloise had his breakfast waiting. Since he had been ill she had made a habit of cooking his breakfast later than usual, and then sharing a cup of tea with him afterwards. He was very fond of Eloise but then, technically, she was distantly related to him through his father.

"Are you feeling better today?" she asked gently as he took his place at the table. She was clearly referring to the previous evening when he had become maudlin during a visit from Sarah, Isobel and Matt. He had grown much more emotional since Tilly had died.

"I am much better, I am going for a walk after breakfast."

"Do you think that is wise?"

"I cannot stay in forever. It is a beautiful day."

"Shall I accompany you?"

"If you do not mind, I will go alone – at my own pace." He nodded his head as if in agreement with himself.

Eloise smiled, her father-in-law had a mind of his own, she could tell he wanted to be alone on his walk – he was not just being considerate of her time. "Well, make sure you wrap up warmly, the sun is nice but it is chilly in the wind. You will need your overcoat." She smiled warmly at him.

He looked fondly at her. He loved all his family dearly. He thought of Isobel and James as his own children and, collectively, with Sarah and Matt, they had given Tilly and himself nine grandchildren – that was including Luke…Yes, he had a good solid family around him.

Eloise helped him on with his boots and overcoat, which felt three times heavier than when he had last worn them. He then returned to the bedroom where he opened a drawer and found the simply painted box that held his Cornelians. He transferred the spare stones from the handkerchief – the one that Tilly had made for him when he was away at school – to the box and put it into his coat pocket. Tilly's little box of stones had been buried with her two years earlier and he had requested his own to be put with him likewise, when his time came.

He was glad that the fever – which had been with him off and on through his bed-ridden three weeks – had now subsided, but it had left him feeling frail and exhausted. An alien condition to him.

After bidding goodbye to Eloise, he set forth from the farmhouse by way of the back door; his big grey overcoat buttoned up high against the fresh, penetrating wind. One of his hands was thrust deep into his pocket where he held the small wooden box, the contents of which had reflected his life from when he was eleven years old. He again looked out over the meadows and the stream. It was a beautiful view; he had always loved it.

He made his way slowly to the road, it felt strange to be out again, he felt as if he were playing truant.

As he passed Uphall Farm he glanced into the yard where the dogs were stretched out in the spring sunshine. They were obviously not feeling the chill in the wind, as he was. They raised themselves and plodded over to the gate hoping for an affectionate pat. Matthew smiled as he indulged them.

Just before the turn off to Poachers Way, he stopped for a rest and leant on the gate which gave access to the meadow and the poppy field beyond, which, in a month or twos time, would be ablaze with vermilion. In his mind's eye he watched as two imaginary children climbed over the stile, ran through the poppies and disappeared into Clancy's Wood.

He wished he could follow them.

Half way down Hill Road, at the gate to the cornfield, he stopped again to get his breath. This was where Matilda had found Richard deep in thought when that first long-awaited letter had arrived. Matilda had told him all about it. He tried to imagine the two of them as they would have been then – so relieved to have heard from him at last but not happy at his news. How he wished he had not needed to have written that letter.

He struggled on, bending himself forward in order to help his balance when the gusts were strongest. He did not enjoy being this frail.

A little further on, at Flintknapper Corner, the old man paused again. This was where he had first met Sarah, his lovely daughter. He let his mind drift to that day long ago. She had been wearing a blue frock which went beautifully with her glossy, black hair, he remembered clearly. He and Matty had given her the ribbons he had bought from Rosa – Rosa, his mother – and Tilly had looked on, almost visibly bursting with pride as she had introduced him to his little girl. He had been full of mixed emotions that day but pride had been uppermost.

Tears trickled down his cheeks as he again forced himself to go on. A little further on, he raised his stick to the men working in the fields, his son and grandsons would be with them, but they were too far away for him to make out who was who.

At the crossroads with the High Street he turned his head to the left, where, a short way down the road, the Vicarage stood – his childhood home, on the doorstep of which he had been left, just one day old – poor Rosa, how desperate she must have felt that day.

Straining his eyes further, he made out the red roof of the old schoolhouse, where he had first met Tilly. She had been such a vibrant child. He could see her now, always full of life and eager to please.

Matthew pulled the collar of his overcoat tighter round his neck. It was very chilly on these crossroads, despite the sun.

As he crossed over the High Street, his shuffling form did not go unnoticed by Mrs Sheldrake.

"You should not be out in this wind, Matthew, and you just up from your bed," she called.

He raised his stick in answer to her, for he had no breath to waste talking, much as he would have liked to have done. He brushed another tear from his eye, why was he crying? Was it because of the genuine concern he had detected in Mrs Sheldrake's voice? Folk were kind, he acknowledged silently. He had inadvertently been the subject of much gossip in the village, but never had any been, in the slightest way, malicious.

As he neared the lych gate of the church, his breath was coming in short, sharp gasps. He leant against the post, willing himself to see his journey through. The churchyard was bathed in spring sunshine but it looked deserted, apart from the young Thompson brothers who were gathering firewood. They stopped what they were doing and watched as the elderly man struggled up the path.

Part way along he stopped and made a short but slow detour to the left, pausing at the foot of an old grave bearing the name 'Walter Fennell'. "Thank you, Walter, my friend, for everything, I will not pass this way again," he said reverently. He bowed his head as he paid his last respects to the old man who had so influenced his life.

Beside Walter was another familiar grave, it was where Edward John Maddon had been laid to rest. Matthew smiled sadly, "Goodbye, Shuffley, you were a great character."

He raised his weather-beaten old face and focused on the yew tree, under which stood the seat he had made in memory of Sebastian. He was tired, very tired, he had never felt so weary in his life, but still he trudged on toward his goal of one of the newer headstones in the churchyard.

Reaching the seat at last, he ran his gnarled, old hands over the carvings he had made twenty-five years earlier, then practically collapsed onto the bench at the foot of the family burial plot.

He blinked his eyes several times quickly as the tears came

easily. He felt at home. He was at last being given a little respite from the biting wind, and the sun felt warm on his face.

Around him were the resting places of his loved ones, Sebastian...Richard...his mother and father – and Tilly, with whom he had shared the past twenty-four years. Then there was his grandson Luke who had not lived long after being brought home, wounded, from France. *That* had been a harrowing time, especially for Matt and Isobel. *His* name was also on the war memorial on the Village Green along with the other local lads who had died for their country. He hoped the world would never see another war. Too many of the boys had never come home or had, like Luke, returned maimed.

He began to feel sleepy, the walk had totally exhausted him and the sun was soothing...twenty-four years...he had seen a lot of changes during that time. Motorised vehicles were now a common sight, they would eventually completely replace the horse as a means of transport, he supposed sadly. He loved horses, there was nothing quite like the warm sweet smell of a horse after it had galloped a mile or two... he took a slow deep breath through his nose, almost bringing the aroma to his senses.

Then there was electricity...*that* was rapidly encroaching on all aspects of life...he was not sure if it were for the better, but that would not stop its advancement.

Yes, the world was changing, but he had no great desire to witness any more of it...it was all too tiring...

He did not know how long he sat there, drifting in and out of sleep but, slowly, he made one last supreme effort to lower himself down onto the grass covering his dear wife. For most of his life he had not been allowed to live with her but, by God, he was going to die with her...outdoors...in the sunshine... with her again...

...and as his face fell back onto the warm, rough stone engraved with Tilly's name, he was back on Winford beach, hearing the crashing waves as they broke and foamed on the shore... washing over his fingers...as he collected the Cornelians.

"Is he dead, John?"
"Yes, I think so."
"Had we better go and fetch our mother?"